What Will He Do with it, Part One

Edward Bulwer-Lytton

ESPRIOS DIGITAL PUBLISHING

WHAT WILL HE DO WITH IT

BY

"PISISTRATUS CAXTON"

(LORD LYTTON)

BOOK I.

CHAPTER I.

In which the history opens with a description of the social manners, habits, and amusements of the English People, as exhibited in an immemorial National Festivity. —Characters to be commemorated in the history, introduced and graphically portrayed, with a nasological illustration. —Original suggestions as to the idiosyncrasies engendered by trades and callings, with other matters worthy of note, conveyed in artless dialogue after the manner of Herodotus, Father of History (mother unknown).

It was a summer fair in one of the prettiest villages in Surrey. The main street was lined with booths, abounding in toys, gleaming crockery, gay ribbons, and gilded ginger bread. Farther on, where the street widened into the ample village-green, rose the more pretending fabrics which lodged the attractive forms of the Mermaid, the Norfolk Giant; the Pig-faced Lady, the Spotted Boy, and the Calf with Two Heads; while high over even these edifices, and occupying the most conspicuous vantage-ground, a lofty stage promised to rural playgoers the "Grand Melodramatic Performance of The Remorseless Baron and the Bandit's Child. " Music, lively if artless, resounded on every side, —drums, fifes, penny-whistles, cat-calls, and a hand-organ played by a dark foreigner, from the height of whose shoulder a cynical but observant monkey eyed the hubbub and cracked his nuts.

It was now sunset, —the throng at the fullest, —an animated, joyous scene. The, day had been sultry; no clouds were to be seen, except low on the western horizon, where they stretched, in lengthened ridges of gold and purple, like the border-land between earth and sky. The tall elms on the green were still, save, near the great stage, one or two, upon which had climbed young urchins, whose laughing faces peered forth, here and there, from the foliage trembling under their restless movements.

Amidst the crowd, as it streamed saunteringly along, were two spectators; strangers to the place, as was notably proved by the attention they excited, and the broad jokes their dress and appearance provoked from the rustic wits, —jokes which they took with amused good-humour, and sometimes retaliated with a zest

1

which had already made them very popular personages. Indeed, there was that about them which propitiated liking. They were young; and the freshness of enjoyment was so visible in their faces, that it begot a sympathy, and wherever they went, other faces brightened round them.

One of the two whom we have thus individualized was of that enviable age, ranging from five-and-twenty to seven-and-twenty, in which, if a man cannot contrive to make life very pleasant, —pitiable indeed must be the state of his digestive organs. But you might see by this gentleman's countenance that if there were many like him, it would be a worse world for the doctors. His cheek, though not highly coloured, was yet ruddy and clear; his hazel eyes were lively and keen; his hair, which escaped in loose clusters from a jean shooting-cap set jauntily on a well-shaped head, was of that deep sunny auburn rarely seen but in persons of vigorous and hardy temperament. He was good-looking on the whole, and would have deserved the more flattering epithet of handsome, but for his nose, which was what the French call "a nose in the air, " —not a nose supercilious, not a nose provocative, as such noses mostly are, but a nose decidedly in earnest to make the best of itself and of things in general, —a nose that would push its way up in life, but so pleasantly that the most irritable fingers would never itch to lay hold of it. With such a nose a man might play the violoncello, marry for love, or even write poetry, and yet not go to the dogs.

Never would he stick in the mud so long as he followed that nose in the air.

By the help of that nose this gentleman wore a black velveteen jacket of foreign cut; a mustache and imperial (then much rarer in England than they have been since the Siege of Sebastopol); and yet left you perfectly convinced that he was an honest Englishman, who had not only no designs on your pocket, but would not be easily duped by any designs upon his own.

The companion of the personage thus sketched might be somewhere about seventeen; but his gait, his air, his lithe, vigorous frame, showed a manliness at variance with the boyish bloom of his face. He struck the eye much more than his elder comrade. Not that he was regularly handsome, —far from it; yet it is no paradox to say that he was beautiful, at least, few indeed were the women who would not have called him so. His hair, long like his friend's, was of a dark chestnut, with gold gleaming through it where the sun fell, inclining to curl, and singularly soft and silken in its texture. His large, clear, dark-blue, happy eyes were fringed with long ebon lashes, and set under brows which already wore the expression of intellectual power, and, better still, of frank courage and open loyalty. His complexion was fair, and somewhat pale, and his lips in laughing showed teeth exquisitely white and even. But though his profile was clearly cut, it was far from the Greek ideal; and he wanted the height of stature which is usually considered essential to the personal pretensions of the male sex. Without being positively short, he was still under middle height, and from the compact development of his proportions, seemed already to have attained his full growth. His dress, though not foreign, like his comrade's, was peculiar: a broad-brimmed straw hat, with a wide blue ribbon; shirt collar turned down, leaving the throat bare; a dark-green jacket of thinner material than cloth; white trousers and waistcoat completed his costume. He looked like a mother's darling, —perhaps he was one.

Scratch across his back went one of those ingenious mechanical contrivances familiarly in vogue at fairs, which are designed to impress upon the victim to whom they are applied, the pleasing conviction that his garment is rent in twain.

The boy turned round so quickly that he caught the arm of the offender, —a pretty village-girl, a year or two younger than himself. "Found in the act, sentenced, punished, " cried he, snatching a kiss, and receiving a gentle slap. "And now, good for evil, here's a ribbon for you; choose. "

The girl slunk back shyly, but her companions pushed her forward, and she ended by selecting a cherry-coloured ribbon, for which the boy paid carelessly, while his elder and wiser friend looked at him with grave, compassionate rebuke, and grumbled out, —"Dr. Franklin tells us that once in his life he paid too dear for a whistle; but then he was only seven years old, and a whistle has its uses. But to pay such a price for a scratch-back! —Prodigal! Come along. "

As the friends strolled on, naturally enough all the young girls who wished for ribbons, and were possessed of scratch-backs, followed in their wake. Scratch went the instrument, but in vain.

"Lasses, " said the elder, turning sharply upon them his nose in the air, "ribbons are plentiful, —shillings scarce; and kisses, though pleasant in private, are insipid in public. What, still! Beware! know that, innocent as we seem, we are women-eaters; and if you follow us farther, you are devoured! " So saying, he expanded his jaws to a width so preternaturally large, and exhibited a row of grinders so formidable, that the girls fell back in consternation. The friends turned down a narrow alley between the booths, and though still pursued by some adventurous and mercenary spirits, were comparatively undisturbed as they threaded their way along the back of the booths, and arrived at last on the village-green, and in front of the Great Stage.

"Oho, Lionel! " quoth the elder friend; "Thespian and classical, — worth seeing, no doubt. " Then turning to a grave cobbler in leathern apron, who was regarding with saturnine interest the motley figures ranged in front of the curtain as the Drumatis Persona, he said, "You seem attracted, sir; you have probably already witnessed the performance. " "Yes, " returned the Cobbler; "this is the third day, and to-morrow's the last. I are n't missed once yet, and I sha' n't miss; but it are n't what it was a while back. "

"'That is sad; but then the same thing is said of everything by everybody who has reached your respectable age, friend. Summers, and suns, stupid old watering-places, and pretty young women, 'are n't what they were a while back. ' If men and things go on degenerating in this way, our grandchildren will have a dull time of it. "

The Cobbler eyed the young man, and nodded approvingly. He had sense enough to comprehend the ironical philosophy of the reply; and our Cobbler loved talk out of the common way. "You speaks truly and cleverly, sir. But if old folks do always say that things are worse than they were, ben't there always summat in what is always said? I'm for the old times; my neighbour, Joe Spruce, is for the new, and says we are all a-progressing. But he 's a pink; I 'm a blue. "

"You are a blue? " said the boy Lionel; "I don't understand. "

"Young 'un, I'm a Tory, —that's blue; and Spruce is a Rad, —that's pink! And, what is more to the purpose, he is a tailor, and I'm a cobbler. "

"Aha! " said the elder, with much interest; "more to the purpose is it? How so? "

The Cobbler put the forefinger of the right hand on the forefinger of the left; it is the gesture of a man about to ratiocinate or demonstrate, as Quintilian, in his remarks on the oratory of fingers, probably observes; or if he has failed to do so, it is a blot in his essay.

"You see, sir, " quoth the Cobbler, "that a man's business has a deal to do with his manner of thinking. Every trade, I take it, has ideas as belong to it. Butchers don't see life as bakers do; and if you talk to a dozen tallow-chandlers, then to a dozen blacksmiths, you will see tallow-chandlers are peculiar, and blacksmiths too. "

"You are a keen observer, " said he of the jean cap, admiringly; "your remark is new to me; I dare say it is true. "

"Course it is; and the stars have summat to do with it; for if they order a man's calling, it stands to reason that they order a man's mind to fit it. Now, a tailor sits on his board with others, and is always a-talking with 'em, and a-reading the news; therefore he thinks, as his fellows do, smart and sharp, bang up to the day, but nothing 'riginal and all his own, like. But a cobbler, " continued the man of leather, with a majestic air, "sits by hisself, and talks with hisself; and what he thinks gets into his head without being put there by another man's tongue. "

"You enlighten me more and more, " said our friend with the nose in the air, bowing respectfully, —"a tailor is gregarious, a cobbler solitary. The gregarious go with the future, the solitary stick by the past. I understand why you are a Tory and perhaps a poet. "

"Well, a bit of one, " said the Cobbler, with an iron smile. "And many 's the cobbler who is a poet, —or discovers marvellous things in a crystal, —whereas a tailor, sir" (spoken with great contempt), "only sees the upper leather of the world's sole in a newspaper. "

Here the conversation was interrupted by a sudden pressure of the crowd towards the theatre. The two young friends looked up, and saw that the new object of attraction was a little girl, who seemed scarcely ten years old, though in truth she was about two years older. She had just emerged from behind the curtain, made her obeisance to the crowd, and was now walking in front of the stage with the prettiest possible air of infantine solemnity. "Poor little thing! " said Lionel. "Poor little thing! " said the Cobbler. And had you been there, my reader, ten to one but you would have said the same. And yet she was attired in white satin, with spangled flounces and a tinsel jacket; and she wore a wreath of flowers (to be sure, the flowers were not real) on her long fair curls, with gaudy bracelets (to be sure, the stones were mock) on her slender arms. Still there was something in her that all this finery could not vulgarize; and since it could not vulgarize, you pitied her for it. She had one of those charming faces that look straight into the hearts of us all, young and old. And though she seemed quite self-possessed, there was no effrontery in her air, but the ease of a little lady, with a simple child's unconsciousness that there was anything in her situation to induce you to sigh, "Poor thing! "

"You should see her act, young gents, " said the Cobbler: "she plays uncommon. But if you had seen him as taught her, —seen him a year ago. "

"Who's he? "

"Waife, sir; mayhap you have heard speak of Waife? "

"I blush to say, no. "

"Why, he might have made his fortune at Common Garden; but that's a long story. Poor fellow! he's broke down now, anyhow. But she takes care of him, little darling: God bless thee! " and the Cobbler here exchanged a smile and a nod with the little girl, whose face brightened when she saw him amidst the crowd.

"By the brush and pallet of Raphael! " cried the elder of the young men, "before I am many hours older I must have that child's head! "

"Her head, man! " cried the Cobbler, aghast.

"In my sketch-book. You are a poet, —I a painter. You know the little girl? "

"Don't I! She and her grandfather lodge with me; her grandfather, — that's Waife, —marvellous man! But they ill-uses him; and if it warn't for her, he'd starve. He fed them all once: he can feed them no longer; he'd starve. That's the world: they use up a genus, and when it falls on the road, push on; that's what Joe Spruce calls a-progressing. But there's the drum! they're a-going to act; won't you look in, gents? "

"Of course, " cried Lionel, —"of course. And, hark ye, Vance, we'll toss up which shall be the first to take that little girl's head. "

"Murderer in either sense of the word! " said Vance, with a smile that would have become Correggio if a tyro had offered to toss up which should be the first to paint a cherub.

CHAPTER II.

The historian takes a view of the British stage as represented by the irregular drama, the regular having (ere the date of the events to which this narrative is restricted) disappeared from the vestiges of creation.

They entered the little theatre, and the Cobbler with them; but the last retired modestly to the threepenny row. The young gentlemen were favoured with reserved seats, price one shilling. "Very dear, " murmured Vance, as he carefully buttoned the pocket to which he restored a purse woven from links of steel, after the fashion of chain mail. Ah, Messieurs and Confreres the Dramatic Authors, do not flatter yourselves that we are about to give you a complacent triumph over the Grand Melodrame of "The Remorseless Baron and the Bandit's Child. " We grant it was horrible rubbish, regarded in an aesthetic point of view, but it was mighty effective in the theatrical. Nobody yawned; you did not even hear a cough, nor the cry of that omnipresent baby, who is always sure to set up an unappeasable wail in the midmost interest of a classical five-act piece, represented for the first time on the metropolitan boards. Here the story rushed on, *per fas aut nefas*, and the audience went with it. Certes, some man who understood the stage must have put the incidents together, and then left it to each illiterate histrio to find the words, — words, my dear confreres, signify so little in an acting play. The movement is the thing. Grand secret! Analyze, practise it, and restore to grateful stars that lost Pleiad the British Acting Drama.

Of course the Bandit was an ill-used and most estimable man. He had some mysterious rights to the Estate and Castle of the Remorseless Baron. That titled usurper, therefore, did all in his power to hunt the Bandit out in his fastnesses and bring him to a bloody end. Here the interest centred itself in the Bandit's child, who, we need not say, was the little girl in the wreath and spangles, styled in the playbill "Miss Juliet Araminta Wife, " and the incidents consisted in her various devices to foil the pursuit of the Baron and save her father. Some of these incidents were indebted to the Comic Muse, and kept the audience in a broad laugh. Her arch playfulness here was exquisite. With what vivacity she duped the High Sheriff, who had the commands of his king to take the Bandit alive or dead, into the belief that the very Lawyer employed by the Baron was the criminal in disguise, and what pearly teeth she showed when the

Lawyer was seized and gagged! how dexterously she ascertained the weak point in the character of the "King's Lieutenant" (jeune premier), who was deputed by his royal master to aid the Remorseless Baron in trouncing the Bandit! how cunningly she learned that he was in love with the Baron's ward (jeune amoureuse), whom that unworthy noble intended to force into a marriage with himself on account of her fortune! how prettily she passed notes to and fro, the Lieutenant never suspecting that she was the Bandit's child, and at last got the king's soldier on her side, as the event proved! And oh, how gayly, and with what mimic art, she stole into the Baron's castle, disguised as a witch, startled his conscience with revelations and predictions, frightened all the vassals with blue lights and chemical illusions, and venturing even into the usurper's own private chamber, while the tyrant was tossing restless on the couch, over which hung his terrible sword, abstracted from his coffer the deeds that proved the better rights of the persecuted Bandit! Then, when he woke before she could escape with her treasure, and pursued her with his sword, with what glee she apparently set herself on fire, and skipped out of the casement in an explosion of crackers! And when the drama approached its *denouement*, when the Baron's men, and the royal officers of justice, had, despite all her arts, tracked the Bandit to the cave, in which, after various retreats, he lay hidden, wounded by shots, and bruised by a fall from a precipice, —with what admirable byplay she hovered around the spot, with what pathos she sought to decoy away the pursuers! it was the skylark playing round the nest. And when all was vain, —when, no longer to be deceived, the enemies sought to seize her, how mockingly she eluded them, bounded up the rock, and shook her slight finger at them in scorn! Surely she will save that estimable Bandit still! Now, hitherto, though the Bandit was the nominal hero of the piece, though you were always hearing of him, —his wrongs, virtues, hairbreadth escapes, —he had never been seen. Not Mrs. Harris, in the immortal narrative, was more quoted and more mythical. But in the last scene there was the Bandit, there in his cavern, helpless with bruises and wounds, lying on a rock. In rushed the enemies, Baron, High Sheriff, and all, to seize him. Not a word spoke the Bandit, but his attitude was sublime, — even Vance cried "bravo; " and just as he is seized, halter round his neck, and about to be hanged, down from the chasm above leaps his child, holding the title-deeds, filched from the Baron, and by her side the King's Lieutenant, who proclaims the Bandit's pardon, with due restoration to his honours and estates, and consigns to the astounded Sheriff the august person of the Remorseless Baron. Then the affecting scene, father and child in each other's arms; and then an exclamation, which had been long hovering about the lips of many of the audience, broke out, "Waife, Waife! " Yes, the Bandit, who appeared but in the last scene, and even then uttered not a word, was the once great actor on that itinerant Thespian stage, known through many a fair for his exuberant humour, his impromptu jokes, his arch eye, his redundant life of drollery, and the strange pathos or dignity with which he could suddenly exalt a jester's part, and call forth tears in the startled hush of laughter; he whom the Cobbler had rightly said, "might have made a fortune at Covent Garden. " There was the remnant of the old popular mime! —all his attributes of eloquence reduced to dumb show! Masterly touch of nature and of art in this representation of him, —touch which all who had ever in former years seen and heard him on that stage felt simultaneously. He came in for his personal portion of dramatic tears. "Waife, Waife! " cried many a village voice, as the little girl led him to the front of the stage.

He hobbled; there was a bandage round his eyes. The plot, in describing the accident that had befallen the Bandit, idealized the genuine infirmities of the man, —infirmities that had befallen him since last seen in that village. He was blind of one eye; he had become crippled; some malady of the trachea or larynx had seemingly broken up the once joyous key of the old pleasant voice. He did not trust himself to speak, even on that stage, but silently bent his head to the rustic audience; and Vance, who was an habitual playgoer, saw in that simple salutation that the man was an artistic actor. All was over, the audience streamed out, much affected, and talking one to the other. It had not been at all like the ordinary stage exhibitions at a village fair. Vance and Lionel exchanged looks of surprise, and then, by a common impulse, moved towards the stage, pushed aside the curtain, which had fallen, and were in that strange world which has so many reduplications, fragments of one broken mirror, whether in the proudest theatre or the lowliest barn, —nay, whether in the palace of kings, the cabinet of statesmen, the home of domestic life, —the world we call "Behind the Scenes. "

CHAPTER III.

Striking illustrations of lawless tyranny and infant avarice exemplified in the social conditions of Great Britain. — Superstitions of the dark ages still in force amongst the trading community, furnishing valuable hints to certain American journalists, and highly suggestive of reflections humiliating to the national vanity.

The Remorseless Baron, who was no other than the managerial proprietor of the stage, was leaning against a side-scene with a pot of porter in his hand. The King's Lieutenant might be seen on the background, toasting a piece of cheese on the point of his loyal sword. The Bandit had crept into a corner, and the little girl was clinging to him fondly as his hand was stroking her fair hair. Vance looked round, and approached the Bandit, —"Sir, allow me to congratulate you; your bow was admirable. I have never seen John Kemble; before my time: but I shall fancy I have seen him now, — seen him on the night of his retirement from the stage. As to your grandchild, Miss Juliet Araminta, she is a perfect chrysolite. "

Before Mr. Waife could reply, the Remorseless Baron stepped up in a spirit worthy of his odious and arbitrary character. "What do you do here, sir? I allow no conspirators behind the scenes earwigging my people. "

"I beg pardon respectfully: I am an artist, —a pupil of the Royal Academy; I should like to make a sketch of Miss Juliet Araminta. "

"Sketch! nonsense. "

"Sir, " said Lionel, with the seasonable extravagance of early youth, "my friend would, I am sure, pay for the sitting—handsomely! "

"Ha! " said the manager, softened, "you speak like a gentleman, sir: but, sir, Miss Juliet Araminta is under my protection; in fact, she is my property. Call and speak to me about it to-morrow, before the first performance begins, which is twelve o'clock. Happy to see any of your friends in the reserved seats. Busy now, and—and—in short—excuse me—servant, sir—servant, sir. "

The Baron's manner left no room for further parley. Vance bowed, smiled, and retreated. But meanwhile his young friend had seized the opportunity to speak both to Waife and his grandchild; and when Vance took his arm and drew him away, there was a puzzled, musing expression on Lionel's face, and he remained silent till they had got through the press of such stragglers as still loitered before the stage, and were in a quiet corner of the sward. Stars and moon were then up, —a lovely summer night.

"What on earth are you thinking of, Lionel? I have put to you three questions, and you have not answered one. "

"Vance, " answered Lionel, slowly, "the oddest thing! I am so disappointed in that little girl, —greedy and mercenary! "

"Precocious villain! how do you know that she is greedy and mercenary? "

"Listen: when that surly old manager came up to you, I said something—civil, of course—to Waife, who answered in a hoarse, broken voice, but in very good language. Well, when I told the manager that you would pay for the sitting, the child caught hold of my arm hastily, pulled me down to her own height, and whispered, 'How much will he give? ' Confused by a question so point-blank, I answered at random, 'I don't know; ten shillings, perhaps. ' You should have seen her face! "

"See her face! radiant, —I should think so. Too much by half! " exclaimed Vance. "Ten shillings! Spendthrift! " "Too much! she looked as you might look if one offered you ten shillings for your picture of 'Julius Caesar considering whether he should cross the Rubicon. ' But when the manager had declared her to be his property, and appointed you to call to-morrow, —implying that he was to be paid for allowing her to sit, —her countenance became overcast, and she muttered sullenly, 'I'll not sit; I'll not! ' Then she turned to her grandfather, and something very quick and close was whispered between the two; and she pulled me by the sleeve, and said in my ear—oh, but so eagerly! —'I want three pounds, sir, — three pounds! —if he would give three pounds; and come to our lodgings, —Mr. Merle, Willow Lane. Three pounds, —three! ' And with those words hissing in my ear, and coming from that fairy mouth, which ought to drop pearls and diamonds, I left her, " added Lionel, as gravely as if he were sixty, "and lost an illusion! "

"Three pounds! " cried Vance, raising his eyebrows to the highest arch of astonishment, and lifting his nose in the air towards the majestic moon, —"three pounds! —a fabulous sum! Who has three pounds to throw away? Dukes, with a hundred thousand a year in acres, have not three pounds to draw out of their pockets in that reckless, profligate manner. Three pounds! —what could I not buy for three pounds? I could buy the Dramatic Library, bound in calf, for three pounds; I could buy a dress coat for three pounds (silk lining not included); I could be lodged for a month for three pounds! And a jade in tinsel, just entering on her teens, to ask three pounds for what? for becoming immortal on the canvas of Francis Vance? — bother! "

Here Vance felt a touch on his shoulder. He turned round quickly, as a man out of temper does under similar circumstances, and beheld the sweat face of the Cobbler.

"Well, master, did not she act fine? —how d'ye like her? "

"Not much in her natural character; but she sets a mighty high value on herself. "

"Anan, I don't take you. "

"She'll not catch me taking her! Three pounds! —three kingdoms! Stay, " cried Lionel to the Cobbler; "did not you say she lodged with you? Are you Mr. Merle? "

"Merle's my name, and she do lodge with me, —Willow Lane. "

"Come this way, then, a few yards down the road, —more quiet. Tell me what the child means, if you can; " and Lionel related the offer of his friend, the reply of the manager, and the grasping avarice of Miss Juliet Araminta.

The Cobbler made no answer; and when the young friends, surprised at his silence, turned to look at him, they saw he was wiping his eyes with his sleeves.

"Poor little thing! " he said at last, and still more pathetically than he had uttered the same words at her appearance in front of the stage; "'tis all for her grandfather; I guess, —I guess. "

"Oh, " cried Lionel, joyfully, "I am so glad to think that. It alters the whole case, you see, Vance. "

"It don't alter the case of the three pounds, " grumbled Vance. "What's her grandfather to me, that I should give his grandchild three pounds, when any other child in the village would have leaped out of her skin to have her face upon my sketch-book and five shillings in her pocket? Hang her grandfather! "

They were now in the main road. The Cobbler seated himself on a lonely milestone, and looked first at one of the faces before him, then at the other; that of Lionel seemed to attract him the most, and in speaking it was Lionel whom he addressed.

"Young master, " he said, "it is now just four years ago, when Mr. Rugge, coming here, as he and his troop had done at fair-time ever sin' I can mind of, brought with him the man you have seen to-night, William Waife; I calls him Gentleman Waife. However that man fell into sick straits, how he came to join sich a caravan, would puzzle most heads. It puzzles Joe Spruce, uncommon; it don't puzzle me. "

"Why? " asked Vance.

"Cos of Saturn! "

"Satan? "

"Saturn, —dead agin his Second and Tenth House, I'll swear. Lord of Ascendant, mayhap; in combustion of the Sun, —who knows? "

"You're not an astrologer? " said Vance, suspiciously, edging off.

"Bit of it; no offence. "

"What does it signify? " said Lionel, impatiently; "go on. So you called Mr. Waife 'Gentleman Waife; ' and if you had not been an astrologer you would have been puzzled to see him in such a calling."

"Ay, that's it; for he warn't like any as we ever see on these boards hereabouts; and yet he warn't exactly like a Lunnon actor, as I have seen 'em in Lunnon, either, but more like a clever fellow who acted for the spree of the thing. He had sich droll jests, and looked so

14

comical, yet not commonlike, but always what I calls a gentleman, — just as if one o' ye two were doing a bit of sport to please your friends. Well, he drew hugely, and so he did, every time he came, so that the great families in the neighbourhood would go to hear him; and he lodged in my house, and had pleasant ways with him, and was what I call a scollard. But still I don't want to deceive ye, and I should judge him to have been a wild dog in his day. Mercury ill-aspected, —not a doubt of it. Last year it so happened that one of the great gents who belong to a Lunnon theatre was here at fair-time. Whether he had heard of Waife chanceways, and come express to judge for hisself, I can't say; like eno'. And when he had seen Gentleman Waife act, he sent for him to the inn—Red Lion—and offered him a power o' money to go to Lunnon, —Common Garden. Well, sir, Waife did not take to it all at once, but hemmed and hawed, and was at last quite coaxed into it, and so he went. But bad luck came on it; and I knew there would, for I saw it all in my crystal. "

"Oh, " exclaimed Vance, "a crystal, too; really it is getting late, and if you had your crystal about you, you might see that we want to sup."

"What happened? " asked Lionel, more blandly, for he saw the Cobbler, who had meant to make a great effect by the introduction of the crystal, was offended.

"What happened? why, just what I foreseed. There was an accident in the railway 'tween this and Lunnon, and poor Waife lost an eye, and was a cripple for life: so he could not go on the Lunnon stage at all; and what was worse, he was a long time atwixt life and death, and got summat bad on his chest wi' catching cold, and lost his voice, and became the sad object you have gazed on, young happy things that ye are. "

"But he got some compensation from the railway, I suppose? " said Vance, with the unfeeling equanimity of a stoical demon.

"He did, and spent it. I suppose the gentleman broke out in him as soon as he had money, and, ill though he was, the money went. Then it seems he had no help for it but to try and get back to Mr. Rugge. But Mr. Rugge was sore and spiteful at his leaving; for Rugge counted on him, and had even thought of taking the huge theatre at York, and bringing out Gentleman Waife as his trump card. But it warn't fated, and Rugge thought himself ill-used, and so at first he would have nothing more to say to Waife. And truth is, what could the poor man do for Rugge? But then Waife produces little Sophy. "

"You mean Juliet Araminta? " said Vance.

"Same—in private life she be Sophy. And Waife taught her to act, and put together the plays for her. And Rugge caught at her; and she supports Waife with what she gets; for Rugge only gives him four shillings a week, and that goes on 'baccy and such like. "

"Such like—drink, I presume? " said Vance.

"No—he don't drink. But he do smoke, and he has little genteel ways with him, and four shillings goes on 'em. And they have been about the country this spring, and done well, and now they be here. But Rugge behaves shocking hard to both on 'em: and I don't believe he has any right to her in law, as he pretends, —only a sort of understanding which she and her grandfather could break if they pleased; and that's what they wish to do, and that's why little Sophy wants the three pounds. "

"How? " cried Lionel, eagerly. "If they had three pounds could they get away? and if they did, how could they live? Where could they go? "

"That's their secret. But I heard Waife say—the first night they came here—I that if he could get three pounds, he had hit on a plan to be independent like. I tell you what put his back up: it was Rugge insisting on his coming on the stage agin, for he did not like to be seen such a wreck. But he was forced to give in; and so he contrived to cut up that play-story, and appear hisself at the last without speaking. "

"My good friend, " cried young Lionel, "we are greatly obliged to you for your story; and we should much like to see little Sophy and her grandfather at your house to-morrow, —can we? "

"Certain sure you can, after the play's over; to-night, if you like. "

"No, to-morrow: you see my friend is impatient to get back now; we will call to-morrow. "

"'T is the last day of their stay, " said the Cobbler. "But you can't be sure to see them safely at my house afore ten o'clock at night; and not a word to Rugge! mum! "

"Not a word to Rugge, " returned Lionel; "good-night to you. "

The young men left the Cobbler still seated on the milestone, gazing on the stars and ruminating. They walked briskly down the road.

"It is I who have had the talk now, " said Lionel, in his softest tone. He was bent on coaxing three pounds out of his richer friend, and that might require some management. For amongst the wild youngsters in Mr. Vance's profession, there ran many a joke at the skill with which he parried irregular assaults on his purse; and that gentleman, with his nose more than usually in the air, having once observed to such scoffers "that they were quite welcome to any joke at his expense, " a wag had exclaimed, "At your expense! Don't fear; if a joke were worth a farthing, you would never give that permission. "

So when Lionel made that innocent remark, the softness of his tone warned the artist of some snake in the grass, and he prudently remained silent. Lionel, in a voice still sweeter, repeated, —"It is I who have all the talk now! "

"Naturally, " then returned Vance, "naturally you have, for it is you, I suspect, who alone have the intention to pay for it, and three pounds appear to be the price. Dearish, eh? "

"Ah, Vance, if I had three pounds! "

"Tush; and say no more till we have supped. I have the hunger of a wolf. "

Just in sight of the next milestone the young travellers turned a few yards down a green lane, and reached a small inn on the banks of the Thames. Here they had sojourned for the last few days, sketching, boating, roaming about the country from sunrise, and returning to supper and bed at nightfall. It was the pleasantest little inn, —an arbour, covered with honeysuckle, between the porch and the river, —a couple of pleasure-boats moored to the bank; and now all the waves rippling under the moonlight.

"Supper and lights in the arbour, " cried Vance to the waiting-maid, "hey, presto, quick! while we turn in to wash our hands. And hark! a quart jug of that capital whiskey-toddy. "

CHAPTER IV.

Being a chapter that links the past to the future by the gradual elucidation of antecedents.

O wayside inns and pedestrian rambles! O summer nights, under honeysuckle arbours, on the banks of starry waves! O Youth, Youth!

Vance ladled out the toddy and lighted his cigar; then, leaning his head on his hand and his elbow on the table, he looked with an artist's eye along the glancing river.

"After all, " said he, "I am glad I am a painter; and I hope I may live to be a great one. "

"No doubt, if you live, you will be a great one, " cried Lionel, with cordial sincerity. "And if I, who can only just paint well enough to please myself, find that it gives a new charm to Nature —"

"Cut sentiment, " quoth Vance, "and go on. "

"What, " continued Lionel, unchilled by the admonitory interruption, "must you feel who can fix a fading sunshine — a fleeting face — on a scrap of canvas, and say 'Sunshine and Beauty, live there forever! '"

VANCE. —"Forever! no! Colours perish, canvas rots. What remains to us of Zeuxis? Still it is prettily said on behalf of the poetic side of the profession; there is a prosaic one; —we'll blink it. Yes; I am glad to be a painter. But you must not catch the fever of my calling. Your poor mother would never forgive me if she thought I had made you a dauber by my example. "

LIONEL (gloomily). —"No. I shall not be a painter! But what can I be? How shall I ever build on the earth one of the castles I have built in the air? Fame looks so far, —Fortune so impossible. But one thing I am bent upon" (speaking with knit brow and clenched teeth), "I will gain an independence somehow, and support my mother. "

VANCE. —"Your mother is supported: she has the pension —"

LIONEL. —"Of a captain's widow; and" (he added with a flushed cheek) "a first floor that she lets to lodgers. "

VANCE. —"No shame in that! Peers let houses; and on the Continent, princes let not only first floors, but fifth and sixth floors, to say nothing of attics and cellars. In beginning the world, friend Lionel, if you don't wish to get chafed at every turn, fold up your pride carefully, put it under lock and key, and only let it out to air upon grand occasions. Pride is a garment all stiff brocade outside, all grating sackcloth on the side next to the skin. Even kings don't wear the dalmaticum except at a coronation. Independence you desire; good. But are you dependent now? Your mother has given you an excellent education, and you have already put it to profit. My dear boy, " added Vance, with unusual warmth, "I honour you; at your age, on leaving school, to have shut yourself up, translated Greek and Latin per sheet for a bookseller, at less than a valet's wages, and all for the purpose of buying comforts for your mother; and having a few pounds in your own pockets, to rove your little holiday with me and pay your share of the costs! Ah, there are energy and spirit and life in all that, Lionel, which will found upon rock some castle as fine as any you have built in air. Your hand, my boy. "

This burst was so unlike the practical dryness, or even the more unctuous humour, of Frank Vance, that it took Lionel by surprise, and his voice faltered as he pressed the hand held out to him. He answered, "I don't deserve your praise, Vance, and I fear the pride you tell me to put under lock and key has the larger share of the merit you ascribe to better motives. Independent? No! I have never been so. "

VANCE. —"Well, you depend on a parent: who, at seventeen does not? "

LIONEL. —"I did not mean my mother; of course, I could not be too proud to take benefits from her. But the truth is simply this—, my father had a relation, not very near, indeed, —a cousin, at about as distant a remove, I fancy, as a cousin well can be. To this gentleman my mother wrote when my poor father died; and he was generous, for it is he who paid for my schooling. I did not know this till very lately. I had a vague impression, indeed, that I had a powerful and wealthy kinsman who took an interest in me, but whom I had never seen. "

VANCE. —"Never seen? "

LIONEL. —"No. And here comes the sting. On leaving school last Christmas, my mother, for the first time, told me the extent of my obligations to this benefactor, and informed me that he wished to know my own choice as to a profession, —that if I preferred Church or Bar, he would maintain me at college. "

VANCE. —"Body o' me! where's the sting in that? Help yourself to toddy, my boy, and take more genial views of life. "

LIONEL. —"You have not heard me out. I then asked to see my benefactor's letters; and my mother, unconscious of the pain she was about to inflict, showed me not only the last one, but all she had received from him. Oh, Vance, they were terrible, those letters! The first began by a dry acquiescence in the claims of kindred, a curt proposal to pay my schooling; but not one word of kindness, and a stern proviso that the writer was never to see nor hear from me. He wanted no gratitude; he disbelieved in all professions of it. His favours would cease if I molested him. 'Molested' was the word; it was bread thrown to a dog. "

VANCE. —"Tut! Only a rich man's eccentricity. A bachelor, I presume? "

LIONEL. —"My mother says he has been married, and is a widower."

VANCE. —"Any children? "

LIONEL. —"My mother says none living; but I know little or nothing about his family. "

Vance looked with keen scrutiny into the face of his boyfriend, and, after a pause, said, drily, —"Plain as a pikestaff. Your relation is one of those men who, having no children, suspect and dread the attention of an heir presumptive; and what has made this sting, as you call it, keener to you is—pardon me—is in some silly words of your mother, who, in showing you the letters, has hinted to you that that heir you might be, if you were sufficiently pliant and subservient. Am I not right? "

Lionel hung his head, without reply.

VANCE (cheeringly). —"So, so; no great harm as yet. Enough of the first letter. What was the last? "

LIONEL. —"Still more offensive. He, this kinsman, this patron, desired my mother to spare him those references to her son's ability and promise, which, though natural to herself, had slight interest to him, —him, the condescending benefactor! As to his opinion, what could I care for the opinion of one I had never seen? All that could sensibly affect my—oh, but I cannot go on with those cutting phrases, which imply but this, 'All I can care for is the money of a man who insults me while he gives it. '"

VANCE (emphatically). —"Without being a wizard, I should say your relative was rather a disagreeable person, —not what is called urbane and amiable, —in fact, a brute. "

LIONEL. —"You will not blame me, then, when I tell you that I resolved not to accept the offer to maintain me at college, with which the letter closed. Luckily Dr. Wallis (the head master of my school), who had always been very kind to me, had just undertaken to supervise a popular translation of the classics. He recommended me, at my request, to the publisher engaged in the undertaking, as not incapable of translating some of the less difficult Latin authors, — subject to his corrections. When I had finished the first instalment of the work thus intrusted to me, my mother grew alarmed for my health, and insisted on my taking some recreation. You were about to set out on a pedestrian tour. I had, as you say, some pounds in my pocket; and thus I have passed with you the merriest days of my life."

VANCE. —"What said your civil cousin when your refusal to go to college was conveyed to him? "

LIONEL. —"He did not answer my mother's communication to that effect till just before I left home, and then, —no, it was not his last letter from which I repeated that withering extract, —no, the last was more galling still, for in it he said that if, in spite of the ability and promise that had been so vaunted, the dulness of a college and the labour of learned professions were so distasteful to me, he had no desire to dictate to my choice, but that as he did not wish one who was, however remotely, of his blood, and bore the name of Haughton, to turn shoeblack or pickpocket—Vance—Vance! "

VANCE. —"Lock up your pride—the sackcloth frets you—and go on; and that therefore he—"

LIONEL. —"Would buy me a commission in the army, or get me an appointment in India. "

VANCE. —"Which did you take? "

LIONEL (passionately). "Which! so offered, —which? —of course neither! But distrusting the tone of my mother's reply, I sat down, the evening before I left home, and wrote myself to this cruel man. I did not show any letter to my mother, —did not tell her of it. I wrote shortly, —that if he would not accept my gratitude, I would not accept his benefits; that shoeblack I might be, —pickpocket, no! that he need not fear I should disgrace his blood or my name; and that I would not rest till, sooner or later, I had paid him back all that I had cost him, and felt relieved from the burdens of an obligation which— which—" The boy paused, covered his face with his hands, and sobbed.

Vance, though much moved, pretended to scold his friend, but finding that ineffectual, fairly rose, wound his arm brother-like round him, and drew him from the arbour to the shelving margin of the river. "Comfort, " then said the Artist, almost solemnly, as here, from the inner depths of his character, the true genius of the man came forth and spoke, —"comfort, and look round; see where the islet interrupts the tide, and how smilingly the stream flows on. See, just where we stand, how the slight pebbles are fretting the wave would the wave if not fretted make that pleasant music? A few miles farther on, and the river is spanned by a bridge, which busy feet now are crossing: by the side of that bridge now is rising a palace; all the men who rule England have room in that palace. At the rear of the palace soars up the old Abbey where kings have their tombs in right of the names they inherit; men, lowly as we, have found tombs there, in right of the names which they made. Think, now, that you stand on that bridge with a boy's lofty hope, with a man's steadfast courage; then turn again to that stream, calm with starlight, flowing on towards the bridge, —spite of islet and pebbles. "

Lionel made no audible answer, though his lips murmured, but he pressed closer and closer to his friend's side; and the tears were already dried on his cheek, though their dew still glistened in his eyes.

CHAPTER V.

Speculations on the moral qualities of the Bandit. —Mr. Vance, with mingled emotions, foresees that the acquisition of the Bandit's acquaintance may be attended with pecuniary loss.

Vance loosened the boat from its moorings, stepped in, and took up the oars. Lionel followed, and sat by the stern. The Artist rowed on slowly, whistling melodiously in time to the dash of the oars. They soon came to the bank of garden-ground surrounding with turf on which fairies might have danced one of those villas never seen out of England. From the windows of the villa the lights gleamed steadily; over the banks, dipping into the water, hung large willows breathlessly; the boat gently brushed aside their pendent boughs, and Vance rested in a grassy cove.

"And faith, " said the Artist, gayly, —"faith, " said he, lighting his third cigar, "it is time we should bestow a few words more on the Remorseless Baron and the Bandit's Child! What a cock-and-a-bull story the Cobbler told us! He must have thought us precious green. "

LIONEL (roused). —"Nay, I see nothing so wonderful in the story, though much that is sad. You must allow that Waife may have been a good actor: you became quite excited merely at his attitude and bow. Natural, therefore, that he should have been invited to try his chance on the London stage; not improbable that he may have met with an accident by the train, and so lost his chance forever; natural, then, that he should press into service his poor little grandchild, natural, also, that, hardly treated and his pride hurt, he should wish to escape. "

VANCE. —"And more natural than all that he should want to extract from our pockets three pounds, the Bandit! No, Lionel, I tell you what is not probable, that he should have disposed of that clever child to a vagabond like Rugge: she plays admirably. The manager who was to have engaged him would have engaged her if he had seen her. I am puzzled. "

LIONEL. —"True, she is an extraordinary child. I cannot say how she has interested me. " He took out his purse, and began counting its contents. "I have nearly three pounds left, " he cried joyously.

"L2. 18s. if I give up the thought of a longer excursion with you, and go quietly home—"

VANCE. —"And not pay your share of the bill yonder? "

LIONEL. —"Ah, I forgot that! But come, I am not too proud to borrow from you: it is not for a selfish purpose. "

VANCE. —"Borrow from me, Cato! That comes of falling in with bandits and their children. No; but let us look at the thing like men of sense. One story is good till another is told. I will call by myself on Rugge to-morrow, and hear what he says; and then, if we judge favourably of the Cobbler's version, we will go at night and talk with the Cobbler's lodgers; and I dare say, " added Vance, kindly, but with a sigh, —"I daresay the three pounds will be coaxed out of me! After all, her head is worth it. I want an idea for Titania. "

LIONEL (joyously). —"My dear Vance, you are the best fellow in the world. "

VANCE. —"Small compliment to humankind! Take the oars: it is your turn now. "

Lionel obeyed; the boat once more danced along the tide—thoro' reeds, —-thoro' waves, skirting the grassy islet—out into pale moonlight. They talked but by fits and starts. What of? —a thousand things! Bright young hearts, eloquent young tongues! No sins in the past; hopes gleaming through the future. O summer nights, on the glass of starry waves! O Youth, Youth!

CHAPTER VI.

Wherein the historian tracks the public characters that fret their hour on the stage, into the bosom of private life. —The reader is invited to arrive at a conclusion which may often, in periods of perplexity, restore ease to his mind; namely, that if man will reflect on all the hopes he has nourished, all the fears he has admitted, all the projects he has formed, the wisest thing he can do, nine times out of ten, with hope, fear, and project, is to let them end with the chapter—in smoke.

It was past nine o'clock in the evening of the following day. The exhibition at Mr. Rugge's theatre had closed for the season in that village, for it was the conclusion of the fair. The final performance had been begun and ended somewhat earlier than on former nights. The theatre was to be cleared from the ground by daybreak, and the whole company to proceed onward betimes in the morning. Another fair awaited them in an adjoining county, and they had a long journey before them.

Gentleman Waife and his Juliet Araminta had gone to their lodgings over the Cobbler's stall. Their rooms were homely enough, but had an air not only of the comfortable, but the picturesque. The little sitting-room was very old-fashioned, —panelled in wood that had once been painted blue, with a quaint chimney-piece that reached to the ceiling. That part of the house spoke of the time of Charles I., it might have been tenanted by a religious Roundhead; and, framed-in over the low door, there was a grim, faded portrait of a pinched-faced saturnine man, with long lank hair, starched band, and a length of upper lip that betokened relentless obstinacy of character, and might have curled in sullen glee at the monarch's scaffold, or preached an interminable sermon to the stout Protector. On a table, under the deep-sunk window, were neatly arrayed a few sober-looking old books; you would find amongst them Colley's "Astrology, " Owen Feltham's "Resolves, " Glanville "On Witches, " the "Pilgrim's Progress, " an early edition of "Paradise Lost, " and an old Bible; also two flower-pots of clay brightly reddened, and containing stocks; also two small worsted rugs, on one of which rested a carved cocoa-nut, on the other an egg-shaped ball of crystal, —that last the pride and joy of the cobbler's visionary soul. A door left wide open communicated with an inner room (very low was its ceiling), in which the Bandit slept, if the severity of his persecutors permitted him to sleep. In the corner of the sitting-room, near that door, was a small horsehair sofa, which, by the aid of sheets and a needlework coverlid, did duty for a bed, and was consigned to the Bandit's child. Here the tenderness of the Cobbler's heart was visible, for over the coverlid were strewed sprigs of lavender and leaves of vervain; the last, be it said, to induce happy dreams, and scare away witchcraft and evil spirits. On another table, near the fireplace, the child was busied in setting out the tea-things for her grandfather. She had left in the property-room of the theatre her robe of spangles and tinsel, and appeared now in a simple frock. She had no longer the look of Titania, but that of a lively, active, affectionate human child; nothing theatrical about her now, yet still, in her graceful movements, so nimble but so noiseless, in her slight fair hands, in her transparent colouring, there was Nature's own lady, — that SOMETHING which strikes us all as well-born and high-bred: not that it necessarily is so; the semblances of aristocracy, in female childhood more especially, are often delusive. The *souvenance* flower, wrought into the collars of princes, springs up wild on field and fell.

Gentleman Waife, wrapped negligently in a gray dressing-gown and seated in an old leathern easy-chair, was evidently out of sorts. He did not seem to heed the little preparations for his comfort, but, resting his cheek on his right hand, his left drooped on his crossed knees, —an attitude rarely seen in a man when his heart is light and his spirits high. His lips moved: he was talking to himself. Though he had laid aside his theatrical bandage over both eyes, he wore a black patch over one, or rather where one had been; the eye exposed was of singular beauty, dark and brilliant. For the rest, the man had a striking countenance, rugged, and rather ugly than otherwise, but by no means unprepossessing; full of lines and wrinkles and strong muscle, with large lips of wondrous pliancy, and an aspect of wistful sagacity, that, no doubt, on occasion could become exquisitely comic, —dry comedy, —the comedy that makes others roar when the comedian himself is as grave as a judge.

You might see in his countenance, when quite in its natural repose, that Sorrow had passed by there; yet the instant the countenance broke into play, you would think that Sorrow must have been sent about her business as soon as the respect due to that visitor, so accustomed to have her own way, would permit. Though the man was old, you could not call him aged. One-eyed and crippled, still, marking the muscular arm, the expansive chest, you would have scarcely called him broken or infirm. And hence there was a certain indescribable pathos in his whole appearance, as if Fate had branded, on face and form, characters in which might be read her agencies on career and mind, —plucked an eye from intelligence, shortened one limb for life's progress, yet left whim sparkling out in the eye she had spared, and a light heart's wild spring in the limb she had maimed not.

"Come, Grandy, come, " said the little girl, coaxingly; "your tea will get quite cold; your toast is ready, and here is such a nice egg; Mr. Merle says you may be sure it is new laid. Come, don't let that hateful man fret you: smile on your own Sophy; come. "

"If, " said Mr. Waife, in a hollow undertone, if I were alone in the world—"

"Oh, Grandy! "

> "'I know a spot on which a bed-post grows,
> And do remember where a roper lives.'

Delightful prospect, not to be indulged; for if I were in peace at one end of the rope, what would chance to my Sophy, left forlorn at the other? "

"Don't talk so, or I shall think you are sorry to have taken care of me."

"Care of thee, oh, child! and what care? It is thou who takest care of me. Put thy hands from thy mouth; sit down, darling, there, opposite, and let us talk. Now, Sophy, thou hast often said that thou wouldst be glad to be out of this mode of life, even for one humbler and harder: think well, is it so? "

"Oh, yes, indeed, grandfather. "

"No more tinsel dresses and flowery wreaths; no more applause; no more of the dear divine stage excitement; the heroine and fairy vanished; only a little commonplace child in dingy gingham, with a purblind cripple for thy sole charge and playmate; Juliet Araminta evaporated evermore into little Sophy! "

"It would be so nice! " answered little Sophy, laughing merrily.

"What would make it nice? " asked the Comedian, turning on her his solitary piercing eye, with curious interest in his gaze.

Sophy left her seat, and placed herself on a stool at her grandfather's knee; on that knee she clasped her tiny hands, and shaking aside her curls, looked into his face with confident fondness. Evidently these two were much more than grandfather and grandchild: they were friends, they were equals, they were in the habit of consulting and prattling with each other. She got at his meaning, however covert his humour; and he to the core of her heart, through its careless babble. Between you and me, Reader, I suspect that, in spite of the Comedian's sagacious wrinkles, the one was as much a child as the other.

"Well, " said Sophy, "I will tell you, Grandy, what would make it nice: no one would vex and affront you, —we should be all by ourselves; and then, instead of those nasty lamps and those dreadful painted creatures, we could go out and play in the fields and gather daisies; and I could run after butterflies, and when I am tired I should come here, where I am now, any time of the day, and you would tell me stories and pretty verses, and teach me to write a little better than I do now, and make such a wise little woman of me; and if I wore gingham—but it need not be dingy, Grandy—it would be all mine, and you would be all mine too, and we'd keep a bird, and you'd teach it to sing; and oh, would it not be nice! "

"But still, Sophy, we should have to live, and we could not live upon daisies and butterflies. And I can't work now; for the matter of that, I never could work: more shame for me, but so it is. Merle says the fault is in the stars, —with all my heart. But the stars will not go to the jail or the workhouse instead of me. And though they want nothing to eat, we do. "

"But, Grandy, you have said every day since the first walk you took after coming here, that if you had three pounds, we could get away and live by ourselves and make a fortune! "

"A fortune! —that's a strong word: let it stand. A fortune! But still, Sophy, though we should be free of this thrice-execrable Rugge, the scheme I have in my head lies remote from daisies and butterflies. We should have to dwell in towns and exhibit! "

"On a stage, Grandy? " said Sophy, resigned, but sorrowful.

"No, not exactly: a room would do. "

"And I should not wear those horrid, horrid dresses, nor mix with those horrid, horrid painted people. "

"No. "

"And we should be quite alone, you and I? "

"Hum! there would be a third. "

"Oh, Grandy, Grandy! " cried Sophy, in a scream of shrill alarm. "I know, I know; you are thinking of joining us with the Pig-faced Lady! "

MR. WAIFE (not a muscle relaxed). —"A well-spoken and pleasing gentlewoman. But no such luck: three pounds would not buy her. "

SOPHIE. —"I am glad of that: I don't care so much for the Mermaid; she's dead and stuffed. But, oh! " (another scream) "perhaps 't is the Spotted Boy? "

MR. WAIFE. —"Calm your sanguine imagination; you aspire too high! But this I will tell you, that our companion, whatsoever or whosoever that companion may be, will be one you will like. "

"I don't believe it, " said Sophy, shaking her head. "I only like you. But who is it? "

"Alas! " said Mr. Waife, "it is no use pampering ourselves with vain hopes: the three pounds are not forthcoming. You heard what that brute Rugge said, that the gentleman who wanted to take your portrait had called on him this morning, and offered 10s. for a sitting, —that is, 5s. for you, 5s. for Rugge; and Rugge thought the terms reasonable. "

"But I said I would not sit. "

"And when you did say it, you heard Rugge's language to me—to you. And now you must think of packing up, and be off at dawn with the rest. And, " added the comedian, colouring high, "I must again parade, to boors and clowns, this mangled form; again set

30

myself out as a spectacle of bodily infirmity, —man's last degradation. And this I have come to—I! "

"No, no, Grandy, it will not last long! we will get the three pounds. We have always hoped on! —hope still! And, besides, I am sure those gentlemen will come here tonight. Mr. Merle said they would, at ten o'clock. It is near ten now, and your tea cold as a stone. "

She hung on his neck caressingly, kissing his furrowed brow, and leaving a tear there, and thus coaxed him till he set-to quietly at his meal; and Sophy shared it—though she had no appetite in sorrowing for him—but to keep him company; that done, she lighted his pipe with the best canaster, —his sole luxury and expense; but she always contrived that he should afford it.

Mr. Waife drew a long whiff, and took a more serene view of affairs. He who doth not smoke hath either known no great griefs, or refuseth himself the softest consolation, next to that which comes from Heaven. "What, softer than woman? " whispers the young reader. Young reader, woman teases as well as consoles. Woman makes half the sorrows which she boasts the privilege to soothe. Woman consoles us, it is true, while we are young and handsome! when we are old and ugly, woman snubs and scolds us. On the whole, then, woman in this scale, the weed in that, Jupiter, hang out thy balance, and weigh them both; and if thou give the preference to woman, all I can say is, the next time Juno ruffles thee, —O Jupiter, try the weed.

CHAPTER VII.

The historian, in pursuance of his stern duties, reveals to the scorn of future ages some of the occult practices which discredit the march of light in the nineteenth century.

"May I come in? " asked the Cobbler, outside the door. "Certainly come in, " said Gentleman Waife. Sophy looked wistfully at the aperture, and sighed to see that Merle was alone. She crept up to him.

"Will they not come? " she whispered. "I hope so, pretty one; it be n't ten yet. "

"Take a pipe, Merle, " said Gentleman Waife, with a Grand Comedian air.

"No, thank you kindly; I just looked in to ask if I could do anything for ye, in case—in case ye must go tomorrow. "

"Nothing: our luggage is small, and soon packed. Sophy has the money to discharge the meaner part of our debt to you. "

"I don't value that, " said the Cobbler, colouring.

"But we value your esteem, " said Mr. Waife, with a smile that would have become a field-marshal. "And so, Merle, you think, if I am a broken-down vagrant, it must be put to the long account of the celestial bodies! "

"Not a doubt of it, " returned the Cobbler, solemnly. "I wish you would give me date and place of Sophy's birth that's what I want; I'd take her horryscope. I'm sure she'd be lucky. "

"I'd rather not, please, " said Sophy, timidly.

"Rather not? —very odd. Why? "

"I don't want to know the future. "

"That is odder and odder, " quoth the Cobbler, staring; "I never heard a girl say that afore. "

"Wait till she's older, Mr. Merle, " said Waife: "girls don't want to know the future till they want to be married. "

"Summat in that, " said the Cobbler. He took up the crystal. "Have you looked into this ball, pretty one, as I bade ye? "

"Yes, two or three times. "

"Ha! and what did you see? "

"My own face made very long, " said Sophy, —"as long as that—, " stretching out her hands.

The Cobbler shook his head dolefully, and screwing up one eye, applied the other to the mystic ball.

MR. WAIFE. —"Perhaps you will see if those two gentlemen are coming. "

SOPHY. —"Do, do! and if they will give us three pounds! "

COBBLER (triumphantly). —"Then you do care to know the future, after all? "

SOPHY. —"Yes, so far as that goes; but don't look any further, pray."

COBBLER (intent upon the ball, and speaking slowly, and in jerks). —"A mist now. Ha! an arm with a besom—sweeps all before it. "

SOPHY (frightened). —"Send it away, please. "

COBBLER—"It is gone. Ha! there's Rugge, —looks very angry, — savage, indeed. "

WAIFE. —"Good sign that! proceed. "

COBBLER. —"Shakes his fist; gone. Ha! a young man, boyish, dark hair. "

SOPHY (clapping her hands). —"That is the young gentleman—the very young one, I mean—with the kind eyes; is he coming? —is he, is he? "

WAIFE—"Examine his pockets! do you see there three pounds? "

COBBLER (testily). —"Don't be a-interrupting. Ha! he is talking with another gentleman, bearded. "

SOPHY (whispering to her grandfather). —"The old young gentleman. "

COBBLER (putting down the crystal, and with great decision). "They are coming here; I see 'd them at the corner of the lane, by the public-house, two minutes' walk to this door. " He took out a great silver watch: "Look, Sophy, when the minute-hand gets there (or before, if they walk briskly), you will hear them knock. "

Sophy clasped her hands in mute suspense, half-credulous, half-doubting; then she went and opened the room-door, and stood on the landing-place to listen. Merle approached the Comedian, and said in a low voice, "I wish for your sake she had the gift. "

WAIFE. —"The gift! —the three pounds! —so do I! "

COBBLER. —"Pooh! worth a hundred times three pounds; the gift, —the spirituous gift. "

WAIFE. —"Spirituous! don't like the epithet, —smells of gin! "

COBBLER. —"Spirituous gift to see in the crystal: if she had that, she might make your fortune. "

WAIFE (with a 'sudden change of countenance). —"Ah! I never thought of that. But if she has not the gift, I could teach it her, —eh?"

COBBLER (indignantly). —"I did not think to hear this from you, Mr. Waife. Teach her, —you! make her an impostor, and of the wickedest kind, inventing lies between earth and them as dwell in the seven spheres! Fie! No, if she hasn't the gift natural, let her alone: what here is not heaven-sent is devil-taught. "

WAIFE (awed, but dubious). —"Then you really think you saw all that you described, in that glass egg? "

COBBLER. —"Think! —am I a liar? I spoke truth, and the proof is— there—! " Rat-tat went the knocker at the door.

"The two minutes are just up, " said the Cobbler; and Cornelius Agrippa could not have said it with more wizardly effect.

"They are come, indeed, " said Sophy, re-entering the room softly: "I hear their voices at the threshold. "

The Cobbler passed by in silence, descended the stairs, and conducted Vance and Lionel into the Comedian's chamber; there he left them, his brow overcast. Gentleman Waife had displeased him sorely.

CHAPTER VIII.

Showing the arts by which a man, however high in the air Nature may have formed his nose, may be led by that nose, and in directions perversely opposite to those which, in following his nose, he might be supposed to take; and, therefore, that nations the most liberally endowed with practical good sense, and in conceit thereof, carrying their noses the most horizontally aloof, when they come into conference with nations more skilled in diplomacy and more practised in "stage-play, " end by the surrender of the precise object which it was intended they should surrender before they laid their noses together.

We all know that Demosthenes said, Everything in oratory was acting, —stage-play. Is it in oratory alone that the saying holds good? Apply it to all circumstances of fife, "stage-play, stage-play, stage-play! "—only *ars est celare artem*, conceal the art. Gleesome in soul to behold his visitors, calculating already on the three pounds to be extracted from them, seeing in that hope the crisis in his own checkered existence, Mr. Waife rose from his seat in superb *upocrisia* or stage-play, and asked, with mild dignity, —"To what am I indebted, gentlemen, for the honour of your visit? "

In spite of his, nose, even Vance was taken aback. Pope says that Lord Bolingbroke had "the nobleman air. " A great comedian Lord Bolingbroke surely was. But, ah, had Pope seen Gentleman Waife! Taking advantage of the impression he had created, the actor added, with the finest imaginable breeding, —"But pray be seated; " and, once seeing them seated, resumed his easy-chair, and felt himself master of the situation.

"Hum! " said Vance, recovering his self-possession, after a pause— "hum! "

"Hem! " re-echoed Gentleman Waife; and the two men eyed each other much in the same way as Admiral Napier might have eyed the fort of Cronstadt, and the fort of Cronstadt have eyed Admiral Napier.

Lionel struck in with that youthful boldness which plays the deuce with all dignified strategical science.

"You must be aware why we come, sir; Mr. Merle will have explained. My friend, a distinguished artist, wished to make a sketch, if you do not object, of this young lady's very" —

"Pretty little face, " quoth Vance, taking up the dis course. "Mr. Rugge, this morning, was willing, —I understand that your grandchild refused. We are come here to see if she will be more complaisant under your own roof, or Under Mr. Merle's, which, I take it, is the same thing for the present. "—Sophy had sidled up to Lionel. He might not have been flattered if he knew why she preferred him to Vance. She looked on him as a boy, a fellow-child; and an instinct, moreover, told her, that more easily through him than his shrewd-looking bearded guest could she attain the object of her cupidity, —"three pounds! "

"Three pounds! " whispered Sophy, with the tones of an angel, into Lionel's thrilling ear.

MR. WAIFE. —"Sir, I will be frank with you. " At that ominous commencement, Mr. Vance recoiled, and mechanically buttoned his trousers pocket. Mr. Waife noted the gesture with his one eye, and proceeded cautiously, feeling his way, as it were, towards the interior of the recess thus protected. "My grandchild declined your flattering proposal with my full approbation. She did not consider — neither did I—that the managerial rights of Mr. Rugge entitled him to the moiety of her face—off the stage. " The Comedian paused, and with a voice, the mimic drollery of which no hoarseness could altogether mar, chanted the old line, —

"'My face is my fortune, sir, ' she said. "

Vance smiled; Lionel laughed; Sophy nestled still nearer to the boy.

GENTLEMAN WAIFE (with pathos and dignity). —"You see before you an old man: one way of life is the same to me as another. But she, —do you think Mr. Rugge's stage the right place for her? "

VANCE. —"Certainly not. Why did you not introduce her to the London Manager who would have engaged yourself? "

Waife could not conceal a slight change of countenance. "How do I know she would have succeeded? She had never then trod the boards. Besides, what strikes you as so good in a village show may be poor enough in a metropolitan theatre. Gentlemen, I do my best for her; you cannot think otherwise, since she maintains me! I am no OEdipus, yet she is my Antigone. "

VANCE. —"You know the classics, sir. Mr. Merle said you were a scholar! —read Sophocles in his native Greek, I presume, sir? "

MR. WAIFE. —"You jeer at the unfortunate: I am used to it. "

VANCE (confused). —"I did not mean to wound you: I beg pardon. But your language and manner are not what—what one might expect to find in a—in a—Bandit persecuted by a remorseless Baron."

MR. WAIFE. —"Sir, you say you are an artist. Have you heard no tales of your professional brethren, —men of genius the highest, who won fame, which I never did, and failed of fortunes, as I have done? Their own fault, perhaps, —improvidence, wild habits, ignorance of the way how to treat life and deal with their fellow-men; such fault may have been mine too. I suffer for it: no matter; I ask none to save me. You are a painter: you would place her features on your canvas; you would have her rank amongst your own creations. She may become a part of your immortality. Princes may gaze on the effigies of the innocent happy childhood, to which your colours lend imperishable glow. They may ask who and what was this fair creature? Will you answer, 'One whom I found in tinsel, and so left, sure that she would die in rags! ' —Save her! "

Lionel drew forth his purse, and poured its contents on the table. Vance covered them with his broad hand, and swept them into his own pocket! At that sinister action Waife felt his heart sink into his shoes; but his face was as calm as a Roman's, only he resumed his pipe with a prolonged and testy whiff.

"It is I who am to take the portrait, and it is I who will pay for it, " said Vance. "I understand that you have a pressing occasion for" —

"Three pounds! " muttered Sophy, sturdily, through the tears which her grandfather's pathos had drawn forth from her downcast eyes, "Three pounds—three—three. "

"You shall have them. But listen: I meant only to take a sketch; I must now have a finished portrait. I cannot take this by candlelight.

You must let me come here to-morrow; and yet to-morrow, I understand, you meant to leave? "

WAIFE. —"If you will generously bestow on us the sum you say, we shall not leave the village till you have completed your picture. It is Mr. Rugge and his company we will leave. "

VANCE. —"And may I venture to ask what you propose to do, towards a new livelihood for yourself and your grandchild, by the help of a sum which is certainly much for me to pay, —enormous, I might say, *quoad* me, —but small for a capital whereon to set up a business? "

WAIFE. —"Excuse me if I do not answer that very natural question at present. Let me assure you that that precise sum is wanted for an investment which promises her and myself an easy existence. But to insure my scheme, I must keep it secret. Do you believe me? "

"I do! " cried Lionel; and Sophy, whom by this time he had drawn upon his lap, put her arm gratefully round his neck.

"There is your money, sir, beforehand, " said Vance, declining downward his betrayed and resentful nose, and depositing three sovereigns on the table.

"And how do you know, " said Waife, smiling, "that I may not be off to-night with your money and your model! "

"Well, " said Vance, curtly, "I think it is on the cards. Still, as John Kemble said when rebuked for too large an alms,

"'It is not often that I do these things,
But when I do, I do them handsomely.'"

"Well applied, and well delivered, sir, " said the Comedian, "only you should put a little more emphasis on the word do. "

"Did I not put enough? I am sure I felt it strongly; no one can feel the do more! "

Waife's pliant face relaxed into a genial brightness. The *equivoque* charmed him. However, not affecting to comprehend it, he thrust back the money, and said, —"No, sir, not a shilling till the picture is completed. Nay, to relieve your mind, I will own that, had I no scruple more delicate, I would rather receive nothing till Mr. Rugge is gone. True, he has no right to any share in it. But you see before you a man who, when it comes to arguing, could never take a wrangler's degree, —never get over the Asses' Bridge, sir. Plucked at it scores of times clean as a feather. But do not go yet. You came to give us money: give us what, were I rich, I should value more highly, —a little of your time. You, sir, are an artist; and you, young gentleman? " addressing Lionel.

LIONEL (colouring). —"I—am nothing as yet. "

WAIFE. —"You are fond of the drama, I presume, both of you? Apropos of John Kemble, you, sir, said that you have never heard him. Allow me, so far as this cracked voice can do it, to give you a faint idea of him. "

"I shall be delighted, " said Vance, drawing nearer to the table, and feeling more at his ease. "But since I see you smoke, may I take the liberty to light my cigar? "

"Make yourself at home, " said Gentleman Waife, with the good-humour of a fatherly host. And, all the while, Lionel and Sophy were babbling together, she still upon his lap.

Waife began his imitation of John Kemble. Despite the cracked voice, it was admirable. One imitation drew on another; then succeeded anecdotes of the Stage, of the Senate, of the Bar. Waife had heard great orators, whom every one still admires for the speeches which nobody nowadays ever reads; he gave a lively idea of each. And then came sayings of dry humour and odd scraps of worldly observation; and time flew on pleasantly till the clock struck twelve, and the young guests tore themselves away.

"Merle, Merle! " cried the Comedian, when they were gone.

Merle appeared.

"We don't go to-morrow. When Rugge sends for us (as he will do at daybreak), say so. You shall lodge us a few days longer, and then— and then—my little Sophy, kiss me, kiss me! You are saved at least from those horrid painted creatures! "

"Ah, ah! " growled Merle from below, "he has got the money! Glad to hear it. But, " he added, as he glanced at sundry weird and astrological symbols with which he had been diverting himself, "that's not it. The true horary question, is, WHAT WILL HE DO WITH IT? "

CHAPTER IX.

The historian shows that, notwithstanding the progressive spirit of the times, a Briton is not permitted, without an effort, "to progress" according to his own inclinations.

Sophy could not sleep. At first she was too happy. Without being conscious of any degradation in her lot amongst the itinerant artists of Mr. Rugge's exhibition, —how could she, when her beloved and revered protector had been one of those artists for years? —yet instinctively she shrank from their contact. Doubtless, while absorbed in some stirring part, she forgot companions, audience, all, and enjoyed what she performed, —necessarily enjoyed, for her acting was really excellent, and where no enjoyment there no excellence; but when the histrionic enthusiasm was not positively at work, she crept to her grandfather with something between loathing and terror of the "painted creatures" and her own borrowed tinsel.

But, more than all, she felt acutely every indignity or affront offered to Gentleman Waife. Heaven knows, these were not few; and to escape from such a life—to be with her grandfather alone, have him all to herself to tend and to pet, to listen to and to prattle with— seemed to her the consummation of human felicity. Ah, but should she be all alone? Just as she was lulling herself into a doze, that question seized and roused her. And then it was not happiness that kept her waking: it was what is less rare in the female breast, curiosity. Who was to be the mysterious third, to whose acquisition the three pounds were evidently to be devoted? What new face had she purchased by the loan of her own? Not the Pig-faced Lady nor the Spotted Boy. Could it be the Norfolk Giant or the Calf with two Heads? Horrible idea! Monstrous phantasmagoria began to stalk before her eyes; and to charm them away, with great fervour she fell to saying her prayers, —an act of devotion which she had forgotten, in her excitement, to perform before resting her head on the pillow, —an omission, let us humbly hope, not noted down in very dark characters by the recording angel.

That act over, her thoughts took a more comely aspect than had been worn by the preceding phantasies, reflected Lionel's kind looks and repeated his gentle words. "Heaven bless him! " she said with emphasis, as a supplement to the habitual prayers; and then tears gathered to her grateful eyelids, for she was one of those beings whose tears come slow from sorrow, quick from affection. And so the gray dawn found her still-wakeful, and she rose, bathed her cheeks in the cold fresh water, and drew them forth with a glow like Hebe's. Dressing herself with the quiet activity which characterized all her movements, she then opened the casement and inhaled the air. All was still in the narrow lane; the shops yet unclosed. But on the still trees behind the shops the birds were beginning to stir and chirp. Chanticleer, from some neighbouring yard, rang out his brisk rereillee. Pleasant English summer dawn in the pleasant English country village. She stretched her graceful neck far from the casement, trying to catch a glimpse of the blue river. She had seen its majestic flow on the day they had arrived at the fair, and longed to gain its banks; then her servitude to the stage forbade her. Now she was to be free! O joy! Now she might have her careless hours of holiday; and, forgetful of Waife's warning that their vocation must be plied in towns, she let her fancy run riot amidst visions of green fields and laughing waters, and in fond delusion gathered the daisies and chased the butterflies. Changeling transferred into that lowest world of Art from the cradle of civil Nature, her human child's heart yearned for the human childlike delights. All children love the country, the flowers, the sward, the birds, the butterflies; or if some do not, despair, O Philanthropy, of their afterlives!

She closed the window, smiling to herself, stole through the adjoining doorway, and saw that her grandfather was still asleep. Then she busied herself in putting the little sitting-room to rights, reset the table for the morning meal, watered the stocks, and finally took up the crystal and looked into it with awe, wondering why the Cobbler could see so much, and she only the distorted reflection of her own face. So interested, however, for once, did she become in the inspection of this mystic globe, that she did not notice the dawn pass into broad daylight, nor hear a voice at the door below, —nor, in short, take into cognition the external world, till a heavy tread shook the floor, and then, starting, she beheld the Remorseless Baron, with a face black enough to have darkened the crystal of Dr. Dee himself.

"Ho, ho, " said Mr. Rugge, in hissing accents which had often thrilled the threepenny gallery with anticipative horror. "Rebellious, eh? —won't come? Where's your grandfather, baggage? "

Sophy let fall the crystal—a mercy it was not brokenand gazed vacantly on the Baron.

"Your vile scamp of a grandfather? "

SOPHY (with spirit). —"He is not vile. You ought to be ashamed of yourself speaking so, Mr. Rugge! "

Here simultaneously, Mr. Waife, hastily indued in his gray dressing-gown, presented himself at the aperture of the bedroom door, and the Cobbler on the threshold of the sitting-room. The Comedian stood mute, trusting perhaps to the imposing effect of his attitude. The Cobbler, yielding to the impulse of untheatric man, put his head doggedly on one side, and with both hands on his hips said,

"Civil words to my lodgers, master, or out you go! "

The Remorseless Baron glared vindictively, first at one and then at the other; at length he strode up to Waife, and said, with a withering grin, "I have something to say to you; shall I say it before your landlord? "

The Comedian waved his hand to the Cobbler.

"Leave us, my friend; I shall not require you. Step this way, Mr. Rugge. " Rugge entered the bedroom, and Waife closed the door behind him.

"Anan, " quoth the Cobbler, scratching his head. "I don't quite take your grandfather's giving in. British ground here! But your Ascendant cannot surely be in such malignant conjunction with that obstreperous tyrant as to bind you to him hand and foot. Let's see what the crystal thinks of it. 'Take it up gently, and come downstairs with me. "

"Please, no; I'll stay near Grandfather, " said Sophy, resolutely. "He sha'n't be left helpless with that rude man. "

The Cobbler could not help smiling. "Lord love you, " said he; "you have a spirit of your own, and if you were my wife I should be afraid of you. But I won't stand here eavesdropping; mayhap your grandfather has secrets I'm not to hear: call me if I'm wanted. " He descended. Sophy, with less noble disdain of eavesdropping, stood in the centre of the room, holding her breath to listen. She heard no sound; she had half a mind to put her ear to the keyhole, but that seemed even to her a mean thing, if not absolutely required by the necessity of the case. So there she still stood, her head bent down, her finger raised: oh, that Vance could have so painted her!

CHAPTER X.

Showing the causes why men and nations, when one man or nation wishes to get for its own arbitrary purposes what the other man or nation does not desire to part with, are apt to ignore the mild precepts of Christianity, shock the sentiments and upset the theories of Peace Societies.

"Am I to understand, " said Mr. Rugge, in a whisper, when Waife had drawn him to the farthest end of the inner room, with the bed-curtains between their position and the door, deadening the sound of their voices, —"am I to understand that, after my taking you and that child to my theatre out of charity, and at your own request, you are going to quit me without warning, —French leave; is that British conduct? "

"Mr. Rugge, " replied Waife, deprecatingly, "I have no engagement with you beyond an experimental trial. We were free on both sides for three months, —you to dismiss us any day, we to leave you. The experiment does not please its: we thank you and depart. "

RUGGE. —"That is not the truth. I said I was free to dismiss you both, if the child did not suit. You, poor helpless creature, could be of no use. But I never heard you say you were to be free too. Stands to reason not! Put my engagements at a Waife's mercy! I, Lorenzo Rugge! —stuff! But I am a just man, and a liberal man, and if you think you ought to have a higher salary, if this ungrateful proceeding is only, as I take it, a strike for wages, I will meet you. Juliet Araminta does play better than I could have supposed; and I'll conclude an engagement on good terms, as we were to have done if the experiment answered, for three years. " Waife shook his head. "You are very good, Mr. Rugge, but it is not a strike. My little girl does not like the life at any price; and, since she supports me, I am bound to please her. Besides, " said the actor, with a stiffer manner, "you have broken faith with me. It was fully understood that I was to appear no more on your stage; all my task was to advise with you in the performances, remodel the plays, help in the stage-management; and you took advantage of my penury, and, when I asked for a small advance, insisted on forcing these relics of what I was upon the public pity. Enough: we part. I bear no malice. "

RUGGE. —"Oh, don't you? No more do I. But I am a Briton, and I have the spirit of one. You had better not make an enemy of me. "

WAIFE. —"I am above the necessity of making enemies. I have an enemy ready made in myself. "

Rugge placed a strong bony hand upon the cripple's arm. "I dare say you have! A bad conscience, sir. How would you like your past life looked into, and blabbed out? "

GENTLEMAN WAIFE (mournfully). —"The last four years of it have been spent in your service, Mr. Rugge. If their record had been blabbed out for my benefit, there would not have been a dry eye in the house. "

RUGGE. "I disdain your sneer. When a scorpion nursed at my bosom sneers at me, I leave it to its own reflections. But I don't speak of the years in which that scorpion has been enjoying a salary and smoking canaster at my expense. I refer to an earlier dodge in its checkered existence. Ha, sir, you wince! I suspect I can find out something about you which would—"

WAIFE (fiercely). —"Would what? "

RUGGE. —"Oh, lower your tone, sir; no bullying me. I suspect! I have good reason for suspicion; and if you sneak off in this way, and cheat me out of my property in Juliet Araminta, I will leave no stone unturned to prove what I suspect: look to it, slight man! Come, I don't wish to quarrel; make it up, and" (drawing out his pocket-book) "if you want cash down, and will have an engagement in black and white for three years for Juliet Araminta, you may squeeze a good sum out of me, and go yourself where you please: you'll never be troubled by me. What I want is the girl. "

All the actor laid aside, Waife growled out, "And hang me; sir, if you shall have the girl! "

At this moment Sophy opened the door wide, and entered boldly. She had heard her grandfather's voice raised, though its hoarse tones did not allow her to distinguish his words. She was alarmed for him. She came in, his guardian fairy, to protect him from the oppressor of six feet high. Rugge's arm was raised, not indeed to strike, but rather to declaim. Sophy slid between him and her grandfather, and, clinging round the latter, flung out her own arm, the forefinger raised menacingly towards the Remorseless Baron. How you would have clapped if you had seen her so at Covent Garden! But I'll swear the child did not know she was acting. Rugge did, and was struck with admiration and regretful rage at the idea of losing her.

"Bravo! " said he, involuntarily. "Come, come, Waife, look at her: she was born for the stage. My heart swells with pride. She is my property, morally speaking; make her so legally; and hark, in your ear, fifty pounds. Take me in the humour, —Golconda opens, —fifty pounds! "

"No, " said the vagrant.

"Well, " said Rugge, sullenly; "let her speak for herself. "

"Speak, child. You don't wish to return to Mr. Rugge, —and without me, too, —do you, Sophy? "

"Without you, Grandy! I'd rather die first. "

"You hear her; all is settled between us. You have had our services up to last night; you have paid us up to last night; and so good morning to you, Mr. Rugge. "

"My dear child, " said the manager, softening his voice as much as he could, "do consider. You shall be so made of without that stupid old man. You think me cross, but 't is he who irritates and puts me out of temper. I 'm uncommon fond of children. I had a babe of my own once, —upon my honour, I had, —and if it had not been for convulsions, caused by teething, I should be a father still. Supply to me the place of that beloved babe. You shall have such fine dresses; all new, —choose 'em yourself, —minced veal and raspberry tarts for dinner every Sunday. In three years, under my care, you will become a great actress, and make your fortune, and marry a lord, — lords go out of their wits for great actresses, —whereas, with him, what will you do? drudge and rot and starve; and he can't live long, and then where will you be? 'T is a shame to hold her so, you idle old vagabond. "

"I don't hold her, " said Waife, trying to push her away. "There's something in what the man says. Choose for yourself, Sophy. "

SOPHY (suppressing a sob). —"How can you have the heart to talk so, Grandy? I tell you, Mr. Rugge, you are a bad man, and I hate you, and all about you; and I'll stay with Grandfather; and I don't care if I do starve: he sha'n't! "

MR. RUGGE (clapping both hands on the crown of his hat, and striding to the door). —"William Waife, beware 't is done. I'm your enemy. As for you, too dear but abandoned infant, stay with him: you'll find out very soon who and what he is; your pride will have a fall, when—"

Waife sprang forward, despite his lameness, —both his fists clenched, his one eye ablaze; his broad burly torso confronted and daunted the stormy manager. Taller and younger though Rugge was, he cowered before the cripple he had so long taunted and humbled. The words stood arrested on his tongue. "Leave the room instantly! " thundered the actor, in a voice no longer broken. "Blacken my name before that child by one word, and I will dash the next down your throat. " Rugge rushed to the door, and keeping it ajar between Waife and himself, he then thrust in his head, hissing forth,

"Fly, caitiff, fly! my revenge shall track your secret and place you in my power. Juliet Araminta shall yet be mine. " With these awful words the Remorseless Baron cleared the stairs in two bounds, and was out of the house.

Waife smiled contemptuously. But as the street-door clanged on the form of the angry manager, the colour faded from the old man's face. Exhausted by the excitement he had gone through, he sank on a chair, and, with one quick gasp as for breath, fainted away.

CHAPTER XI.

Progress of the Fine Arts. —Biographical anecdotes. —Fluctuations in the value of money. —Speculative tendencies of the time.

Whatever the shock which the brutality of the Remorseless Baron inflicted on the nervous system of the persecuted but triumphant Bandit, it had certainly subsided by the time Vance and Lionel entered Waife's apartment; for they found grandfather and grandchild seated near the open window, at the corner of the table (on which they had made room for their operations by the removal of the carved cocoanut, the crystal egg, and the two flower-pots), eagerly engaged, with many a silvery laugh from the lips of Sophy, in the game of dominos.

Mr. Waife had been devoting himself, for the last hour and more, to the instruction of Sophy in the mysteries of that intellectual amusement; and such pains did he take, and so impressive were his exhortations, that his happy pupil could not help thinking to herself that this was the new art upon which Waife depended for their future livelihood. She sprang up, however, at the entrance of the visitors, her face beaming with grateful smiles; and, running to Lionel and taking him by the hand, while she courtesied with more respect to Vance, she exclaimed, "We are free! thanks to you, thanks to you both! He is gone! Mr. Rugge is gone! "

"So I saw on passing the green; stage and all, " said Vance, while Lionel kissed the child and pressed her to his side. It is astonishing how paternal he felt, —how much she had crept into his heart.

"Pray, sir, " asked Sophy, timidly, glancing to Vance, "has the Norfolk Giant gone too? "

VANCE. —"I fancy so—all the shows were either gone or going. "

SOPHY. —"The Calf with Two Heads? "

VANCE. —"Do you regret it? "

SOPHY. —"Oh, dear, no. "

Waife, who after a profound bow, and a cheery "Good day, gentlemen, " had hitherto remained silent, putting away the dominoes, now said, "I suppose, sir, you would like at once to begin your sketch? "

VANCE. —"Yes; I have brought all my tools; see, even the canvas. I wish it were larger, but it is all I have with me of that material: 't is already stretched; just let me arrange the light. "

WAIFE. —"If you don't want me, gentlemen, I will take the air for half-an-hour or so. In fact, I may now feel free to look after my investment. "

SOPHY (whispering Lionel). —"You are sure the Calf has gone as well as the Norfolk Giant? "

Lionel wonderingly replied that he thought so; and Waife disappeared into his room, whence he soon emerged, having doffed his dressing-gown for a black coat, by no means threadbare, and well brushed. Hat, stick, and gloves in hand, he really seemed respectable, —more than respectable, —Gentleman Waife every inch of him; and saying, "Look your best, Sophy, and sit still, if you can, " nodded pleasantly to the three, and hobbled down the stairs. Sophy—whom Vance had just settled into a chair, with her head bent partially down (three-quarters), as the artist had released

"The loose train of her amber-dropping hair, "

and was contemplating aspect and position with a painter's meditative eye-started up, to his great discomposure, and rushed to the window. She returned to her seat with her mind much relieved. Waife was walking in an opposite direction to that which led towards the whilolm quarters of the Norfolk Giant and the Two-headed Calf.

"Come, come, " said Vance, impatiently, "you have broken an idea in half. I beg you will not stir till I have placed you; and then, if all else of you be still, you may exercise your tongue. I give you leave to talk. "

SOPHY (penitentially). —"I am so sorry—I beg pardon. Will that do, sir? "

51

VANCE. —"Head a little more to the right, —so, Titania watching Bottom asleep. Will you lie on the floor, Lionel, and do Bottom? "

LIONEL (indignantly). —"Bottom! Have I an ass's head? "

VANCE. —"Immaterial! I can easily imagine that you have one. I want merely an outline of figure, —something sprawling and ungainly. "

LIONEL (sulkily). —"Much obliged to you; imagine that too. "

VANCE. —"Don't be so disobliging. It is necessary that she should look fondly at something, —expression in the eye. " Lionel at once reclined himself incumbent in a position as little sprawling and ungainly as he could well contrive.

VANCE. —"Fancy, Miss Sophy, that this young gentleman is very dear to you. Have you got a brother? "

SOPHY. —"Ah, no, sir. "

VANCE. —"Hum. But you have, or have had, a doll? "

SOPHY. —"Oh, yes; Grandfather gave me one. "

VANCE. —"And you were fond of that doll? "

SOPHY. —"Very. "

VANCE. —"Fancy that young gentleman is your doll grown big, that it is asleep, and you are watching that no one hurts it; Mr. Rugge, for instance. Throw your whole soul into that thought, —love for doll, apprehension of Rugge. Lionel, keep still, and shut your eyes; do. "

LIONEL (grumbling). —"I did not come here to be made a doll of. "

VANCE. —"Coax him to be quiet, Miss Sophy, and sleep peaceably, or I shall do him a mischief. I can be a Rugge, too, if I am put out. "

SOPHY (in the softest tones). —"Do try and sleep, sir: shall I get you a pillow? "

LIONEL. —"No, thank you: I'm very comfortable now, " settling his head upon his arm; and after one upward glance towards Sophy, the lids closed reluctantly over his softened eyes. A ray of sunshine came aslant through the half-shut window, and played along the boy's clustering hair and smooth pale cheek. Sophy's gaze rested on him most benignly.

"Just so, " said Vance; "and now be silent till I have got the attitude and fixed the look. "

The artist sketched away rapidly with a bold practised hand, and all was silent for about half-an-hour, when he said, "You May get up, Lionel; I have done with you for the present. "

SOPHY. —"And me too—may I see? "

VANCE. —"No, but you may talk now. So you had a doll? What has become of it? "

SOPHY. —"I left it behind, sir. Grandfather thought it would distract me from attending to his lessons and learning my part. "

VANCE. —"You love your grandfather more than the doll? "

SOPHY. —"Oh! a thousand million million times more. "

VANCE. —"He brought you up, I suppose? Have you no father, — no mother? "

SOPHY. —"I have only Grandfather. "

LIONEL. —"Have you always lived with him? "

SOPHY. —"Dear me, no; I was with Mrs. Crane till Grandfather came from abroad, and took me away, and put me with some very kind people; and then, when Grandfather had that bad accident, I came to stay with him, and we have been together ever since. "

LIONEL. —"Was Mrs. Crane no relation of yours? "

SOPHY. —"No, I suppose not, for she was not kind; I was so miserable: but don't talk of it; I forget that now. I only wish to

53

remember from the time Grandfather took me in his lap, and told me to be a good child and love him; and I have been happy ever since. "

"You are a dear good child, " said Lionel, emphatically, "and I wish I had you for my sister. "

VANCE. —"When your grandfather has received from me that exorbitant—not that I grudge it—sum, I should like to ask, What will he do with it? As he said it was a secret, I must not pump you. "

SOPHY. —"What will he do with it? I should like to know, too, sir; but whatever it is I don't care, so long as I and Grandfather are together. "

Here Waife re-entered. "Well, how goes on the picture? "

VANCE. —"Tolerably, for the first sitting; I require two more. "

WAIFE. —"Certainly; only—only" (he drew aside Vance, and whispered), "only the day after to-morrow, I fear I shall want the money. It is an occasion that never will occur again: I would seize it."

VANCE. —"Take the money now. "

WAIFE. —"Well, thank you, sir; you are sure now that we shall not run away; and I accept your kindness; it will make all safe. "

Vance, with surprising alacrity, slipped the sovereigns into the old man's hand; for truth to say, though thrifty, the artist was really generous. His organ of caution was large, but that of acquisitiveness moderate. Moreover, in those moments when his soul expanded with his art, he was insensibly less alive to the value of money. And strange it is that, though States strive to fix for that commodity the most abiding standards, yet the value of money to the individual who regards it shifts and fluctuates, goes up and down half-a-dozen times a day. For any part, I honestly declare that there are hours in the twenty-four—such, for instance, as that just before breakfast, or that succeeding a page of this History in which I have been put out of temper with my performance and myself—when any one in want of five shillings at my disposal would find my value of that sum put it quite out of his reach; while at other times—just after dinner, for instance, or when I have effected what seems to me a happy stroke, or a good bit of colour, in this historical composition—the value of those five shillings is so much depreciated that I might be, —I think so, at least, —I might be almost tempted to give them away for nothing. Under some such mysterious influences in the money-market, Vance therefore felt not the loss of his three sovereigns; and returning to his easel, drove away Lionel and Sophy, who had taken that opportunity to gaze on the canvas.

"Don't do her justice at all, " quoth Lionel; "all the features exaggerated. "

"And you pretend to paint! " returned Vance, in great scorn, and throwing a cloth over his canvas. "To-morrow, Mr. Waife, the same hour. Now, Lionel, get your hat, and come away. "

Vance carried off the canvas, and Lionel followed slowly. Sophy gazed at their departing forms from the open window; Waife stumped about the room, rubbing his hands, "He'll do; he 'll do: I always thought so. " Sophy turned: "Who'll do? —the young gentleman? Do what? "

WAIFE. -"The young gentleman? -as if I was thinking of him! Our new companion; I have been with him this last hour. Wonderful natural gifts. "

SOPHY (ruefully). —"It is alive, then? "

WAIFE. —"Alive! yes, I should think so. "

SOPHY (half-crying.)—"I am very sorry; I know I shall hate it. "

WAIFF. —"Tut, darling: get me my pipe; I'm happy. "

SOPHY (cutting short her fit of ill-humour). —"Are you? then I am, and I will not hate it. "

CHAPTER XII.

In which it is shown that a man does this or declines to do that for reasons best known to himself, —a reserve which is extremely conducive to the social interests of a community, since the conjecture into the origin and nature of those reasons stimulates the inquiring faculties, and furnishes the staple of modern conversation. And as it is not to be denied that, if their neighbours left them nothing to guess at, three-fourths of civilized humankind, male or female, would have nothing to talk about; so we cannot too gratefully encourage that needful curiosity termed by the inconsiderate tittle-tattle or scandal, which saves the vast majority of our species from being reduced to the degraded condition of dumb animals.

The next day the sitting was renewed: but Waife did not go out, and the conversation was a little more restrained; or rather, Waife had the larger share in it. The Comedian, when he pleased, could certainly be very entertaining. It was not so much in what he said as his manner of saying it. He was a strange combination of sudden extremes, at one while on a tone of easy but not undignified familiarity with his visitors, as if their equal in position, their superior in years; then abruptly, humble, deprecating, almost obsequious, almost servile; and then again, jerked as it were into pride and stiffness, falling back, as if the effort were impossible, into meek dejection. Still the prevalent character of the man's mood and talk was social, quaint, cheerful. Evidently he was by original temperament a droll and joyous humourist, with high animal spirits; and, withal, an infantine simplicity at times, like the clever man who never learns the world and is always taken in.

A circumstance, trifling in itself, but suggestive of speculation either as to the character or antecedent circumstances of Gentleman Waife, did not escape Vance's observation. Since his rupture with Mr. Rugge, there was a considerable amelioration in that affection of the trachea, which, while his engagement with Rugge lasted, had rendered the Comedian's dramatic talents unavailable on the stage. He now expressed himself without the pathetic hoarseness or cavernous wheeze which had previously thrown a wet blanket over his efforts at discourse. But Vance put no very stern construction on the dissimulation which his change seemed to denote. Since Waife was still one-eyed and a cripple, he might very excusably shrink from reappearance on the stage, and affect a third infirmity to save his pride from the exhibition of the two infirmities that were genuine.

That which most puzzled Vance was that which had most puzzled the Cobbler, —What could the man once have been? how fallen so low? —for fall it was, that was clear. The painter, though not himself of patrician extraction, had been much in the best society. He had been a petted favourite in great houses. He had travelled. He had seen the world. He had the habits and instincts of good society.

Now, in what the French term the *beau monde*, there are little traits that reveal those who have entered it, —certain tricks of phrase, certain modes of expression, —even the pronunciation of familiar words, even the modulation of an accent. A man of the most refined bearing may not have these peculiarities; a man, otherwise coarse and brusque in his manner, may. The slang of the *beau monde* is quite apart from the code of high breeding. Now and then, something in Waife's talk seemed to show that he had lighted on that beau-world; now and then, that something wholly vanished. So that Vance might have said, "He has been admitted there, not inhabited it. "

Yet Vance could not feel sure, after all; comedians are such takes in. But was the man, by the profession of his earlier life, a comedian? Vance asked the question adroitly.

"You must have taken to the stage young? " said he.

"The stage! " said Waife; "if you mean the public stage, no. I have acted pretty often in youth, even in childhood, to amuse others, never professionally to support myself, till Mr. Rugge civilly engaged me four years ago. "

"Is it possible, —with your excellent education! But pardon me; I have hinted my surprise at your late vocation before, and it displeased you. "

"Displeased me! " said Waife, with an abject, depressed manner; "I hope I said nothing that would have misbecome a poor broken vagabond like me. I am no prince in disguise, —a good-for-nothing varlet who should be too grateful to have something to keep himself from a dunghill. "

LIONEL. —"Don't talk so. And but for your accident you might now be the great attraction on the metropolitan stage. Who does not respect a really fine actor? "

WAIFE (gloomily). —"The metropolitan stage! I was talked into it: I am glad even of the accident that saved me; say no more of that, no more of that. But I have spoiled your sitting. Sophy, you see, has left her chair. "

"I have done for to-day, " said Vance; "to-morrow, and my task is ended. "

Lionel came up to Vance and whispered him; the painter, after a pause, nodded silently, and then said to Waife,

"We are going to enjoy the fine weather on the Thames (after I have put away these things), and shall return to our inn—not far hence—to sup, at eight o'clock. Supper is our principal meal; we rarely spoil our days by the ceremonial of a formal dinner. Will you do us the favour to sup with us? Our host has a wonderful whiskey, which when raw is Glenlivat, but refined into toddy is nectar. Bring your pipe, and let us hear John Kemble again. "

Waife's face lighted up. "You are most kind; nothing I should like so much. But—" and the light fled, the face darkened—"but no; I cannot—you don't know—that is—I—I have made a vow to myself to decline all such temptations. I humbly beg you'll excuse me. "

VANCE. —"Temptations! of what kind, —the whiskey toddy? "

WAIFE (puffing away a sigh). —"Ah, yes; whiskey toddy, if you please. Perhaps I once loved a glass too well, and could not resist a glass too much now; and if I once broke the rule and became a tippler, what would happen to Juliet Araminta? For her sake don't press me. "

"Oh, do go, Grandy; he never drinks, —never anything   stronger than tea, I assure you, sir: it can't be that. "

"It is, silly child, and nothing else, " said Waife, positively, drawing himself up, —"excuse me. "

Lionel began brushing his hat with his sleeve, and his face worked; at last he said, "Well, sir, then may I ask another favour? Mr. Vance and I are going to-morrow, after the sitting, to see Hampton Court; we have kept that excursion to the last before leaving these parts. Would you and little Sophy come with us in the boat? We will have no whiskey toddy, and we will bring you both safe home. "

WAIFE. —"What—I! what—I! You are very young, sir, —a gentleman born and bred, I'll swear; and you to be seen, perhaps by some of your friends or family, with an old vagrant like me, in the Queen's palace, —the public gardens! I should be the vilest wretch if I took such advantage of your goodness. 'Pretty company, ' they would say, 'you had got into. ' With me! with me! Don't be alarmed, Mr. Vance not to be thought of. "

The young men were deeply affected.

"I can't accept that reason, " said Lionel, tremulously, "though I must not presume to derange your habits. But she may go with us, mayn't she? We'll take care of her, and she is dressed so plainly and neatly, and looks such a little lady" (turning to Vance).

"Yes, let her come with us, " said the artist, benevolently; though he by no means shared in Lionel's enthusiastic desire for her company. He thought she would be greatly in their way.

"Heaven bless you both! " answered Waife; "and she wants a holiday; she shall have it. "

"I'd rather stay with you, Grandy: you'll be so lone. "

"No, I wish to be out all to-morrow, -the investment! I shall not be alone; making friends with our future companion, Sophy. "

"And can do without me already? heigh-ho! "

VANCE. —"So that's settled; good-by to you. "

CHAPTER XIII.

Inspiring effect of the Fine Arts: the vulgar are moved by their exhibition into generous impulses and flights of fancy, checked by the ungracious severities of their superiors, as exemplified in the instance of Cobbler Merle and his servant of-all-work.

The next day, perhaps with the idea of removing all scruple from Sophy's mind, Waife had already gone after his investment when the friends arrived. Sophy at first was dull and dispirited, but by degrees she brightened up; and when, the sitting over and the picture done (save such final touches as Vance reserved for solitary study), she was permitted to gaze at her own effigy, she burst into exclamations of frank delight. "Am I like that! is it possible? Oh, how beautiful! Mr. Merle, Mr. Merle, Mr. Merle! " and running out of the room before Vance could stop her, she returned with the Cobbler, followed, too, by a thin gaunt girl, whom he pompously called his housekeeper, but who in sober truth was servant-of-all-work. Wife he had none: his horoscope, he said, having Saturn in square to the Seventh House, forbade him to venture upon matrimony. All gathered round the picture; all admired, and with justice: it was a chef-d'oeuvre. Vance in his maturest day never painted more charmingly. The three pounds proved to be the best outlay of capital he had ever made. Pleased with his work, he was pleased even with that unsophisticated applause.

"You must have Mercury and Venus very strongly aspected, " quoth the Cobbler; "and if you have the Dragon's Head in the Tenth House, you may count on being much talked of after you are dead. "

"After I am dead! —sinister omen! " said Vance, discomposed. "I have no faith in artists who count on being talked of after they are dead. Never knew a dauber who did not! But stand back: time flies; tie up your hair; put on your bonnet, Titania. You have a shawl? — not tinsel, I hope! quieter the better. You stay and see to her, Lionel. "

Said the gaunt servant-of-all-work to Mr. Merle, "I'd let the gentleman paint me, if he likes: shall I tell him, master? "

"Go back to the bacon, foolish woman. Why, he gave L3 for her likeness, 'cause of her Benefics! But you'd have to give him three years' wages afore he'd look you straight in the face, 'cause, you see, your Aspects are crooked. And, " added the Cobbler, philosophizing, "when the Malefics are dead agin a girl's mug, man is so constituted by natur' that he can't take to that mug unless it has a golden handle. Don't fret, 't is not your fault: born under Scorpio, —coarse-limbed, —dull complexion; and the Head of the Dragon aspected of Infortunes in all your Angles. "

CHAPTER XIV.

The historian takes advantage of the summer hours vouchsafed to the present life of Mr. Waife's grandchild, in order to throw a few gleams of light on her past. —He leads her into the palace of our kings, and moralizes thereon; and, entering the Royal Gardens, shows the uncertainty of human events, and the insecurity of British laws, by the abrupt seizure and constrained deportation of an innocent and unforeboding Englishman.

Such a glorious afternoon! The capricious English summer was so kind that day to the child and her new friends! When Sophy's small foot once trod the sward, had she been really Queen of the Green People, sward and footstep could not more joyously have met together. The grasshopper bounded in fearless trust upon the hem of her frock; she threw herself down on the grass and caught him, but, oh, so tenderly! and the gay insect, dear to poet and fairy, seemed to look at her from that quaint sharp face of his with sagacious recognition, resting calmly on the palm of her pretty hand; then when he sprang off, little moth-like butterflies peculiar to the margins of running waters quivered up from the herbage, fluttering round her. And there, in front, lay the Thames, glittering through the willows, Vance getting ready the boat, Lionel seated by her side, a child like herself, his pride of incipient manhood all forgotten; happy in her glee; she loving him for the joy she felt, and blending his image evermore in her remembrance with her first summer holiday, —with sunny beams, glistening leaves, warbling birds, fairy wings, sparkling waves. Oh, to live so in a child's heart, —innocent, blessed, angel-like, —better, better than the troubled reflection upon woman's later thoughts, better than that mournful illusion, over which tears so bitter are daily shed, —better than First Love! They entered the boat. Sophy had never, to the best of her recollection, been in a boat before. All was new to her: the lifelike speed of the little vessel; that world of cool green weeds, with the fish darting to and fro; the musical chime of oars; those distant stately swans. She was silent now—her heart was very full.

"What are you thinking of, Sophy? " asked Lionel, resting on the oar.

"Thinking! —I was not thinking. "

"What then? "

"I don't know, —feeling, I suppose. "

"Feeling what? "

"As if between sleeping and waking; as the water perhaps feels, with the sunlight on it! "

"Poetical, " said Vance, who, somewhat of a poet himself, naturally sneered at poetical tendencies in others; "but not so bad in its way. Ah, have I hurt your vanity? there are tears in your eyes. "

"No, sir, " said Sophy, falteringly. "But I was thinking then. "

"Ah, " said the artist, "that's the worst of it; after feeling ever comes thought; what was yours? "

"I was sorry poor Grandfather was not here, that's all. "

"It was not our fault: we pressed him cordially, " said Lionel.

"You did indeed, sir, thank you! And I don't know why he refused you. " The young men exchanged compassionate glances.

Lionel then sought to make her talk of her past life, tell him more of Mrs. Crane. Who and what was she?

Sophy could not or would not tell. The remembrances were painful; she had evidently tried to forget them. And the people with whom Waife had placed her, and who had been kind?

The Misses Burton; and they kept a day-school, and taught Sophy to read, write, and cipher. They lived near London, in a lane opening on a great common, with a green rail before the house, and had a good many pupils, and kept a tortoise shell cat and a canary. Not much to enlighten her listener did Sophy impart here.

And now they neared that stately palace, rich in associations of storm and splendour, —of the grand Cardinal; the iron-clad Protector; Dutch William of the immortal memory, whom we tried so hard to like, and in spite of the great Whig historian, that Titian of English prose, can only frigidly respect. Hard task for us Britons to like a Dutchman who dethrones his father-in-law, and drinks schnaps! Prejudice certainly; but so it is. Harder still to like Dutch

William's unfilial Fran! Like Queen Mary! I could as soon like Queen Goneril! Romance flies from the prosperous phlegmatic AEneas; flies from his plump Lavinia, his "fidus Achates, " Bentinck; flies to follow the poor deserted fugitive Stuart, with all his sins upon his head. Kings have no rights divine, except when deposed and fallen; they are then invested with the awe that belongs to each solemn image of mortal vicissitude, —vicissitude that startles the Epicurean, "insanientis sapientiae consultus, " and strikes from his careless lyre the notes that attest a god! Some proud shadow chases another from the throne of Cyrus, and Horace hears in the thunder the rush of Diespiter, and identifies Providence with the Fortune that snatches off the diadem in her whirring swoop. But fronts discrowned take a new majesty to generous natures: in all sleek prosperity there is something commonplace; in all grand adversity, something royal.

The boat shot to the shore; the young people landed, and entered the arch of the desolate palace. They gazed on the great hall and the presence-chamber, and the long suite of rooms with faded portraits; Vance as an artist, Lionel as an enthusiastic, well-read boy, Sophy as a wondering, bewildered, ignorant child. And then they emerged into the noble garden, with its regal trees. Groups were there of well dressed persons. Vance heard himself called by name. He had forgotten the London world, —forgotten, amidst his midsummer ramblings, that the London season was still ablaze; and there, stragglers from the great focus, fine people, with languid tones and artificial jaded smiles, caught him in his wanderer's dress, and walking side by side with the infant wonder of Mr. Rugge's show, exquisitely neat indeed, but still in a coloured print, of a pattern familiar to his observant eye in the windows of many a shop lavish of tickets, and inviting you to come in by the assurance that it is "selling off. " The artist stopped, coloured, bowed, answered the listless questions put to him with shy haste: he then attempted to escape; they would not let him.

"You MUST come back and dine with us at the Star and Garter, " said Lady Selina Vipont. "A pleasant party, —you know most of them, —the Dudley Slowes, dear old Lady Frost, those pretty Ladies Prymme, Janet and Wilhelmina. "

"We can't let you off, " said, sleepily, Mr. Crampe, a fashionable wit, who rarely made more than one bon mot in the twenty-four hours, and spent the rest of his time in a torpid state.

VANCE. —"Really you are too kind, but I am not even dressed for —
"

LADY SELINA. —"So charmingly dressed-so picturesque! Besides, what matters? Every one knows who you are. Where on earth have you been? "

VANCE. —"Rambling about, taking sketches. "

LADY SELINA (directing her eyeglass towards Lionel and Sophy, who stood aloof). —"But your companions, your brother? and that pretty little girl, —your sister, I suppose? "

VANCE (shuddering). —"No, not relations. I took charge of the boy, —clever young fellow; and the little girl is—"

LADY SELINA. —"Yes. The little girl is—"

VANCE. —"A little girl, as you see: and very pretty, as you say, — subject for a picture. "

LADY SELINA (indifferently). —"Oh, let the children go and amuse themselves somewhere. Now we have found you; positively you are our prisoner. "

Lady Selina Vipont was one of the queens of London; she had with her that habit of command natural to such royalties. Frank Vance was no tuft-hunter, but once under social influences, they had their effect on him, as on most men who are blest with noses in the air. Those great ladies, it is true, never bought his pictures; but they gave him the position which induced others to buy them. Vance loved his art; his art needed its career. Its career was certainly brightened and quickened by the help of rank and fashion.

In short, Lady Selina triumphed, and the painter stepped back to Lionel. "I must go to Richmond with these people. I know you'll excuse me. I shall be back to-night somehow. By the by, as you are going to the post-office here for the letter you expect from your mother, ask for my letters too. You will take care of little Sophy, and [in a whisper] hurry her out of the garden, or that Grand Mogul feminine, Lady Selina, whose condescension would crush the Andes, will be stopping her as my *protege*, falling in raptures with that horrid coloured print, saying, 'Dear, what pretty sprigs! where can such things be got? ' and learning perhaps how Frank Vance saved the Bandit's Child from the Remorseless Baron. 'T is your turn now. Save your friend. The Baron was a lamb compared to a fine lady. " He pressed Lionel's unresponding hand, and was off to join the polite merrymaking of the Frosts, Slowes, and Prymmes.

Lionel's pride ran up to the fever-heat of its thermometer; more roused, though, on behalf of the unconscious Sophy than himself.

"Let us come into the town, lady-bird, and choose a doll. You may have one now, without fear of distracting you from what I hate to think you ever stooped to perform. "

As Lionel, his crest erect and nostril dilated, and holding Sophy firmly by the hand, took his way out from the gardens, he was obliged to pass the patrician party, of whom Vance now made one.

His countenance and air, as he swept by, struck them all, especially Lady Selina. "A very distinguished-looking boy, " said she. "What a fine face! Who did you say he was, Mr. Vance? "

VANCE. —"His name is Haughton, —Lionel Haughton. "

LADY SELINA. —"Haughton! Haughton! Any relation to poor dear Captain Haughton, —Charlie Haughton, as he was generally called?"

Vance, knowing little more of his young friend's parentage than that his mother let lodgings, at which, once domiciliated himself, he had made the boy's acquaintance, and that she enjoyed the pension of a captain's widow, replied carelessly, —

"His father was a captain, but I don't know whether he was a Charlie. "

MR. CRAMPE (the wit). —"Charlies are extinct! I have the last in a fossil, —box and all. "

General laugh. Wit shut up again.

LADY SELINA. —"He has a great look of Charlie Haughton. Do you know if he is connected with that extraordinary man, Mr. Darrell? "

VANCE. —"Upon my word, I do not. What Mr. Darrell do you mean? "

Lady Selina, with one of those sublime looks of celestial pity with which personages in the great world forgive ignorance of names and genealogies in those not born within its orbit, replied, "Oh, to be sure. It is not exactly in the way of your delightful art to know Mr. Darrell, one of the first men in Parliament, a connection of mine. "

LADY FROST (nippingly). —"You mean Guy Darrell, the lawyer. "

LADY SELINA. —"Lawyer—true; now I think of it, he was a lawyer. But his chief fame was in the House of Commons. All parties agreed that he might have commanded any station; but he was too rich perhaps to care sufficiently about office. At all events, Parliament was dissolved when he was at the height of his reputation, and he refused to be re-elected. "

One SIR GREGORY STOLLHEAD (a member of the House of Commons, young, wealthy, a constant attendant, of great promise, with speeches that were filled with facts, and emptied the benches). —"I have heard of him. Before my time; lawyers not much weight in the House now. "

LADY SELINA. —"I am told that Mr. Darrell did not speak like a lawyer. But his career is over; lives in the country, and sees nobody; a thousand pities; a connection of mine, too; great loss to the country. Ask your young friend, Mr. Vance, if Mr. Darrell is not his relation. I hope so, for his sake. Now that our party is in power, Mr. Darrell could command anything for others, though he has ceased to act with us. Our party is not forgetful of talent. "

LADY FROST (with icy crispness). —"I should think not: it has so little of that kind to remember. "

SIR GREGORY. —"Talent is not wanted in the House of Commons now; don't go down, in fact. Business assembly. "

LADY SELINA (suppressing a yawn). —"Beautiful day! We had better think of going back to Richmond. "

General assent, and slow retreat.

CHAPTER XV.

The historian records the attachment to public business which distinguishes the British legislator. —Touching instance of the regret which ever in patriotic bosoms attends the neglect of a public duty.

From the dusty height of a rumble-tumble affixed to Lady Selina Vipont's barouche, and by the animated side of Sir Gregory Stollhead, Vance caught sight of Lionel and Sophy at a corner of the spacious green near the Palace. He sighed; he envied them. He thought of the boat, the water, the honeysuckle arbour at the little inn, —pleasures he had denied himself, —pleasures all in his own way. They seemed still more alluring by contrast with the prospect before him; formal dinner at the Star and Garter, with titled Prymmes, Slowes, and Frosts, a couple of guineas a head, including light wines, which he did not drink, and the expense of a chaise back by himself. But such are life and its social duties, —such, above all, ambition and a career. Who that would leave a name on his tombstone can say to his own heart, "Perish Stars and Garters: my existence shall pass from day to day in honeysuckle arbours! "

Sir Gregory Stollhead interrupted Vance's revery by an impassioned sneeze. "Dreadful smell of hay! " said the legislator, with watery eyes. "Are you subject to the hay fever? I am! A-tisha-tisha-tisha [sneezing]—country frightfully unwholesome at this time of year. And to think that I ought now to be in the House, —in my committee-room; no smell of hay there; most important committee. "

VANCE (rousing himself). —"Ah—on what? "

SIR GREGORY (regretfully). —"Sewers. "

CHAPTER XVI.

Signs of an impending revolution, which, like all revolutions, seems to come of a sudden, though its causes have long been at work; and to go off in a tantrum, though its effects must run on to the end of a history.

Lionel could not find in the toy-shops of the village a doll good enough to satisfy his liberal inclinations, but he bought one which amply contented the humbler aspirations of Sophy. He then strolled to the post-office. There were several letters for Vance; one for himself in his mother's handwriting. He delayed opening it for the moment. The day was far advanced Sophy must be hungry. In vain she declared she was not. They passed by a fruiterer's stall. The strawberries and cherries were temptingly fresh; the sun still very powerful. At the back of the fruiterer's was a small garden, or rather orchard, smiling cool through the open door; little tables laid out there. The good woman who kept the shop was accustomed to the wants and tastes of humble metropolitan visitors. But the garden was luckily now empty: it was before the usual hour for tea-parties; so the young folks had the pleasantest table under an apple-tree, and the choice of the freshest fruit. Milk and cakes were added to the fare. It was a banquet, in Sophy's eyes, worthy that happy day. And when Lionel had finished his share of the feast, eating fast, as spirited, impatient boys formed to push on in life and spoil their digestion are apt to do; and while Sophy was still lingering over the last of the strawberries, he threw himself back on his chair and drew forth his letter. Lionel was extremely fond of his mother, but her letters were not often those which a boy is over-eager to read. It is not all mothers who understand what boys are, —their quick susceptibilities, their precocious manliness, all their mystical ways and oddities. A letter from Mrs. Haughton generally somewhat fretted and irritated Lionel's high-strung nerves, and he had instinctively put off the task of reading the one he held, till satisfied hunger and cool-breathing shadows, and rest from the dusty road, had lent their soothing aid to his undeveloped philosophy.

He broke the seal slowly; another letter was enclosed within. At the first few words his countenance changed; he uttered a slight exclamation, read on eagerly; then, before concluding his mother's epistle, hastily tore open that which it had contained, ran his eye over its contents, and, dropping both letters on the turf below, rested his face on his hand in agitated thought. Thus ran his mother's letter:

MY DEAR BOY, —How could you! Do it slyly!! Unknown to your own mother!! I could not believe it of you!!!! Take advantage of my confidence in showing you the letters of your father's cousin, to write to himself—clandestinely! —you, who I thought had such an open character, and who ought to appreciate mine. Every one who knows me says I am a woman in ten thousand, —not for beauty and talent (though I have had my admirers for them too), but for GOODNESS I As a wife and mother, I may say I have been exemplary. I had sore trials with the dear captain—and IMMENSE temptations. But he said on his death-bed, "Jessica, you are an angel. " And I have had offers since, —IMMENSE offers, —but I devoted myself to my child, as you know. And what I have put up with, letting the first floor, nobody can tell; and only a widow's pension, —going before a magistrate to get it paid! And to think my own child, for whom I have borne so much, should behave so cruelly to me! Clandestine! that is that which stabs me. Mrs. Inman found me crying, and said, "What is the matter? —you who are such an angel, crying like a baby! " And I could not help saying, "'T is the serpent's tooth, Mrs. L" What you wrote to your benefactor (and I had hoped patron) I don't care to guess; something very rude and imprudent it must be, judging by the few lines he addressed to me. I don't mind copying them for you to read. All my acts are aboveboard, as often and often Captain H. used to say, "Your heart is in a glass case, Jessica; " and so it is! but my son keeps his under lock and key.

"Madam [this is what he writes to me], your son has thought fit to infringe the condition upon which I agreed to assist you on his behalf. I enclose a reply to himself, which I beg you will give to his own hands without breaking the seal. Since it did not seem to you indiscreet to communicate to a boy of his years letters written solely to yourself, you cannot blame me if I take your implied estimate of his capacity to judge for himself of the nature of a correspondence, and of the views and temper of, madam, your very obedient servant." And that's all to me.

I send his letter to you, —seal unbroken. I conclude he has done with you forever, and your CAREER is lost! But if it be so, oh, my poor, poor child I at that thought I have not the heart to scold you further. If it be so, come home to me, and I 'll work and slave for you, and you shall keep up your head and be a gentleman still, as you are, every inch of you. Don't mind what I've said at the beginning, dear: don't you know I'm hasty; and I was hurt. But you could not mean to be sly and underhand: 'twas only your high spirit, and it was my fault; I should not have shown you the letters. I hope you are well, and have quite lost that nasty cough, and that Mr. Vance treats you with proper respect. I think him rather too pushing and familiar, though a pleasant young man on the whole. But, after all, he is only a painter Bless you, my child, and don't have secrets again from your poor mother.

JESSICA HAUGHTON.

The enclosed letter was as follows: —

LIONEL HAUGHTON, —Some men might be displeased at receiving such a letter as you have addressed to me; I am not. At your years, and under the same circumstances, I might have written a letter much in the same spirit. Relieve your mind: as yet you owe me no obligations; you have only received back a debt due to you. My father was poor; your grandfather, Robert Haughton, assisted him in the cost of my education. I have assisted your father's son; we are quits. Before, however, we decide on having done with each other for the future, I suggest to you to pay me a short visit. Probably I shall not like you, nor you me. But we are both gentlemen, and need not show dislike too coarsely. If you decide on coming, come at once, or possibly you may not find me here. If you refuse, I shall have a poor opinion of your sense and temper, and in a week I shall have forgotten your existence. I ought to add that your father and I were once warm friends, and that by descent I am the head not only of my own race, which ends with me, but of the Haughton family, of which, though your line assumed the name, it was but a younger branch. Nowadays young men are probably not brought up to care for these things: I was. Yours,

GUY HAUGHTON DARRELL.

MANOR HOUSE, FAWLEY.

Sophy picked up the fallen letters, placed them on Lionel's lap, and looked into his face wistfully. He smiled, resumed his mother's epistle, and read the concluding passages, which he had before omitted. Their sudden turn from reproof to tenderness melted him.

He began to feel that his mother had a right to blame him for an act of concealment. Still she never would have consented to his writing such a letter; and had that letter been attended with so ill a result? Again he read Mr. Darrell's blunt but not offensive lines. His pride was soothed: why should he not now love his father's friend? He rose briskly, paid for the fruit, and went his way back to the boat with Sophy. As his oars cut the wave he talked gayly, but he ceased to interrogate Sophy on her past. Energetic, sanguine, ambitious, his own future entered now into his thoughts. Still, when the sun sank as the inn came partially into view from the winding of the banks and the fringe of the willows, his mind again settled on the patient, quiet little girl, who had not ventured to ask him one question in return for all he had put so unceremoniously to her. Indeed, she was silently musing over words he had inconsiderately let fall, —"What I hate to think you had ever stooped to perform. " Little could Lionel guess the unquiet thoughts which those words might hereafter call forth from the brooding deepening meditations of lonely childhood! At length said the boy abruptly, as he had said once before,

"I wish, Sophy, you were my sister. " He added in a saddened tone, "I never had a sister: I have so longed for one! However, surely we shall meet again. You go to-morrow so must I. "

Sophy's tears flowed softly, noiselessly.

"Cheer up, lady-bird, I wish you liked me half as much as I like you!"

"I do like you: oh, so much! " cried Soppy, passionately. "Well, then, you can write, you say? "

"A little. "

"You shall write to me now and then, and I to you. I'll talk to your grandfather about it. Ah, there he is, surely! " The boat now ran into the shelving creek, and by the honeysuckle arbour stood Gentleman Waife, leaning on his stick.

"You are late, " said the actor, as they landed, and Sophy sprang into his arms. "I began to be uneasy, and came here to inquire after you. You have not caught cold, child? "

SOPHY. —"Oh, no. "

LIONEL. —"She is the best of children. Pray, come into the inn, Mr. Waife; no toddy, but some refreshment. "

WAIFE. —"I thank you, —no, sir; I wish to get home at once. I walk slowly; it will be dark soon. "

Lionel tried in vain to detain him. There was a certain change in Mr. Waife's manner to him: it was much more distant; it was even pettish, if not surly. Lionel could not account for it; thought it mere whim at first: but as he walked part of the way back with them towards the village, this asperity continued, nay increased. Lionel was hurt; he arrested his steps.

"I see you wish to have your grandchild to yourself now. May I call early to-morrow? Sophy will tell you that I hope we may not altogether lose sight of each other. I will give you my address when I call. "

"What time to-morrow, sir? "

"About nine. "

Waife bowed his head and walked on, but Sophy looked back towards her boy friend, sorrowfully, gratefully; twilight in the skies that had been so sunny, —twilight in her face that had been so glad! She looked back once, twice, thrice, as Lionel halted on the road and kissed his hand. The third time Waife said with unwonted crossness,—

"Enough of that, Sophy; looking after young men is not proper! What does he mean about 'seeing each other, and giving me his address'? "

"He wished me to write to him sometimes and he would write to me. "

Waife's brow contracted; but if, in the excess of grandfatherly caution, he could have supposed that the bright-hearted boy of seventeen meditated ulterior ill to that fairy child in such a scheme for correspondence, he must have been in his dotage, and he had not hitherto evinced any signs of that.

Farewell, pretty Sophy! the evening star shines upon yon elm-tree that hides thee from view. Fading-fading grows the summer landscape; faded already from the landscape thy gentle image! So ends a holiday in life. Hallow it, Sophy; hallow it, Lionel! Life's holidays are not too many!

CHAPTER XVII.

By this chapter it appeareth that he who sets out on a career can scarcely expect to walk in perfect comfort, if he exchanges his own thick-soled shoes for dress-boots which were made for another man's measure, and that the said boots may not the less pinch for being brilliantly varnished. —It also showeth, for the instruction of Men and States, the connection between democratic opinion and wounded self-love; so that, if some Liberal statesman desire to rouse against an aristocracy the class just below it, he has only to persuade a fine lady to be exceedingly civil "to that sort of people."

Vance, returning late at night, found his friend still up in the little parlour, the windows open, pacing the floor with restless strides, stopping now and then to look at the moon upon the river.

"Such a day as I have had! and twelve shillings for the fly, 'pikes not included, " said Vance, much out of humour—

"'I fly from plate, I fly from pomp,

I fly from falsehood's specious grin; ' I forget the third line. I know the last is—"

'To find my welcome at an inn. '

You are silent: I annoyed you by going—could not help it—pity me, and lock up your pride. "

"No, my dear Vance, I was hurt for a moment, but that's long since over! "

"Still you seem to have something on your mind, " said Vance, who had now finished reading his letters, lighted his cigar, and was leaning against the window as the boy continued to walk to and fro.

"That is true: I have. I should like your advice. Read that letter. Ought I to go? Would it look mercenary, grasping? You know what I mean. "

Vance approached the candles and took the letter. He glanced first at the signature. "Darrell, " he exclaimed. "Oh, it is so, then! " He read with great attention, put down the letter, and shook Lionel by the hand. "I congratulate you: all is settled as it should be. Go? of course: you would be an ill-mannered lout if you did not. Is it far from hence must you return to town first? "

LIONEL. —"No, I find I can get across the country, —two hours by the railway. There is a station at the town which bears the post-mark of the letter. I shall make for that, if you advise it. "

"You knew I should advise it, or you would not have tortured your intellect by those researches into Bradshaw. "

"Shrewdly said, " answered Lionel, laughing; "but I wished for your sanction of my crude impressions. "

"You never told me your cousin's name was Darrell: not that I should have been much wiser if you had; but, thunder and lightning, Lionel! do you know that your cousin Darrell is a famous man? "

LIONEL. —"Famous! —Nonsense. I suppose he was a good lawyer, for I have heard my mother say, with a sort of contempt, that he had made a great fortune at the bar. "

VANCE. —"But he was in Parliament. "

LIONEL. —"Was he? I did not know. "

VANCE. —"And this is senatorial fame! You never heard your schoolfellows talk of Mr. Darrell? —they would not have known his name if you had boasted of it? "

LIONEL. —"Certainly not. "

VANCE. —"Would your schoolfellows have known the names of Wilkie, of Landseer, of Turner, Maclise? I speak of painters. "

LIONEL. —"I should think so, indeed. "

VANCE (soliloquizing). —"And yet Her Serene Sublimity-ship, Lady Selina Vipont, says to me with divine compassion, 'Not in the way of your delightful art to know such men as Mr. Darrell! ' Oh, as if I did not see through it, too, when she said, *a propos* of my jean cap and velveteen jacket, 'What matters how you dress? Every one knows who you are! ' Would she have said that to the earl of Dunder, or even to Sir Gregory Stollhead? No. I am the painter Frank Vance, —nothing more nor less; and if I stood on my head in a check shirt and a sky-coloured apron, Lady Selina Vipont would kindly murmur, 'Only Frank Vance the painter: what does it signify? ' Aha! —and they think to put me to use, puppets and lay figures! it is I who put them to use! Hark ye, Lionel, you are nearer akin to these fine folks than I knew of. Promise me one thing: you may become of their set, by right of your famous Mr. Darrell; if ever you hear an artist, musician, scribbler, no matter what, ridiculed as a tuft-hunter, —seeking the great, and so forth, —before you join in the laugh, ask some great man's son, with a pedigree that dates from the Ark, 'Are you not a toad-eater too? Do you want political influence; do you stand contested elections; do you curry and fawn upon greasy Sam the butcher and grimy Tom the blacksmith for a vote? Why? useful to your career, necessary to your ambition? Aha! is it meaner to curry and fawn upon white-handed women and elegant coxcombs? Tut, tut! useful to a career, necessary to ambition! '" Vance paused, out of breath. The spoiled darling of the circles, —he, to talk such republican rubbish! Certainly he must have taken his two guineas' worth out of those light wines. Nothing so treacherous! they inflame the brain like fire, while melting on the palate like ice. All inhabitants of lightwine countries are quarrelsome and democratic.

LIONEL (astounded). —"No one, I am sure, could have meant to call you a tuft-hunter; of course, every one knows that a great painter—"

VANCE. —"Dates from Michael Angelo, if not from Zeuxis! Common individuals trace their pedigree from their own fathers! the children of Art from Art's founders! "

Oh, Vance, Vance, you are certainly drunk! If that comes from dining with fine people at the Star and Garter, you would be a happier man and as good a painter if your toddy were never sipped save in honeysuckle arbours.

"But, " said Lionel, bewildered, and striving to turn his friend's thoughts, "what has all this to do with Mr. Darrell? "

VANCE. —"Mr. Darrell might have been one of the first men in the kingdom. Lady Selina Vipout says so, and she is related, I believe, to every member in the Cabinet. Mr. Darrell can push you in life, and make your fortune, without any great trouble on your own part. Bless your stars, and rejoice that you are not a painter! "

Lionel flung his arm round the artist's broad breast. "Vance, you are cruel! " It was his turn to console the painter, as the painter had three nights before *a propos* of the same Mr. Darrell consoled him. Vance gradually sobered down, and the young men walked forth in the moonlight. And the eternal stars had the same kind looks for Vance as they had vouchsafed to Lionel.

"When do you start? " asked the painter, as they mounted the stairs to bed.

"To-morrow evening. I miss the early train, for I must call first and take leave of Sophy. I hope I may see her again in after life. "

"And I hope, for your sake, that if so, she may not be in the same coloured print, with Lady Selina Vipont's eyeglass upon her! "

"What! " said Lionel, laughing; "is Lady Selina Vipont so formidably rude? "

"Rude! nobody is rude in that delightful set. Lady Selina Vipont is excruciatingly—civil. "

CHAPTER XVIII.

Being devoted exclusively to a reflection, not inapposite to the events in this history nor to those in any other which chronicles the life of men.

There is one warning lesson in life which few of us have not received, and no book that I can call to memory has noted down with an adequate emphasis. It is this: "Beware of parting! " The true sadness is not in the pain of the parting, it is in the When and the How you are to meet again with the face about to vanish from your view! From the passionate farewell to the woman who has your heart in her keeping, to the cordial good-by exchanged with pleasant companions at a watering-place, a country-house, or the close of a festive day's blithe and careless excursion, —a cord, stronger or weaker, is snapped asunder in every parting, and Time's busy fingers are not practised in re-splicing broken ties. Meet again you may; will it be in the same way? —with the same sympathies? — with the same sentiments? Will the souls, hurrying on in diverse paths, unite once more, as if the interval had been a dream? Rarely, rarely! Have you not, after even a year, even a month's absence, returned to the same place, found the same groups reassembled, and yet sighed to yourself, "But where is the charm that once breathed from the spot, and once smiled from the faces? " A poet has said, "Eternity itself cannot restore the loss struck from the minute. " Are you happy in the spot on which you tarry with the persons whose voices are now melodious to your ear? beware of parting; or, if part you must, say not in insolent defiance to Time and Destiny, "What matters! —we shall soon meet again. "

Alas, and alas! when we think of the lips which murmured, "Soon meet again, " and remember how in heart, soul, and thought, we stood forever divided the one from the other, when, once more face to face, we each inly exclaimed, "Met again! "

The air that we breathe makes the medium through which sound is conveyed; be the instrument unchanged, be the force which is applied to it the same, still the air that thou seest not, the air to thy ear gives the music.

Ring a bell underneath an exhausted receiver, thou wilt scarce hear the sound; give the bell due vibration by free air in warm daylight, or sink it down to the heart of the ocean, where the air, all compressed, fills the vessel around it, ' and the chime, heard afar, starts thy soul, checks thy footstep, unto deep calls the deep, —a voice from the ocean is borne to thy soul.

Where then the change, when thou sayest, "Lo, the same metal, — why so faint-heard the ringing? " Ask the air that thou seest not, or above thee in sky, or below thee in ocean. Art thou sure that the bell, so faint-heard, is not struck underneath an exhausted receiver?

CHAPTER XIX.

The wandering inclinations of nomad tribes not to be accounted for on the principles of action peculiar to civilized men, who are accustomed to live in good houses and able to pay the income tax. — When the money that once belonged to a man civilized vanishes into the pockets of a nomad, neither lawful art nor occult science can, with certainty, discover what he will do with it. —Mr. Vance narrowly escapes well-merited punishment from the nails of the British Fair—Lionel Haughton, in the temerity of youth, braves the dangers of a British Railway.

The morning was dull and overcast, rain gathering in the air, when Vance and Lionel walked to Waife's lodging. As Lionel placed his hand on the knocker of the private door, the Cobbler, at his place by the window in the stall beside, glanced towards him, and shook his head.

"No use knocking, gentlemen. Will you kindly step in? —this way. "

"Do you mean that your lodgers are out? " asked Vance.

"Gone! " said the Cobbler, thrusting his awl with great vehemence through the leather destined to the repair of a ploughman's boot.

"Gone—for good! " cried Lionel; "you cannot mean it. I call by appointment. "

"Sorry, sir, for your trouble. Stop a bit; I have a letter here for you. " The Cobbler dived into a drawer, and from a medley of nails and thongs drew forth a letter addressed to L. Haughton, Esq.

"Is this from Waife? How on earth did he know my surname? you never mentioned it, Vance? "

"Not that I remember. But you said you found him at the inn, and they knew it there. It is on the brass-plate of your knapsack. No matter, —what does he say? " and Vance looked over his friend's shoulder and read.

SIR, —I most respectfully thank you for your condescending kindness to me and my grandchild; and your friend, for his timely and generous aid. You will pardon me that the necessity which knows no law obliges me to leave this place some hours before the time of your proposed visit. My grandchild says you intended to ask her sometimes to write to you. Excuse me, sir—on reflection, you will perceive how different your ways of life are from those which she must tread with me. You see before you a man who— but I forget; you see him no more, and probably never will.

Your most humble and most obliged, obedient servant,

W. W.

VANCE. —"Who never more may trouble you—trouble you! Where have they gone? "

COBBLER. —"Don't know; would you like to take a peep in the crystal—perhaps you've the gift, unbeknown? "

VANCE. —"Not I—bah! Come away, Lionel. "

"Did not Sophy even leave any message for me? " asked the boy, sorrowfully.

"To be sure she did; I forgot-no, not exactly a message, but this—I was to be sure to give it to you. " And out of his miscellaneous receptacle the Cobbler extracted a little book. Vance looked and laughed, —"The Butterflies' Ball and the Grasshoppers' Feast. "

Lionel did not share the laugh. He plucked the book to himself, and read on the fly-leaf, in a child's irregular scrawl, blistered, too, with the unmistakable trace of fallen tears, these words: —

Do not Scorn it. I have nothing else I can think of which is All Mine. Miss Jane Burton gave it me for being Goode. Grandfather says you are too high for us, and that I shall not see you More; but I shall never forget how kind you were, never—never. Sophy.

Said the Cobbler, his awl upright in the hand which rested on his knee, "What a plague did the 'Stronomers discover Herschel for? You see, sir, " addressing Vance, "things odd and strange all come along o' Herschel. "

"What! —Sir John? "

"No, the star he poked out. He's a awful star for females! hates 'em like poison! I suspect he's been worriting hisself into her nativity, for I got out from her the year, month, and day she was born, hour unbeknown, but, calkeiating by noon, Herschel was dead agin her in the Third and Ninth House, —Voyages, Travels, Letters, News, Church Matters, and such like. But it will all come right after he's transited. Her Jupiter must be good. But I only hope, " added the Cobbler, solemnly, "that they won't go a-discovering any more stars. The world did a deal better without the new one, and they do talk of a Neptune—as bad as Saturn! "

"And this is the last of her! " said Lionel, sadly, putting the book into his breast-pocket. "Heaven shield her wherever she goes! "

VANCE. —"Don't you think Waife and the poor little girl will come back again? "

COBBLER. —"P'raps; I know he was looking hard into the county map at the stationer's over the way; that seems as if he did not mean to go very far. P'raps he may come back. "

VANCE. —"Did he take all his goods with him? "

COBBLER. —"Barrin' an old box, —nothing in it, I expect, but theatre rubbish, —play-books, paints, an old wig, and sick like. He has good clothes, —always had; and so has she, but they don't make more than a bundle. "

VANCE. "But surely you must know what the old fellow's project is. He has got from me a great sum: what will he do with it? "

COBBLER. —"Just what has been a-bothering me. What will he do with it? I cast a figure to know; could not make it out. Strange signs in Twelfth House. Enemies and Big Animals. Well, well, he's a marbellous man, and if he warn't a misbeliever in the crystal, I should say he was under Herschel; for you see, sir" (laying hold of Vance's button, as he saw that gentleman turning to escape), —"you see Herschel, though he be a sinister chap eno', specially in affairs connected with t' other sex, disposes the native to dive into the mysteries of natur'. I'm a Herschel man, out and outer; born in March, and—"

"As mad as its hares, " muttered Vance, wrenching his button from the Cobbler's grasp, and impatiently striding off. But he did not effect his escape so easily, for, close at hand, just at the corner of the lane, a female group, headed by Merle's gaunt housekeeper, had been silently collecting from the moment the two friends had paused at the Cobbler's door. And this petticoated divan suddenly closing round the painter, one pulled him by the sleeve, another by the jacket, and a third, with a nose upon which somebody had sat in early infancy, whispered, "Please, sir, take my picter fust. "

Vance stared aghast, —"Your picture, you drab! " Here another model of rustic charms, who might have furnished an ideal for the fat scullion in "Tristram Shandy, " bobbing a courtesy put in her rival claim.

"Sir, if you don't objex to coming into the kitching after the family has gone to bed, I don't care if I lets you make a minnytur of me for two pounds. "

"Miniature of you, porpoise! "

"Polly, sir, not Porpus, —ax pardon. I shall clean myself, and I have a butyful new cap, —Honeytun, and —"

"Let the gentleman go, will you? " said a third; "I am surprised at ye, Polly. The kitching, unbeknown! Sir, I'm in the nussery; yes, sir; and Alissus says you may take me any time, purvided you'll take the babby, in the back parlour; yes, sir, No. 5 in the High Street. Mrs. Spratt, —yes, sir. Babby has had the small-pox; in case you're a married gentleman with a family; quite safe there; yes, sir. "

Vance could endure no more, and, forgetful of that gallantry which should never desert the male sex, burst through the phalanx with an anathema, blackening alike the beauty and the virtue of those on whom it fell, that would have justified a cry of shame from every manly bosom, and which at once changed into shrill wrath the supplicatory tones with which he had been hitherto addressed. Down the street he hurried and down the street followed the insulted fair. "Hiss—hiss—no gentleman, no gentleman! Aha-skulk off—do—low blaggurd! " shrieked Polly. From their counters shop-folks rushed to their doors. Stray dogs, excited by the clamour, ran wildly after the fugitive man, yelping "in madding bray"! Vance, fearing to be clawed by the females if he merely walked, sure to be bitten by the dogs if he ran, ambled on, strove to look composed, and carry his nose high in its native air, till, clearing the street, he saw a hedgerow to the right; leaped it with an agility which no stimulus less preternatural than that of self-preservation could have given to his limbs, and then shot off like an arrow, and did not stop, till, out of breath, he dropped upon the bench in the sheltering honeysuckle arbour. Here he was still fanning himself with his cap, and muttering unmentionable expletives, when he was joined by Lionel, who had tarried behind to talk more about Sophy to the Cobbler, and who, unconscious that the din which smote his ear was caused by his ill-starred friend, had been enticed to go upstairs and look after Sophy in the crystal, —vainly. When Vance had recited his misadventures, and Lionel had sufficiently condoled with him, it became time for the latter to pay his share of the bill, pack up his knapsack, and start for the train. Now, the station could only be reached by penetrating the heart of the village, and Vance swore that he had had enough of that. "Peste! " said he; "I should pass right before No. 5 in the High Street, and the nuss and the babby will be there on the threshold, like Virgil's picture of the infernal regions,

"'Infantumque anima; flentes in limine primo. '

We will take leave of each other here. I shall go by the boat to Chertsey whenever I shall have sufficiently recovered my shaken nerves. There are one or two picturesque spots to be seen in that neighbourhood. In a few days I shall be in town! write to me there, and tell me how you get on. Shake hands, and Heaven speed you. But, ah! now you have paid your moiety of the bill, have you enough left for the train? "

"Oh, yes, the fare is but a few shillings; but, to be sure, a fly to Fawley? I ought not to go on foot" (proudly); "and, too, supposing he affronts me, and I have to leave his house suddenly? May I borrow a sovereign? My mother will call and repay it. "

VANCE (magnificently). —"There it is, and not much more left in my purse, —that cursed Star and Garter! and those three pounds! "

LIONEL (sighing). —"Which were so well spent! Before you sell that picture, do let me make a copy. "

VANCE. —"Better take a model of your own. Village full of them; you could bargain with a porpoise for half the money which I was duped into squandering away on a chit! But don't look so grave; you may copy me if you can! "

"Time to start, and must walk brisk, sir, " said the jolly landlord, looking in.

"Good-by, good-by. "

And so departed Lionel Haughton upon an emprise as momentous to that youth-errant as Perilous Bridge or Dragon's Cave could have been to knight-errant of old.

"Before we decide on having done with each other, a short visit, " — so ran the challenge from him who had everything to give unto him who had everything to gain. And how did Lionel Haughton, the ambitious and aspiring, contemplate the venture in which success would admit him within the gates of the golden Carduel an equal in the lists with the sons of paladins, or throw him back to the arms of the widow who let a first floor in the back streets of Pimlico? Truth to say, as he strode musingly towards the station for starting, where the smoke-cloud now curled from the wheel-track of iron, truth to say, the anxious doubt which disturbed him was not that which his friends might have felt on his behalf. In words, it would have shaped itself thus, —"Where is that poor little Sophy! and what will become of her—what? " But when, launched on the journey, hurried on to its goal, the thought of the ordeal before him forced itself on his mind, he muttered inly to himself, "Done with each other; let it be as he pleases, so that I do not fawn on his pleasure. Better a million times enter life as a penniless gentleman, who must work his way up like a man, than as one who creeps on his knees into fortune, shaming birthright of gentleman or soiling honour of man. " Therefore taking into account the poor cousin's vigilant pride on the *qui vive* for offence, and the rich cousin's temper (as judged by his letters) rude enough to resent it, we must own that if Lionel Haughton has at this moment what is commonly called "a chance, " the question as yet is not, What is that chance? but, What will he do with it? And as the reader advances in this history, he will acknowledge that there are few questions in this world so frequently agitated, to which the solution is more important to each puzzled mortal than that upon which starts every sage's discovery, every novelist's plot, —that which applies to MAN'S LIFE, from its first sleep in the cradle, "WHAT WILL HE DO WITH IT? "

BOOK II.

CHAPTER I.

Primitive character of the country in certain districts of Great Britain. —Connection between the features of surrounding scenery and the mental and moral inclinations of man, after the fashion of all sound ethnological historians. —A charioteer, to whom an experience of British laws suggests an ingenious mode of arresting the progress of Roman Papacy, carries Lionel Haughton and his fortunes to a place which allows of description and invites repose.

In safety, but with naught else rare enough, in a railway train, to deserve commemoration, Lionel reached the station to which he was bound. He there inquired the distance to Fawley Manor House; it was five miles. He ordered a fly, and was soon wheeled briskly along a rough parish road, through a country strongly contrasting the gay river scenery he had so lately quitted, —quite as English, but rather the England of a former race than that which spreads round our own generation like one vast suburb of garden-ground and villas. Here, nor village nor spire, nor porter's lodge came in sight. Rare even were the cornfields; wide spaces of unenclosed common opened, solitary and primitive, on the road, bordered by large woods, chiefly of beech, closing the horizon with ridges of undulating green. In such an England, Knights Templars might have wended their way to scattered monasteries, or fugitive partisans in the bloody Wars of the Roses have found shelter under leafy coverts.

The scene had its romance, its beauty—half savage, half gentle— leading perforce the mind of any cultivated and imaginative gazer far back from the present day, waking up long-forgotten passages from old poets. The stillness of such wastes of sward, such deeps of woodland, induced the nurture of revery, gravely soft and lulling. There, Ambition might give rest to the wheel of Ixion, Avarice to the sieve of the Danaids; there, disappointed Love might muse on the brevity of all human passions, and count over the tortured hearts that have found peace in holy meditation, or are now stilled under grassy knolls. See where, at the crossing of three roads upon the waste, the landscape suddenly unfolds, an upland in the distance, and on the upland a building, the first sign of social man. What is the building? only a silenced windmill, the sails dark and sharp against the dull leaden sky.Lionel touched the driver, —"Are we yet on Mr.

Darrell's property? " Of the extent of that property he had involuntarily conceived a vast idea.

"Lord, sir, no; we be two miles from Squire Darrell's. He han't much property to speak of hereabouts. But he bought a good bit o' land, too, some years ago, ten or twelve mile t' other side o' the county. First time you are going to Fawley, sir? "

"Yes. "

"Ah! I don't mind seeing you afore; and I should have known you if I had, for it is seldom indeed I have a fare to Fawley old Manor House. It must be, I take it, four or five years ago sin' I wor there with a gent, and he went away while I wor feeding the horse; did me out o' my back fare. What bisness had he to walk when he came in my fly? Shabby. "

"Mr. Darrell lives very retired, then? sees few persons? " "S'pose so. I never seed him as I knows on; see'd two o' his hosses though, — rare good uns; " and the driver whipped on his own horse, took to whistling, and Lionel asked no more.

At length the chaise stopped at a carriage gate, receding from the road, and deeply shadowed by venerable trees, —no lodge. The driver, dismounting, opened the gate.

"Is this the place? "

The driver nodded assent, remounted, and drove on rapidly through what night by courtesy he called a park. The enclosure was indeed little beyond that of a good-sized paddock; its boundaries were visible on every side: but swelling uplands covered with massy foliage sloped down to its wild, irregular turf soil, —soil poor for pasturage, but pleasant to the eye; with dell and dingle, bosks of fantastic pollards; dotted oaks of vast growth; here and there a weird hollow thorn-tree; patches of fern and gorse. Hoarse and loud cawed the rooks; and deep, deep as from the innermost core of the lovely woodlands came the mellow note of the cuckoo. A few moments more a wind of the road brought the house in sight. At its rear lay a piece of water, scarcely large enough to be styled a lake; too winding in its shaggy banks, its ends too concealed by tree and islet, to be called by the dull name of pond. Such as it was it arrested the eye before the gaze turned towards the house: it had an air of tranquillity so sequestered, so solemn. A lively man of the world would have been seized with spleen at the first glimpse of it; but he who had known some great grief, some anxious care, would have drunk the calm into his weary soul like an anodyne. The house, —small, low, ancient, about the date of Edward VI., before the statelier architecture of Elizabeth. Few houses in England so old, indeed, as Fawley Manor House. A vast weight of roof, with high gables; windows on the upper story projecting far over the lower part; a covered porch with a coat of half-obliterated arms deep panelled over the oak door. Nothing grand, yet all how venerable! But what is this? Close beside the old, quiet, unassuming Manor House rises the skeleton of a superb and costly pile, —a palace uncompleted, and the work evidently suspended, —perhaps long since, perhaps now forever. No busy workmen nor animated scaffolding. The perforated battlements roofed over with visible haste, —here with slate, there with tile; the Elizabethan mullion casements unglazed; some roughly boarded across, —some with staring forlorn apertures, that showed floorless chambers, for winds to whistle through and rats to tenant. Weeds and long grass were growing over blocks of stone that lay at hand. A wallflower had forced itself into root on the sill of a giant oriel. The effect was startling. A fabric which he who conceived it must have founded for posterity, —so solid its masonry, so thick its walls, —and thus abruptly left to moulder; a palace constructed for the reception of crowding guests, the pomp of stately revels, abandoned to owl and bat. And the homely old house beside it, which that lordly hall was doubtless designed to replace, looking so safe and tranquil at the baffled presumption of its spectral neighbour.

The driver had rung the bell, and now turning back to the chaise met Lionel's inquiring eye, and said, "Yes; Squire Darrell began to build that—many years ago—when I was a boy. I heerd say it was to be the show-house of the whole county. Been stopped these ten or a dozen years. "

"Why? —do you know? "

"No one knows. Squire was a laryer, I b'leve: perhaps he put it into Chancery. My wife's grandfather was put into Chancery jist as he was growing up, and never grew afterwards: never got out o' it; nout ever does. There's our churchwarden comes to me with a petition to sign agin the Pope. Says I, 'That old Pope is always in trouble: what's he bin doin' now? ' Says he, 'Spreading! He's a-got into Parlyment, and he's now got a colledge, and we pays for it. I does n't know how to stop him. ' Says I, 'Put the Pope into Chancery, along with wife's grandfather, and he'll never spread agin. '"

The driver had thus just disposed of the Papacy, when an elderly servant out of livery opened the door. Lionel sprang from the chaise, and paused in some confusion: for then, for the first time, there darted across him the idea that he had never written to announce his acceptance of Mr. Darrell's invitation; that he ought to have done so; that he might not be expected. Meanwhile the servant surveyed him with some surprise. "Mr. Darrell? " hesitated Lionel, inquiringly.

"Not at home, sir, " replied the man, as if Lionel's business was over, and he had only to re-enter his chaise. The boy was naturally rather bold than shy, and he said, with a certain assured air, "My name is Haughton. I come here on Mr. Darrell's invitation. "

The servant's face changed in a moment; he bowed respectfully. "I beg pardon, sir. I will look for my master; he is somewhere on the grounds. " The servant then approached the fly, took out the knapsack, and, observing Lionel had his purse in his hand, said, "Allow me to save you that trouble, sir. Driver, round to the stable-yard. " Stepping back into the house, the servant threw open a door to the left, on entrance, and advanced a chair. "If you will wait here a moment, sir, I will seek for my master. "

CHAPTER II.

Guy Darrell—and Stilled Life.

The room in which Lionel now found himself was singularly quaint. An antiquarian or architect would have discovered at a glance that at some period it had formed part of the entrance-hall; and when, in Elizabeth's or James the First's day, the refinement in manners began to penetrate from baronial mansions to the homes of the gentry, and the entrance-hall ceased to be the common refectory of the owner and his dependants, this apartment had been screened off by perforated panels, which for the sake of warmth and comfort had been filled up into solid wainscot by a succeeding generation. Thus one side of the room was richly carved with geometrical designs and arabesque pilasters, while the other three sides were in small simple panels, with a deep fantastic frieze in plaster, depicting a deer-chase in relief and running be tween woodwork and ceiling. The ceiling itself was relieved by long pendants without any apparent meaning, and by the crest of the Darrells, —a heron, wreathed round with the family motto, "Ardua petit Ardea. " It was a dining-room, as was shown by the character of the furniture. But there was no attempt on the part of the present owner, and there had clearly been none on the part of his predecessor, to suit the furniture to the room. The furniture, indeed, was of the heavy, graceless taste of George the First, —cumbrous chairs in walnut-tree, with a worm-eaten mosaic of the heron on their homely backs, and a faded blue worsted on their seats; a marvellously ugly sideboard to match, and on it a couple of black shagreen cases, the lids of which were flung open, and discovered the pistol-shaped handles of silver knives. The mantelpiece reached to the ceiling, in panelled compartments, with heraldic shields, and supported by rude stone Caryatides. On the walls were several pictures, —family portraits, for the names were inscribed on the frames. They varied in date from the reign of Elizabeth to that of George I. A strong family likeness pervaded them all, —high features, dark hair, grave aspects, —save indeed one, a Sir Ralph Haughton Darrell, in a dress that spoke him of the holiday date of Charles II., —all knots, lace, and ribbons; evidently the beau of the race; and he had blue eyes, a blonde peruke, a careless profligate smile, and looked altogether as devil-me-care, rakehelly, handsome, good-for-nought, as ever swore at a drawer, beat a watchman, charmed a lady, terrified a husband, and hummed a song as he pinked his man.

Lionel was still gazing upon the effigies of this airy cavalier when the door behind him opened very noiselessly, and a man of imposing presence stood on the threshold, —stood so still, and the carved mouldings of the doorway so shadowed, and as it were cased round his figure, that Lionel, on turning quickly, might have mistaken him for a portrait brought into bold relief from its frame by a sudden fall of light. We hear it, indeed, familiarly said that such a one is like an old picture. Never could it be more appositely said than of the face on which the young visitor gazed, much startled and somewhat awed. Not such as inferior limners had painted in the portraits there, though it had something in common with those family lineaments, but such as might have looked tranquil power out of the canvas of Titian.

The man stepped forward, and the illusion passed. "I thank you, " he said, holding out his hand, "for taking me at my word, and answering me thus in person. " He paused a moment, surveying Lionel's countenance with a keen but not unkindly eye, and added softly, "Very like your father. "

At these words Lionel involuntarily pressed the hand which he had taken. That hand did not return the pressure. It lay an instant in Lionel's warm clasp—not repelling, not responding—and was then very gently withdrawn.

"Did you come from London? "

"No, sir; I found your letter yesterday at Hampton Court. I had been staying some days in that neighbourhood. I came on this morning: I was afraid too unceremoniously; your kind welcome reassures me there. "

The words were well chosen and frankly said. Probably they pleased the host, for the expression of his countenance was, on the whole, propitious; but he merely inclined his head with a kind of lofty indifference, then, glancing at his watch, he rang the bell. The servant entered promptly. "Let dinner be served within an hour. "

"Pray, sir, " said Lionel, "do not change your hours on my account. "

Mr. Darrell's brow slightly contracted. Lionel's tact was in fault there; but the great man answered quietly, "All hours are the same to me; and it were strange if a host could be deranged by consideration to his guest, —on the first day too. Are you tired? Would you like to go to your room, or look out for half an hour? The sky is clearing. "

"I should so like to look out, sir. "

"This way then. "

Mr. Darrell, crossing the hall, threw open a door opposite to that by which Lionel entered, and the lake (we will so call it) lay before them, —separated from the house only by a shelving gradual declivity, on which were a few beds of flowers, —not the most in vogue nowadays, and disposed in rambling old-fashioned parterres. At one angle, a quaint and dilapidated sun-dial; at the other, a long bowling-alley, terminated by one of those summer-houses which the Dutch taste, following the Revolution of 1688, brought into fashion. Mr. Darrell passed down this alley (no bowls there now), and observing that Lionel looked curiously towards the summer-house, of which the doors stood open, entered it. A lofty room with coved ceiling, painted with Roman trophies of helms and fasces, alternated with crossed fifes and fiddles, painted also.

"Amsterdam manners, " said Mr. Darrell, slightly shrugging his shoulders. "Here a former race heard music, sang glees, and smoked from clay pipes. That age soon passed, unsuited to English energies, which are not to be united with Holland phlegm! But the view from the window-look out there. I wonder whether men in wigs and women in hoops enjoyed that. It is a mercy they did not clip those banks into a straight canal! "

The view was indeed lovely, —the water looked so blue and so large and so limpid, woods and curving banks reflected deep on its peaceful bosom.

"How Vance would enjoy this! " cried Lionel. "It would come into a picture even better than the Thames. "

"Vance? who is Vance? "

"The artist, —a great friend of mine. Surely, sir, you have heard of him or seen his pictures! "

"Himself and his pictures are since my time. Days tread down days for the recluse, and he forgets that celebrities rise with their suns, to wane with their moons,

"'Truditur dies die,
Novaeque pergunt interire lunae'"

"All suns do not set; all moons do not wane! " cried Lionel, with blunt enthusiasm. "When Horace speaks elsewhere of the Julian star, he compares it to a moon—'inter ignes minores'—and surely Fame is not among the orbs which 'pergunt interire, '—hasten on to perish! "

"I am glad to see that you retain your recollections of Horace, " said Mr. Darrell, frigidly, and without continuing the allusion to celebrities; "the most charming of all poets to a man of my years, and" (he very dryly added) "the most useful for popular quotation to men at any age. "

Then sauntering forth carelessly, he descended the sloping turf, came to the water-side, and threw himself at length on the grass: the wild thyme which he crushed sent up its bruised fragrance. There, resting his face on his hand, Darrell gazed along the water in abstracted silence. Lionel felt that he was forgotten; but he was not hurt. By this time a strong and admiring interest for his cousin had sprung up within his breast: he would have found it difficult to explain why. But whosoever at that moment could have seen Guy Darrell's musing countenance, or whosoever, a few minutes before, could have heard the very sound of his voice, sweetly, clearly full; each slow enunciation unaffectedly, mellowly distinct, —making musical the homeliest; roughest word, would have understood and shared the interest which Lionel could not explain. There are living human faces, which, independently of mere physical beauty, charm and enthrall us more than the most perfect lineaments which Greek sculptor ever lent to a marble face; there are key-notes in the thrilling human voice, simply uttered, which can haunt the heart, rouse the passions, lull rampant multitudes, shake into dust the thrones of guarded kings, and effect more wonders than ever yet have been wrought by the most artful chorus or the deftest quill.

In a few minutes the swans from the farther end of the water came sailing swiftly towards the bank on which Darrell reclined. He had evidently made friends with them, and they rested their white breasts close on the margin, seeking to claim his notice with a low hissing salutation, which, it is to be hoped, they changed for something less sibilant in that famous song with which they depart this life.

Darrell looked up. "They come to be fed, " said he, "smooth emblems of the great social union. Affection is the offspring of utility. I am useful to them: they love me. " He rose, uncovered, and bowed to the birds in mock courtesy: "Friends, I have no bread to give you. "

LIONEL. —"Let me run in for some. I would be useful too. "

MR. DARRELL. —"Rival! —useful to my swans? "

LIONEL (tenderly). —"Or to you, sir. "

He felt as if he had said too much, and without waiting for permission, ran indoors to find some one whom he could ask for the bread.

"Sonless, childless, hopeless, objectless! " said Darrell, murmuringly to himself, and sank again into revery.

By the time Lionel returned with the bread, another petted friend had joined the master. A tame doe had caught sight of him from her covert far away, came in light bounds to his side, and was pushing her delicate nostril into his drooping hand. At the sound of Lionel's hurried step, she took flight, trotted off a few paces, then turned, looking.

"I did not know you had deer here. "

"Deer! —in this little paddock! —of course not; only that doe. Fairthorn introduced her here. By the by, " continued Darrell, who was now throwing the bread to the swans, and had resumed his careless, unmeditative manner, "you were not aware that I have a brother hermit, —a companion be sides the swans and the doe. Dick Fairthorn is a year or two younger than myself, the son of my father's bailiff. He was the cleverest boy at his grammar-school. Unluckily he took to the flute, and unfitted himself for the present century. He condescends, however, to act as my secretary, —a fair classical scholar, plays chess, is useful to me, —I am useful to him. We have an affection for each other. I never forgive any one who laughs at him. The half-hour bell, and you will meet him at dinner. Shall we come in and dress? "

They entered the house; the same man-servant was in attendance in the hall. "Show Mr. Haughton to his room. " Darrell inclined his head — I use that phrase, for the gesture was neither bow nor nod — turned down a narrow passage and disappeared.

Led up an uneven staircase of oak, black as ebony, with huge balustrades, and newel-posts supporting clumsy balls, Lionel was conducted to a small chamber, modernized a century ago by a faded Chinese paper, and a mahogany bedstead, which took up three-fourths of the space, and was crested with dingy plumes, that gave it the cheerful look of a hearse; and there the attendant said, "Have you the key of your knapsack, sir? shall I put out your things to dress? " Dress! Then for the first time the boy remembered that he had brought with him no evening dress, — nay, evening dress, properly so called, he possessed not at all in any corner of the world. It had never yet entered into his modes of existence. Call to mind when you were a boy of seventeen, "betwixt two ages hovering like a star, " and imagine Lionel's sensations. He felt his cheek burn as if he had been detected in a crime. "I have no dress things, " he said piteously; "only a change of linen, and this, " glancing at the summer jacket. The servant was evidently a most gentleman-like man: his native sphere that of groom of the chambers. "I will mention it to Mr. Darrell; and if you will favour me with your address in London, I will send to telegraph for what you want against to-morrow. "

"Many thanks, " answered Lionel, recovering his presence of mind; "I will speak to Mr. Darrell myself. "

"There is the hot water, sir; that is the bell. I have the honour to be placed at your commands. " The door closed, and Lionel unlocked his knapsack; other trousers, other waistcoat had he, — those worn at the fair, and once white. Alas! they had not since then passed to the care of the laundress. Other shoes, — double-soled for walking. There was no help for it but to appear at dinner, attired as he had been before, in his light pedestrian jacket, morning waistcoat flowered with sprigs, and a fawn-coloured nether man. Could it signify much, — only two men? Could the grave Mr. Darrell regard such trifles? — Yes, if they intimated want of due respect.

"Durum! sed fit levius Patientia
Quicquid corrigere est nefas."

On descending the stairs, the same high-bred domestic was in waiting to show him into the library. Mr. Darrell was there already, in the simple but punctilious costume of a gentleman who retains in seclusion the habits customary in the world. At the first glance Lionel thought he saw a slight cloud of displeasure on his host's brow. He went up to Mr. Darrell ingenuously, and apologized for the deficiencies of his itinerant wardrobe. "Say the truth, " said his host; "you thought you were coming to an old churl, with whom ceremony was misplaced. "

"Indeed no! " exclaimed Lionel. "But—but I have so lately left school. "

"Your mother might have thought for you. "

"I did not stay to consult her, indeed, sir; I hope you are not offended. "

"No, but let me not offend you if I take advantage of my years and our relationship to remark that a young man should be careful not to let himself down below the standard of his own rank. If a king could bear to hear that he was only a ceremonial, a private gentleman may remember that there is but a ceremonial between himself and—his hatter! "

Lionel felt the colour mount his brow; but Darrell pressing the distasteful theme no further, and seemingly forgetting its purport, turned his remarks carelessly towards the weather. "It will be fair to-morrow: there is no mist on the hill yonder. Since you have a painter for a friend, perhaps you yourself are a draughtsman. There are some landscape effects here which Fairthorn shall point out to you. "

"I fear, Mr. Darrell, " said Lionel, looking down, "that to-morrow I must leave you. "

"So soon? Well, I suppose the place must be very dull. "

"Not that—not that; but I have offended you, and I would not repeat the offence. I have not the 'ceremonial' necessary to mark me as a gentleman, —either here or at home. "

97

"So! Bold frankness and ready wit command ceremonials, " returned Darrell, and for the first time his lip wore a smile. "Let me present to you Mr. Fairthorn, " as the door, opening, showed a shambling awkward figure, with loose black knee-breeches and buckled shoes. The figure made a strange sidelong bow; and hurrying in a lateral course, like a crab suddenly alarmed, towards a dim recess protected by a long table, sank behind a curtain fold, and seemed to vanish as a crab does amidst the shingles.

"Three minutes yet to dinner, and two before the lettercarrier goes, " said the host, glancing at his watch. "Mr. Fairthorn, will you write a note for me? " There was a mutter from behind the curtain. Darrell walked to the place, and whispered a few words, returned to the hearth, rang the bell. "Another letter for the post, Mills: Mr. Fairthorn is sealing it. You are looking at my book-shelves, Lionel. As I understand that your master spoke highly of you, I presume that you are fond of reading. "

"I think so, but I am not sure, " answered Lionel, whom his cousin's conciliatory words had restored to ease and good-humour.

"You mean, perhaps, that you like reading, if you may choose your own books. "

"Or rather, if I may choose my own time to read them, and that would not be on bright summer days. "

"Without sacrificing bright summer days, one finds one has made little progress when the long winter nights come. "

"Yes, sir. But must the sacrifice be paid in books? I fancy I learned as much in the play-ground as I did n the schoolroom, and for the last few months, in much my own master, reading hard in the forenoon, it is true, for many hours at a stretch, and yet again for a few hours at evening, but rambling also through the streets, or listening to a few friends whom I have contrived to make, —I think, if I can boast of any progress at all, the books have the smaller share in it. "

"You would, then, prefer an active life to a studious one? "

"Oh, yes—yes. "

"Dinner is served, " said the decorous Mr. Mills, throwing open the door.

CHAPTER III.

In our happy country every man's house is his castle. But however stoutly he fortify it, Care enters, as surely as she did in Horace's time, through the porticos of a Roman's villa. Nor, whether ceilings be fretted with gold and ivory, or whether only coloured with whitewash, does it matter to Care any more than it does to a house-fly. But every tree, be it cedar or blackthorn, can harbour its singing-bird; and few are the homes in which, from nooks least suspected, there starts not a music. Is it quite true that, "non avium citharaeque cantus somnum reducent"? Would not even Damocles himself have forgotten the sword, if the lute-player had chanced on the notes that lull?

The dinner was simple enough, but well dressed and well served. One footman, in plain livery, assisted Mr. Mills. Darrell ate sparingly, and drank only water, which was placed by his side iced, with a single glass of wine at the close of the repast, which he drank on bending his head to Lionel, with a certain knightly grace, and the prefatory words of "Welcome here to a Haughton. " Mr. Fairthorn was less abstemious; tasted of every dish, after examining it long through a pair of tortoise-shell spectacles, and drank leisurely through a bottle of port, holding up every glass to the light. Darrell talked with his usual cold but not uncourteous indifference. A remark of Lionel on the portraits in the room turned the conversation chiefly upon pictures, and the host showed himself thoroughly accomplished in the attributes of the various schools and masters. Lionel, who was very fond of the art, and indeed painted well for a youthful amateur, listened with great delight.

"Surely, sir, " said he, struck much with a very subtile observation upon the causes why the Italian masters admit of copyists with greater facility than the Flemish, —"surely, sir, you yourself must have practised the art of painting? "

"Not I; but I instructed myself as a judge of pictures, because at one time I was a collector. "

Fairthorn, speaking for the first time: "The rarest collection, —such Albert Durers! such Holbeins! and that head by Leonardo da Vinci! " He stopped; looked extremely frightened; helped himself to the port, turning his back upon his host, to hold, as usual, the glass to the light.

"Are they here, sir? " asked Lionel.

Darrell's face darkened, and he made no answer; but his head sank on his breast, and he seemed suddenly absorbed in gloomy thought. Lionel felt that he had touched a wrong chord, and glanced timidly towards Fairthorn; but that gentleman cautiously held up his finger, and then rapidly put it to his lip, and as rapidly drew it away. After that signal the boy did not dare to break the silence, which now lasted uninterruptedly till Darrell rose, and with the formal and superfluous question, "Any more wine? " led the way back to the library. There he ensconced himself in an easy-chair, and saying, "Will you find a book for yourself, Lionel? " took a volume at random from the nearest shelf, and soon seemed absorbed in its contents. The room, made irregular by baywindows, and shelves that projected as in public libraries, abounded with nook and recess. To one of these Fairthorn sidled himself, and became invisible. Lionel looked round the shelves. No belles lettres of our immediate generation were found there; none of those authors most in request in circulating libraries and literary institutes. The shelves disclosed no poets, no essayists, no novelists, more recent than the Johnsonian age. Neither in the lawyer's library were to be found any law books; no, nor the pamphlets and parliamentary volumes that should have spoken of the once eager politician. But there were superb copies of the ancient classics. French and Italian authors were not wanting, nor such of the English as have withstood the test of time. The larger portions of the shelves seemed, however, devoted to philosophical works. Here alone was novelty admitted, the newest essays on science, or the best editions of old works thereon. Lionel at length made his choice, —a volume of the "Faerie Queene. " Coffee was served; at a later hour tea. The clock struck ten. Darrell laid down his book.

"Mr. Fairthorn, the flute! "

From the recess a mutter; and presently—the musician remaining still hidden—there came forth the sweetest note, —so dulcet, so plaintive! Lionel's ear was ravished. The music suited well with the enchanted page through which his fancy had been wandering dreamlike, —the flute with the "Faerie Queene. " As the air flowed liquid on, Lionel's eyes filled with tears. He did not observe that

Darrell was intently watching him. When the music stopped, he turned aside to wipe the tears from his eyes. Somehow or other, what with the poem, what with the flute, his thoughts had wandered far, far hence to the green banks and blue waves of the Thames, —to Sophy's charming face, to her parting childish gift! And where was she now? Whither passing away, after so brief a holiday, into the shadows of forlorn life? Darrell's bell-like voice smote his ear.

"Spenser; you love him! Do you write poetry? " "No, sir: I only feel it! "

"Do neither! " said the host, abruptly. Then, turning away, he lighted his candle, murmured a quick good-night, and disappeared through a side-door which led to his own rooms.

Lionel looked round for Fairthorn, who now emerged *ab anqulo* from his nook.

"Oh, Mr. Fairthorn, how you have enchanted me! I never believed the flute could have been capable of such effects! "

Mr. Fairthorn's grotesque face lighted up. He took off his spectacles, as if the better to contemplate the face of his eulogist. "So you were pleased! really? " he said, chuckling a strange, grim chuckle, deep in his inmost self.

"Pleased! it is a cold word! Who would not be more than pleased? "

"You should hear me in the open air. "

"Let me do so-to-morrow. "

"My dear young sir, with all my heart. Hist! " —gazing round as if haunted, —"I like you. I wish him to like you. Answer all his questions as if you did not care how he turned you inside out. Never ask him a question, as if you sought to know what he did not himself confide. So there is some thing, you think, in a flute, after all? There are people who prefer the fiddle. "

"Then they never heard your flute, Mr. Fairthorn. " The musician again emitted his discordant chuckle, and, nodding his head nervously and cordially, shambled away without lighting a candle, and was engulfed in the shadows of some mysterious corner.

CHAPTER IV.

The old world and the new.

It was long before Lionel could sleep. What with the strange house and the strange master, what with the magic flute and the musician's admonitory caution, what with tender and regretful reminiscences of Sophy, his brain had enough to work on. When he slept at last, his slumber was deep and heavy, and he did not wake till gently shaken by the well-bred arm of Mr. Mills. "I humbly beg pardon: nine o'clock, sir, and the breakfast-bell going to ring. " Lionel's toilet was soon hurried over; Mr. Darrell and Fairthorn were talking together as he entered the breakfast-room, —the same room as that in which they had dined.

"Good morning, Lionel, " said the host. "No leave-taking to-day, as you threatened. I find you have made an appointment with Mr. Fairthorn, and I shall place you under his care. You may like to look over the old house, and make yourself"—Darrell paused "at home, " jerked out Mr. Fairthorn, filling up the hiatus. Darrell turned his eye towards the speaker, who evidently became much frightened, and, after looking in vain for a corner, sidled away to the window and poked himself behind the curtain. "Mr. Fairthorn, in the capacity of my secretary, has learned to find me thoughts, and put them in his own words, " said Darrell, with a coldness almost icy. He then seated himself at the breakfast-table; Lionel followed his example, and Mr. Fairthorn, courageously emerging, also took a chair and a roll. "You are a true diviner, Mr. Darrell, " said Lionel; "it is a glorious day. "

"But there will be showers later. The fish are at play on the surface of the lake, " Darrell added, with a softened glance towards Fairthorn, who was looking the picture of misery. "After twelve, it will be just the weather for trout to rise; and if you fish, Mr. Fairthorn will lend you a rod. He is a worthy successor of Izaak Walton, and loves a companion as Izaak did, but more rarely gets one. "

"Are there trout in your lake, sir? "

"The lake! You must not dream of invading that sacred water. The inhabitants of rivulets and brooks not within my boundary are beyond the pale of Fawley civilization, to be snared and slaughtered like Caifres, red men, or any other savages, for whom we bait with a missionary and whom we impale on a bayonet. But I regard my lake as a politic community, under the protection of the law, and leave its denizens to devour each other, as Europeans, fishes, and other cold-blooded creatures wisely do, in order to check the overgrowth of population. To fatten one pike it takes a great many minnows. Naturally I support the vested rights of pike. I have been a lawyer. "

It would be in vain to describe the manner in which Mr. Darrell vented this or similar remarks of mocking irony or sarcastic spleen. It was not bitter nor sneering, but in his usual mellifluous level tone and passionless tranquillity.

The breakfast was just over as a groom passed in front of the windows with a led horse. "I am going to leave you, Lionel, " said the host, "to make—friends with Mr. Fairthorn, and I thus complete, according to my own original intention, the sentence which he diverted astray. " He passed across the hall to the open house-door, and stood by the horse, stroking its neck and giving some directions to the groom. Lionel and Fairthorn followed to the threshold, and the beauty of the horse provoked the boy's admiration: it was a dark muzzled brown, of that fine old-fashioned breed of English roadster which is now so seldom seen, —showy, bownecked, long-tailed, stumbling, reedy hybrids, born of bad barbs, ill-mated, having mainly supplied their place. This was, indeed, a horse of great power, immense girth of loin, high shoulder, broad hoof; and such a head! the ear, the frontal, the nostril! you seldom see a human physiognomy half so intelligent, half so expressive of that high spirit and sweet generous temper, which, when united, constitute the ideal of thorough-breeding, whether in horse or man. The English rider was in harmony with the English steed. Darrell at this moment was resting his arm lightly on the animal's shoulder, and his head still uncovered. It has been said before that he was, of imposing presence; the striking attribute of his person, indeed, was that of unconscious grandeur; yet, though above the ordinary height, he was not very tall-five feet eleven at the utmost-and far from being very erect. On the contrary, there was that habitual bend in his proud neck which men who meditate much and live alone almost invariably contract. But there was, to use an expression common with our older writers, that "great air" about him which filled the eye, and gave him the dignity of elevated stature, the commanding aspect that accompanies the upright carriage. His figure was inclined to be slender, though broad of shoulder and deep of chest; it was the figure of a young man and probably little changed from what it might have been at five-and-twenty. A certain youthfulness still lingered even on the countenance, —strange, for sorrow is supposed to expedite the work of age; and Darrell had known sorrow of a kind most adapted to harrow his peculiar nature, as great in its degree as ever left man's heart in ruins. No gray was visible in the dark brown hair, that, worn short behind, still retained in front the large Jove-like curl. No wrinkle, save at the corner of the eyes, marred the pale bronze of the firm cheek; the forehead was smooth as marble, and as massive. It was that forehead which chiefly contributed to the superb expression of his whole aspect. It was high to a fault; the perceptive organs, over a dark, strongly-marked, arched eyebrow, powerfully developed, as they are with most eminent lawyers; it did not want for breadth at the temples; yet, on the whole, it bespoke more of intellectual vigour and dauntless will than of serene philosophy or all-embracing benevolence. It was the forehead of a man formed to command and awe the passions and intellect of others by the strength of passions in himself, rather concentred than chastised, and by an intellect forceful from the weight of its mass rather than the niceness of its balance. The other features harmonized with that brow; they were of the noblest order of aquiline, at once high and delicate. The lip had a rare combination of exquisite refinement and inflexible resolve. The eye, in repose, was cold, bright, unrevealing, with a certain absent, musing, self-absorbed expression, that often made the man's words appear as if spoken mechanically, and assisted towards that seeming of listless indifference to those whom he addressed, by which he wounded vanity without, perhaps, any malice prepense. But it was an eye in which the pupil could suddenly expand, the hue change from gray to dark, and the cold still brightness flash into vivid fire. It could not have occurred to any one, even to the most commonplace woman, to have described Darrell's as a handsome face; the expression would have seemed trivial and derogatory; the words that would have occurred to all, would have been somewhat to this effect: "What a magnificent countenance! What a noble head! " Yet an experienced physiognomist might have noted that the same lineaments which bespoke a virtue bespoke also its neighbouring vice; that with so much will there went stubborn obstinacy; that with that power of grasp there would be the tenacity in adherence which narrows, in astringing, the intellect; that a prejudice once conceived, a passion once cherished, would resist all rational argument for relinquishment. When men of this mould do relinquish prejudice or passion, it is by their own impulse, their own sure conviction that what they hold is worthless: then they do not yield it graciously;

they fling it from them in scorn, but not a scorn that consoles. That which they thus wrench away had "grown a living part of themselves; " their own flesh bleeds; the wound seldom or never heals. Such men rarely fail in the achievement of what they covet, if the gods are neutral; but, adamant against the world, they are vulnerable through their affections. Their love is intense, but undemonstrative; their hatred implacable, but unrevengeful, —too proud to revenge, too galled to pardon.

There stood Guy Darrell, to whom the bar had destined its highest honours, to whom the senate had accorded its most rapturous cheers; and the more you gazed on him as he there stood, the more perplexed became the enigma, —how with a career sought with such energy, advanced with such success, the man had abruptly subsided into a listless recluse, and the career had been voluntarily resigned for a home without neighbours, a hearth without children.

"I had no idea, " said Lionel, as Darrell rode slowly away, soon lost from sight amidst the thick foliage of summer trees, —"I had no idea that my cousin was so young! "

"Oh, yes, " said Mr. Fairthorn; "he is only a year older than I am! "

"Older than you! " exclaimed Lionel, staring in blunt amaze at the elderly-looking personage beside him; "yet true, he told me so himself. "

"And I am fifty-one last birthday. " "Mr. Darrell fifty-two! Incredible! "

"I don't know why we should ever grow old, the life we lead, " observed Mr. Fairthorn, readjusting his spectacles. "Time stands so still! Fishing, too, is very conducive to longevity. If you will follow me, we will get the rods; and the flute, —you are quite sure you would like the flute? Yes! thank you, my dear young sir. And yet there are folks who prefer the fiddle! "

"Is not the sun a little too bright for the fly at present; and will you not, in the meanwhile, show me over the house? "

"Very well; not that this house has much worth seeing. The other indeed would have had a music-room! But, after all, nothing like the open air for the flute. This way. "

I spare thee, gentle reader, the minute inventory of Fawley Manor House. It had nothing but its antiquity to recommend it. It had a great many rooms, all, except those used as the dining-room and library, very small, and very low, —innumerable closets, nooks, — unexpected cavities, as if made on purpose for the venerable game of hide-and-seek. Save a stately old kitchen, the offices were sadly defective even for Mr. Darrell's domestic establishment, which consisted but of two men and four maids (the stablemen not lodging in the house). Drawing-room properly speaking that primitive mansion had none. At some remote period a sort of gallery under the gable roofs (above the first floor), stretching from end to end of the house, might have served for the reception of guests on grand occasions; for fragments of mouldering tapestry still here and there clung to the walls; and a high chimney-piece, whereon, in plaster relief, was commemorated the memorable fishing party of Antony and Cleopatra, retained patches of colour and gilding, which must when fresh have made the Egyptian queen still more appallingly hideous, and the fish at the end of Antony's hook still less resembling any creature known to ichthyologists.

The library had been arranged into shelves from floor to roof by Mr. Darrell's father, and subsequently, for the mere purpose of holding as many volumes as possible, brought out into projecting wings (college-like) by Darrell himself, without any pretension to mediaeval character. With this room communicated a small reading-closet, which the host reserved to himself; and this, by a circular stair cut into the massive wall, ascended first into Mr. Darrell's sleeping-chamber, and thence into a gable recess that adjoined the gallery, and which the host had fitted up for the purpose of scientific experiments in chemistry or other branches of practical philosophy. These more private rooms Lionel was not permitted to enter. Altogether the house was one of those cruel tenements which it would be a sin to pull down, or even materially to alter, but which it would be an hourly inconvenience for a modern family to inhabit. It was out of all character with Mr. Darrell's former position in life, or with the fortune which Lionel vaguely supposed him to possess, and considerably underrated. Like Sir Nicholas Bacon, the man had grown too large for his habitation.

"I don't wonder, " said Lionel, as, their wanderings over, he and Fairthorn found themselves in the library, "that Mr. Darrell began to build a new house. But it would have been a great pity to pull down this for it. "

"Pull down this! Don't hint at such an idea to Mr. Darrell. He would as soon have pulled down the British Monarchy! Nay, I suspect, sooner. "

"But the new building must surely have swallowed up the old one? "

"Oh, no; Mr. Darrell had a plan by which he would have enclosed this separately in a kind of court, with an open screen-work or cloister; and it was his intention to appropriate it entirely to mediaeval antiquities, of which he has a wonderful collection. He had a notion of illustrating every earlier reign in which his ancestors flourished, —different apartments in correspondence with different dates. It would have been a chronicle of national manners. "

"But, if it be not an impertinent question, where is this collection? In London? "

"Hush! hush! I will give you a peep of some of the treasures, only don't betray me. "

Fairthorn here, with singular rapidity, considering that he never moved in a straightforward direction, undulated into the open air in front of the house, described a rhomboid towards a side-buttress in the new building, near to which was a postern-door; unlocked that door from a key in his pocket, and, motioning Lionel to follow him, entered within the ribs of the stony skeleton. Lionel followed in a sort of supernatural awe, and beheld, with more substantial alarm, Mr. Fairthorn winding up an inclined plank which lie embraced with both arms, and by which he ultimately ascended to a timber joist in what should have been an upper floor, only flooring there was none. Perched there, Fairthorn glared down on Lionel through his spectacles. "Dangerous, " he said whisperingly; "but one gets used to everything! If you feel afraid, don't venture! "

Lionel, animated by that doubt of his courage, sprang up the plank, balancing himself schoolboy fashion, with outstretched arms, and gained the side of his guide.

"Don't touch me! " exclaimed Mr. Fairthorn, shrinking, "or we shall both be over. Now observe and imitate. " Dropping himself, then, carefully and gradually, till he dropped on the timber joist as if it were a velocipede, his long legs dangling down, he with thigh and hand impelled himself onward till he gained the ridge of a wall, on which he delivered his person, and wiped his spectacles.

Lionel was not long before he stood in the same place. "Here we are," said Fairthorn.

"I don't see the collection, " answered Lionel, first peering down athwart the joists upon the rugged ground overspread with stones and rubbish, then glancing up through similar interstices above to the gaunt rafters.

"Here are some, —most precious, " answered Fairthorn, tapping behind him. "Walled up, except where these boards, cased in iron, are nailed across, with a little door just big enough to creep through; but that is locked, —Chubb's lock, and Mr. Darrell keeps the key! — treasures for a palace! No, you can't peep through here—not a chink; but come on a little further, —mind your footing. "

Skirting the wall, and still on the perilous ridge, Fairthorn crept on, formed an angle, and stopping short, clapped his eye to the crevice of some planks nailed rudely across a yawning aperture. Lionel found another crevice for himself, and saw, piled up in admired disorder, pictures, with their backs turned to a desolate wall, rare cabinets, and articles of curious furniture, chests, boxes, crates, — heaped pell-mell. This receptacle had been roughly floored in deal, in order to support its miscellaneous contents, and was lighted from a large window (not visible in front of the house), glazed in dull rough glass, with ventilators.

"These are the heavy things, and least costly things, that no one could well rob. The pictures here are merely curious as early specimens, intended for the old house, all spoiling and rotting; Mr. Darrell wishes them to do so, I believe! What he wishes must be done! my dear young sir: a prodigious mind; it is of granite! "

"I cannot understand it, " said Lionel, aghast. "The last man I should have thought capriciously whimsical. "

"Whimsical! Bless my soul! don't say such a word, don't, pray! or the roof will fall down upon us! Come away. You have seen all you can see. You must go first now; mind that loose stone there! "

Nothing further was said till they were out of the building; and Lionel felt like a knight of old who had been led into sepulchral halls by a wizard.

CHAPTER V.

The annals of empire are briefly chronicled in family records brought down to the present day, showing that the race of men is indeed "like leaves on trees, now green in youth, now withering on the ground. " Yet to the branch the most bare will green leaves return, so long as the sap can remount to the branch from the root; but the branch which has ceased to take life from the root—hang it high, hang it low—is a prey to the wind and the woodman.

It was mid-day. The boy and his new friend were standing apart, as becomes silent anglers, on the banks of a narrow brawling rivulet, running through green pastures, half a mile from the house. The sky was overcast, as Darrell had predicted, but the rain did not yet fall. The two anglers were not long before they had filled a basket with small trout. Then Lionel, who was by no means fond of fishing, laid his rod on the bank, and strolled across the long grass to his companion.

"It will rain soon, " said he. "Let us take advantage of the present time, and hear the flute, while we can yet enjoy the open air. No, not by the margin, or you will be always looking after the trout. On the rising ground, see that old thorn tree; let us go and sit under it. The new building looks well from it. What a pile it would have been! I may not ask you, I suppose, why it is left uncompleted. Perhaps it would have cost too much, or would have been disproportionate to the estate. "

"To the present estate it would have been disproportioned, but not to the estate Mr. Darrell intended to add to it. As to cost, you don't know him. He would never have undertaken what he could not afford to complete; and what he once undertook, no thoughts of the cost would have scared him from finishing. Prodigious mind, — granite! And so rich! " added Fairthorn, with an air of great pride. "I ought to know; I write all his letters on money matters. How much do you think he has, without counting land? "

"I cannot guess. "

"Nearly half a million; in two years it will be more than half a million. And he had not three hundred a year when he began life; for Fawley was sadly mortgaged. "

"Is it possible! Could any lawyer make half a million at the bar? "

"If any man could, Mr. Darrell would. When he sets his mind on a thing, the thing is done; no help for it. But his fortune was not all made at the bar, though a great part of it was. An old East Indian bachelor of the same name, but who had never been heard of hereabouts till he wrote from Calcutta to Mr. Darrell (inquiring if they were any relation, and Mr. Darrell referred him to the College-at-Arms, which proved that they came from the same stock ages ago), left him all his money. Mr. Darrell was not dependent on his profession when he stood up in Parliament. And since we have been here, such savings! Not that Mr. Darrell is avaricious, but how can he spend money in this place? You should have seen the establishment we kept in Carlton Gardens. Such a cook too, —a French gentleman, looked like a marquis. Those were happy days, and proud ones! It is true that I order the dinner here, but it can't be the same thing. Do you like fillet of veal? —we have one to-day. "

"We used to have fillet of veal at school on Sundays. I thought it good then. "

"It makes a nice mince, " said Mr. Fairthorn, with a sensual movement of his lips. "One must think of dinner when one lives in the country: so little else to think of! Not that Mr. Darrell does, but then he is granite! "

"Still, " said Lionel, smiling, "I do not get my answer. Why was the house uncompleted? and why did Mr. Darrell retire from public life?"

"He took both into his head; and when a thing once gets there, it is no use asking why. But, " added Fairthorn, and his innocent ugly face changed into an expression of earnest sadness, —"but no doubt he had his reasons. He has reasons for all he does, only they lie far, far away from what appears on the surface, —far as that rivulet lies from its source! My dear young sir, Mr. Darrell has known griefs on which it does not become you and me to talk. He never talks of them. The least I can do for my benefactor is not to pry into his secrets, nor babble them out. And he is so kind, so good, never gets into a passion; but it is so awful to wound him, —it gives him such pain; that's why he frightens me, —frightens me horribly; and so he will you when you come to know him. Prodigious mind! —granite, —

overgrown with sensitive plants. Yes, a little music will do us both good. "

Mr. Fairthorn screwed his flute, an exceedingly handsome one. He pointed out its beauties to Lionel—a present from Mr. Darrell last Christmas—and then he began. Strange thing, Art! especially music. Out of an art, a man may be so trivial you would mistake him for an imbecile, —at best a grown infant. Put him into his art, and how high he soars above you! How quietly he enters into a heaven of which he has become a denizen, and unlocking the gates with his golden key, admits you to follow, a humble reverent visitor.

In his art, Fairthorn was certainly a master, and the air he now played was exquisitely soft and plaintive; it accorded with the clouded yet quiet sky, with the lone but summer landscape, with Lionel's melancholic but not afflicted train of thought. The boy could only murmur "Beautiful! " when the musician ceased.

"It is an old air, " said Fairthorn; "I don't think it is known. I found its scale scrawled down in a copy of the 'Eikon Basilike, ' with the name of 'Joannes Darrell, Esq., Aurat, ' written under it. That, by the date, was Sir John Darrell, the cavalier who fought for Charles I., father of the graceless Sir Ralph, who flourished under Charles II. Both their portraits are in the dining-room. "

"Tell me something of the family; I know so little about it, —not even how the Haughtons and Darrells seem to have been so long connected. I see by the portraits that the Haughton name was borne by former Darrells, then apparently dropped, now it is borne again by my cousin. "

"He bears it only as a Christian name. Your grandfather was his sponsor. But he is nevertheless the head of your family. "

"So he says. How? "

Fairthorn gathered himself up, his knees to his chin, and began in the tone of a guide who has got his lesson by heart; though it was not long before he warmed into his subject.

"The Darrells are supposed to have got their name from a knight in the reign of Edward III., who held the lists in a joust victoriously against all comers, and was called, or called himself, John the Dare-all; or, in old spelling, the Der-all. They were amongst the most powerful families in the country; their alliances were with the highest houses, —Montfichets, Nevilles, Mowbrays; they descended through such marriages from the blood of Plantagenet kings. You'll find their names in chronicles in the early French wars. Unluckily they attached themselves to the fortunes of Earl Warwick, the king-maker, to whose blood they were allied; their representative was killed in the fatal field of Barnet; their estates were of course confiscated; the sole son and heir of that ill-fated politician passed into the Low Countries, where he served as a soldier. His son and grandson followed the same calling under foreign banners. But they must have kept up the love of the old land; for in the latter part of the reign of Henry VIII., the last male Darrell returned to England with some broad gold pieces saved by himself or his exiled fathers, bought some land in this county, in which the ancestral possessions had once been large, and built the present house, of a size suited to the altered fortunes of a race that in a former age had manned castles with retainers. The baptismal name of the soldier who thus partially refounded the old line in England was that now borne by your cousin, Guy, —a name always favoured by Fortune in the family annals; for in Elizabeth's time, from the rank of small gentry, to which their fortune alone lifted them since their return to their native land, the Darrells rose once more into wealth and eminence under a handsome young Sir Guy, —we have his picture in black flowered velvet, —who married the heiress of the Haughtons, a family that had grown rich under the Tudors, and was in high favour with the Maiden-Queen. This Sir Guy was befriended by Essex and knighted by Elizabeth herself. Their old house was then abandoned for the larger mansion of the Haughtons, which had also the advantage of being nearer to the Court, The renewed prosperity of the Darrells was of short duration. The Civil Wars came on, and Sir John Darrell took the losing side. He escaped to France with his only son. He is said to have been an accomplished, melancholy man; and my belief is, that he composed that air which you justly admire for its mournful sweetness. He turned Roman Catholic and died in a convent. But the son, Ralph, was brought up in France with Charles II, and other gay roisterers. On the return of the Stuart, Ralph ran off with the daughter of the Roundhead to whom his estates had been given, and, after getting them back, left his wife in the country, and made love to other men's wives in town. Shocking profligate! no fruit could thrive upon such a branch. He squandered all he could squander, and would have left his children beggars, but that he was providentially slain in a tavern brawl for boasting of a lady's favours

to her husband's face. The husband suddenly stabbed him, —no fair duello, for Sir Ralph was invincible with the small sword. Still the family fortune was much dilapidated, yet still the Darrells lived in the fine house of the Haughtons, and left Fawley to the owls. But Sir Ralph's son, in his old age, married a second time, a young lady of high rank, an earl's daughter. He must have been very much in love with her, despite his age, for to win her consent or her father's he agreed to settle all the Haughton estates on her and the children she might bear to him. The smaller Darrell property had already been entailed on his son by his first marriage. This is how the family came to split. Old Darrell had children by his second wife; the eldest of those children took the Haughton name and inherited the Haughton property. The son by the first marriage had nothing but Fawley and the scanty domain round it. You descend from the second marriage, Mr. Darrell from the first. You understand now, my dear young sir?"
"Yes, a little; but I should very much like to know where those fine Haughton estates are now? "

"Where they are now? I can't say. They were once in Middlesex. Probably much of the land, as it was sold piecemeal, fell into small allotments, constantly changing hands. But the last relics of the property were, I know, bought on speculation by Cox the distiller; for, when we were in London, by Mr. Darrell's desire I went to look after them, and inquire if they could be repurchased. And I found that so rapid in a few years has been the prosperity of this great commercial country, that if one did buy them back, one would buy twelve villas, several streets, two squares, and a paragon! But as that symptom of national advancement, though a proud thought in itself, may not have any pleasing interest for you, I return to the Darrells. From the time in which the Haughton estate had parted from them, they settled back in their old house of Fawley. But they could never again hold up their heads with the noblemen and great squires in the county. As much as they could do to live at all upon the little patrimony; still the reminiscence of what they had been made them maintain it jealously and entail it rigidly. The eldest son would never have thought of any profession or business; the younger sons generally became soldiers, and being always a venturesome race, and having nothing particular to make them value their existence, were no less generally killed off betimes. The family became thoroughly obscure, slipped out of place in the county, seldom rose to be even justices of the peace, never contrived to marry heiresses again, but only the daughters of some neighbouring parson or squire as poor as themselves, but always of gentle blood. Oh, they were as proud as Spaniards in that respect! So from father to son, each generation grew obscurer and poorer; for, entail the estate as they might, still some settlements on it were necessary, and no settlements were ever brought into it; and thus entails were cut off to admit some new mortgage, till the rent-roll was somewhat less than L300 a year when Mr. Darrell's father came into possession. Yet somehow or other he got to college, where no Darrell had been since the time of the Glorious Revolution, and was a learned man and an antiquary, —A GREAT ANTIQUARY! You may have read his works. I know there is one copy of them in the British Museum, and there is another here, but that copy Mr. Darrell keeps under lock and key. "

"I am ashamed to say I don't even know the titles of those works. "

"There were 'Popular Ballads on the Wars of the Roses; ' 'Darrelliana, ' consisting of traditional and other memorials of the Darrell family; 'Inquiry into the Origin of Legends Connected with Dragons; ' 'Hours amongst Monumental Brasses, ' and other ingenious lucubrations above the taste of the vulgar; some of them were even read at the Royal Society of Antiquaries. They cost much to print and publish. But I have heard my father, who was his bailiff, say that he was a pleasant man, and was fond of reciting old scraps of poetry, which he did with great energy; indeed, Mr. Darrell declares that it was the noticing, in his father's animated and felicitous elocution, the effects that voice, look, and delivery can give to words, which made Mr. Darrell himself the fine speaker he is. But I can only recollect the antiquary as a very majestic gentleman, with a long pigtail—awful, rather, not so much so as his son, but still awful—and so sad-looking; you would not have recovered your spirits for a week if you had seen him, especially when the old house wanted repairs, and he was thinking how he could pay for them! "

"Was Mr. Darrell, the present one, an only child? "

"Yes, and much with his father, whom he loved most dearly, and to this day he sighs if he has to mention his father's name! He has old Mr. Darrell's portrait over the chimney-piece in his own reading-room; and he had it in his own library in Carlton Gardens. Our Mr. Darrell's mother was very pretty, even as I remember her: she died when he was about ten years old. And she too was a relation of yours, —a Haughton by blood, —but perhaps you will be ashamed of her, when I say she was a governess in a rich mercantile family.

She had been left an orphan. I believe old Mr. Darrell (not that he was old then) married her because the Haughtons could or would do nothing for her, and because she was much snubbed and put upon, as I am told governesses usually are, —married her because, poor as he was, he was still the head of both families, and bound to do what he could for decayed scions. The first governess a Darrell, ever married; but no true Darrell would have called that a mesalliance since she was still a Haughton and 'Fors non mutat genus, '—Chance does not change race. "

"But how comes it that the Haughtons, my grandfather Haughton, I suppose, would do nothing for his own kinswoman? "

"It was not your grandfather Robert Haughton, who was a generous man, —he was then a mere youngster, hiding himself for debt, —but your great—grandfather, who was a hard man and on the turf. He never had money to give, —only money for betting. He left the Haughton estates sadly clipped. But when Robert succeeded, he came forward, was godfather to our Mr. Darrell, insisted on sharing the expense of sending him to Eton, where he became greatly distinguished; thence to Oxford, where he increased his reputation; and would probably have done more for him, only Mr. Darrell, once his foot on the ladder, wanted no help to climb to the top. "

"Then my grandfather, Robert, still had the Haughton estates? Their last relics had not been yet transmuted by Mr. Cox into squares and a paragon? "

"No; the grand old mansion, though much dilapidated, with its park, though stripped of salable timber, was still left with a rental from farms that still appertained to the residence, which would have sufficed a prudent man for the luxuries of life, and allowed a reserve fund to clear off the mortgages gradually. Abstinence and self-denial for one or two generations would have made a property, daily rising in value as the metropolis advanced to its outskirts, a princely estate for a third. But Robert Haughton, though not on the turf, had a grand way of living; and while Guy Darrell went into the law to make a small patrimony a large fortune, your father, my dear young sir, was put into the Guards to reduce a large patrimony—into Mr. Cox's distillery. "

Lionel coloured, but remained silent.

Fairthorn, who was as unconscious in his zest of narrator that he was giving pain as an entomologist in his zest for collecting when he pins a live moth in his cabinet, resumed: "Your father and Guy Darrell were warm friends as boys and youths. Guy was the elder of the two, and Charlie Haughton (I beg your pardon, he was always called Charlie) looked up to him as to an elder brother. Many's the scrape Guy got him out of; and many a pound, I believe, when Guy had some funds of his own, did Guy lend to Charlie. "

"I am very sorry to hear that, " said Lionel, sharply. Fairthorn looked frightened. "I 'm afraid I have made a blunder. Don't tell Mr. Darrell."

"Certainly not; I promise. But how came my father to need this aid, and how came they at last to quarrel? "

Your father Charlie became a gay young man about town, and very much the fashion. He was like you in person, only his forehead was lower, and his eye not so steady. Mr. Darrell studied the law in chambers. When Robert Haughton died, what with his debts, what with his father's, and what with Charlie's post-obits and I O U's, there seemed small chance indeed of saving the estate to the Haughtons. But then Mr. Darrell looked close into matters, and with such skill did he settle them that he removed the fear of foreclosure; and what with increasing the rental here and there, and replacing old mortgages by new at less interest, he contrived to extract from the property an income of nine hundred pounds a year to Charlie (three times the income Darrell had inherited himself), where before it had seemed that the debts were more than the assets. Foreseeing how much the land would rise in value, he then earnestly implored Charlie (who unluckily had the estate in fee-simple, as Mr. Darrell has this, to sell if he pleased) to live on his income, and in a few years a part of the property might be sold for building purposes, on terms that would save all the rest, with the old house in which Darrells and Haughtons both had once reared generations. Charlie promised, I know, and I've no doubt, my dear young sir, quite sincerely; but all men are not granite! He took to gambling, incurred debts of honour, sold the farms one by one, resorted to usurers, and one night, after playing six hours at piquet, nothing was left for him but to sell all that remained to Mr. Cox the distiller, unknown to Mr. Darrell, who was then married himself, working hard, and living quite out of news of the fashionable world. Then Charlie Haughton sold out of the Guards, spent what he got for his commission, went into the

Line; and finally, in a country town, in which I don't think he was quartered, but having gone there on some sporting speculation, was unwillingly detained, married —"

"My mother! " said Lionel, haughtily; "and the best of women she is. What then? "

"Nothing, my dear young sir, —nothing, except that Mr. Darrell never forgave it. He has his prejudices: this marriage shocked one of them. "

"Prejudice against my poor mother! I always supposed so! I wonder why? The most simple-hearted, inoffensive, affectionate woman. "

"I have not a doubt of it; but it is beginning to rain. Let us go home. I should like some luncheon: it breaks the day. "

"Tell me first why Mr. Darrell has a prejudice against my mother. I don't think that he has even seen her. Unaccountable caprice! Shocked him, too, —what a word! Tell me—I beg—I insist. "

"But you know, " said Fairthorn, half piteously, half snappishly, "that Mrs. Haughton was the daughter of a linendraper, and her father's money got Charlie out of the county jail; and Mr. Darrell said, 'Sold even your name! ' My father heard him say it in the hall at Fawley. Mr. Darrell was there during a long vacation, and your father came to see him. Your father fired up, and they never saw each other, I believe, again. "

Lionel remained still as if thunder-stricken. Something in his mother's language and manner had at times made him suspect that she was not so well born as his father. But it was not the discovery that she was a tradesman's daughter that galled him; it was the thought that his father was bought for the altar out of the county jail! It was those cutting words, "Sold even your name. " His face, before very crimson, became livid; his head sank on his breast. He walked towards the old gloomy house by Fairthorn's side, as one who, for the first time in life, feels on his heart the leaden weight of an hereditary shame.

CHAPTER VI.

Showing how sinful it is in a man who does not care for his honour to beget children.

When Lionel saw Mr. Fairthorn devoting his intellectual being to the contents of a cold chicken-pie, he silently stepped out of the room and slunk away into a thick copse at the farthest end of the paddock. He longed to be alone. The rain descended, not heavily, but in penetrating drizzle; he did not feel it, or rather he felt glad that there was no gaudy mocking sunlight. He sat down forlorn in the hollows of a glen which the copse covered, and buried his face in his clasped hands.

Lionel Haughton, as the reader may have noticed, was no premature man, —a manly boy, but still a habitant of the twilight, dreamy, shadow-land of boyhood. Noble elements were stirring fitfully within him, but their agencies were crude and undeveloped. Sometimes, through the native acuteness of his intellect, he apprehended truths quickly and truly as a man; then, again, through the warm haze of undisciplined tenderness, or the raw mists of that sensitive pride in which objects, small in themselves, loom large with undetected outlines, he fell back into the passionate dimness of a child's reasoning. He was intensely ambitious; Quixotic in the point of honour; dauntless in peril: but morbidly trembling at the very shadow of disgrace, as a foal, destined to be the war-horse and trample down levelled steel, starts in its tranquil pastures at the rustling of a leaf. Glowingly romantic, but not inclined to vent romance in literary creations, his feelings were the more high-wrought and enthusiastic because they had no outlet in poetic channels. Most boys of great ability and strong passion write verses—it is Nature's relief to brain and heart at the critical turning age. Most boys thus gifted do so; a few do not, and out of those few Fate selects the great men of action, —those large luminous characters that stamp poetry on the world's prosaic surface. Lionel had in him the pith and substance of Fortune's grand nobodies, who become Fame's abrupt somebodies when the chances of life throw suddenly in their way a noble something, to be ardently coveted and boldly won. But I repeat, as yet he was a boy; so he sat there, his hands before his face, an unreasoning self-torturer. He knew now why this haughty Darrell had written with so little tenderness and respect to his beloved mother. Darrell looked on her as the cause of his ignoble kinsman's "sale of name; " nay, most probably ascribed to her not the fond girlish love which levels all disparities of rank, but the vulgar cold-blooded design to exchange her father's bank-notes for a marriage beyond her station. And he was the debtor to this supercilious creditor, as his father had been before him. His father! till then he had been so proud of that relationship! Mrs. Haughton had not been happy with her captain; his confirmed habits of wild dissipation had embittered her union, and at last worn away her wifely affections. But she had tended and nursed him in his last illness as the lover of her youth; and though occasionally she hinted at his faults, she ever spoke of him as the ornament of all society, —poor, it is true, harassed by unfeeling creditors, but the finest of fine gentlemen. Lionel had never heard from her of the ancestral estates sold for a gambling debt; never from her of the county jail nor the mercenary misalliance. In boyhood, before we have any cause to be proud of ourselves, we are so proud of our fathers, if we have a decent excuse for it. Of his father could Lionel Haughton be proud now? And Darrell was cognizant of his paternal disgrace, had taunted his father in yonder old hall—for what? —the marriage from which Lionel sprang! The hands grew tighter and tighter before that burning face. He did not weep, as he had done in Vance's presence at a thought much less galling. Not that tears would have misbecome him. Shallow judges of human nature are they who think that tears in themselves ever misbecome boy or even man. Well did the sternest of Roman writers place the arch distinction of humanity aloft from all meaner of Heaven's creatures, in the prerogative of tears! Sooner mayst thou trust thy purse to a professional pickpocket than give loyal friendship to the man who boasts of eyes to which the heart never mounts in dew! Only, when man weeps he should be alone, —not because tears are weak, but because they should be sacred. Tears are akin to prayers. Pharisees parade prayer! impostors parade tears. O Pegasus, Pegasus, —softly, softly, —thou hast hurried me off amidst the clouds: drop me gently down—there, by the side of the motionless boy in the shadowy glen.

CHAPTER VII.

Lionel Haughton, having hitherto much improved his chance of fortune, decides the question, "What will he do with it? "

"I have been seeking you everywhere, " said a well-known voice; and a hand rested lightly on Lionel's shoulder. The boy looked up, startled, but yet heavily, and saw Guy Darrell, the last man on earth he could have desired to see. "Will you come in for a few minutes? you are wanted. "

"What for? I would rather stay here. Who can want me? "

Darrell, struck by the words and the sullen tone in which they were uttered, surveyed Lionel's face for an instant, and replied in a voice involuntarily more kind than usual, —

"Some one very commonplace, but since the Picts went out of fashion, very necessary to mortals the most sublime. I ought to apologize for his coming. You threatened to leave me yesterday because of a defect in your wardrobe. Mr. Fairthorn wrote to my tailor to hasten hither and repair it. He is here. I commend him to your custom! Don't despise him because he makes for a man of my remote generation. Tailors are keen observers and do not grow out of date so quickly as politicians. "

The words were said with a playful good-humour very uncommon to Mr. Darrell. The intention was obviously kind and kinsmanlike. Lionel sprang to his feet; his lip curled, his eye flashed, and his crest rose.

"No, sir; I will not stoop to this! I will not be clothed by your charity, —yours! I will not submit to an implied taunt upon my poor mother's ignorance of the manners of a rank to which she was not born! You said we might not like each other, and, if so, we should part forever. I do not like you, and I will go! " He turned abruptly, and walked to the house—magnanimous. If Mr. Darrell had not been the most singular of men, he might well have been offended. As it was, though few were less accessible to surprise, he was surprised. But offended? Judge for yourself. "I declare, " muttered Guy Darrell, gazing on the boy's receding figure, "I declare that I almost feel as if I could once again be capable of an emotion! I hope I am not going to like that boy! The old Darrell blood in his veins, surely. I might have spoken as he did at his age, but I must have had some better reason for it. What did I say to justify such an explosion?

"*Quid feci? —ubi lapsus?* Gone, no doubt, to pack up his knapsack, and take the Road to Ruin! Shall I let him go? Better for me, if I am really in danger of liking him; and so be at his mercy to sting—what? my heart! I defy him; it is dead. No; he shall not go thus. I am the head of our joint houses. Houses! I wish he had a house, poor boy! And his grandfather loved me. Let him go? I will beg his pardon first; and he may dine in his drawers if that will settle the matter. "

Thus, no less magnanimous than Lionel, did this misanthropical man follow his ungracious cousin. "Ha! " cried Darrell, suddenly, as, approaching the threshold, he saw Mr. Fairthorn at the dining-room window occupied in nibbing a pen upon an ivory thumb-stall—"I have hit it! That abominable Fairthorn has been shedding its prickles! How could I trust flesh and blood to such a bramble? I'll know what it was this instant! " Vain menace! No sooner did Mr. Fairthorn catch glimpse of Darrell's countenance within ten yards of the porch, than, his conscience taking alarm, he rushed incontinent from the window, the apartment, and, ere Darrell could fling open the door, was lost in some lair—"nullis penetrabilis astris"—in that sponge-like and cavernous abode wherewith benignant Providence had suited the locality to the creature.

CHAPTER VIII.

New imbroglio in that ever-recurring, never-to-be-settled question, "What will he do with it? "

With a disappointed glare and a baffled shrug of the shoulder, Mr. Darrell turned from the dining-room, and passed up the stairs to Lionel's chamber, opened the door quickly, and extending his hand said, in that tone which had disarmed the wrath of ambitious factions, and even (if fame lie not) once seduced from the hostile Treasury-bench a placeman's vote, "I must have hurt your feelings, and I come to beg your pardon! "

But before this time Lionel's proud heart, in which ungrateful anger could not long find room, had smitten him for so ill a return to well-meant and not indelicate kindness. And, his wounded egotism appeased by its very outburst, he had called to mind Fairthorn's allusions to Darrell's secret griefs, —griefs that must have been indeed stormy so to have revulsed the currents of a life. And, despite those griefs, the great man had spoken playfully to him, —playfully in order to make light of obligations. So when Guy Darrell now extended that hand, and stooped to that apology, Lionel was fairly overcome. Tears, before refused, now found irresistible way. The hand he could not take, but, yielding to his yearning impulse, he threw his arms fairly round his host's neck, leaned his young cheek upon that granite breast, and sobbed out incoherent words of passionate repentance, honest, venerating affection. Darrell's face changed, looking for a moment wondrous soft; and then, as by an effort of supreme self-control, it became severely placid. He did not return that embrace, but certainly he in no way repelled it; nor did he trust himself to speak till the boy had exhausted the force of his first feelings, and had turned to dry his tears.

Then he said, with a soothing sweetness: "Lionel Haughton, you have the heart of a gentleman that can never listen to a frank apology for unintentional wrong but what it springs forth to take the blame to itself and return apology tenfold. Enough! A mistake no doubt, on both sides. More time must elapse before either can truly say that he does not like the other. Meanwhile, " added Darrell, with almost a laugh, —and that concluding query showed that even on trifles the man was bent upon either forcing or stealing his own will upon others, —"meanwhile must I send away the tailor? " I need not repeat Lionel's answer.

.

CHAPTER IX.

DARRELL—mystery in his past life—What has he done with it?

Some days passed, each day varying little from the other. It was the habit of Darrell if he went late to rest to rise early. He never allowed himself more than five hours sleep. A man greater than Guy Darrell—Sir Walter Raleigh—carved from the solid day no larger a slice for Morpheus. And it was this habit perhaps, yet more than temperance in diet, which preserved to Darrell his remarkable youthfulness of aspect and frame, so that at fifty-two he looked, and really was, younger than many a strong man of thirty-five. For, certain it is, that on entering middle life, he who would keep his brain clear, his step elastic, his muscles from fleshiness, his nerves from tremor, —in a word, retain his youth in spite of the register, — should beware of long slumbers. Nothing ages like laziness. The hours before breakfast Darrell devoted first to exercise, whatever the weather; next to his calm scientific pursuits. At ten o'clock punctually he rode out alone and seldom returned till late in the afternoon. Then he would stroll forth with Lionel into devious woodlands, or lounge with him along the margin of the lake, or lie down on the tedded grass, call the boy's attention to the insect populace which sports out its happy life in the summer months, and treat of the ways and habits of each varying species, with a quaint learning, half humorous, half grave. He was a minute observer and an accomplished naturalist. His range of knowledge was, indeed, amazingly large for a man who has had to pass his best years in a dry and absorbing study: necessarily not so profound in each section as that of a special professor; but if the science was often on the surface, the thoughts he deduced from what he knew were as often original and deep. A maxim of his, which he dropped out one day to Lionel in his careless manner, but pointed diction, may perhaps illustrate his own practice and its results "Never think it enough to have solved the problem started by another mind till you have deduced from it a corollary of your own. "

After dinner, which was not over till past eight o'clock, they always adjourned to the library, Fairthorn vanishing into a recess, Darrell and Lionel each with his several book, then an air on the flute, and each to his own room before eleven. No life could be more methodical; yet to Lionel it had an animating charm, for his interest in his host daily increased, and varied his thoughts with perpetual

126

occupation. Darrell, on the contrary, while more kind and cordial, more cautiously on his guard not to wound his young guest's susceptibilities than he had been before the quarrel and its reconciliation, did not seem to feel for Lionel the active interest which Lionel felt for him. He did not, as most clever men are apt to do in their intercourse with youth, attempt to draw him out, plumb his intellect, or guide his tastes. If he was at times instructive, it was because talk fell on subjects on which it pleased himself to touch, and in which he could not speak without involuntarily instructing. Nor did he ever allure the boy to talk of his school-days, of his friends, of his predilections, his hopes, his future. In short, had you observed them together, you would have never supposed they were connections, that one could and ought to influence and direct the career of the other. You would have said the host certainly liked the guest, as any man would like a promising, warm-hearted, high-spirited, graceful boy, under his own roof for a short time, but who felt that that boy was nothing to him; would soon pass from his eye; form friends, pursuits, aims, with which he could be in no way commingled, for which he should be wholly irresponsible. There was also this peculiarity in Darrell's conversation; if he never spoke of his guest's past and future, neither did he ever do more than advert in the most general terms to his own. Of that grand stage on which he had been so brilliant an actor he imparted no reminiscences; of those great men, the leaders of his age, with whom he had mingled familiarly, he told no anecdotes. Equally silent was he as to the earlier steps in his career, the modes by which he had studied, the accidents of which he had seized advantage, —silent there as upon the causes he had gained, or the debates he had adorned. Never could you have supposed that this man, still in the prime of public life, had been the theme of journals and the boast of party. Neither did he ever, as men who talk easily at their own hearths are prone to do, speak of projects in the future, even though the projects be no vaster than the planting of a tree or the alteration of a parterre, —projects with which rural life so copiously and so innocently teems. The past seemed as if it had left to him no memory, the future as if it stored for him no desire. But did the past leave no memory? Why then at intervals would the book slide from his eye, the head sink upon the breast, and a shade of unutterable dejection darken over the grand beauty of that strong stern countenance? Still that dejection was not morbidly fed and encouraged, for he would fling it from him with a quick impatient gesture of the head, resume the book resolutely, or change it for another which induced fresh trains of thought, or look over Lionel's shoulder, and make some subtile comment on his choice, or call on Fairthorn for the flute; and in a few minutes the face was severely serene again. And be it here said, that it is only in the poetry of young gentlemen, or the prose of lady novelists, that a man in good health and of sound intellect wears the livery of unvarying gloom. However great his causes of sorrow, he does not forever parade its ostentatious mourning, nor follow the hearse of his hopes with the long face of an undertaker. He will still have his gleams of cheerfulness, his moments of good humour. The old smile will sometimes light the eye, and awake the old playfulness of the lip. But what a great and critical sorrow does leave behind is often far worse than the sorrow itself has been. It is a change in the inner man, which strands him, as Guy Darrell seemed stranded, upon the shoal of the Present; which the more he strives manfully to bear his burden warns him the more from dwelling on the Past; and the more impressively it enforces the lesson of the vanity of human wishes strikes the more from his reckoning illusive hopes in the Future. Thus out of our threefold existence two parts are annihilated, —the what has been, the what shall be. We fold our arms, stand upon the petty and steep cragstone, which alone looms out of the Measureless Sea, and say to ourselves, looking neither backward nor beyond, "Let us bear what is; " and so for the moment the eye can lighten and the lip can smile.

Lionel could no longer glean from Mr. Fairthorn any stray hints upon the family records. That gentleman had evidently been reprimanded for indiscretion, or warned against its repetition, and he became as reserved and mum as if he had just emerged from the cave of Trophonius. Indeed he shunned trusting himself again alone to Lionel, and affecting a long arrear of correspondence on behalf of his employer, left the lad during the forenoons to solitary angling, or social intercourse with the swans and the tame doe. But from some mystic concealment within doors would often float far into the open air the melodies of that magic flute; and the boy would glide back, along the dark-red mournful walls of the old house, or the futile pomp of pilastered arcades in the uncompleted new one, to listen to the sound: listening, he, blissful boy, forgot the present; he seized the unchallenged royalty of his years. For him no rebels in the past conspired with poison to the wine-cup, murder to the sleep. No deserts in the future, arresting the march of ambition, said, "Here are sands for a pilgrim, not fields for a conqueror. "

CHAPTER X.

In which chapter the history quietly moves on to the next.

Thus nearly a week had gone, and Lionel began to feel perplexed as to the duration of his visit. Should he be the first to suggest departure? Mr. Darrell rescued him from that embarrassment. On the seventh day, Lionel met his host in a lane near the house, returning from his habitual ride. The boy walked home by the side of the horseman, patting the steed, admiring its shape, and praising the beauty of another saddle-horse, smaller and slighter, which he had seen in the paddock exercised by a groom. "Do you ever ride that chestnut? I think it even handsomer than this. "

"Half our preferences are due to the vanity they flatter. Few can ride this horse; any one, perhaps, that. "

"There speaks the Dare-all! " said Lionel, laughing. The host did not look displeased.

"Where no difficulty, there no pleasure, " said he in his curt laconic diction. "I was in Spain two years ago. I had not an English horse there, so I bought that Andalusian jennet. What has served him at need, no *preux chevalier* would leave to the chance of ill-usage. So the jennet came with me to England. You have not been much accustomed to ride, I suppose? "

"Not much; but my dear mother thought I ought to learn. She pinched for a whole year to have me taught at a riding-school during one school vacation. "

"Your mother's relations are, I believe, well off. Do they suffer her to pinch? "

"I do not know that she has relations living; she never speaks of them. "

"Indeed! " This was the first question on home matters that Darrell had ever directly addressed to Lionel. He there dropped the subject, and said, after a short pause, "I was not aware that you are a horseman, or I would have asked you to accompany me; will you do so to-morrow, and mount the jennet? "

"Oh, thank you; I should like it so much. "

Darrell turned abruptly away from the bright, grateful eyes. "I am only sorry, " he added, looking aside, "that our excursions can be but few. On Friday next I shall submit to you a proposition; if you accept it, we shall part on Saturday, —liking each other, I hope: speaking for myself, the experiment has not failed; and on yours? "

"On mine! —oh, Mr. Darrell, if I dared but tell you what recollections of yourself the experiment will bequeath to me! "

"Do not tell me, if they imply a compliment, " answered Darrell, with the low silvery laugh which so melodiously expressed indifference and repelled affection. He entered the stable-yard, dismounted; and on returning to Lionel, the sound of the flute stole forth, as if from the eaves of the gabled roof. "Could the pipe of Horace's Faunus be sweeter than that flute? " said Darrell,

> "'Utcunque dulci, Tyndare, fistula,
> Valles,' etc.

What a lovely ode that is! What knowledge of town life! what susceptibility to the rural! Of all the Latins, Horace is the only one with whom I could wish to have spent a week. But no! I could not have discussed the brief span of human life with locks steeped in Malobathran balm and wreathed with that silly myrtle. Horace and I would have quarrelled over the first heady bowl of Massie. We never can quarrel now! Blessed subject and poet-laureate of Queen Proserpine, and, I dare swear, the most gentlemanlike poet she ever received at court; henceforth his task is to uncoil the asps from the brows of Alecto, and arrest the ambitious Orion from the chase after visionary lions. "

CHAPTER XI.

Showing that if a good face is a letter of recommendation, a good heart is a letter of credit.

The next day they rode forth, host and guest, and that ride proved an eventful crisis in the fortune of Lionel Haughton. Hitherto I have elaborately dwelt on the fact that whatever the regard Darrell might feel for him, it was a regard apart from that interest which accepts a responsibility and links to itself a fate. And even if, at moments, the powerful and wealthy man had felt that interest, he had thrust it from him. That he meant to be generous was indeed certain, and this he had typically shown in a very trite matter-of-fact way. The tailor, whose visit had led to such perturbation, had received instructions beyond the mere supply of the raiment for which he had been summoned; and a large patent portmanteau, containing all that might constitute the liberal outfit of a young man in the rank of gentleman, had arrived at Fawley, and amazed and moved Lionel, whom Darrell had by this time thoroughly reconciled to the acceptance of benefits. The gift denoted this: "In recognizing you as kinsman, I shall henceforth provide for you as gentleman. " Darrell indeed meditated applying for an appointment in one of the public offices, the settlement of a liberal allowance, and a parting shake of the hand, which should imply, "I have now behaved as becomes me: the rest belongs to you. We may never meet again. There is no reason why this good-by may not be forever. "

But in the course of that ride, Darrell's intentions changed. Wherefore? You will never guess! Nothing so remote as the distance between cause and effect, and the cause for the effect here was — poor little Sophy.

The day was fresh, with a lovely breeze, as the two riders rode briskly over the turf of rolling commons, with the feathery boughs of neighbouring woodlands tossed joyously to and fro by the sportive summer wind. The exhilarating exercise and air raised Lionel's spirits, and released his tongue from all trammels; and when a boy is in high spirits, ten to one but he grows a frank egotist, feels the teeming life of his individuality, and talks about himself. Quite unconsciously, Lionel rattled out gay anecdotes of his school-days; his quarrel with a demoniacal usher; how he ran away; what befell him; how the doctor went after, and brought him back; how splendidly the doctor behaved, —neither flogged nor expelled him, but after patiently listening, while he rebuked the pupil, dismissed the usher, to the joy of the whole academy; how he fought the head boy in the school for calling the doctor a sneak; how, licked twice, he yet fought that head boy a third time, and licked him; how, when head boy himself, he had roused the whole school into a civil war, dividing the boys into Cavaliers and Roundheads; how clay was rolled out into cannon-balls and pistol-shots, sticks shaped into swords, the playground disturbed to construct fortifications; how a slovenly stout boy enacted Cromwell; how he himself was elevated into Prince Rupert; and how, reversing all history, and infamously degrading Cromwell, Rupert would not consent to be beaten; and Cromwell at the last, disabled by an untoward blow across the knuckles, ignominiously yielded himself prisoner, was tried by a court-martial, and sentenced to be shot! To all this rubbish did Darrell incline his patient ear, —not encouraging, not interrupting, but sometimes stifling a sigh at the sound of Lionel's merry laugh, or the sight of his fair face, with heightened glow on his cheeks, and his long silky hair, worthy the name of lovelocks, blown by the wind from the open loyal features, which might well have graced the portrait of some youthful Cavalier. On bounded the Spanish jennet, on rattled the boy rider. He had left school now, in his headlong talk; he was describing his first friendship with Frank Vance, as a lodger at his mother's; how example fired him, and he took to sketch-work and painting; how kindly Vance gave him lessons; how at one time he wished to be a painter; how much the mere idea of such a thing vexed his mother, and how little she was moved when he told her that Titian was of a very ancient family, and that Francis I., archetype of gentleman, visited Leonardo da Vinci's sick-bed; and that Henry VIII. had said to a pert lord who had snubbed Holbein, "I can make a lord any day, but I cannot make a Holbein! " how Mrs. Haughton still confounded all painters in the general image of the painter and the plumber who had cheated her so shamefully in the renewed window-sashes and redecorated walls, which Time and the four children of an Irish family had made necessary to the letting of the first floor. And these playful allusions to the maternal ideas were still not irreverent, but contrived so as rather to prepossess Darrell in Mrs. Haughton's favour by bringing out traits of a simple natural mother, too proud, perhaps, of her only son, not caring what she did, how she worked, so that he might not lose caste as a born Haughton. Darrell understood, and nodded his head approvingly. "Certainly, " he said, speaking almost for the first time, "Fame confers a rank above that of gentlemen and of kings; and as soon as she issues her patent of nobility, it matters not a straw whether the recipient be the son of a Bourbon or of a tallow-chandler. But if Fame withhold her patent; if a well-born man paint aldermen, and be not famous (and I dare say you would have been neither a Titian nor a Holbein), — why, he might as well be a painter and plumber, and has a better chance even of bread and cheese by standing to his post as gentleman. Mrs. Haughton was right, and I respect her. "

"Quite right. If I lived to the age of Methuselah, I could not paint a head like Frank Vance. "

"And even he is not famous yet. Never heard of him. "

"He will be famous: I am sure of it; and if you lived in London, you would hear of him even now. Oh, sir! such a portrait as he painted the other day! But I must tell you all about it. " And therewith Lionel plunged at once, medias res, into the brief broken epic of little Sophy, and the eccentric infirm Belisarius for whose sake she first toiled and then begged; with what artless eloquence he brought out the colours of the whole story, —now its humour, now its pathos; with what beautifying sympathy he adorned the image of the little vagrant girl, with her mien of gentlewoman and her simplicity of child; the river excursion to Hampton Court; her still delight; how annoyed he felt when Vance seemed ashamed of her before those fine people; the orchard scene in which he had read Darrell's letter, that, for the time, drove her from the foremost place in his thoughts; the return home, the parting, her wistful look back, the visit to the Cobbler's next day; even her farewell gift, the nursery poem, with the lines written on the fly-leaf, he had them by heart! Darrell, the grand advocate, felt he could not have produced on a jury, with those elements, the effect which that boy-narrator produced on his granite self.

"And, oh, sir! " cried Lionel, checking his horse, and even arresting Darrell's with bold right hand—"oh, " said he, as he brought his moist and pleading eyes in full battery upon the shaken fort to which he had mined his way—"oh, sir! you are so wise and rich and kind, do rescue that poor child from the penury and hardships of such a life! If you could but have seen and heard her! She could never have been born to it! You look away: I offend you! I have no right to tax your benevolence for others; but, instead of showering favours upon me, so little would suffice for her! —if she were but above positive want, with that old man (she would not be happy without him), safe in such a cottage as you give to your own peasants! I am a man, or shall be one soon; I can wrestle with the world, and force my way somehow; but that delicate child, a village show, or a beggar on the high road! —no mother, no brother, no one but that broken-down cripple, leaning upon her arm as his crutch. I cannot bear to think of it. I am sure I shall meet her again somewhere; and when I do, may I not write to you, and will you not come to her help? Do speak; do say 'Yes, ' Mr. Darrell. "

The rich man's breast heaved slightly; he closed his eyes, but for a moment. There was a short and sharp struggle with his better self, and the better self conquered.

"Let go my reins; see, my horse puts down his ears; he may do you a mischief. Now canter on: you shall be satisfied. Give me a moment to—to unbutton my coat: it is too tight for me. "

CHAPTER XII.

Guy Darrell gives way to an impulse, and quickly decides what he will do with it.

"Lionel Haughton, " said Guy Darrell, regaining his young cousin's side, and speaking in a firm and measured voice, "I have to thank you for one very happy minute; the sight of a heart so fresh in the limpid purity of goodness is a luxury you cannot comprehend till you have come to my age; journeyed, like me, from Dan to Beersheba, and found all barren. Heed me: if you had been half-a-dozen years older, and this child for whom you plead had been a fair young woman, perhaps just as innocent, just as charming, —more in peril, —my benevolence would have lain as dormant as a stone. A young man's foolish sentiment for a pretty girl, —as your true friend, I should have shrugged my shoulders and said, 'Beware! ' Had I been your father, I should have taken alarm and frowned. I should have seen the sickly romance which ends in dupes and deceivers. But at your age, you, hearty, genial, and open-hearted boy, —you, caught but by the chivalrous compassion for helpless female childhood, —oh, that you were my son, —oh, that my dear father's blood were in those knightly veins! I had a son once! God took him; " the strong man's lips quivered: he hurried on. "I felt there was manhood in you, when you wrote to fling my churlish favours in my teeth; when you would have left my roof-tree in a burst of passion which might be foolish, but was nobler than the wisdom of calculating submission, manhood, but only perhaps man's pride as man, —man's heart not less cold than winter. To-day you have shown me something far better than pride; that nature which constitutes the heroic temperament is completed by two attributes, —unflinching purpose, disinterested humanity. I know not yet if you have the first; you reveal to me the second. Yes! I accept the duties you propose to me; I will do more than leave to you the chance of discovering this poor child. I will direct my solicitor to take the right steps to do so. I will see that she is safe from the ills you feel for her. Lionel, more still, I am impatient till I write to Mrs. Haughton. I did her wrong. Remember, I have never seen her. I resented in her the cause of my quarrel with your father, who was once dear to me. Enough of that. I disliked the tone of her letters to me. I disliked it in the mother of a boy who had Darrell blood; other reasons too, —let them pass. But in providing for your education; I certainly thought her relations provided for her support. She never

135

asked me for help there; and, judging of her hastily, I thought she would not have scrupled to do so, if my help there had not been forestalled. You have made me understand her better; and, at all events, three-fourths of what we are in boyhood most of us owe to our mothers! You are frank, fearless, affectionate, a gentleman. I respect the mother who has such a son. "

Certainly praise was rare upon Darrell's lips; but when he did praise, he knew how to do it! And no man will ever command others who has not by nature that gift! It cannot be learned. Art and experience can only refine its expression.

CHAPTER XIII.

He who sees his heir in his own child, carries his eye over hopes and possessions lying far beyond his gravestone, viewing his life, even here, as a period but closed with a comma. He who sees his heir in another man's child, sees the full stop at the end of the sentence.

Lionel's departure was indefinitely postponed; nothing more was said of it. Meanwhile Darrell's manner towards him underwent a marked change. The previous indifference the rich kinsman had hitherto shown as to the boy's past life, and the peculiarities of his intellect and character, wholly vanished. He sought now, on the contrary, to plumb thoroughly the more hidden depths which lurk in the nature of every human being, and which, in Lionel, were the more difficult to discern from the vivacity and candour which covered with so smooth and charming a surface a pride tremulously sensitive, and an ambition that startled himself in the hours when solitude and revery reflect upon the visions of youth the giant outline of its own hopes.

Darrell was not dissatisfied with the results of his survey; yet often, when perhaps most pleased, a shade would pass over his countenance; and had a woman who loved him been by to listen, she would have heard the short slight sigh which came and went too quickly for the duller sense of man's friendship to recognize it as the sound of sorrow.

In Darrell himself, thus insensibly altered, Lionel daily discovered more to charm his interest and deepen his affection. In this man's nature there were, indeed, such wondrous under-currents of sweetness, so suddenly gushing forth, so suddenly vanishing again! And exquisite in him were the traits of that sympathetic tact which the world calls fine breeding, but which comes only from a heart at once chivalrous and tender, the more bewitching in Darrell from their contrast with a manner usually cold, and a bearing so stamped with masculine, self-willed, haughty power. Thus—days went on as if Lionel had become a very child of the house. But his sojourn was in truth drawing near to a close not less abrupt and unexpected than the turn in his host's humours to which he owed the delay of his departure.

One bright afternoon, as Darrell was standing at the window of his private study, Fairthorn, who had crept in on some matter of business, looked at his countenance long and wistfully, and then, shambling up to his side, put one hand on his shoulder with a light timid touch, and, pointing with the other to Lionel, who was lying on the grass in front of the casement reading the "Faerie Queene, " said, "Why do you take him to your heart if he does not comfort it? "

Darrell winced and answered gently, "I did not know you were in the room. Poor Fairthorn; thank you! "

"Thank me! — what for? "

"For a kind thought. So, then, you like the boy? "

"Mayn't I like him? " asked Fairthorn, looking rather frightened; "surely you do! "

"Yes, I like him much; I am trying my best to love him. But, but" — Darrell turned quickly, and the portrait of his father over the mantelpiece came full upon his sight, —an impressive, a haunting face, —sweet and gentle, yet with the high narrow brow and arched nostril of pride, with restless melancholy eyes, and an expression that revealed the delicacy of intellect, but not its power. There was something forlorn, but imposing, in the whole effigy. As you continued to look at the countenance, the mournful attraction grew upon you. Truly a touching and a most lovable aspect. Darrell's eyes moistened.

"Yes, my father, it is so! " he said softly. "All my sacrifices were in vain. The race is not to be rebuilt! No grandchild of yours will succeed me, —me, the last of the old line! Fairthorn, how can I love that boy? He may be my heir, and in his veins not a drop of my father's blood! "

"But he has the blood of your father's ancestors; and why must you think of him as your heir? —you, who, if you would but go again into the world, might yet find a fair wi—"

With such a stamp came Darrell's foot upon the floor that the holy and conjugal monosyllable dropping from Fairthorn's lips was as much cut in two as if a shark had snapped it. Unspeakably frightened, the poor man sidled away, thrust himself behind a tall reading-desk, and, peering aslant from that covert, whimpered out, "Don't, don't now, don't be so awful; I did not mean to offend, but I'm always saying something I did not mean; and really you look so young still" (coaxingly), "and, and—"

Darrell, the burst of rage over, had sunk upon a chair, his face bowed over his hands, and his breast heaving as if with suppressed sobs.

The musician forgot his fear; he sprang forward, almost upsetting the tall desk; he flung himself on his knees at Darrell's feet, and exclaimed in broken words, "Master, master, forgive me! Beast that I was! Do look up—do smile or else beat me—kick me. "

Darrell's right hand slid gently from his face, and fell into Fairthorn's clasp.

"Hush, hush, " muttered the man of granite; "one moment, and it will be over. "

One moment! That might be but a figure of speech; yet before Lionel had finished half the canto that was plunging him into fairyland, Darrell was standing by him with his ordinary tranquil mien; and Fairthorn's flute from behind the boughs of a neighbouring lime-tree was breathing out an air as dulcet as if careless Fauns still piped in Arcady, and Grief were a far dweller on the other side of the mountains, of whom shepherds, reclining under summer leaves, speak as we speak of hydras and unicorns, and things in fable.

On, on swelled the mellow, mellow, witching music; and now the worn man with his secret sorrow, and the boy with his frank glad laugh, are passing away, side by side, over the turf, with its starry and golden wild-flowers, under the boughs in yon Druid copse, from which they start the ringdove, —farther and farther, still side by side, now out of sight, as if the dense green of the summer had closed around them like waves. But still the flute sounds on, and still they hear it, softer and softer as they go. Hark! do you not hear it— you?

CHAPTER XIV.

There are certain events which to each man's life are as comets to the earth, seemingly strange and erratic portents; distinct from the ordinary lights which guide our course and mark our seasons, yet true to their own laws, potent in their own influences. Philosophy speculates on their effects, and disputes upon their uses; men who do not philosophize regard them as special messengers and bodes of evil.

They came out of the little park into a by-lane; a vast tract of common land, yellow with furze and undulated with swell and hollow, spreading in front; to their right the dark beechwoods, still beneath the weight of the July noon. Lionel had been talking about the "Faerie Queene, " knight-errantry, the sweet impossible dream-life that, safe from Time, glides by bower and hall, through magic forests and by witching eaves in the world of poet-books. And Darrell listened, and the flute-notes mingled with the atmosphere faint and far off, like voices from that world itself.

Out then they came, this broad waste land before them; and Lionel said merrily, —

"But this is the very scene! Here the young knight, leaving his father's hall, would have checked his destrier, glancing wistfully now over that green wild which seems so boundless, now to the 'umbrageous horror' of those breathless woodlands, and questioned himself which way to take for adventure. "

"Yes, " said Darrell, coming out from his long reserve on all that concerned his past life, —"Yes, and the gold of the gorse-blossoms tempted me; and I took the waste land. " He paused a moment, and renewed: "And then, when I had known cities and men, and snatched romance from dull matter-of-fact, then I would have done as civilization does with romance itself, —I would have enclosed the waste land for my own aggrandizement. Look, " he continued, with a sweep of the hand round the width of prospect, "all that you see to the verge of the horizon, some fourteen years ago, was to have been thrown into the pretty paddock we have just quitted, and serve as park round the house I was then building. Vanity of human wishes! What but the several proportions of their common folly distinguishes the baffled squire from the arrested conqueror? Man's characteristic cerebral organ must certainly be acquisitiveness. "

"Was it his organ of acquisitiveness that moved Themistocles to boast that 'he could make a small state great'? " "Well remembered, —ingeniously quoted, " returned Darrell, with the polite bend of his stately head. "Yes, I suspect that the coveting organ had much to do with the boast. To build a name was the earliest dream of Themistocles, if we are to accept the anecdote that makes him say, 'The trophies of Miltiades would not suffer him to sleep, ' To build a name, or to create a fortune, are but varying applications of one human passion. The desire of something we have not is the first of our childish remembrances: it matters not what form it takes, what object it longs for; still it is to acquire! it never deserts us while we live. "

"And yet, if I might, I should like to ask, what you now desire that you do not possess? "

"I—nothing; but I spoke of the living! I am dead. Only, " added Darrell, with his silvery laugh, "I say, as poor Chesterfield said before me, 'It is a secret: keep it. '"

Lionel made no reply; the melancholy of the words saddened him: but Darrell's manner repelled the expression of sympathy or of interest; and the boy fell into conjecture, what had killed to the world this man's intellectual life?

And thus silently they continued to wander on till the sound of the flute had long been lost to their ears. Was the musician playing still?

At length they came round to the other end of Fawley village, and Darrell again became animated.

"Perhaps, " said he, returning to the subject of talk that had been abruptly suspended, —"perhaps the love of power is at the origin of each restless courtship of Fortune: yet, after all, who has power with less alloy than the village thane? With so little effort, so little thought, the man in the manor-house can make men in the cottage happier here below and more fit for a hereafter yonder. In leaving the world I come from contest and pilgrimage, like our sires the Crusaders, to reign at home. "

As he spoke, he entered one of the cottages. An old paralytic man was seated by the fire, hot though the July sun was out of doors; and his wife, of the same age, and almost as helpless, was reading to him a chapter in the Old Testament, —the fifth chapter in Genesis, containing the genealogy, age, and death of the patriarchs before the Flood. How the faces of the couple brightened when Darrell entered. "Master Guy! " said the old man, tremulously rising. The world-weary orator and lawyer was still Master Guy to him.

"Sit down, Matthew, and let, me read you a chapter. " Darrell took the Holy Book, and read the Sermon on the Mount. Never had Lionel heard anything like that reading; the feeling which brought out the depth of the sense, the tones, sweeter than the flute, which clothed the divine words in music. As Darrell ceased, some beauty seemed gone from the day. He lingered a few minutes, talking kindly and familiarly, and then turned into another cottage, where lay a sick woman. He listened to her ailments, promised to send her something to do her good from his own stores, cheered up her spirits, and, leaving her happy, turned to Lionel with a glorious smile, that seemed to ask, "And is there not power in this? "

Put it was the sad peculiarity of this remarkable man that all his moods were subject to rapid and seemingly unaccountable variations. It was as if some great blow had fallen on the mainspring of his organization, and left its original harmony broken up into fragments each impressive in itself, but running one into the other with an abrupt discord, as a harp played upon by the winds. For, after this evident effort at self-consolation or self-support in soothing or strengthening others, suddenly Darrell's head fell again upon his breast, and he walked on, up the village lane, heeding no longer either the open doors of expectant cottagers or the salutation of humble passers-by. "And I could have been so happy here! " he said suddenly. "Can I not be so yet? Ay, perhaps, when I am thoroughly old, —tied to the world but by the thread of an hour. Old men do seem happy; behind them, all memories faint, save those of childhood and sprightly youth; before them, the narrow ford, and the sun dawning up through the clouds on the other shore. 'T is the critical descent into age in which man is surely most troubled; griefs gone, still rankling; nor-strength yet in his limbs, passion yet in his heart-reconciled to what loom nearest in the prospect, —the armchair and the palsied head. Well! life is a quaint puzzle. Bits the most incongruous join into each other, and the scheme thus gradually becomes symmetrical and clear; when, lo! as the infant claps his hands and cries, 'See! see! the puzzle is made out! ' all the pieces are swept back into the box, —black box with the gilded nails. Ho! Lionel, look up; there is our village church, and here, close at my right, the churchyard! "

Now while Darrell and his young companion were directing their gaze to the right of the village lane, towards the small gray church, —towards the sacred burial-ground in which, here and there amongst humbler graves, stood the monumental stone inscribed to the memory of some former Darrell, for whose remains the living sod had been preferred to the family vault; while both slowly neared the funeral spot, and leaned, silent and musing, over the rail that fenced it from the animals turned to graze on the sward of the surrounding green, —a foot-traveller, a stranger in the place, loitered on the threshold of the small wayside inn, about fifty yards off to the left of the lane, and looked hard at the still figures of the two kinsmen.

Turning then to the hostess, who was standing somewhat within the threshold, a glass of brandy-and-water in her hand, the third glass that stranger had called for during his half hour's rest in the hostelry, quoth the man,

"The taller gentleman yonder is surely your squire, is he not? but who is the shorter and younger person? "

The landlady put forth her head.

"Oh! that is a relation of the squire down on a visit, sir. I heard coachman say that the squire's taken to him hugely; and they do think at the Hall that the young gentleman will be his heir. "

"Aha! —indeed—his heir! What is the lad's name? What relation can he be to Mr. Darrell? "

"I don't know what relation exactly, sir; but he is one of the Haughtons, and they've been kin to the Fawley folks time out of mind. "

"Haughton? —aha! Thank you, ma'am. Change, if you please. "

The stranger tossed off his dram, and stretched his hand for his change.

"Beg pardon, sir, but this must be forring money, " said the landlady, turning a five-franc piece on her palm with suspicious curiosity.

"Foreign! Is it possible? " The stranger dived again into his pocket, and apparently with some difficulty hunted out half-a-crown.

"Sixpence more, if you please, sir; three brandies, and bread-and-cheese and the ale too, sir. "

"How stupid I am! I thought that French coin was a five shilling piece. I fear I have no English money about me but this half-crown; and I can't ask you to trust me, as you don't know me. "

"Oh, sir, 't is all one if you know the squire. You may be passing this way again. "

"I shall not forget my debt when I do, you may be sure, " said the stranger; and, with a nod, he walked away in the same direction as Darrell and Lionel had already taken, through a turnstile by a public path that, skirting the churchyard and the neighbouring parsonage, led along a cornfield to the demesnes of Fawley.

The path was narrow, the corn rising on either side, so that two persons could not well walk abreast. Lionel was some paces in advance, Darrell walking slow. The stranger followed at a distance: once or twice he quickened his pace, is if resolved to overtake Darrell; then apparently his mind misgave him, and he again fell back.

There was something furtive and sinister about the man. Little could be seen of his face, for he wore a large hat of foreign make, slouched deep over his brow, and his lips and jaw were concealed by a dark and full mustache and beard. As much of the general outline of the countenance as remained distinguishable was nevertheless decidedly handsome; but a complexion naturally rich in colour seemed to have gained the heated look which comes with the earlier habits of intemperance before it fades into the leaden hues of the later.

His dress bespoke pretension to a certain rank: but its component parts were strangely ill-assorted, out of date, and out of repair; pearl-coloured trousers, with silk braids down their sides; brodequins to match, —Parisian fashion three years back, but the trousers shabby, the braiding discoloured, the brodequins in holes. The coat-once a black evening dress-coat—of a cut a year or two anterior to that of the trousers; satin facing, -cloth napless, satin stained. Over all, a sort of summer travelling-cloak, or rather large cape of a waterproof silk, once the extreme mode with the lions of the Chaussee d'Autin whenever they ventured to rove to Swiss cantons or German spas; but which, from a certain dainty effeminacy in its shape and texture, required the minutest elegance in the general costume of its wearer as well as the cleanliest purity in itself. Worn by this traveller, and well-nigh worn out too, the cape became a finery mournful as a tattered pennon over a wreck.

Yet in spite of this dress, however unbecoming, shabby, obsolete, a second glance could scarcely fail to note the wearer as a man wonderfully well-shaped, —tall, slender in the waist, long of limb, but with a girth of chest that showed immense power; one of those rare figures that a female eye would admire for grace, a recruiting sergeant for athletic strength.

But still the man's whole bearing and aspect, even apart from the dismal incongruities of his attire, which gave him the air of a beggared spendthrift, marred the favourable effect that physical comeliness in itself produces. Difficult to describe how, —difficult to say why, —but there is a look which a man gets, and a gait which he contracts when the rest of mankind cut him; and this man had that look and that gait.

"So, so, " muttered the stranger. "That boy his heir? so, so. How can I get to speak to him? In his own house he would not see me: it must be as now, in the open air; but how catch him alone? and to lurk in the inn, in his own village, —perhaps for a day, —to watch an occasion; impossible! Besides, where is the money for it? Courage, courage! " He quickened his pace, pushed back his hat. "Courage! Why not now? Now or never! "

While the man thus mutteringly soliloquized, Lionel had reached the gate which opened into the grounds of Fawley, just in the rear of the little lake. Over the gate he swung himself lightly, and, turning back to Darrell cried, "Here is the doe waiting to welcome you. "

Just as Darrell, scarcely heeding the exclamation, and with his musing eyes on the ground, approached the gate, a respectful hand opened it wide, a submissive head bowed low, a voice artificially soft faltered forth words, broken and, indistinct, but of which those most audible were—"Pardon, me; something to communicate, — important; hear me. "

Darrell started, just as the traveller almost touched him, started, recoiled, as one on whose path rises a wild beast. His bended head became erect, haughty, indignant, defying; but his cheek was pale, and his lip quivered. "You here! You in England-at Fawley! You presume to accost me! You, sir, —you! "

Lionel just caught the sound of the voice as the doe had come timidly up to him. He turned round sharply, and beheld Darrell's stern, imperious countenance, on which, stern and imperious though it was, a hasty glance could discover, at once, a surprise that almost bordered upon fear. Of the stranger still holding the gate he saw but the back, and his voice he did not hear, though by the man's gesture he was evidently replying. Lionel paused a moment irresolute; but as the man continued to speak, he saw Darrell's face grow paler and paler, and in the impulse of a vague alarm he hastened towards him; but just within three feet of the spot, Darrell arrested his steps.

"Go home, Lionel; this person would speak to me in private. " Then, in a lower tone, he said to the stranger, "Close the gate, sir; you are standing upon the land of my fathers. If you would speak with me, this way; " and, brushing through the corn, Darrell strode towards a patch of waste land that adjoined the field: the man followed him, and both passed from Lionel's eyes. The doe had come to the gate to greet her master; she now rested her nostrils on the bar, with a look disappointed and plaintive.

"Come, " said Lionel, "come. " The doe would not stir.

So the boy walked on alone, not much occupied with what had just passed. "Doubtless, " thought he, "some person in the neighbourhood upon country business. "

He skirted the lake, and seated himself on a garden bench near the house. What did he there think of? —who knows? Perhaps of the Great World; perhaps of little Sophy! Time fled on: the sun was receding in the west when Darrell hurried past him without speaking, and entered the house.

The host did not appear at dinner, nor all that evening. Mr. Mills made an excuse: Mr. Darrell did not feel very well.

Fairthorn had Lionel all to himself, and having within the last few days reindulged in open cordiality to the young guest, he was especially communicative that evening. He talked much on Darrell, and with all the affection that, in spite of his fear, the poor flute-player felt for his ungracious patron. He told many anecdotes of the stern man's tender kindness to all that came within its sphere. He told also anecdotes more striking of the kind man's sternness where some obstinate prejudice, some ruling passion, made him "granite. "

"Lord, my dear young sir, " said Fairthorn, "be his most bitter open enemy, and fall down in the mire, the first hand to help you would be Guy Darrell's; but be his professed friend, and betray him to the worth of a straw, and never try to see his face again if you are wise, —the most forgiving and the least forgiving of human beings. But—"

The study door noiselessly opened, and Darrell's voice called out, "Fairthorn, let me speak with you. "

CHAPTER XV.

Every street has two sides, the shady side and the sunny. When two men shake hands and part, mark which of the two takes the sunny side: he will be the younger man of the two.

The next morning, neither Darrell nor Fairthorn appeared at breakfast; but as soon as Lionel had concluded that meal, Mr. Mills informed him, with customary politeness, that Mr. Darrell wished to speak with him in the study. Study, across the threshold of which Lionel had never yet set footstep! He entered it now with a sentiment of mingled curiosity and awe. Nothing in it remarkable, save the portrait of the host's father over the mantelpiece. Books strewed tables, chairs, and floors in the disorder loved by habitual students. Near the window was a glass bowl containing gold-fish, and close by, in its cage, a singing-bird. Darrell might exist without companionship in the human species, but not without something which he protected and cherished, —a bird, even a fish.

Darrell looked really ill: his keen eye was almost dim, and the lines in his face seemed deeper. But he spoke with his usual calm, passionless melody of voice.

"Yes, " he said, in answer to Lionel's really anxious inquiry; "I am ill. Idle persons like me give way to illness. When I was a busy man, I never did; and then illness gave way to me. My general plans are thus, if not actually altered, at least hurried to their consummation sooner than I expected. Before you came here, I told you to come soon, or you might not find me. I meant to go abroad this summer; I shall now start at once. I need the change of scene and air. You will return to London to-day. "

"To-day! You are not angry with me? "

"Angry! boy and cousin—no! " resumed Darrell, in a tone of unusual tenderness. "Angry-fie! But since the parting must be, 't is well to abridge the pain of long farewell. You must wish, too, to see your mother, and thank her for rearing you up so that you may step from poverty into ease with a head erect. You will give to Mrs. Haughton this letter: for yourself, your inclinations seem to tend towards the army. But before you decide on that career, I should like you to see something more of the world. Call to-morrow on Colonel Morley, in

Curzon Street: this is his address. He will receive by to-day's post a note from me, requesting him to advise you. Follow his counsels in what belongs to the world. He is a man of the world, —a distant connection of mine, who will be kind to you for my sake. Is there more to say? Yes. It seems an ungracious speech; but I should speak it. Consider yourself sure from me of an independent income. Never let idle sycophants lead you into extravagance by telling you that you will have more. But indulge not the expectation, however plausible, that you will be my heir. "

"Mr. Darrell—oh, sir—"

"Hush! the expectation would be reasonable; but I am a strange being. I might marry again, —have heirs of my own. Eh, sir, —Oh why not? " Darrell spoke these last words almost fiercely, and fixed his eyes on Lionel as he repeated, —"Why not? " But seeing that the boy's face evinced no surprise, the expression of his own relaxed, and he continued calmly, —"Enough; what I have thus rudely said was kindly meant. It is a treason to a young man to let him count on a fortune which at last is left away from him. Now, Lionel, go; enjoy your spring of life! Go, hopeful and light-hearted. If sorrow reach you, battle with it; if error mislead you, come fearlessly to me for counsel. Why, boy, what is this? —tears? Tut, tut. "

"It is your goodness, " faltered Lionel. "I cannot help it. And is there nothing I can do for you in return? "

"Yes, much. Keep your name free from stain, and your heart open to such noble emotions as awaken tears like those. Ah, by the by, I heard from my lawyer to-day about your poor little protegee. Not found yet, but he seems sanguine of quick success. You shall know the moment I hear more. "

"You will write to me, then, sir, and I may write to you? "

"As often as you please. Always direct to me here. "

"Shall you be long abroad? "

Darrell's brows met. "I don't know, " said he, curtly. "Adieu. "

He opened the door as he spoke.

Lionel looked at him with wistful yearning, filial affection, through his swimming eyes. "God bless you, sir, " he murmured simply, and passed away.

"That blessing should have come from me! " said Darrell to himself, as he turned back, and stood on his solitary hearth. "But they on whose heads I once poured a blessing, where are they, —where? And that man's tale, reviving the audacious fable which the other, and I verily believe the less guilty knave of the two, sought to palm on me years ago! Stop; let me weigh well what he said. If it were true! Oh, shame, shame! "

Folding his arms tightly on his breast, Darrell paced the room with slow, measured strides, pondering deeply. He was, indeed, seeking to suppress feeling, and to exercise only judgment; and his reasoning process seemed at length fully to satisfy him, for his countenance gradually cleared, and a triumphant smile passed across it. "A lie, — certainly a palpable and gross lie; lie it must and shall be. Never will I accept it as truth. Father" (looking full at the portrait over the mantel-shelf), "Father, fear not—never—never! "

BOOK III.

CHAPTER I.

Certes, the lizard is a shy and timorous creature. He runs into chinks and crannies if you come too near to him, and sheds his very tail for fear, if you catch it by the tip. He has not his being in good society: no one cages him, no one pets. He is an idle vagrant. But when he steals through the green herbage, and basks unmolested in the sun, he crowds perhaps as much enjoyment into one summer hour as a parrot, however pampered and erudite, spreads over a whole drawing-room life spent in saying "How dye do" and "Pretty Poll. "

ON that dull and sombre summer morning in which the grandfather and grandchild departed from the friendly roof of Mr. Merle, very dull and very sombre were the thoughts of little Sophy. She walked slowly behind the gray cripple, who had need to lean so heavily on his staff, and her eye had not even a smile for the golden buttercups that glittered on dewy meads alongside the barren road.

Thus had they proceeded apart and silent till they had passed the second milestone. There, Waife, rousing from his own reveries, which were perhaps yet more dreary than those of the dejected child, halted abruptly, passed his hand once or twice rapidly over his forehead, and, turning round to Sophy, looked into her face with great kindness as she came slowly to his side.

"You are sad, little one? " said he.

"Very sad, Grandy. "

"And displeased with me? Yes, displeased that I have taken you suddenly away from the pretty young gentleman, who was so kind to you, without encouraging the chance that you were to meet with him again. "

"It was not like you, Grandy, " answered Sophy; and her under-lip slightly pouted, while the big tears swelled to her eye.

"True, " said the vagabond; "anything resembling common-sense is not like me. But don't you think that I did what I felt was best for

151

you? Must I not have some good cause for it, whenever I have the heart deliberately to vex you? "

Sophy took his hand and pressed it, but she could not trust herself to speak, for she felt that at such effort she would have burst out into hearty crying. Then Waife proceeded to utter many of those wise sayings, old as the hills, and as high above our sorrows as hills are from the valley in which we walk. He said how foolish it was to unsettle the mind by preposterous fancies and impossible hopes. The pretty young gentleman could never be anything to her, nor she to the pretty young gentleman. It might be very well for the pretty young gentleman to promise to correspond with her, but as soon as he returned to his friends he would have other things to think of, and she would soon be forgotten; while she, on the contrary, would be thinking of him, and the Thames and the butterflies, and find hard life still more irksome. Of all this, and much more, in the general way of consolers who set out on the principle that grief is a matter of logic, did Gentleman Waife deliver himself with a vigour of ratiocination which admitted of no reply, and conveyed not a particle of comfort. And feeling this, that great actor—not that he was acting then-suddenly stopped, clasped the child in his arms, and murmured in broken accents, —"But if I see you thus cast down, I shall have no strength left to hobble on through the world; and the sooner I lie down, and the dust is shovelled over me, why, the better for you; for it seems that Heaven sends you friends, and I tear you from them. "

And then Sophy fairly gave way to her sobs: she twined her little arms round the old man's neck convulsively, kissed his rough face with imploring pathetic fondness, and forced out through her tears, "Don't talk so! I've been ungrateful and wicked. I don't care for any one but my own dear, dear Grandy. "

After this little scene, they both composed themselves, and felt much lighter of heart. They pursued their journey, no longer apart, but side by side, and the old man leaning, though very lightly, on the child's arm. But there was no immediate reaction from gloom to gayety. Waife began talking in softened undertones, and vaguely, of his own past afflictions; and partial as was the reference, how vast did the old man's sorrows seem beside the child's regrets; and yet he commented on them as if rather in pitying her state than grieving for his own.

"Ah, at your age, my darling, I had not your troubles and hardships. I had not to trudge these dusty roads on foot with a broken-down good-for-nothing scatterling; I trod rich carpets, and slept under silken curtains. I took the air in gay carriages, —I such a scapegrace; and you, little child, you so good! All gone, all melted away from me, and not able now to be sure that you will have a crust of bread this day week. "

"Oh, yes! I shall have bread, and you too, Grandy, " cried Sophy, with cheerful voice. "It was you who taught me to pray to God, and said that in all your troubles God had been good to you: and He has been so good to me since I prayed to Him; for I have no dreadful Mrs. Crane to beat me now, and say things more hard to bear than beating; and you have taken me to yourself. How I prayed for that! And I take care of you too, Grandy, —don't I? I prayed for that too; and as to carriages, " added Sophy, with superb air, "I don't care if I am never in a carriage as long as I live; and you know I have been in a van, which is bigger than a carriage, and I didn't like that at all. But how came people to behave so ill to you, Grandy? "

"I never said people behaved ill to me, Sophy. "

"Did not they take away the carpets and silk curtains, and all the fine things you had as a little boy? "

"I don't know, " replied Waife, with a puzzled look, "that people actually took them away; but they melted away.

"However, I had much still to be thankful for: I was so strong, and had such high spirits, Sophy, and found people not behaving ill to me, —quite the contrary, so kind. I found no Crane (she monster) as you did, my little angel. Such prospects before me, if I had walked straight towards them! But I followed my own fancy, which led me zigzag; and now that I would stray back into the high road, you see before you a man whom a Justice of the Peace could send to the treadmill for presuming to live without a livelihood. "

SOPHY. —"Not without a livelihood! —the what did you call it? — independent income, —that is, the Three Pounds, Grandy? "

WAIFE (admiringly). —"Sensible child. That is true. Yes, Heaven is very good to me still. Ah! what signifies fortune? How happy I was with my dear Lizzy, and yet no two persons could live more from hand to mouth. "

SOPHY (rather jealously). —"tizzy? "

WAIFE (with moistened eyes, and looking down). —"My wife. She was only spared to me two years: such sunny years! And how grateful I ought to be that she did not live longer. She was saved— such—such—such shame and misery! " A long pause.

Waife resumed, with a rush from memory, as if plucking himself from the claws of a harpy, —"What's the good of looking back? A man's gone self is a dead thing. It is not I—now tramping this road, with you to lean upon—whom I see, when I would turn to look behind on that which I once was: it is another being, defunct and buried; and when I say to myself, 'that being did so and so, ' it is like reading an epitaph on a tombstone. So, at last, solitary and hopeless, I came back to my own land; and I found you, —a blessing greater than I had ever dared to count on. And how was I to maintain you, and take you from that long-nosed alligator called Crane, and put you in womanly gentle hands; for I never thought then of subjecting you to all you have since undergone with me, —I who did not know one useful thing in life by which a man can turn a penny. And then, as I was all alone in a village ale-house, on my way back from—it does not signify from what, or from whence, but I was disappointed and despairing, Providence mercifully threw in my way—Mr. Rugge, and ordained me to be of great service to that ruffian, and that ruffian of great use to me. "

Sorfiy. —"Ah, how was that? "

WAIFE. —"It was fair time in the village wherein I stopped, and Rugge's principal actor was taken off by delirium tremens, which is Latin for a disease common to men who eat little and drink much. Rugge came into the alehouse bemoaning his loss. A bright thought struck me. Once in my day I had been used to acting. I offered to try my chance on Mr. Rugge's stage: he caught at me, I at him. I succeeded: we came to terms, and my little Sophy was thus taken from that ringleted crocodile, and placed with Christian females who wore caps and read their Bible. Is not Heaven good to us, Sophy; and to me too—me, such a scamp? "

"And you did all that, —suffered all that for my sake? "

"Suffered, but I liked it. And, besides, I must have done something; and there were reasons—in short, I was quite happy; no, not actually happy, but comfortable and merry. Providence gives thick hides to animals that must exist in cold climates; and to the man whom it reserves for sorrow, Providence gives a coarse, jovial temper. Then, when by a mercy I was saved from what I most disliked and dreaded, and never would have thought of but that I fancied it might be a help to you, —I mean the London stage, —and had that bad accident on the railway, how did it end? Oh! in saving you" (and Waife closed his eyes and shuddered), "in saving your destiny from what might be much worse for you, body and soul, than the worst that has happened to you with me. And so we have been thrown together; and so you have supported me; and so, when we could exist without Mr. Rugge, Providence got rid of him for us. And so we are now walking along the high road; and through yonder trees you can catch a peep of the roof under which we are about to rest for a while; and there you will learn what I have done with the Three Pounds! "

"It is not the Spotted Boy, Grandy? "

"No, " said Waife, sighing; "the Spotted Boy is a handsome income; but let us only trust in Providence, and I should not wonder if our new acquisition proved a monstrous—"

"Monstrous! "

"Piece of good fortune. "

CHAPTER II.

The investment revealed.

Gentleman Waife passed through a turnstile, down a narrow lane, and reached a solitary cottage. He knocked at the door; an old peasant woman opened it, and dropped him a civil courtesy. "Indeed, sir, I am glad you are come. I 'se most afeared he be dead. "

"Dead! " exclaimed Waife. "Oh, Sophy, if he should be dead! "

"Who? "

Waife did not heed the question. "What makes you think him dead? " said he, fumbling in his pockets, from which he at last produced a key. "You have not been disobeying my strict orders, and tampering with the door? "

"Lor' love ye, no, sir. But he made such a noise at fust—awful! And now he's as still as a corpse. And I did peep through the keyhole, and he was stretched stark. "

"Hunger, perhaps, " said the Comedian; "'t is his way when he has been kept fasting much over his usual hours. Follow me, Sophy. " He put aside the woman, entered the sanded kitchen, ascended a stair that led from it; and Sophy following, stopped at a door and listened: not a sound. Timidly he unlocked the portals and crept in, when, suddenly such a rush, —such a spring, and a mass of something vehement yet soft, dingy yet whitish, whirled past the actor, and came pounce against Sophy, who therewith uttered a shriek. "Stop him, stop him, for heaven's sake, " cried Waife. "Shut the door below, —seize him. " Downstairs, however, went the mass, and downstairs after it hobbled Waife, returning in a few moments with the recaptured and mysterious fugitive. "There, " he cried triumphantly to Sophy, who, standing against the wall with her face buried in her frock, long refused to look up, —"there, —tame as a lamb, and knows me. See! " he seated himself on the floor, and Sophy, hesitatingly opening her eyes, beheld gravely gazing at her from under a profusion of shaggy locks an enormous—

CHAPTER III.

Denoumente!
POODLE!

CHAPTER IV.

Zoology in connection with history.

"Walk to that young lady, sir, —walk, I say. " The poodle slowly rose on his hind legs, and, with an aspect inexpressibly solemn, advanced towards Sophy, who hastily receded into the room in which the creature had been confined.

"Make a bow—no—a bow, sir; that is right: you can shake hands another time. Run down, Sophy, and ask for his dinner. "

"Yes; that I will; " and Sophy flew down the stairs.

The dog, still on his hind legs, stood in the centre of the floor dignified, but evidently expectant.

"That will do; lie down and die. Die this moment, sir. " The dog stretched himself out, closed his eyes, and to all appearance gave up the ghost. "A most splendid investment, " said Waife, with enthusiasm; "and upon the whole, clog cheap. Ho! you are not to bring up his dinner; it is not you who are to make friends with the dog; it is my little girl; send her up; Sophy, Sophy! "

"She be fritted, sir, " said the woman, holding a plate of canine comestibles; "but lauk, sir, bent he really dead? "

"Sophy, Sophy"

"Please let me stay here, Grandy, " said Sophy's voice from the foot of the stairs.

"Nonsense! it is sixteen hours since he has had a morsel to eat. And he will never bite the hand that feeds him now. Come up, I say. "

Sophy slowly reascended, and Waife summoning the poodle to life, insisted upon the child's feeding him. And indeed, when that act of charity was performed, the dog evinced his gratitude by a series of unsophisticated bounds and waggings of the tail, which gradually removed Sophy's apprehensions, and laid the foundation for that intimate friendship which is the natural relation between child and dog.

"And how did you come by him? " asked Sophy; "and is this really the—the INVESTMENT? "

"Shut the door carefully, but see first that the woman is not listening. Lie down, sir, there, at the feet of the young lady. Good dog! How did I come by him? I will tell you. The first day we arrived at the village which we have just left I went into the tobacconist's. While I was buying my ounce of canaster that dog entered the shop. In his mouth was a sixpence wrapped in paper. He lifted himself on his hind legs, and laid his missive on the counter. The shopwoman— you know her, Mrs. Traill—unfolded the paper and read the order. 'Clever dog that, sir, ' said she. 'To fetch and carry? ' said I, indifferently. 'More than that, sir; you shall see. The order is for two penn'orth of snuff. The dog knows he is to take back fourpence. I will give him a penny short. ' So she took the sixpence and gave the dog threepence out of it. The dog shook his head and looked gravely into her face. 'That's all you'll get, ' said she. The dog shook his head again, and tapped his paw once on the counter, as much as to say, 'I'm not to be done: a penny more, if you please. ' 'If you'll not take that, you shall have nothing, ' said Mrs. Traill, and she took back the threepence. "

"Dear! and what did the dog do then, —snarl or bite? " "Not so; he knew he was in his rights, and did not lower himself by showing bad temper. The dog looked quietly round, saw a basket which contained two or three pounds of candles lying in a corner for the shop boy to take to some customer; took up the basket in his mouth, and turned tail, as much as to say, 'Tit for tat then. ' He understood, you see, what is called 'the law of reprisals. ' 'Come back this moment, ' cried Mrs. Traill. The dog walked out of the shop; then she ran after him, and counted the fourpence before him, on which he dropped the basket, picked up the right change, and went off demurely. 'To whom does that poodle belong? ' said I. 'To a poor drunken man, ' said Mrs. Traill; 'I wish it was in better hands. ' 'So do I, ma'am, ' answered I; 'did he teach it? ' 'No, it was taught by his brother, who was an old soldier, and died in his house two weeks ago. It knows a great many tricks, and is quite young. It might make a fortune as a show, sir. ' So I was thinking. I inquired the owner's address, called on him, and found him disposed to sell the dog. But he asked L3, a sum that seemed out of the question then. Still I kept the dog in my eye; called every day to make friends with it, and ascertain its capacities. And at last, thanks to you, Sophy, I bought the dog; and what is more, as soon as I had two golden sovereigns to show, I got him for that sum, and we have still L1. left (besides small savings from our lost salaries) to go to the completion of his education, and the advertisement of his merits. I kept this a secret from Merle, — from all. I would not even let the drunken owner know where I took the dog to yesterday. I brought him here, where, I learned in the village, there were two rooms to let, locked him up, and my story is told. "

"But why keep it such a secret? "

"Because I don't want Rugge to trace us. He might do one a mischief; because I have a grand project of genteel position and high prices for the exhibition of that dog. And why should it be known where we come from, or what we were? And because, if the owner knew where to find the dog, he might decoy it back from us. Luckily he had not made the dog so fond of him but what, unless it be decoyed, it will accustom itself to us. And now I propose that we should stay a week or so here, and devote ourselves exclusively to developing the native powers of this gifted creature. Get out the dominos. "

"What is his name? "

"Ha! that is the first consideration. What shall be his name? "

"Has he not one already? "

"Yes, —trivial and unattractive, —Mop! In private life it might pass. But in public life—give a dog a bad name and hang him. Mop, indeed! "

Therewith Mop, considering himself appealed to, rose and stretched himself.

"Right, " said Gentleman Waife; "stretch yourself—you decidedly require it. "

CHAPTER V.

Mop becomes a personage. —Much thought is bestowed on the verbal dignities, without which a personage would become a mop. —The importance of names is apparent in all history. —If Augustus had called himself king, Rome would have risen against him as a Tarquin; so he remained a simple equestrian, and modestly called himself Imperator. —Mop chooses his own title in a most mysterious manner, and ceases to be Mop.

"The first noticeable defect in your name of Mop, " said Gentleman Waife, "is, as you yourself denote, the want of elongation. Monosyllables are not imposing, and in striking compositions their meaning is elevated by periphrasis; that is to say, Sophy, that what before was a short truth, an elegant author elaborates into a long stretch. "

"Certainly, " said Sophy, thoughtfully; "I don't think the name of Mop would draw! Still he is very like a mop. "

"For that reason the name degrades him the more, and lowers him from an intellectual phenomenon to a physical attribute, which is vulgar. I hope that that dog will enable us to rise in the scale of being. For whereas we in acting could only command a threepenny audience—reserved seats a shilling—he may aspire to half-crowns and dress-boxes; that is, if we can hit on a name which inspires respect. Now, although the dog is big, it is not by his size that he is to become famous, or we might call him Hercules or Goliath; neither is it by his beauty, or Adonis would not be unsuitable. It is by his superior sagacity and wisdom. And there I am puzzled to find his prototype amongst mortals; for, perhaps, it may be my ignorance of history—"

"You ignorant, indeed, Grandfather! "

"But considering the innumerable millions who have lived on the earth, it is astonishing how few I can call to mind who have left behind them a proverbial renown for wisdom. There is, indeed, Solomon, but he fell off at the last; and as he belongs to sacred history, we must not take a liberty with his name. Who is there very, very wise, besides Solomon? Think, Sophy, —Profane History. "

Sophy (after a musing pause). —"Puss in Boots. "

"Well, he was wise; but then he was not human; he was a cat. Ha! Socrates. Shall we call him Socrates, Socrates, Socrates? "

SOPHY. —"Socrates, Socrates! " Mop yawned.

WAIFE. —"He don't take to Socrates, —prosy! "

SOPHY. —"Ah, Mr. Merle's book about the Brazen Head, Friar Bacon! He must have been very wise. "

WAIFE. —"Not bad; mysterious, but not recondite; historical, yet familiar. What does Mop say to it? Friar, Friar, Friar Bacon, sir, — Friar! "

SOPHY (coaxingly). —"Friar! "

Mop, evidently conceiving that appeal is made to some other personage, canine or human, not present, rouses up, walks to the door, smells at the chink, returns, shakes his head, and rests on his haunches, eying his two friends superciliously.

SOPHY. —"He does not take to that name. "

WAIFE. —"He has his reasons for it; and indeed there are many worthy persons who disapprove of anything that savours of magical practices. Mop intimates that on entering public life one should beware of offending the respectable prejudices of a class. "

Mr. Waife then, once more resorting to the recesses of scholastic memory, plucked therefrom, somewhat by the head and shoulders, sundry names reverenced in a by-gone age. He thought of the seven wise men of Greece, but could only recall the nomenclature of two out of the—even, —a sad proof of the distinction between collegiate fame and popular renown. He called Thales; he called Bion. Mop made no response. "Wonderful intelligence! " said Waife; "he knows that Thales and Bion would not draw! —obsolete. "

Mop was equally mute to Aristotle. He pricked up his cars at Plato, perhaps because the sound was not wholly dissimilar from that of Ponto, —a name of which he might have had vague reminiscences. The Romans not having cultivated an original philosophy, though they contrived to produce great men without it, Waife passed by that perished people. He crossed to China, and tried Confucius. Mop had evidently never heard of him.

"I am at the end of my list, so far as the wise men are concerned, " said Waife, wiping his forehead. "If Mop were to distinguish himself by valour, one would find heroes by the dozen, —Achilles, and Hector, and Julius Caesar, and Pompey, and Bonaparte, and Alexander the Great, and the Duke of Marlborough. Or, if he wrote poetry, we could fit him to a hair. But wise men certainly are scarce, and when one has hit on a wise man's name it is so little known to the vulgar that it would carry no more weight with it than Spot or Toby. But necessarily some name the dog must have, and take to sympathetically. "

Sophy meanwhile had extracted the dominos from Waife's bundle, and with the dominos an alphabet and a multiplication-table in printed capitals. As the Comedian's one eye rested upon the last, he exclaimed, "But after all, Mop's great strength will probably be in arithmetic, and the science of numbers is the root of all wisdom. Besides, every man, high and low, wants to make a fortune, and associations connected with addition and multiplication are always pleasing. Who, then, is the sage at computation most universally known? Unquestionably Cocker! He must take to that, Cocker, Cocker" (commandingly), —"C-o-c-k-e-r" (with persuasive sweetness).

Mop looked puzzled; he put his head first on one side, then on the other.

SOPHY (with mellifluous endearment). —"Cocker, good Cocker; Cocker dear! "

BOTH. —"Cocker, Cocker, Cocker! "

Excited and bewildered, Mop put up his head, and gave vent to his perplexities in a long and lugubrious howl, to which certainly none who heard it could have desired addition or multiplication.

"Stop this instant, sir, —stop; I shoot you! You are dead, —down! " Waife adjusted his staff to his shoulder gun-wise; and at the word of command, "Down, " Mop was on his side, stiff and lifeless. "Still, " said Waife, "a name connected with profound calculation would be the most appropriate; for instance, Sir Isaac—"

Before the. Comedian could get out the word Newton, Mop had sprung to his four feet, and, with wagging tail and wriggling back, evinced a sense of beatified recognition.

"Astounding! " said Waife, rather awed. "Can it be the name? Impossible. Sir Isaac, Sir Isaac! "

"Bow-wow! " answered Mop, joyously.

"If there be any truth in the doctrine of metempsychosis, " faltered Gentleman Waife, "if the great Newton could have transmigrated into that incomparable animal! Newton, Newton! " To that name Mop made no obeisance, but, evidently still restless, walked round the room, smelling at every corner, and turning to look back with inquisitive earnestness at his new master.

"He does not seem to catch at the name of Newton, " said Waife, trying it thrice again, and vainly, "and yet he seems extremely well versed in the principle of gravity. Sir Isaac! " The dog bounded towards him, put his paws on his shoulder, and licked his face. "Just cut out those figures carefully, my dear, and see if we can get him to tell us how much twice ten are—I mean by addressing him as Sir Isaac. "

Sophy cut the figures from the multiplication table, and arranged them, at Waife's instruction, in a circle on the floor. "Now, Sir Isaac. " Mop lifted a paw, and walked deliberately round the letters. "Now, Sir Isaac, how much are ten times two? " Mop deliberately made his survey and calculation, and, pausing at twenty, stooped, and took the letters in his mouth.

"It is not natural, " cried Sophy, much alarmed. "It must be wicked, and I'd rather have nothing to do with it, please. "

"Silly child! He was but obeying my sign. He had been taught that trick already under the name of Mop. The only strange thing is, that he should do it also under the name of Sir Isaac, and much more cheerfully too. However, whether he has been the great Newton or not, a live dog is better than a dead lion. But it is clear that, in acknowledging the name of Sir Isaac, he does not encourage us to take that of Newton; and he is right: for it might be thought unbecoming to apply to an animal, however extraordinary, who by the severity of fortune is compelled to exhibit his talents for a small pecuniary reward, the family name of so great a philosopher. Sir Isaac, after all, is a vague appellation; any dog has a right to be Sir Isaac—Newton may be left conjectural. Let us see if we can add to our arithmetical information. Look at me, Sir Isaac. " Sir Isaac looked and grinned affectionately; and under that title learned a new combination with a facility that might have relieved Sophy's mind of all superstitious belief that the philosopher was resuscitated in the dog, had she known that in life that great master of calculations the most abstruse could not accurately cast up a simple sum in addition. Nothing brought him to the end of his majestic tether like dot and carry one. Notable type of our human incompleteness, where men might deem our studies had made us most complete! Notable type, too, of that grandest order of all human genius which seems to arrive at results by intuition, which a child might pose by a row of figures on a slate, while it is solving the laws that link the stars to infinity! But *revenons a nos moutons*, what was the astral attraction that incontestably bound the reminiscences of Mop to the cognominal distinction of Sir Isaac? I had prepared a very erudite and subtle treatise upon this query, enlivened by quotations from the ancient Mystics, —such as Iamblicus and Proclus, —as well as by a copious reference to the doctrine of the more modern Spiritualists, from Sir Kenelm Digby and Swedenborg, to Monsieur Cahagnet and Judge Edwards. It was to be called Inquiry into the Law of Affinities, by Philomopsos: when, unluckily for my treatise, I arrived at the knowledge of a fact which, though it did not render the treatise less curious, knocked on the head the theory upon which it was based. The baptismal name of the old soldier, Mop's first proprietor and earliest preceptor, was Isaac; and his master being called in the homely household by that Christian name, the sound had entered into Mop's youngest and most endeared associations. His canine affections had done much towards ripening his scholastic education. "Where is Isaac? " "Call Isaac! " "Fetch Isaac his hat, " etc. Stilled was that name when the old soldier died; but when heard again, Mop's heart was moved, and in missing the old master, he felt more at home with the new. As for the title, "Sir, " it was a mere expletive in his ears. Such was the fact, and such the deduction to be drawn from it. Not that it will satisfy every one. I know that philosophers who deny all that they have not witnessed, and refuse to witness what they resolve to deny, will reject the story in toto; and will prove, by reference to their own dogs, that a dog never recognizes the name of his master, —never yet could be taught arithmetic. I know also that there are Mystics who will prefer to believe that Mop was in direct spiritual communication with unseen Isaacs, or in a state of clairvoyance, or under the influence of the odic fluid. But did we ever yet find in human reason a question with only one side to it? Is not truth a polygon? Have not sages arisen in our day to deny even the principle of gravity, for which we bad been so long contentedly taking the word of the great Sir Isaac? It is that blessed spirit of controversy which keeps the world going; and it is that which, perhaps, explains why Mr. Waife, when his memory was fairly put to it, could remember, out of the history of the myriads who have occupied our planet from the date of Adam to that in which I now write, so very few men whom the world will agree to call wise, and out of that very few so scant a percentage with names sufficiently known to make them more popularly significant of pre-eminent sagacity than if they had been called—Mops.

CHAPTER VI.

The vagrant having got his dog, proceeds to hunt fortune with it, leaving behind him a trap to catch rats. —What the trap does catch is "just like his luck. "

Sir Isaac, to designate him by his new name, improved much upon acquaintance. He was still in the ductile season of youth, and took to learning as an amusement to himself. His last master, a stupid sot, had not gained his affections; and perhaps even the old soldier, though gratefully remembered and mourned, had not stolen into his innermost heart, as Waife and Sophy gently contrived to do. In short, in a very few days he became perfectly accustomed and extremely attached to them. When Waife had ascertained the extent of his accomplishments, and added somewhat to their range in matters which cost no great trouble, he applied himself to the task of composing a little drama which might bring them all into more interesting play, and in which though Sophy and himself were performers the dog had the premier role. And as soon as this was done, and the dog's performances thus ranged into methodical order and sequence, he resolved to set off to a considerable town at some distance, and to which Mr. Rugge was no visitor.

His bill at the cottage made but slight inroad into his pecuniary resources; for in the intervals of leisure from his instructions to Sir Isaac, Waife had performed various little services to the lone widow with whom they lodged, which Mrs. Saunders (such was her name) insisted upon regarding as money's worth. He had repaired and regulated to a minute an old clock which had taken no note of time for the last three years; he had mended all the broken crockery by some cement of his own invention, and for which she got him the materials. And here his ingenuity was remarkable, for when there was only a fragment to be found of a cup and a fragment or two of a saucer, he united them both into some pretty form, which, if not useful, at all events looked well on a shelf. He bound, in smart showy papers, sundry tattered old books which had belonged to his landlady's defunct husband, a Scotch gardener, and which she displayed on a side table, under the japan tea-tray. More than all, he was of service to her in her vocation; for Mrs. Saunders eked out a small pension—which she derived from the affectionate providence of her Scotch husband, in insuring his life in her favour—by the rearing and sale of poultry; and Waife saved her the expense of a carpenter by the construction of a new coop, elevated above the reach of the rats, who had hitherto made sad ravage amongst the chickens; while he confided to her certain secrets in the improvement of breed and the cheaper processes of fattening, which excited her gratitude no less than her wonder. "The fact is, " said Gentleman Waife, "that my life has known makeshifts. Once, in a foreign country, I kept poultry, upon the principle that the poultry should keep me. "

Strange it was to notice such versatility of invention, such readiness of resource, such familiarity with divers nooks and crannies in the practical experience of life, in a man now so hard put to it for a livelihood. There are persons, however, who might have a good stock of talent, if they did not turn it all into small change. And you, reader, know as well as I do, that when a sovereign or a shilling is once broken into, the change scatters and dispends itself in a way quite unaccountable. Still coppers are useful in household bills; and when Waife was really at a pinch, somehow or other, by hook or by crook, he scraped together intellectual halfpence enough to pay his way.

Mrs. Saunders grew quite fond of her lodgers. Waife she regarded as a prodigy of genius; Sophy was the prettiest and best of children. Sir Isaac, she took for granted, was worthy of his owners. But the Comedian did not confide to her his dog's learning, nor the use to which he designed to put it. And in still greater precaution, when he took his leave, he extracted from Mrs. Saunders a solemn promise that she would set no one on his track in case of impertinent inquiries.

"You see before you, " said he, "a man who has enemies, such as rats are to your chickens: chickens despise rats when raised, as yours are now, above the reach of claws and teeth. Some day or other I may so raise a coop for that little one: I am too old for coops. Meanwhile, if a rat comes sneaking here after us, send it off the wrong way, with a flea in its ear. "

Mrs. Saunders promised, between tears and laughter; blessed Waife, kissed Sophy, patted Sir Isaac, and stood long at her threshold watching the three, as the early sun lit their forms receding in the narrow green lane, —dewdrops sparkling on the hedgerows, and the skylark springing upward from the young corn.

Then she slowly turned indoors, and her home seemed very solitary. We can accustom ourselves to loneliness, but we should beware of infringing the custom. Once admit two or three faces seated at your hearthside, or gazing out from your windows on the laughing sun, and when they are gone, they carry off the glow from your grate and the sunbeam from your panes. Poor Mrs. Saunders! in vain she sought to rouse herself, to put the rooms to rights, to attend to the chickens to distract her thoughts. The one-eyed cripple, the little girl, the shaggy-faced dog, still haunted her; and when at noon she dined all alone off the remnants of the last night's social supper, the very click of the renovated clock seemed to say, "Gone, gone; " and muttering, "Ah! gone, " she reclined back on her chair, and indulged herself in a good womanlike cry. From this luxury she was startled by a knock at the door. "Could they have come back? " No; the door opened, and a genteel young man, in a black coat and white neckcloth, stepped in.

"I beg your pardon, ma'am—your name 's Saunders—sell poultry? "

"At your service, sir. Spring chickens? " Poor people, whatever their grief, must sell their chickens, if they have any to sell.

"Thank you, ma'am; not at this moment. The fact is, that I call to make some inquiries Have not you lodgers here? "

Lodgers! at that word the expanding soul of Mrs. Saunders reclosed hermetically; the last warning of Waife revibrated in her ears this white neckclothed gentleman, was he not a rat?

"No, sir, I ha'n't no lodgers. "

"But you have had some lately, eh? a crippled elderly man and a little girl. "

"Don't know anything about them; leastways, " said Mrs. Saunders, suddenly remembering that she was told less to deny facts than to send inquirers upon wrong directions, "leastways, at this blessed time. Pray, sir, what makes you ask? "

"Why, I was instructed to come down to — — —, and find out where this person, one William Waife, had gone. Arrived yesterday, ma'am. All I could hear is, that a person answering to his description left the place several days ago, and had been seen by a boy, who was tending sheep, to come down the lane to your house, and you were supposed to have lodgers (you take lodgers sometimes, I think, ma'am), because you had been buying some trifling articles of food not in your usual way of custom. Circumstantial evidence, ma'am: you can have no motive to conceal the truth. "

"I should think not indeed, sir, " retorted Mrs. Saunders, whom the ominous words "circumstantial evidence" set doubly on her guard. "I did see a gentleman such as you mention, and a pretty young lady, about ten days agone, or so, and they did lodge here a night or two, but they are gone to—"

"Yes, ma'am, —gone where? "

"Lunnon. "

"Really—very likely. By the train or on foot? "

"On foot, I s'pose. "

"Thank you, ma'am. If you should see them again, or hear where they are, oblige me by conveying this card to Mr. Waife. My employer, ma'am, Mr. Gotobed, Craven Street, Strand, —eminent solicitor. He has something of importance to communciate to Mr. Waife. "

"Yes, sir, —a lawyer; I understand. " And as of all ratlike animals in the world Mrs. Saunders had the ignorance to deem a lawyer was the most emphatically devouring, she congratulated herself with her whole heart on the white lies she had told in favour of the intended victims.

The black-coated gentleman having thus obeyed his instructions and attained his object, nodded, went his way, and regained the fly which he had left at the turnstile. "Back to the inn, " cried he, "quick: I must be in time for the three o'clock train to London. "

And thus terminated the result of the great barrister's first instructions to his eminent solicitor to discover a lame man and a little girl. No inquiry, on the whole, could have been more skilfully conducted. Mr. Gotobed sends his head clerk; the head clerk employs the policeman of the village; gets upon the right track;

comes to the right house; and is altogether in the wrong, —in a manner highly creditable to his researches.

"In London, of course: all people of that kind come back to London, " said Mr. Gotobed. "Give me the heads in writing, that I may report to my distinguished client. Most satisfactory. That young man will push his way, —businesslike and methodical. "

CHAPTER VII.

The cloud has its silver lining.

Thus turning his back on the good fortune which he had so carefully cautioned Mrs. Saunders against favouring on his behalf, the vagrant was now on his way to the ancient municipal town of Gatesboro', which, being the nearest place of fitting opulence and population, Mr. Waife had resolved to honour with the debut of Sir Isaac as soon as he had appropriated to himself the services of that promising quadruped. He had consulted a map of the county before quitting Mr. Merle's roof, and ascertained that he could reach Gatesboro' by a short cut for foot-travellers along fields and lanes. He was always glad to avoid the high road: doubtless for such avoidance he had good reasons. But prudential reasons were in this instance supported by vagrant inclinations. High roads are for the prosperous. By-paths and ill-luck go together. But by-paths have their charm, and ill-luck its pleasant moments.

They passed then from the high road into a long succession of green pastures, through which a straight public path conducted them into one of those charming lanes never seen out of this bowery England, —a lane deep sunk amidst high banks with overhanging oaks, and quivering ash, gnarled wych-elm, vivid holly and shaggy brambles, with wild convolvulus and creeping woodbine forcing sweet life through all. Sometimes the banks opened abruptly, leaving patches of green sward, and peeps through still sequestered gates, or over moss-grown pales, into the park or paddock of some rural thane. New villas or old manor-houses on lawny uplands, knitting, as it were, together England's feudal memories with England's freeborn hopes, —the old land with its young people; for England is so old, and the English are so young! And the gray cripple and the bright-haired child often paused, and gazed upon the demesnes and homes of owners whose lots were cast in such pleasant places. But there was no grudging envy in their gaze; perhaps because their life was too remote from those grand belongings. And therefore they could enjoy and possess every banquet of the eye. For at least the beauty of what we see is ours for the moment, on the simple condition that we do not covet the thing which gives to our eyes that beauty. As the measureless sky and the unnumbered stars are equally granted to king and to beggar; and in our wildest ambition we do not sigh for a monopoly of the empyrean, or the fee-simple of the planets: so the earth too, with all its fenced gardens and embattled walls, all its landmarks of stern property and churlish ownership, is ours too by right of eye. Ours to gaze on the fair possessions with such delight as the gaze can give; grudging to the unseen owner his other, and, it may be, more troubled rights, as little as we grudge an astral proprietor his acres of light in Capricorn. Benignant is the law that saith, "Thou shalt not covet. "

When the sun was at the highest our wayfarers found a shadowy nook for their rest and repast. Before them ran a shallow limpid trout-stream; on the other side its margin, low grassy meadows, a farmhouse in the distance, backed by a still grove, from which rose a still church tower and its still spire. Behind them, a close-shaven sloping lawn terminated the hedgerow of the lane; seen clearly above it, with parterres of flowers on the sward, drooping lilacs and laburnums farther back, and a pervading fragrance from the brief-lived and rich syringas. The cripple had climbed over a wooden rail that separated the lane from the rill, and seated himself under the shade of a fantastic hollow thorn-tree. Sophy, reclined beside him, was gathering some pale scentless violets from a mound which the brambles had guarded from the sun. The dog had descended to the waters to quench his thirst, but still stood knee-deep in the shallow stream, and appeared lost in philosophical contemplation of a swarm of minnows, which his immersion had disturbed, but which now made itself again visible on the farther side of the glassy brook, undulating round and round a tiny rocklet which interrupted the glide of the waves, and caused them to break into a low melodious murmur. "For these and all thy mercies, O Lord, make us thankful, " said the victim of ill-luck, in the tritest words of a pious custom. But never, perhaps, at aldermanic feasts was the grace more sincerely said.

And then he untied the bundle, which the dog, who had hitherto carried it by the way, had now carefully deposited at his side. "As I live, " ejaculated Waife, "Mrs. Saunders is a woman in ten thousand. See, Sophy, not contented with the bread and cheese to which I bade her stint her beneficence, a whole chicken, —a little cake too for you, Sophy; she has not even forgotten the salt. Sophy, that woman deserves the handsomest token of our gratitude; and we will present her with a silver teapot the first moment we can afford it. "

His spirits exhilarated by the unexpected good cheer, the Comedian gave way to his naturally blithe humour; and between every mouthful he rattled or rather drolled on, now infant-like, now sage-like. He cast out the rays of his liberal humour, careless where they fell, —on the child, on the dog, on the fishes that played beneath the wave, on the cricket that chirped amidst the grass; the woodpecker tapped the tree, and the cripple's merry voice answered it in bird-like mimicry. To this riot of genial babble there was a listener, of whom neither grandfather nor grandchild was aware. Concealed by thick brushwood a few paces farther on, a young angler, who might be five or six and twenty, had seated himself, just before the arrival of our vagrant to those banks and waters, for the purpose of changing an unsuccessful fly. At the sound of voices, perhaps suspecting an unlicensed rival, for that part of the stream was preserved, —he had suspended his task, and noiselessly put aside the clustering leaves to reconnoitre. The piety of Waife's simple grace seemed to surprise him pleasingly, for a sweet approving smile crossed his lips. He continued to look and to listen. He forgot the fly, and a trout sailed him by unheeded. But Sir Isaac, having probably satisfied his speculative mind as to the natural attributes of minnows, now slowly reascended the bank, and after a brief halt and a sniff, walked majestically towards the hidden observer, looked at him with great solemnity, and uttered an inquisitive bark, —a bark not hostile, not menacing; purely and dryly interrogative. Thus detected, the angler rose; and Waife, whose attention was directed that way by the bark, saw him, called to Sir Isaac, and said politely, "There is no harm in my dog, sir. "

The young man muttered some inaudible reply, and, lifting up his rod as in sign of his occupation or excuse for his vicinity, came out from the intervening foliage, and stepped quietly to Waife's side. Sir Isaac followed him, sniffed again, seemed satisfied; and seating himself on his haunches, fixed his attention upon the remains of the chicken which lay defenceless on the grass. The new comer was evidently of the rank of gentleman; his figure was slim and graceful, his face pale, meditative, refined. He would have impressed you at once with the idea of what he really was, —an Oxford scholar; and you would perhaps have guessed him designed for the ministry of the Church, if not actually in orders.

CHAPTER VIII.

Mr. Waife excites the admiration, and benignly pities the infirmity, of an Oxford scholar.

"You are str-str-strangers? " said the Oxonian, after a violent exertion to express himself, caused by an impediment in his speech.

WAIFE. —"Yes, sir, travellers. I trust we are not trespassing: this is not private ground, I think? "

OXONIAN. —"And if-f-f-f—it were, my f-f-father would not war-n-n you off-ff—f. "

"Is it your father's ground, then? Sir, I beg you a thousand pardons."

The apology was made in the Comedian's grandest style: it imposed greatly on the young scholar. Waife might have been a duke in disguise; but I will do the angler the justice to say that such discovery of rank would have impressed him little more in the vagrant's favour. It had been that impromptu "grace" —that thanksgiving which the scholar felt was for something more than the carnal food—which had first commanded his respect and wakened his interest. Then that innocent careless talk—part uttered to dog and child, part soliloquized, part thrown out to the ears of the lively teeming Nature—had touched a somewhat kindred chord in the angler's soul; for he was somewhat of a poet and much of a soliloquist, and could confer with Nature, nor feel that impediment in speech which obstructed his intercourse with men. Having thus far indicated that oral defect in our new acquaintance, the reader will cheerfully excuse me for not enforcing it over much. Let it be among the things *subaudita*, as the sense of it gave to a gifted and aspiring nature, thwarted in the sublime career of Preacher, an exquisite mournful pain. And I no more like to raise a laugh at his infirmity behind his back, than I should before his pale, powerful, melancholy face; therefore I suppress the infirmity in giving the reply.

OXONIAN. —"On the other side the lane, where the garden slopes downward, is my father's house. This ground is his property certainly, but he puts it to its best use, in lending it to those who so piously acknowledge that Father from whom all good comes. Your child, I presume, sir? "

175

"My grandchild. "

"She seems delicate: I hope you have not far to go? "

"Not very far, thank you, sir. But my little girl looks more delicate than she is. You are not tired, darling? "

"Oh, not at all! " There was no mistaking the looks of real love interchanged between the old man and the child; the scholar felt much interested and somewhat puzzled.

"Who and what could they be? so unlike foot wayfarers! " On the other hand, too, Waife took a liking to the courteous young man, and conceived a sincere pity for his physical affliction. But he did not for those reasons depart from the discreet caution he had prescribed to himself in seeking new fortunes and shunning old perils, so he turned the subject.

"You are an angler, sir? I suppose the trout in the stream run small?"

"Not very: a little higher up I have caught them at four pounds weight. "

WAIFE. —"There goes a fine fish yonder, —see! balancing himself between those weeds. "

OXONIAN. —"Poor fellow, let him be safe to-day. After all, it is a cruel sport, and I should break myself of it. But it is strange that whatever our love for Nature we always seek some excuse for trusting ourselves alone to her. A gun, a rod, a sketch-book, a geologist's hammer, an entomologist's net, a something. "

WAIFE. —"Is it not because all our ideas would run wild if not concentrated on a definite pursuit? Fortune and Nature are earnest females, though popular beauties; and they do not look upon coquettish triflers in the light of genuine wooers. "

The Oxonian, who, in venting his previous remark, had thought it likely he should be above his listener's comprehension, looked surprised. What pursuits, too, had this one-eyed philosopher?

"You have a definite pursuit, sir? "

"I—alas! when a man moralizes, it is a sign that he has known error: it is because I have been a trifler that I rail against triflers. And talking of that, time flies, and we must be off and away. "

Sophy re-tied the bundle. Sir Isaac, on whom, meanwhile, she had bestowed the remains of the chicken, jumped up and described a circle.

"I wish you success in your pursuit, whatever it be, " stuttered out the angler.

"And I no less heartily, sir, wish you success in yours. "

"Mine! Success there is beyond my power. "

"How, sir? Does it rest so much with others? "

"No, my failure is in myself. My career should be the Church, my pursuit the cure of souls, and—and—this pitiful infirmity! How can I speak the Divine Word—I—I—a stutterer! "

The young man did not pause for an answer, but plunged through the brushwood that bespread the banks of the rill, and his hurried path could be traced by the wave of the foliage through which he forced his way.

"We all have our burdens, " said Gentleman Waife, as Sir Isaac took up the bundle and stalked on, placid and refreshed.

CHAPTER IX.

The nomad, entering into civilized life, adopts its arts, shaves his poodle, and puts on a black coat. —Hints at the process by which a Cast-off exalts himself into a Take-in.

At twilight they stopped at a quiet inn within eight miles of Gatesboro'. Sophy, much tired, was glad to creep to bed. Waife sat up long after her; and, in preparation for the eventful morrow, washed and shaved Sir Isaac. You would not have known the dog again; he was dazzling. Not Ulysses, rejuvenated by Pallas Athene, could have been more changed for the better. His flanks revealed a skin most daintily mottled; his tail became leonine, with an imperial tuft; his mane fell in long curls like the beard of a Ninevite king; his boots were those of a courtier in the reign of Charles II. ; his eyes looked forth in dark splendour from locks white as the driven snow. This feat performed, Waife slept the sleep of the righteous, and Sir Isaac, stretched on the floor beside the bed, licked his mottled flanks and shivered: *"il faut souffrir pour etre beau. "* Much marvelling, Sophy the next morning beheld the dog; but, before she was up, Waife had paid the bill and was waiting for her on the road, impatient to start. He did not heed her exclamation, half compassionate, half admiring; he was absorbed in thought. Thus they proceeded slowly on till within two miles of the town, and then Waife turned aside, entered a wood, and there, with the aid of Sophy, put the dog upon a deliberate rehearsal of the anticipated drama. The dog was not in good spirits, but he went through his part with mechanical accuracy, though slight enthusiasm.

"He is to be relied upon, in spite of his French origin, " said Waife. "All national prejudice fades before the sense of a common interest. And we shall always find more genuine solidity of character in a French poodle than in an English mastiff, whenever a poodle is of use to us and the mastiff is not. But oh, waste of care! oh, sacrifice of time to empty names! oh, emblem of fashionable education! It never struck me before, —does it not, child though thou art, strike thee now, —by the necessities of our drama, this animal must be a French dog? "

"Well, Grandfather? "

"And we have given him an English name! Precious result of our own scholastic training, taught at preparatory academies precisely that which avails us naught when we are to face the world! What is to be done? Unlearn him his own cognomen, —teach him another name, —too late, too late. We cannot afford the delay. "

"I don't see why he should be called any name at all. He observes your signs just as well without. "

"If I had but discovered that at the beginning. Pity! Such a fine name too. Sir Isaac! *Vanitas vanitatum!* What desire chiefly kindles the ambitious? To create a name, perhaps bequeath a title, —exalt into Sir Isaacs a progeny of slops! And, after all, it is possible (let us hope it in this instance) that a sensible young dog may learn his letters and shoulder his musket just as well, though all the appellations by which humanity knows him be condensed into a pitiful monosyllable. Nevertheless (as you will find when you are older), people are obliged in practice to renounce for themselves the application of those rules which they philosophically prescribe for others. Thus, while I grant that a change of name for that dog is a question belonging to the policy of Ifs and Buts, commonly called the policy of Expediency, about which one may differ from others and one's own self every quarter of an hour, a change of name for me belongs to the policy of Must and Shall; namely the policy of Necessity, against which let no dog bark, —though I have known dogs howl at it! William Waife is no more: he is dead; he is buried; and even Juliet Araminta is the baseless fabric of a vision. "

Sophy raised inquiringly her blue guileless eyes.

"You see before you a man who has used up the name of Waife, and who on entering the town of Gatesboro' becomes a sober, staid, and respectable personage, under the appellation of Chapman. You are Miss Chapman. Rugge and his Exhibition 'leave not a wrack behind.'"

Sophy smiled, and then sighed, —the smile for her grandfather's gay spirits; wherefore the sigh? Was it that some instinct in that fresh, loyal nature revolted from the thought of these aliases, which, if requisite for safety, were still akin to imposture? If so, poor child, she had much yet to set right with her conscience! All I can say is, that after she had smiled she sighed. And more reasonably might a reader ask his author to subject a zephyr to the microscope than a female's sigh to analysis.

"Take the dog with you, my dear, back into the lane; I will join you in a few minutes. You are neatly dressed, and, if not, would look so. I, in this old coat, have the air of a pedler, so I will change it, and enter the town of Gatesboro' in the character of—a man whom you will soon see before you. Leave those things alone, de-Isaacized Sir Isaac! Follow your mistress, —go! "

Sophy left the wood, and walked on slowly towards the town, with her hand pensively resting on Sir Isaac's head. In less than ten minutes she was joined by Waife, attired in respectable black; his hat and shoes well brushed; a new green shade to his eye; and with his finest air of *Pere noble*. He was now in his favourite element. HE WAS ACTING: call it not imposture. Was Lord Chatham an impostor when he draped his flannels into the folds of the toga, and arranged the curls of his wig so as to add more sublime effect to the majesty of his brow and the terrors of its nod? And certainly, considering that Waife, after all, was but a professional vagabond, considering all the turns and shifts to which he has been put for bread and salt, the wonder is, not that he is full of stage tricks and small deceptions, but that he has contrived to retain at heart so much childish simplicity. When a man for a series of years has only had his wits to live by, I say not that he is necessarily a rogue, —he may be a good fellow; but you can scarcely expect his code of honour to be precisely the same as Sir Philip Sidney's. Homer expresses through the lips of Achilles that sublime love of truth which even in those remote times was the becoming characteristic of a gentleman and a soldier. But then, Achilles is well off during his whole life, which, though distinguished, is short. On the other hand Ulysses, who is sorely put to it, kept out of his property in Ithaca, and, in short, living on his wits, is not the less befriended by the immaculate Pallas because his wisdom savours somewhat of stage trick and sharp practice. And as to convenient aliases and white fibs, where would have been the use of his wits, if Ulysses had disdained such arts, and been magnanimously munched up by Polyphemus? Having thus touched on the epic side of Mr. Waife's character with the clemency due to human nature, but with the caution required by the interests of society, permit him to resume a "duplex course, " sanctioned by ancient precedent, but not commended to modern imitation.

Just as our travellers neared the town, the screech of a railway whistle resounded towards the right, —a long train rushed from the jaws of a tunnel and shot into the neighbouring station.

"How lucky! " exclaimed Waife; "make haste, my dear! "

Was he going to take the train? Pshaw! he was at his journey's end. He was going to mix with the throng that would soon stream through those white gates into the town; he was going to purloin the respectable appearance of a passenger by the train. And so well did he act the part of a bewildered stranger just vomited forth into unfamiliar places by one of those panting steam monsters, —so artfully, amidst the busy competition of nudging elbows, over-bearing shoulders, and the impedimenta of carpet-bags, portmanteaus, babies in arms, and shin-assailing trucks, did he look round, consequentially, on the *qui vive*, turning his one eye, now on Sophy, now on Sir Isaac, and griping his bundle to his breast as if he suspected all his neighbours to be Thugs, condottieri, and swellmob, —that in an instant fly-men, omnibus drivers, cads, and porters marked him for their own. "Gatesboro' Arms, " "Spread Eagle, " "Royal Hotel, " "Saracen's Head; very comfortable, centre of High Street, opposite the Town Hall, "—were shouted, bawled, whispered, or whined into his ear.

"Is there an honest porter? " asked the Comedian, piteously. An Irishman presented himself. "And is it meself can serve your honour? "—"Take this bundle, and walk on before me to the High Street. "—"Could not I take the bundle, Grandfather? The man will charge so much, " said the prudent Sophy. "Hush! you indeed! " said the Pere Noble, as if addressing an exiled Altesse royale, —"you take a bundle—Miss—Chapman! "

They soon gained the High Street. Waife examined the fronts of the various inns which they passed by with an eye accustomed to decipher the physiognomy of hostelries. The Saracen's Head pleased him, though its imposing size daunted Sophy. He arrested the steps of the porter, "Follow me close, " and stepped across the open threshold into the bar. The landlady herself was there, portly and imposing, with an auburn toupet, a silk gown, a cameo brooch, and an ample bosom.

"You have a private sitting-room, ma'am? " said the Comedian, lifting his hat. There are so many ways of lifting a hat, -for instance, the way for which Louis XIV. was so renowned. But the Comedian's way on the present occasion rather resembled that of the late Duke of B————, not quite royal, but as near to royalty as becomes a subject. He added, recovering his head, —"And on the first floor? " The landlady did not courtesy, but she bowed, emerged from the bar, and set foot on the broad stairs; then, looking back graciously, her eyes rested on Sir Isaac, who had stalked forth in advance and with expansive nostrils sniffed. She hesitated. "Your dog, sir! shall Boots take it round to the stables? "

"The stables, ma'am—the stables, my dear, " turning to Sophy, with a smile more ducal than the previous bow; "what would they say at home if they heard that noble animal was consigned to-stables? Ma'am, my dog is my companion, and as much accustomed to drawing-rooms as I am myself. " Still the landlady paused. The dog might be accustomed to drawing-rooms, but her drawing-room was not accustomed to dogs. She had just laid down a new carpet. And such are the strange and erratic affinities in nature, such are the incongruous concatenations in the cross-stitch of ideas, that there are associations between dogs and carpets, which, if wrongful to the owners of dogs, beget no unreasonable apprehensions in the proprietors of carpets. So there stood the landlady, and there stood the dog! and there they might be standing to this day had not the Comedian dissolved the spell. "Take up my effects again, " said he, turning to the porter; "doubtless they are more habituated to distinguish between dog and dog at the Royal Hotel. "

The landlady was mollified in a moment. Nor was it only the rivalries that necessarily existed between the Saracen's Head and the Royal Hotel that had due weight with her. A gentleman who could not himself deign to carry even that small bundle must be indeed a gentleman! Had he come with a portmanteau—even with a carpet-bag—the porter's service would have been no evidence of rank; but accustomed as she was chiefly to gentlemen engaged in commercial pursuits, it was new to her experience, —a gentleman with effects so light, and hands so aristocratically helpless. Herein were equally betokened the two attributes of birth and wealth; namely, the habit of command and the disdain of shillings. A vague remembrance of the well-known story how a man and his dog had arrived at the Granby Hotel, at Harrowgate, and been sent away roomless to the other and less patrician establishment, because, while he had a dog, he had not a servant; when, five minutes after such dismissal, came carriages and lackeys and an imperious valet, asking for his grace the

Duke of A———, who had walked on before with his dog, and who, oh, everlasting thought of remorse! had been sent away to bring the other establishment into fashion, —a vague reminiscence of that story, I say, flashed upon the landlady's mind, and she exclaimed, "I only thought, sir, you might prefer the stables; of course, it is as you please. This way, sir. He is a fine animal, indeed, and seems mild. "

"You may bring up the bundle, porter, " quoth the Pere Noble. "Take my arm, my dear; these steps are very steep. "

The landlady threw open the door of a handsome sitting-room, —her best: she pulled down the blinds to shut out the glare of the sun; then retreating to the threshold awaited further orders.

"Rest yourself, my dear, " said the Actor, placing Sophy on a couch with that tender respect for sex and childhood which so specially belongs to the high-bred. "The room will do, ma'am. I will let you know later whether we shall require beds. As to dinner, I am not particular, —a cutlet, a chicken, what you please, at seven o'clock. Stay, I beg your pardon for detaining you, but where does the Mayor live? "

"His private residence is a mile out of the town, but his counting-house is just above the Town Hall, —to the right, sir. "

"Name? "

"Mr. Hartopp! "

"Hartopp! Ah! to be sure! Hartopp. His political opinions, I think, are" (ventures at a guess) "enlightened? "

LANDLADY. —"Very much so, sir. Mr. Hartopp is highly respected."

WAIFE. —"The chief municipal officer of a town so thriving—fine shops and much plate glass—must march with the times. I think I have heard that Mr. Hartopp promotes the spread of intelligence and the propagation of knowledge. "

LANDLADY (rather puzzled). —"I dare say, sir. The Mayor takes great interest in the Gatesboro' Athemeum and Literary Institute. "

WAIFE. —"Exactly what I should have presumed from his character and station. I will detain you no longer, ma'am" (ducal bow). The landlady descended the stairs. Was her guest a candidate for the representation of the town at the next election? March with the times! —spread of intelligence! All candidates she ever knew had that way of expressing themselves, —"March" and "Spread. " Not an address had parliamentary aspirant put forth to the freemen and electors of Gatesboro' but what "March" had been introduced by the candidate, and "Spread" been suggested by the committee. Still she thought that her guest, upon the whole, looked and bowed more like a member of the Upper House, —perhaps one of the amiable though occasionally prosy peers who devote the teeth of wisdom to the cracking of those very hard nuts, "How to educate the masses, " "What to do with our criminals, " and such like problems, upon which already have been broken so many jawbones tough as that with which Samson slew the Philistines.

"Oh, Grandfather! " sighed Sophy, "what are you about? We shall be ruined, you, too, who are so careful not to get into debt. And what have we left to pay the people here? "

"Sir Isaac! and THIS! " returned the Comedian, touching his forehead. "Do not alarm yourself: stay here and repose; and don't let Sir Isaac out of the room on any account! "

He took off his hat, brushed the nap carefully with his sleeve, replaced it on his head, —not jauntily aside, not like a jeune premier, but with equilateral brims, and in composed fashion, like a *pere noble*; then, making a sign to Sir Isaac to rest quiet, he passed to the door; there he halted, and turning towards Sophy, and, meeting her wistful eyes, his own eye moistened. "Ah! " he murmured, "Heaven grant I may succeed now, for if I do, then you shall indeed be a little lady! "

He was gone.

CHAPTER X.

Showing with what success Gentleman Waife assumes the pleasing part of friend to the enlightenment of the age and the progress of the people.

On the landing-place, Waife encountered the Irish porter, who, having left the bundle in the drawing-room, was waiting patiently to be paid for his trouble.

The Comedian surveyed the good-humoured shrewd face, on every line of which was writ the golden maxim, "Take things asy. " "I beg your pardon, my friend; I had almost forgotten you. Have you been long in this town? "

"Four years, and long life to your honour! "

"Do you know Mr. Hartopp, the Mayor? "

"Is it his worship the Mayor? Sure and it is the Mayor as has made a man o' Mike Callaghan. "

The Comedian evinced urbane curiosity to learn the history of that process, and drew forth a grateful tale. Four summers ago Mike had resigned the "first gem of the sea" in order to assist in making hay for a Saxon taskmaster.

Mr. Hartopp, who farmed largely, had employed him in that rural occupation. Seized by a malignant fever, Mr. Hartopp had helped him through it, and naturally conceived a liking for the man he helped. Thus, as Mike became convalescent, instead of passing the poor man back to his own country, which at that time gave little employment to the surplus of its agrarian population beyond an occasional shot at a parson, —an employment, though animated, not lucrative, he exercised Mike's returning strength upon a few light jobs in his warehouse; and finally, Mike marrying imprudently the daughter of a Gatesboro' operative, Mr. Hartopp set him up in life as a professional messenger and porter, patronized by the Corporation. The narrative made it evident that Mr. Hartopp was a kind and worthy man, and the Comedian's heart warmed towards him.

"An honour to our species, this Mr. Hartopp! " said Waife, striking his staff upon the floor; "I covet his acquaintance. Would he see you if you called at his counting-house? "

Mike replied in the affirmative with eager pride. "Mr. Hartopp would see him at once. Sure, did not the Mayor know that time was money? Mr. Hartopp was not a man to keep the poor waiting. "

"Go down and stay outside the hall door; you shall take a note for me to the Mayor. "

Waife then passed into the bar, and begged the favour of a sheet of note-paper. The landlady seated him at her own desk, and thus wrote the Comedian:

"Mr. Chapman presents his compliments to the Mayor of Gatesboro', and requests the Honour of a very short interview. Mr. Chapman's deep interest in the permanent success of those literary institutes which are so distinguished a feature of this enlightened age, and Mr. Mayor's well-known zeal in the promotion of those invaluable societies, must be Mr. Chapman's excuse for the liberty he ventures to take in this request. Mr. C. may add that of late he has earnestly directed his attention to the best means of extracting new uses from those noble but undeveloped institutions.

"Saracens Head, &c. "

This epistle, duly sealed and addressed, Waife delivered to the care of Mike Callaghan; and simultaneously he astounded that functionary with no less a gratuity than half a crown. Cutting short the fervent blessings which this generous donation naturally called forth, the Comedian said, with his happiest combination of suavity and loftiness, "And should the Mayor ask you what sort of person I am, —for I have not the honour to be known to him, and there are so many adventurers about, that he might reasonably expect me to be one, perhaps you can say that I don't look like a person he need be afraid to admit. You know a gentleman by sight! Bring back an answer as soon as may be; perhaps I sha'n't stay long in the town. You will find me in the High Street, looking at the shops. "

The porter took to his legs, impatient to vent his overflowing heart upon the praises of this munificent stranger. A gentleman, indeed! Mike should think so! If Mike's good word with the Mayor was worth money, Gentleman Waife had put his half-crown out upon famous interest.

The Comedian strolled along the High Street, and stopped before a stationer's shop, at the window of which was displayed a bill, entitled,

GATESBORO' ATHENIEUM
AND LITERARY INSTITUTE.

LECTURE ON CONCHOLOGY.

BY PROFESSOR LONG.
Author of "Researches into the Natural
History of Limpets."

Waife entered the shop, and lifted his hat, —"Permit me, sir, to look at that hand-bill. "

"Certainly, sir; but the lecture is over; you can see by the date: it came off last week. We allow the bills of previous proceedings at our Athenaeum to be exposed at the window till the new bills are prepared, —keeps the whole thing alive, sir. "

"Conchology, " said the Comedian, "is a subject which requires deep research, and on which a learned man may say much without fear of contradiction. But how far is Gatesboro' from the British Ocean? "

"I don't know exactly, sir, —a long way. "

"Then, as shells are not familiar to the youthful remembrances of your fellow-townsmen, possibly the lecturer may have found an audience rather select than numerous. "

"It was a very attentive audience, sir, and highly respectable: Miss Grieve's young ladies' (the genteelest seminary in the town) attended. "

WAIFE. —"Highly creditable to the young ladies. But, pardon me, is your Athenaeum a Mechanics' institute? "

SHOPMAN. —"It was so called at first. But, somehow or other, the mere operatives fell off, and it was thought advisable to change the word 'Mechanics' into the word 'Literary. ' Gatesboro' is not a manufacturing town, and the mechanics here do not realize the expectations of that taste for abstract science on which the originators of these societies founded their—"

WAIFE (insinuatingly interrupting). —"Their calculations of intellectual progress and their tables of pecuniary return. Few of these societies, I am told, are really self-supporting: I suppose Professor Long is! —and if he resides in Gatesboro', and writes on limpets, he is probably a man of independent fortune. "

SHOPMAN. —"Why, sir, the professor was engaged from London, —five guineas and his travelling expenses. The funds of the society could ill afford such outlay; but we have a most worthy mayor, who, assisted by his foreman, Mr. Williams, our treasurer, is, I may say, the life and soul of the institute. "

"A literary man himself, your mayor? "

The shopman smiled. "Not much in that way, sir; but anything to enlighten the working classes. This is Professor Long's great work upon limpets, two vols. post octavo. The Mayor has just presented it to the library of the institute. I was cutting the leaves when you came in. "

"Very prudent in you, sir. If limpets were but able to read printed character in the English tongue, this work would have more interest for them than the ablest investigations upon the political and social history of man. But, " added the Comedian, shaking his head mournfully, "the human species is not testaceous; and what the history of man might be to a limpet, the history of limpets is to a man. " So saying, Mr. Waife bought a sheet of cardboard and some gilt foil, relifted his hat, and walked out.

The shopman scratched his head thoughtfully; he glanced from his window at the form of the receding stranger, and mechanically resumed the task of cutting those leaves, which, had the volumes reached the shelves of the library uncut, would have so remained to the crack of doom.

Mike Callaghan now came in sight, striding fast; "Mr. Mayor sends his love—bother-o'-me—his respex; and will be happy to see your honour. "

In three minutes more the Comedian was seated in a little parlour that adjoined Mr. Hartopp's counting-house, — Mr. Hartopp seated also, vis-a-vis. The Mayor had one of those countenances upon which good-nature throws a sunshine softer than Claude ever shed upon canvas. Josiah Hartopp had risen in life by little other art than that of quiet kindliness. As a boy at school, he had been ever ready to do a good turn to his school-fellows; and his school-fellows at last formed themselves into a kind of police, for the purpose of protecting Jos. Hartopp's pence and person from the fists and fingers of each other. He was evidently so anxious to please his master, not from fear of the rod, but the desire to spare that worthy man the pain of inflicting it, that he had more trouble taken with his education than was bestowed on the brightest intellect that school ever reared; and where other boys were roughly flogged, Jos. Hartopp was soothingly patted on the head, and told not to be cast down, but try again. The same even-handed justice returned the sugared chalice to his lips in his apprenticeship to an austere leather-seller, who, not bearing the thought to lose sight of so mild a face, raised him into partnership, and ultimately made him his son-in-law and residuary legatee. Then Mr. Hartopp yielded to the advice of friends who desired his exaltation, and from a leather-seller became a tanner. Hides themselves softened their asperity to that gentle dealer, and melted into golden fleeces. He became rich enough to hire a farm for health and recreation. He knew little of husbandry, but he won the heart of a bailiff who might have reared a turnip from a deal table. Gradually the farm became his fee-simple, and the farmhouse expanded into a villa. Wealth and honours flowed in from a brimmed horn. The surliest man in the town would have been ashamed of saying a rude thing to Jos. Hartopp. If he spoke in public, though he hummed and hawed lamentably, no one was so respectfully listened to. As for the parliamentary representation of the town, he could have returned himself for one seat and Mike Callaghan for the other, had he been so disposed. But he was too full of the milk of humanity to admit into his veins a drop from the gall of party. He suffered others to legislate for his native land, and (except on one occasion when he had been persuaded to assist in canvassing, not indeed the electors of Gatesboro', but those of a distant town in which he possessed some influence, on behalf of a certain eminent orator) Jos. Hartopp was only visible in politics whenever Parliament was to be petitioned in favour of some humane measure, or against a tax that would have harassed the poor.

If anything went wrong with him in his business, the whole town combined to set it right for him. Was a child born to him, Gatesboro' rejoiced as a mother. Did measles or scarlatina afflict his neighbourhood, the first anxiety of Gatesboro' was for Mr. Hartopp's nursery. No one would have said Mrs. Hartopp's nursery; and when in such a department the man's name supersedes the woman's, can more be said in proof of the tenderness he excites? In short, Jos. Hartopp was a notable instance of a truth not commonly recognized; namely, that affection is power, and that, if you do make it thoroughly and unequivocally clear that you love your neighbours, though it may not be quite so well as you love yourself, —still, cordially and disinterestedly, you will find your neighbours much better fellows than Mrs. Grundy gives them credit for, —but always provided that your talents be not such as to excite their envy, nor your opinions such as to offend their prejudices.

MR. HARTOPP. —"You take an interest, you say, in literary institutes, and have studied the subject? "

THE COMEDIAN. —"Of late, those institutes have occupied my thoughts as representing the readiest means of collecting liberal ideas into a profitable focus. "

MR. HARTOPP. —"Certainly it is a great thing to bring classes together in friendly union. "

THE COMEDIAN. —"For laudable objects. "

MR. HARTOPP. —"To cultivate their understandings. "

THE COMEDIAN. —"To warm their hearts. "

MR. HARTOPP. —"To give them useful knowledge. "

THE COMEDIAN. —"And pleasurable sensations. "

MR. HARTOPP. —"In a word, to instruct them. "

THE COMEDIAN. —"And to amuse. "

"Eh! " said the Mayor, —"amuse! "

Now, every one about the person of this amiable man was on the constant guard to save him from the injurious effects of his own benevolence; and accordingly his foreman, hearing that he was closeted with a stranger, took alarm, and entered on pretence of asking instructions about an order for hides, in reality, to glower upon the intruder, and keep his master's hands out of imprudent pockets.

Mr. Hartopp, who, though not brilliant, did not want for sense, and was a keener observer than was generally supposed, divined the kindly intentions of his assistant. "A gentleman interested in the Gatesboro' Athenaeum. My foreman, sir, —Mr. Williams, the treasurer of our institute. Take a chair, Williams. "

"You said to amuse, Mr. Chapman, but —"

"You did not find Professor Long on conchology amusing. "

"Why, " said the Mayor, smiling blandly, "I myself am not a man of science, and therefore his lecture, though profound, was a little dry to me. "

"Must it not have been still more dry to your workmen, Mr. Mayor?"

"They did not attend, " said Williams. "Up-hill task we have to secure the Gatesboro' mechanics, when anything really solid is to be addressed to their understandings. "

"Poor things, they are so tired at night, " said the Mayor, compassionately; "but they wish to improve themselves, and they take books from the library. "

"Novels, " quoth the stern Williams: "it will be long before they take out that valuable 'History of Limpets. "

"If a lecture were as amusing as a novel, would not they attend it? " asked the Comedian.

"I suppose they would, " returned Mr. Williams. "But our object is to instruct; and instruction, sir —"

"Could be made amusing. If, for instance, the lecturer could produce a live shell-fish, and, by showing what kindness can do towards developing intellect and affection in beings without soul, —make man himself more kind to his fellow-man? "

Mr. Williams laughed grimly. "Well, sir! "

"This is what I should propose to do. "

"With a shell-fish! " cried the Mayor.

"No, sir; with a creature of nobler attributes, —A DOG! "

The listeners stared at each other like dumb animals as Waife continued, —"By winning interest for the individuality of a gifted quadruped, I should gradually create interest in the natural history of its species. I should lead the audience on to listen to comparisons with other members of the great family which once associated with Adam. I should lay the foundation for an instructive course of natural history, and from vertebrated mammifers who knows but we might gradually arrive at the nervous system of the molluscous division, and produce a sensation by the production of a limpet? "

"Theoretical, " said Mr. Williams.

"Practical, sir; since I take it for granted that the Athenaeum, at present, is rather a tax upon the richer subscribers, including Mr. Mayor. "

"Nothing to speak of, " said the mild Hartopp. Williams looked towards his master with unspeakable love, and groaned. "Nothing indeed—oh! "

"These societies should be wholly self-supporting, " said the Comedian, "and inflict no pecuniary loss upon Mr. Mayor. "

"Certainly, " said Williams, "that is the right principle. Mr. Mayor should be protected. "

"And if I show you how to make these societies self-supporting—"

"We should be very much obliged to you. "

"I propose, then, to give an exhibition at your rooms. " Mr. Williams nudged the Mayor, and coughed, the Comedian not appearing to remark cough nor nudge.

"Of course gratuitously. I am not a professional lecturer, gentlemen."

Mr. Williams looked charmed to hear it.

"And when I have made my first effort successful, as I feel sure it will be, I will leave it to you, gentlemen, to continue my undertaking. But I cannot stay long here. If the day after to-morrow—"

"That is our ordinary soiree night, " said the Mayor. "But you said a dog, sir, —dogs not admitted, -eh, Williams? "

MR. WILLIAMS. —"A mere by-law, which the subcommittee can suspend if necessary. But would not the introduction of a live animal be less dignified than—"

"A dead failure, " put in the Comedian, gravely. The Mayor would have smiled, but he was afraid of doing so lest he might hurt the feelings of Mr. Williams, who did not seem to take the joke.

"We are a purely intellectual body, " said the latter gentleman, "and a dog—"

"A learned dog, I presume, " observed the Mayor.

MR. WILLIAMS (nodding). —"Might form a dangerous precedent for the introduction of other quadrupeds. We might thus descend even to the level of a learned pig. We are not a menagerie, Mr. — Mr. —"

"Chapman, " said the Mayor, urbanely.

"Enough, " said the Comedian, rising with his grand air; "if I considered myself at liberty, gentlemen, to say who and what I am, you would be sure that I am not trifling with what I consider a very grave and important subject. As to suggesting anything derogatory to the dignity of science, and the eminent repute of the Gatesboro' Athenaeum, it would be idle to vindicate myself. These gray hairs are—"

He did not conclude that sentence, save by a slight wave of the hand. The two burgesses bowed reverentially, and the Comedian went on, —

"But when you speak of precedent, Mr. Williams, allow me to refer you to precedents in point. Aristotle wrote to Alexander the Great for animals to exhibit to the Literary Institute of Athens. At the colleges in Egypt lectures were delivered on a dog called Anubis, as inferior, I boldly assert, to that dog which I have referred to, as an Egyptian Colleg to a British Institute. The ancient Etrurians, as is shown by the erudite Schweighduser in that passage—you understand Greek, I presume, Mr. Williams? "

Mr. Williams could not say he did.

THE COMEDIAN. —"Then I will not quote that passage in Schweighauser upon the Molossian dogs in general, and the dog of Alcibiades in particular. But it proves beyond a doubt, that, in every ancient literary institute, learned dogs were highly estimated; and there was even a philosophical Academy called the Cynic, —that is, Doggish, or Dog-school, of which Diogenes was the most eminent professor. He, you know, went about with a lantern looking for an honest man, and could not find one! Why? Because the Society of Dogs had raised his standard of human honesty to an impracticable height. But I weary you; otherwise I could lecture on in this way for the hour together, if you think the Gatesboro' operatives prefer erudition to amusement. "

"A great scholar, " whispered Mr. Williams. —Aloud: "and I've nothing to say against your precedents, sir. I think you have made out that part of the case. But, after all, a learned dog is not so very uncommon as to be in itself the striking attraction which you appear to suppose. "

"It is not the mere learning of my dog of which I boast, " replied the Comedian. "Dogs may be learned, and men too; but it is the way that learning is imparted, whether by dog or man, for the edification of the masses, in order, as Pope expresses himself, 'to raise the genius and to mend the heart' that alone adorns the possessor, exalts the species, interests the public, and commands the respect of such judges as I see before me. " The grand bow.

"Ah! " said Mr. Williams, hesitatingly, "sentiments that do honour to your head and heart; and if we could, in the first instance, just see the dog privately. "

"'Nothing easier! " said the Comedian. "Will you do me the honour to meet him at tea this evening? "

"Rather will you not come and take tea at my house? " said the Mayor, with a shy glance towards Mr. Williams.

THE COMEDIAN. —"You are very kind; but my time is so occupied that I have long since made it a rule to decline all private invitations out of my own home. At my years, Mr. Mayor, one may be excused for taking leave of society and its forms; but you are comparatively young men. I presume on the authority of these gray hairs, and I shall expect you this evening, —say at nine o'clock. " The Actor waved his hand graciously and withdrew.

"A scholar AND a gentleman, " said Williams, emphatically. And the Mayor, thus authorized to allow vent to his kindly heart, added, "A humourist, and a pleasant one. Perhaps he is right, and our poor operatives would thank us more for a little innocent amusement than for those lectures, which they may be excused for thinking rather dull, since even you fell asleep when Professor Long got into the multilocular shell of the very first class of cephalous mollusca; and it is my belief that harmless laughter has a good moral effect upon the working class, —only don't spread it about that I said so, for we know excellent persons of a serious turn of mind whose opinions that sentiment might shock. "

CHAPTER XI.

HISTORICAL PROBLEM: "Is Gentleman Waife a swindler or a man of genius? " ANSWER: "Certainly a swindler, if he don't succeed. " Julius Caesar owed two millions when he risked the experiment of being general in Gaul. If Julius Caesar had not lived to cross the Rubicon and pay off his debts, what would his creditors have called Julius Caesar?

I need not say that Mr. Hartopp and his foreman came duly to tea, but the Comedian exhibited Sir Isaac's talents very sparingly, —just enough to excite admiration without sating curiosity. Sophy, whose pretty face and well-bred air were not unappreciated, was dismissed early to bed by a sign from her grandfather, and the Comedian then exerted his powers to entertain his visitors, so that even Sir Isaac was soon forgotten. Hard task, by writing, to convey a fair idea of this singular vagrant's pleasant vein. It was not so much what he said as the way of saying it, which gave to his desultory talk the charm of humour. He had certainly seen an immense deal of life somehow or other; and without appearing at the time to profit much by observation, without perhaps being himself conscious that he did profit, there was something in the very *enfantillage* of his loosest prattle, by which, with a glance of the one lustrous eye and a twist of the mobile lip, he could convey the impression of an original genius playing with this round world of ours—tossing it up, catching it again—easily as a child plays with its party-coloured ball. His mere book-knowledge was not much to boast of, though early in life he must have received a fair education. He had a smattering of the ancient classics, sufficient, perhaps, to startle the unlearned. If he had not read them, he had read about them; and at various odds and ends of his life he had picked up acquaintance with the popular standard modern writers. But literature with him was the smallest stripe in the party-coloured ball. Still it was astonishing how far and wide the Comedian could spread the sands of lore that the winds had drifted round the door of his playful, busy intellect. Where, for instance, could he ever have studied the nature and prospects of Mechanics' Institutes? and yet how well he seemed to understand them. Here, perhaps, his experience in one kind of audience helped him to the key to all miscellaneous assemblages. In fine, the man was an actor; and if he had thought fit to act the part of Professor Long himself, he would have done it to the life.

The two burghers had not spent so pleasant an evening for many years. As the clock struck twelve, the Mayor, whose gig had been in waiting a whole hour to take him to his villa, rose reluctantly to depart.

"And, " said Williams, "the bills must be out to-morrow. What shall we advertise? "

"The simpler the better, " said Waife; "only pray head the performance with the assurance that it is under the special patronage of his worship the Mayor. "

The Mayor felt his breast swell as if he had received some overwhelming personal obligation.

"Suppose it run thus, " continued the Comedian, —"Illustrations from Domestic Life and Natural History, with LIVE examples: PART FIRST—THE DOG! "

"It will take, " said the Mayor: "dogs are such popular animals! "

"Yes, " said Williams; "and though for that very reason some might think that by the 'live example of a dog' we compromised the dignity of the Institute, still the importance of Natural History —"

"And, " added the Comedian, "the sanctifying influences of domestic life—"

"May, " concluded Mr. Williams, "carry off whatever may seem to the higher order of minds a too familiar attraction in the—dog! "

"I do not fear the result, " said Waife, "provided the audience be sufficiently numerous; for that (which is an indispensable condition to a fair experiment) I issue hand-bills, only where distributed by the Mayor. "

"Don't be too sanguine. I distributed bills on behalf of Professor Long, and the audience was not numerous. How ever, I will do my best. Is there nothing more in which I can be of use to you, Mr. Chapman? "

"Yes, later. " Williams took alarm, and approached the Mayor's breast-pocket protectingly. The Comedian withdrew him aside and

197

whispered, "I intend to give the Mayor a little outline of the exhibition, and bring him into it, in order that his fellow-townsmen may signify their regard for him by a cheer; it will please his good heart, and be touching, you'll see—mum! " Williams shook the Comedian by the hand, relieved, affected, and confiding.

The visitors departed; and the Comedian lighted his hand-candlestick, whistled to Sir Isaac, and went to bed without one compunctious thought upon the growth of his bill and the deficit in his pockets. And yet it was true, as Sophy implied, that the Comedian had an honest horror of incurring debt. He generally thought twice before he risked owing even the most trifling bill; and when the bill came in, if it left him penniless, it was paid. And, now, what reckless extravagance! The best apartments! dinner, tea, in the first hotel of the town! half-a-crown to a porter! That lavish mode of life renewed with the dawning sun! not a care for the morrow; and I dare not conjecture how few the shillings in that purse. What aggravation, too, of guilt! Bills incurred without means under a borrowed name! I don't pretend to be a lawyer; but it looks to me very much like swindling. Yet the wretch sleeps. But are we sure that we are not shallow moralists? Do we carry into account the right of genius to draw bills upon the Future? Does not the most prudent general sometimes burn his ships? Does not the most upright merchant sometimes take credit on the chance of his ventures? May not that peaceful slumberer be morally sure that he has that argosy afloat in his own head, which amply justifies his use of the "Saracen's"? If his plan should fail? He will tell you that is impossible! But if it should fail, you say. Listen; there runs a story-I don't vouch for its truth: I tell it as it was told to me—there runs a story that in the late Russian war a certain naval veteran, renowned for professional daring and scientific invention, was examined before some great officials as to the chances of taking Cronstadt. "If you send me, " said the admiral, "with so many ships of the line, and so many gunboats, Cronstadt of course will be taken. " "But, " said a prudent lord, "suppose it should not be taken? " "That is impossible: it must be taken! " "Yes, " persisted my lord, "you think so, no doubt; but still, if it should not be taken, —what then? " "What then? —why, there's an end of the British fleet! " The great men took alarm, and that admiral was not sent. But they misconstrued the meaning of his answer. He meant not to imply any considerable danger to the British fleet. He meant to prove that one hypothesis was impossible by the suggestion of a counter-impossibility more self-evident. "It is impossible but what I shall take Cronstadt! " "But if you don't take it! " "It is impossible but what I shall take it; for if I don't take it, there's an end of the British fleet; and as it is impossible that there should be an end of the British fleet, it is impossible that I should not take Cronstadt! " —Q. E.D.

CHAPTER XII.

In which everything depends on Sir Isaac's success in discovering the law of attraction.

On the appointed evening, at eight o'clock, the great room of the Gatesboro' Athenaeum was unusually well filled. Not only had the Mayor exerted himself to the utmost for that object, but the hand-bill itself promised a rare relief from the prosiness of abstract enlightenment and elevated knowledge. Moreover, the stranger himself had begun to excite speculation and curiosity. He was an amateur, not a cut-and-dry professor. The Mayor and Mr. Williams had both spread the report that there was more in him than appeared on the surface; prodigiously learned, but extremely agreeable, fine manners, too! —Who could he be? Was Chapman his real name? etc.

The Comedian had obtained permission to arrange the room beforehand. He had the raised portion of it for his stage, and he had been fortunate enough to find a green curtain to be drawn across it. From behind this screen he now emerged and bowed. The bow redoubled the first conventional applause. He then began a very short address, —extremely well delivered, as you may suppose, but rather in the conversational than the oratorical style. He said it was his object to exhibit the intelligence of that Universal Friend of Man, the Dog, in some manner appropriate, not only to its sagacious instincts, but to its affectionate nature, and to convey thereby the moral that talents, however great, learning, however deep, were of no avail, unless rendered serviceable to Man. (Applause.) He must be pardoned then, if, in order to effect this object, he was compelled to borrow some harmless effects from the stage. In a word, his dog could represent to them the plot of a little drama. And he, though he could not say that he was altogether unaccustomed to public speaking (here a smile, modest, but august as that of some famous parliamentary orator who makes his first appearance at a vestry), still wholly new to its practice in the special part he had undertaken, would rely on their indulgence to efforts aspiring to no other merit than that of aiding the Hero of the Piece in a familiar illustration of those qualities in which dogs might give a lesson to humanity. Again he bowed, and retired behind the curtain. A pause of three minutes! the curtain drew up. Could that be the same Mr. Chapman whom the spectators beheld before them? Could three minutes suffice to change the sleek, respectable, prosperous-looking gentleman who had just addressed them into that image of threadbare poverty and hunger-pinched dejection? Little aid from theatrical costume: the clothes seemed the same, only to have grown wondrous aged and rusty. The face, the figure, the man, —these had undergone a transmutation beyond the art of the mere stage wardrobe, be it ever so amply stored, to effect. But for the patch over the eye, you could not have recognized Mr. Chapman. There was, indeed, about him, still, an air of dignity; but it was the dignity of woe, —a dignity, too, not of an affable civilian, but of some veteran soldier. You could not mistake. Though not in uniform, the melancholy man must have been a warrior! The way the coat was buttoned across the chest, the black stock tightened round the throat, the shoulders thrown back in the disciplined habit of a life, though the head bent forward in the despondency of an eventful crisis, —all spoke the decayed but not ignoble hero of a hundred fields.

There was something foreign, too, about the veteran's air. Mr. Chapman had looked so thoroughly English: that tragical and meagre personage looked so unequivocally French.

Not a word had the Comedian yet said; and yet all this had the first sight of him conveyed to the audience. There was an amazed murmur, then breathless stillness; the story rapidly unfolded itself, partly by words, much more by look and action. There sat a soldier who had fought under Napoleon at Marengo and Austerlitz, gone through the snows of Muscovy, escaped the fires of Waterloo, —the soldier of the Empire! Wondrous ideal of a wondrous time! and nowhere winning more respect and awe than in that land of the old English foe, in which with slight knowledge of the Beautiful in Art, there is so reverent a sympathy for all that is grand in Man! There sat the soldier, penniless and friendless, there, scarcely seen, reclined his grandchild, weak and slowly dying for the want of food; and all that the soldier possesses wherewith to buy bread for the day, is his cross of the Legion of Honour. It was given to him by the hand of the Emperor: must he pawn or sell it? Out on the pomp of decoration which we have substituted for the voice of passionate nature on our fallen stage! Scenes so faithful to the shaft of a column, —dresses by which an antiquary can define a date to a year! Is delusion there? Is it thus we are snatched from Thebes to Athens? No; place a really fine actor on a deal board, and for Thebes and Athens you may hang up a blanket! Why, that very cross which the old soldier holds—away from his sight—in that tremulous hand, is but patched up from the foil and cardboard bought at the stationer's shop. You might see it was nothing more, if you tried to see. Did a soul present think of such minute investigation? Not one. In the actor's hand that trumpery became at once the glorious thing by which Napoleon had planted the sentiment of knightly heroism in the men whom Danton would have launched upon earth ruthless and bestial, as galley-slaves that had burst their chain.

The badge, wrought from foil and cardboard, took life and soul: it begot an interest, inspired a pathos, as much as if it had been made — oh! not of gold and gems, but of flesh and blood. And the simple broken words that the veteran addressed to it! The scenes, the fields, the hopes, the glories it conjured up! And now to be wrenched away, —sold to supply Man's humblest, meanest wants, —sold—the last symbol of such a past! It was indeed *"propter vitam vivendi perdere causas.* " He would have starved rather, —but the child? And then the child rose up and came into play. She would not suffer such a sacrifice, —she was not hungry, —she was not weak; and when her voice failed her, she looked up into that iron face and smiled, — nothing but a smile. Outcame the pocket-handkerchiefs! The soldier seizes the cross, and turns away. It shall be sold! As he opens the door, a dog enters gravely, —licks his hand, approaches the table, raises itself on its hind legs, surveys the table dolefully, shakes its head, whines, comes to its master, pulls him by the skirt, looks into his face inquisitively.

What does all this mean? It soon comes out, and very naturally. The dog belonged to an old fellow-soldier, who had gone to the Isle of France to claim his share in the inheritance of a brother who had settled and died there, and who, meanwhile, had confided it to the care of our veteran, who was then in comparatively easy circumstances, since ruined by the failure and fraud of a banker to whom he had intrusted his all; and his small pension, including the yearly sum to which his cross entitled him, had been forestalled and mortgaged to pay the petty debts which, relying on his dividend from the banker, he had innocently incurred. The dog's owner had been gone for months; his return might be daily expected. Meanwhile the dog was at the hearth, but the wolf at the door. Now, this sagacious animal had been taught to perform the duties of messenger and major-domo. At stated intervals he applied to his master for sous, and brought back the supplies which the sous purchased. He now, as usual, came to the table for the accustomed coin—the last sou was gone, —the dog's occupation was at an end.

But could not the dog be sold? Impossible: it was the property of another, —a sacred deposit; one would be as bad as the fraudulent banker if one could apply to one's own necessities the property one holds in trust. These little biographical particulars came out in that sort of bitter and pathetic humour which a study of Shakspeare, or the experience of actual life, had taught the Comedian to be a natural relief to an intense sorrow. The dog meanwhile aided the narrative by his by-play. Still intent upon the sous, he thrust his nose into his master's pockets; he appealed touchingly to the child, and finally put back his head and vented his emotion in a lugubrious and elegiacal howl. Suddenly there is heard without the sound of a showman's tin trumpet! Whether the actor had got some obliging person to perform on that instrument, or whether, as more likely, it was but a trick of ventriloquism, we leave to conjecture. At that note, an idea seemed to seize the dog. He ran first to his master, who was on the threshold about to depart; pulled him back into the centre of the room: next he ran to the child, dragging her towards the same spot, though with great tenderness, and then, uttering a joyous bark, he raised himself on his hind legs and, with incomparable solemnity, performed a minuet step! The child catches the idea from the dog. Was he not more worth seeing than the puppet-show in the streets? might not people give money to see him, and the old soldier still keep his cross? To-day there is a public fete in the gardens yonder: that showman must be going thither; why not go too? What! he the old soldier, —he stoop to show off a dog! he! he! The dog looked at him deprecatingly and stretched himself on the floor—lifeless.

Yes, that is the alternative—shall his child die too, and he be too proud to save her? Ah! and if the cross can be saved also! But pshaw! what did the dog know that people would care to see? Oh, much, much. When the child was alone and sad, it would come and play with her. See those old dominos! She ranged them on the floor, and the dog leaped up and came to prove his skill. Artfully, then, the Comedian had planned that the dog should make some sad mistakes, alternated by some marvellous surprises. No, he would not do: yes, he would do. The audience took it seriously, and became intensely interested in the dog's success; so sorry for his blunders, so triumphant in his lucky hits. And then the child calmed the hasty irritable old man so sweetly, and corrected the dog so gently, and talked to the animal; told it how much they relied on it, and produced her infant alphabet, and spelt out "Save us. " The dog looked at the letters meditatively, and henceforth it was evident that he took more pains. Better and better; he will do, he will do! The child shall not starve, the cross shall not be sold. Down drops the curtain. End of Act I.

Act II. opens with a dialogue spoken off the stage. Invisible dramatis persona, that subsist, with airy tongues, upon the mimetic art of the Comedian. You understand that there is a vehement dispute going on. The dog must not be admitted into a part of the gardens where a more refined and exclusive section of the company have hired seats, in order to contemplate, without sharing, the rude dances or jostling promenade of the promiscuous merry-makers. Much hubbub, much humour; some persons for the dog, some against him; privilege and decorum here, equality and fraternity there. A Bonapartist colonel sees the cross on the soldier's breast, and, *mille tonnerres!* he settles the point. He pays for three reserved seats, — one for the soldier, one for the child, and a third for the dog. The veteran enters, — the child, not strong enough to have pushed through the crowd, raised on his shoulder, Rolla-like; the dog led by a string. He enters erect and warrior-like; his spirit has been roused by contest; his struggles have been crowned by victory. But (and here the art of the drama and the actor culminated towards the highest point)—but he now at once includes in the list of his dramatis persona the whole of his Gatesboro' audience. They are that select company into which he has thus forced his way. As he sees them seated before him, so calm, orderly, and dignified, *mauvaise honte* steals over the breast more accustomed to front the cannon than the battery of ladies' eyes. He places the child in a chair abashed and humbled; he drops into a seat beside her shrinkingly; and the dog, with more self-possession and sense of his own consequence, brushes with his paw some imaginary dust from a third chair, as in the superciliousness of the well dressed, and then seats himself, and looks round with serene audacity.

The chairs were skilfully placed on one side of the stage, as close as possible to the front row of the audience. The soldier ventures a furtive glance along the lines, and then speaks to his grandchild in whispered, bated breath: "Now they are there, what are they come for? To beg? He can never have the boldness to exhibit an animal for sous, — impossible; no, no, let them slink back again and sell the cross. " And the child whispers courage; bids him look again along the rows; those faces seem very kind. He again lifts his eyes, glances round, and with an extemporaneous tact that completed the illusion to which the audience were already gently lending themselves, made sundry complimentary comments on the different faces actually before him, selected most felicitously. The audience, taken by surprise, as some fair female, or kindly burgess, familiar to their associations, was thus pointed out to their applause, became heartily genial in their cheers and laughter. And the Comedian's face, unmoved by such demonstrations, —so shy and sad, insinuated its pathos underneath cheer and laugh. You now learned through the child that a dance, on which the company had been supposed to be gazing, was concluded, and that they would not be displeased by an interval of some other diversion. Now was the tune! The dog, as if to convey a sense of the prevalent ennui, yawned audibly, patted the child on the shoulder, and looked up in her face. "A game of dominos, " whispered the little girl. The dog gleefully grinned assent. Timidly she stole forth the old dominos, and ranged them on the ground; on which she slipped from her chair, the dog slipped from his; they began to play. The experiment was launched; the soldier saw that the curiosity of the company was excited, that the show would commence, the sons follow; and as if he at least would not openly shame his service and his Emperor, he turned aside, slid his hand to his breast, tore away his cross, and hid it. Scarce a murmured word accompanied the action, the acting said all; and a noble thrill ran through the audience. Oh, sublime art of the mime!

The Mayor sat very near where the child and dog were at play. The Comedian had (as he before implied he would do) discreetly prepared that gentleman for direct and personal appeal. The little girl turned her blue eyes innocently towards Mr. Hartopp, and said, "The dog beats me, sir; will you try what you can do? "

A roar, and universal clapping of hands, amidst which the worthy magistrate stepped on the stage. At the command of its young mistress the dog made the magistrate a polite bow, and straight to the game went magistrate and dog. From that time the interest became, as it were, personal to all present. "Will you come, sir, " said the child to a young gentleman, who was straining his neck to see how the dominos were played, "and observe that it is all fair? You, too, sir? " to Mr. Williams. The Comedian stood beside the dog, whose movements he directed with undetected skill, while appearing only to fix his eyes on the ground in conscious abasement. Those on the rows from behind now pressed forward; those in advance either came on the stage, or stood up intently contemplating. The Mayor was defeated, the crowd became too thick, and the caresses bestowed on the dog seemed to fatigue him. He rose and retreated to a corner haughtily. "Manners, sir, " said the soldier; "it is not for the like of us to be proud; excuse him, ladies and gentlemen. He only wishes to please all, " said the child, deprecatingly. "Say how many would you have round us at a time, so that the rest may not be prevented seeing you. " She spread the multiplication figures before the dog; the dog put his paw on 10. "Astonishing! " said the Mayor.

"Will you choose them yourself, sir? "

The dog nodded, walked leisurely round, keeping one eye towards the one eye of his master and selected ten persons, amongst whom were the Mayor, Mr. Williams, and three pretty young ladies who had been induced to ascend the stage. The others were chosen no less judiciously.

The dog was then artfully led on from one accomplishment to another, much within the ordinary range which bounds the instruction of learned animals. He was asked to say how many ladies were on the stage: he spelt three. What were their names? "The Graces. " Then he was asked who was the first magistrate in the town. The dog made a bow to the Mayor. "What had made that gentleman first magistrate? " The dog looked to the alphabet and spelt "Worth. " "Were there any persons present more powerful than the Mayor? " The dog bowed to the three young ladies. "What made them more powerful? " The dog spelt "Beauty. " When ended the applause these answers received, the dog went through the musket exercise with the soldier's staff; and as soon as he had performed that, he came to the business part of the exhibition, seized the hat which his master had dropped on the ground, and carried it round to each person on the stage. They looked at one another. "He is a poor soldier's dog, " said the child, hiding her face. "No, no; a soldier cannot beg, " cried the Comedian. The Mayor dropped a coin in the hat; others did the same or affected to do it. The dog took the hat to his master, who waved him aside. There was a pause. The dog laid the hat softly at the soldier's feet, and looked up at the child beseechingly. "What, " asked she, raising her head proudly — "what secures WORTH and defends BEAUTY? " The dog took up the staff and shouldered it. "And to what can the soldier look for aid when he starves and will not beg? " The dog seemed puzzled, —the suspense was awful. "Good heavens, " thought the Comedian, "if the brute should break down after all! —and when I took such care that the words should lie undisturbed-right before his nose! " With a deep sigh the veteran started from his despondent attitude, and crept along the floor as if for escape—so broken-down, so crestfallen.

Every eye was on that heartbroken face and receding figure; and the eye of that heartbroken face was on the dog, and the foot of that receding figure seemed to tremble, recoil, start, as it passed by the alphabetical letters which still lay on the ground as last arranged. "Ah! to what should he look for aid? " repeated the grandchild, clasping her little hands. The dog had now caught the cue, and put his paw first upon "WORTH, " and then upon "BEAUTY. "

"Worth! " cried the ladies—"Beauty! " exclaimed the Mayor. "Wonderful, wonderful! "

"Take up the hat, " said the child, and turning to the Mayor—"Ah! tell him, sir, that what Worth and Beauty give to Valour in distress is not alms but tribute. "

The words were little better than a hack claptrap; but the sweet voice glided through the assembly, and found its way into every heart.

"Is it so? " asked the old soldier, as his hand hoveringly passed above the coins. "Upon my honour it is, sir! " said the Mayor, with serious emphasis. The audience thought it the best speech he had ever made in his life, and cheered him till the roof rang again. "Oh! bread, bread, for you, darling! " cried the veteran, bowing his head over the child, and taking out his cross and kissing it with passion; "and the badge of honour still for me! "

While the audience was in the full depth of its emotion, and generous tears in many an eye, Waife seized his moment, dropped the actor, and stepped forth to the front as the man—simple, quiet, earnest man—artless man!

"This is no mimic scene, ladies and gentlemen. It is a tale in real life that stands out before you. I am here to appeal to those hearts that are not vainly open to human sorrows. I plead for what I have represented. True, that the man who needs your aid is not one of that soldiery which devastated Europe. But he has fought in battles as severe, and been left by fortune to as stern a desolation. True, he is not a Frenchman; he is one of a land you will not love less than France, —it is your own. He, too, has a child whom he would save from famine. He, too, has nothing left to sell or to pawn for bread, — except—oh, not this gilded badge, see, this is only foil and cardboard, —except, I say, the thing itself, of which you respect even so poor a symbol, —nothing left to sell or to pawn but Honour! For these I have pleaded this night as a showman; for these, less haughty than the Frenchman, I stretch my hands towards you without shame; for these I am a beggar. "

He was silent. The dog quietly took up the hat and approached the Mayor again. The Mayor extracted the half-crown he had previously deposited, and dropped into the hat two golden sovereigns. Who does not guess the rest? All crowded forward, —youth and age, man and woman. And most ardent of all were those whose life stands most close to vicissitude, most exposed to beggary, most sorely tried in the alternative between bread and honour. Not an operative there but spared his mite.

CHAPTER XIII.

Omne ignotum pro magnifico. —Rumour, knowing nothing of his antecedents, exalts Gentleman Waife into Don Magnifico.

The Comedian and his two coadjutors were followed to the Saracen's Head inn by a large crowd, but at respectful distance. Though I know few things less pleasing than to have been decoyed and entrapped into an unexpected demand upon one's purse, —when one only counted, too, upon an agreeable evening, —and hold, therefore, in just abhorrence the circulating plate which sometimes follows a public oration, homily, or other eloquent appeal to British liberality; yet, I will venture to say, there was not a creature whom the Comedian had surprised into impulsive beneficence who regretted his action, grudged its cost, or thought he had paid too dear for his entertainment. All had gone through a series of such pleasurable emotions that all had, as it were, wished a vent for their gratitude; and when the vent was found, it became an additional pleasure. But, strange to say, no one could satisfactorily explain to himself these two questions, —for what, and to whom had he given his money? It was not a general conjecture that the exhibitor wanted the money for his own uses. No; despite the evidence in favour of that idea, a person so respectable, so dignified, addressing them, too, with that noble assurance to which a man who begs for himself is not morally entitled, —a person thus characterized must be some high-hearted philanthropist who condescended to display his powers at an Institute purely intellectual, perhaps on behalf of an eminent but decayed author, whose name, from the respect due to letters, was delicately concealed. Mr. Williams, considered the hardest head and most practical man in the town, originated and maintained that hypothesis. Probably the stranger was an author himself, a great and affluent author. Had not great and affluent authors—men who are the boast of our time and land—acted, yea, on a common stage, and acted inimitably too, on behalf of some lettered brother or literary object? Therefore in these guileless minds, with all the pecuniary advantages of extreme penury and forlorn position, the Comedian obtained the respect due to prosperous circumstances and high renown. But there was one universal wish expressed by all who had been present, as they took their way homeward; and that wish was to renew the pleasure they had experienced, even if they paid the same price for it. Could not the long-closed theatre be re-opened, and the great man be induced by philanthropic motives, and an assured sum raised by voluntary subscriptions, to gratify the whole town, as he had gratified its selected intellect? Mr. Williams, in a state of charitable thaw, now softest of the soft, like most hard men when once softened, suggested this idea to the Mayor. The Mayor said evasively that he would think of it, and that he intended to pay his respects to Mr. Chapman before he returned home, that very night: it was proper. Mr. Williams and many others wished to accompany his worship. But the kind magistrate suggested that Mr. Chapman would be greatly fatigued: that the presence of many might seem more an intrusion than a compliment; that he, the Mayor, had better go alone, and at a somewhat later hour, when Mr. Chapman, though not retired to bed, might have had time for rest and refreshment. This delicate consideration had its weight; and the streets were thin when the Mayor's gig stopped, on its way villa-wards, at the Saracen's Head.

CHAPTER XIV.

It is the interval between our first repinings and our final resignation, in which, both with individuals and communities, is to be found all that makes a history worth telling. Ere yet we yearn for what is out of our reach, we are still in the cradle. When wearied out with our yearnings, desire again falls asleep; we are on the deathbed.

Sophy (leaning on her grandfather's arm as they ascend the stair of the Saracen's Head). —"But I am so tired, Grandy: I'd rather go to bed at once, please! "

GENTLEMAN WAIFE. —"Surely you could take something to eat first—something nice, —Miss Chapman? "—(Whispering close), "We can live in clover now, —a phrase which means" (aloud to the landlady, who crossed the landing-place above) "grilled chicken and mushrooms for supper, ma'am! Why don't you smile, Sopby? Oh, darling, you are ill! "

"No, no, Grandy, dear; only tired: let me go to bed. I shall be better to-morrow; I shall indeed! "

Waife looked fondly into her face, but his spirits were too much exhilarated to allow him to notice the unusual flush upon her cheek, except with admiration of the increased beauty which the heightened colour gave to her soft features.

"Well, " said he, "you are a pretty child! —a very pretty child, and you act wonderfully. You would make a fortune on the stage; but—"

SOPHY (eagerly). —"But—no, no, never! —not the stage! "

WAIFE. —"I don't wish you to go on the stage, as you know. A private exhibition—like the one to-night, for instance—has" (thrusting his hand into his pocket) "much to recommend it. "

SOPHY (with a sigh). —"Thank Heaven! that is over now; and you'll not be in want of money for a long, long time! Dear Sir Isaac! "

She began caressing Sir Isaac, who received her attentions with solemn pleasure. They were now in Sophy's room; and Waife, after again pressing the child in vain to take some refreshment, bestowed on her his kiss and blessing, and whistled "*Malbrook s'en va-t-en guerre*" to Sir Isaac, who, considering that melody an invitation to supper, licked his lips, and stalked forth, rejoicing, but decorous.

Left alone, the child breathed long and hard, pressing her hands to her bosom, and sank wearily on the foot of the bed. There were no shutters to the window, and the moonlight came in gently, stealing across that part of the wall and floor which the ray of the candle left in shade. The girl raised her eyes slowly towards the window, — towards the glimpse of the blue sky, and the slanting lustre of the moon. There is a certain epoch in our childhood, when what is called the romance of sentiment first makes itself vaguely felt. And ever with the dawn of that sentiment the moon and the stars take a strange and haunting fascination. Few persons in middle life-even though they be genuine poets—feel the peculiar spell in the severe stillness and mournful splendour of starry skies which impresses most of us, even though no poets at all, in that mystic age when Childhood nearly touches upon Youth, and turns an unquiet heart to those marvellous riddles within us and without, which we cease to conjecture when experience has taught us that they have no solution upon this side the grave. Lured by the light, the child rose softly, approached the window, and, resting her upturned face upon both hands, gazed long into the heavens, communing evidently with herself, for her lips moved and murmured indistinctly. Slowly she retired from the casement, and again seated herself at the foot of the bed, disconsolate. And then her thoughts ran somewhat thus, though she might not have shaped them exactly in the same words: "No, I cannot understand it. Why was I contented and happy before I knew him? Why did I see no harm, no shame in this way of life — not even on that stage with those people—until he said, 'It was what he wished I had never stooped to'? And Grandfather says our paths are so different they cannot cross each other again. There is a path of life, then, which I can never enter; there is a path on which I must always, always walk, always, always, always that path, —no escape! Never to come into that other one where there is no disguise, no hiding, no false names, —never, never! " she started impatiently, and with a wild look, —"It is killing me! "

Then, terrified by her own impetuosity, she threw herself on the bed, weeping low. Her heart had now gone back to her grandfather; it was smiting her for ingratitude to him. Could there be shame or wrong in what he asked, —what he did? And was she to murmur if she aided him to exist? What was the opinion of a stranger boy compared to the approving sheltering love of her sole guardian and tried fostering friend? And could people choose their own callings and modes of life? If one road went this way, another that, and they on the one road were borne farther and farther away from those on the other—as that idea came, consolation stopped, and in her noiseless weeping there was a bitterness as of despair. But the tears ended by relieving the grief that caused them. Wearied out of conjecture and complaint, her mind relapsed into the old native, childish submission. With a fervour in which there was self-reproach she repeated her meek, nightly prayer, that God would bless her dear grandfather, and suffer her to be his comfort and support. Then mechanically she undressed, extinguished the candle, and crept into bed. The moonlight became bolder and bolder; it advanced tip the floors, along the walls; now it floods her very pillow, and seems to her eyes to take a holy loving kindness, holier and more loving as the lids droop beneath it. A vague remembrance of some tale of "guardian spirits, " with which Waife had once charmed her wonder, stirred through her lulling thoughts, linking itself with the presence of that encircling moonlight. There! see the eyelids are closed, no tear upon their fringe. See the dimples steal out as the sweet lips are parted. She sleeps, she dreams already! Where and what is the rude world of waking now? Are there not guardian spirits? Deride the question if thou wilt, stern man, the reasoning and self-reliant; but thou, O fair mother, who hast marked the strange happiness on the face of a child that has wept itself to sleep, what sayest thou to the soft tradition, which surely had its origin in the heart of the earliest mother?

CHAPTER XV.

There is no man so friendless but what he can find a friend sincere enough to tell him disagreeable truths.

Meanwhile the Comedian had made himself and Sir Isaac extremely comfortable. No unabstemious man by habit was Gentleman Waife. He could dine on a crust, and season it with mirth; and as for exciting drinks, there was a childlike innocence in his humour never known to a brain that has been washed in alcohol. But on this special occasion, Waife's heart was made so bounteous by the novel sense of prosperity that it compelled him to treat himself. He did honour to the grilled chicken to which he had vainly tempted Sophy. He ordered half a pint of port to be mulled into negus. He helped himself with a bow, as if himself were a guest, and nodded each time he took off his glass, as much as to say, "Your health, Mr. Waife! " He even offered a glass of the exhilarating draught to Sir Isaac, who, exceedingly offended, retreated under the sofa, whence he peered forth through his deciduous ringlets, with brows knit in grave rebuke. Nor was it without deliberate caution—a whisker first, and then a paw—that he emerged from his retreat, when a plate heaped with the remains of the feast was placed upon the hearth-rug.

The supper over, and the attendant gone, the negus still left, Waife lighted his pipe, and, gazing on Sir Isaac, thus addressed that canine philosopher: "Illustrious member of the Quadrupedal Society of Friends to Man, and, as possessing those abilities for practical life which but few friends to man ever display in his service, promoted to high rank—Commissary-General of the Victualling Department, and Chancellor of the Exchequer—I have the honour to inform you that a vote of thanks in your favour has been proposed in this house, and carried unanimously. " Sir Isaac, looking shy, gave another lick to the plate, and wagged his tail. "It is true that thou wert once (shall I say it?) in fault at 'Beauty and Worth, '—thy memory deserted thee; thy peroration was on the verge of a breakdown; but 'Nemo mortalium omnibus horis sapit, I as the Latin grammar philosophically expresseth it. Mortals the wisest, not only on two legs but even upon four, occasionally stumble. The greatest general, statesman, sage, is not he who commits no blunder, but he who best repairs a blunder and converts it to success. This was thy merit and distinction! It hath never been mine! I recognize thy superior genius. I place in thee unqualified confidence; and consigning thee to the arms of Morpheus, since I see that panegyric acts on thy nervous system as a salubrious soporific, I now move that this House do resolve itself into a Committee of Ways and Means for the Consideration of the Budget! "

Therewith, while Sir Isaac fell into a profound sleep the Comedian deliberately emptied his pockets on the table; and arranging gold and silver before him, thrice carefully counted the total, and then divided it into sundry small heaps.

"That's for the bill, " quoth he, —"Civil List! —a large item. That's for Sophy, the darling! She shall have a teacher, and learn Music, — Education Grant; Current Expenses for the next fortnight; Miscellaneous Estimates; tobacco, —we'll call that Secret-service Money. Ah, scamp, vagrant, is not Heaven kind to thee at last? A few more such nights, and who knows but thine old age may have other roof than the workhouse? And Sophy? —Ah, what of her? Merciful Providence, spare my life till she has outgrown its uses! " A tear came to his eye; he brushed it away quickly, and, recounting his money, hummed a joyous tune.

The door opened; Waife looked up in surprise, sweeping his hand over the coins, and restoring them to his pocket. The Mayor entered.

As Mr. Hartopp walked slowly up the room, his eye fixed Waife's; and that eye was so searching, though so mild, that the Comedian felt himself change colour. His gay spirits fell, —falling lower and lower, the nearer the Mayor's step came to him; and when Hartopp, without speaking, took his hand, —not in compliment, not in congratulation, but pressed it as if in deep compassion, still looking him full in the face, with those pitying, penetrating eyes, the actor experienced a sort of shock as if he were read through, despite all his histrionic disguises, read through to his heart's core; and, as silent as his visitor, sank back in his chair, —abashed, disconcerted.

MR. HARTOPP. —"Poor man! "

THE COMEDIAN (rousing himself with an effort, but still confused). —"Down, Sir Isaac, down! This visit, Mr. Mayor, is an honour which may well take a dog by surprise! Forgive him! "

MR. HARTOPP (patting Sir Isaac, who was inquisitively sniffing his garments, and drawing a chair close to the actor, who thereon edged his own chair a little away, —in vain; for, on that movement, Mr. Hartopp advanced in proportion). —"Your dog is a very admirable and clever animal; but in the exhibition of a learned dog there is something which tends to sadden one. By what privations has he been forced out of his natural ways? By what fastings and severe usage have his instincts been distorted into tricks? Hunger is a stern teacher, Mr. Chapman; and to those whom it teaches, we cannot always give praise unmixed with pity. "

THE COMEDIAN (ill at ease under this allegorical tone, and surprised at a quicker intelligence in Mr. Hartopp than he had given that person credit for). —"You speak like an oracle, Mr. Mayor; but that dog, at least, has been mildly educated and kindly used. Inborn genius, sir, will have its vent. Hum! a most intelligent audience honoured us to-night; and our best thanks are due to you. "

MR. HARTOPP. —"Mr. Chapman, let us be frank with each other. I am not a clever man; perhaps a dull one. If I had set up for a clever man, I should not be where I am now. Hush! no compliments. But my life has brought me into frequent contact with those who suffer; and the dullest of us gain a certain sharpness in the matters to which our observation is habitually drawn. You took me in at first, it is true. I thought you were a philanthropical humourist, who might have crotchets, as many benevolent men, with time on their hands and money in their pockets, are apt to form. But when it came to the begging hat (I ask your pardon; don't let me offend you), when it came to the begging hat, I recognized the man who wants philanthropy from others, and whose crotchets are to be regarded in a professional point of view. Sir, I have come here alone, because I alone perhaps see the case as it really is. Will you confide in me? you may do it safely. To be plain, who and what are you? "

THE COMEDIAN (evasively). —"What do you take me for, Mr. Mayor? What can I be other than an itinerant showman, who has had resort to a harmless stratagem in order to obtain an audience, and create a surprise that might cover the naked audacity of the 'begging hat'! "

MR. HARTOPP (gravely). —"When a man of your ability and education is reduced to such stratagems, he must have committed some great faults. Pray Heaven it be no worse than faults! "

THE COMEDIAN (bitterly). —"That is always the way with the prosperous. Is a man unfortunate? They say, 'Why don't he help himself? ' Does he try to help himself? They say, 'With so much ability, why does not he help himself better? ' Ability and education! Snares and springes, Mr. Mayor! Ability and education! the two worst mantraps that a poor fellow can put his foot into! Aha! Did not you say if you had set up to be clever, you would not be where you now are: ' A wise saying; I admire you for it. Well, well, I and my dog have amused your townsfolk; they have amply repaid us. We are public servants; according as we act in public—hiss us or applaud. Are we to submit to an inquisition into our private character? Are you to ask how many mutton bones has that dog stolen? how many cats has he worried? or how many shirts has the showman in his wallet? how many debts has he left behind him? what is his rent-roll on earth, and his account with Heaven? Go and put those questions to ministers, philosophers, generals, poets. When they have acknowledged your right to put them, come to me and the other dog. "

MR. HARTOPP (rising and drawing on his gloves). —"I beg your pardon! I have done, sir. And yet I conceived an interest in you. It is because I have no talents myself that I admire those who have. I felt a mournful anxiety, too, for your poor little girl, —so young, so engaging. And is it necessary that you should bring up that child in a course of life certainly equivocal, and to females dangerous? "

The Comedian lifted his eyes suddenly, and stared hard at the face of his visitor, and in that face there was so much of benevolent humanity, so much sweetness contending with authoritative rebuke, that the vagabond's hardihood gave way! He struck his breast, and groaned aloud.

MR. HARTOPP (pressing on the advantage he had gained). —"And have you no alarm for her health? Do you not see how delicate she is? Do you not see that her very talent comes from her susceptibility to emotions which must wear her away? "

WAIFE. -"No, no! stop, stop, stop! you terrify me, you break my heart. Man, man! it is all for her that I toil and show and beg, —if you call it begging. Do you think I care what becomes of this battered hulk? Not a straw. What am I to do? What! what! You tell me to confide in you; wherefore? How can you help me? Would you give me employment? What am I fit for? Nothing! You could find work and bread for an Irish labourer, nor ask who or what he was; but to a man who strays towards you, seemingly from a sphere in which, if Poverty enters, she drops a courtesy, and is called 'genteel, ' you cry, 'Hold, produce your passport; where are your credentials, references? ' I have none. I have slipped out of the world I once moved in. I can no more appeal to those I knew in it than if I had transmigrated from one of yon stars, and said, 'See there what I was once! ' Oh, but you do not think she looks ill! —do you? do you? Wretch that I am! And I thought to save her! "

The old man trembled from head to foot, and his cheek was as pale as ashes.

Again the good magistrate took his hand, but this time the clasp was encouraging. "Cheer up: where there is a will there is a way; you justify the opinion I formed in your favour despite all circumstances to the contrary. When I asked you to confide in me, it was not from curiosity, but because I would serve you if I can. Reflect on what I have said. True, you can know but little of me. Learn what is said of me by my neighbours before you trust me further. For the rest, to-morrow you will have many proposals to renew your performance. Excuse me if I do not actively encourage it. I will not, at least, interfere to your detriment; but—"

"But, " exclaimed Waife, not much heeding this address, "but you think she looks ill? you think this is injuring her? you think I am murdering my grandchild, —my angel of life, my all? "

"Not so; I spoke too bluntly. Yet still—"

"Yes, yes, yet still—"

"Still, if you love her so dearly, would you blunt her conscience and love of truth? Were you not an impostor tonight? Would you ask her to reverence and imitate and pray for an impostor? "

"I never saw it in that light! " faltered Waife, struck to the soul; "never, never, so help me Heaven! "

"I felt sure you did not, " said the Mayor; "you saw but the sport of the thing; you took to it as a schoolboy. I have known many such men, with high animal spirits like yours. Such men err thoughtlessly;

but did they ever sin consciously, they could not keep those high spirits! Good night, Mr. Chapman, I shall hear from you again. "

The door closed on the form of the visitor; Waife's head sank on his breast, and all the deep lines upon brow and cheek stood forth, records of mighty griefs revived, —a countenance so altered, now its innocent arch play was gone, that you would not have known it. At length he rose very quietly, took up the candle, and stole into Sophy's room. Shading the light with careful hand, he looked on her face as she slept. The smile was still upon the parted lip: the child was still in the fairyland of dreams. But the cheek was thinner than it had been weeks ago, and the little hand that rested on the coverlet seemed wasted. Waife took that hand noiselessly into his own! it was hot and dry. He dropped it with a look of unutterable fear and anguish, and, shaking his head piteously; stole back again. Seating himself by the table at which he had been caught counting his gains, he folded his arms, and rooted his gaze on the floor; and there, motionless, and as if in stupefied suspense of thought itself, he sat till the dawn crept over the sky, —till the sun shone into the windows. The dog, crouched at his feet, sometimes started up and whined as to attract his notice: he did not heed it. The clock struck six; the house began to stir. The chambermaid came into the room. Waife rose and took his hat, brushing its nap mechanically with his sleeve. "Who did you say was the best here? " he asked with a vacant smile, touching the chambermaid's arm.

"Sir! the best—what? "

"The best doctor, ma'am; none of your parish apothecaries, —the best physician, —Dr. Gill, —did you say Gill? Thank you; his address, High Street. Close by, ma'am. " With his grand bow, —such is habit! —Gentleman Waife smiled graciously, and left the room. Sir Isaac stretched himself and followed.

CHAPTER XVI.

In every civilized society there is found a race of men who retain the instincts of the aboriginal cannibal, and live upon their fellow-men as a natural food. These interesting but formidable bipeds, having caught their victim, invariably select one part of his body on which to fasten their relentless grinders. The part thus selected is peculiarly susceptible, Providence having made it alive to the least nibble; it is situated just above the hip-joint, it is protected by a tegument of exquisite fibre, vulgarly called "THE BREECHES POCKET. " The thoroughbred Anthropophagite usually begins with his own relations and friends; and so long as he confines his voracity to the domestic circle, the law interferes little, if at all, with his venerable propensities. But when he has exhausted all that allows itself to be edible in the bosom of private life, the man-eater falls loose on society, and takes to prowling, —then "Sauve qui peut! " the laws rouse themselves, put on their spectacles, call for their wigs and gowns, and the Anthropophagite turned prowler is not always sure of his dinner. It is when he has arrived at this stage of development that the man- eater becomes of importance, enters into the domain of history, and occupies the thoughts of Moralists.

On the same morning in which Waife thus went forth from the Saracen's Head in quest of the doctor, but at a later hour, a man, who, to judge by the elaborate smartness of his attire, and the jaunty assurance of his saunter, must have wandered from the gay purlieus of Regent Street, threaded his way along the silent and desolate thoroughfares that intersect the remotest districts of Bloomsbury. He stopped at the turn into a small street still more sequestered than those which led to it, and looked up to the angle on the wall whereon the name of the street should have been inscribed. But the wall had been lately whitewashed, and the whitewash had obliterated the expected epigraph. The man muttered an impatient execration; and, turning round as if to seek a passenger of whom to make inquiry, beheld on the opposite side of the way another man apparently engaged in the same research. Involuntarily each crossed over the road towards the other.

"Pray, sir, " quoth the second wayfarer in that desert, "can you tell me if this is a street that is called a Place, —Podden Place, Upper? "

"Sir, " returned the sprucer wayfarer, "it is the question I would have asked of you. "

"Strange! "

"Very strange indeed that more than one person can, in this busy age, employ himself in discovering a Podden Place! Not a soul to inquire of, —not a shop that I see, not an orange-stall! "

"Ha! " cried the other, in a hoarse sepulchral voice, "Ha! there is a pot-boy! Boy! boy! boy! I say. Hold, there! hold! Is this Podden Place, —Upper? "

"Yes, it be, " answered the pot-boy, with a sleepy air, caught in that sleepy atmosphere; and chiming his pewter against an area rail with a dull clang, he chanted forth "Pots oho! " with a note as dirge-like as that which in the City of the Plague chanted "Out with the dead! "

Meanwhile the two wayfarers exchanged bows and parted; the sprucer wayfarer whether from the indulgence of a reflective mood, or from an habitual indifference to things and persons not concerning him, ceased to notice his fellow-solitary, and rather busied himself in sundry little coquetries appertaining to his own person. He passed his hand through his hair, re-arranged the cock of his hat, looked complacently at his boots, which still retained the gloss of the morning's varnish, drew down his wristbands, and, in a word, gave sign of a man who desires to make an effect, and feels that he ought to do it. So occupied was he in this self-commune that when he stopped at length at one of the small doors in the small street and lifted his hand to the knocker, he started to see that Wayfarer the Second was by his side. The two men now examined each other briefly but deliberately. Wayfarer the First was still young, —certainly handsome, but with an indescribable look about the eye and lip, from which the other recoiled with an instinctive awe, —a hard look, a cynical look, —a sidelong, quiet, defying, remorseless look. His clothes were so new of gloss that they seemed put on for the first time, were shaped to the prevailing fashion, and of a taste for colours less subdued than is usual with Englishmen, yet still such as a person of good mien could wear without incurring the charge of vulgarity, though liable to that of self-conceit. If you doubted that the man were a gentleman, you would have been puzzled to guess what else he could be. Were it not for the look we have mentioned, and which was perhaps not habitual, his

221

appearance might have been called prepossessing. In his figure there was the grace, in his step the elasticity which come from just proportions and muscular strength. In his hand he carried a supple switch-stick, slight and innocuous to appearance, but weighted at the handle after the fashion of a life-preserver. The tone of his voice was not displeasing to the ear, though there might be something artificial in the swell of it, —the sort of tone men assume when they desire to seem more frank and off-hand than belongs to their nature, —a sort of rollicking tone which is to the voice what swagger is to, the gait. Still that look! it produced on you the effect which might be created by some strange animal, not without beauty, but deadly to man. Wayfarer the Second was big and burly, middle-aged, large-whiskered, his complexion dirty. He wore a wig, —a wig evident, unmistakable, —a wig curled and rusty, —over the wig a dingy white hat. His black stock fitted tight round his throat, and across his breast he had thrown the folds of a Scotch plaid.

WAYFARER THE FIRST. —"YOU call here, too, —on Mrs. Crane? "

WAYFARER THE SECOND. —"Mrs. Crane? you too? Strange! "

WAYFARER THE FIRST (with constrained civility). —"Sir, I call on business, —private business. "

WAYFARER THE SECOND (with candid surliness). —"So do I. "

WAYFARER THE FIRST. —"Oh! "

WAYFARER THE SECOND. —"Ha! the locks unbar! "

The door opened, and an old meagre woman-servant presented herself.

WAYFARER THE FIRST (gliding before the big man with a serpent's undulating celerity of movement). —"Mrs. Crane lives here? "—"Yes! " "She's at home I suppose? "—"Yes! "—"Take up my card; say I come alone, not with this gentleman. "

Wayfarer the Second seems to have been rather put out by the manner of his rival. He recedes a step.

"You know the lady of this mansion well, sir? " "Extremely well. "

"Ha! then I yield you the precedence; I yield it, sir, but conditionally. You will not be long? "

"Not a moment longer than I can help; the land will be clear for you in an hour or less. "

"Or less, so please you, let it be or less. Servant, sir. "

"Sir, yours: come, my Hebe, track the dancers; that is, go up the stairs, and let me renew the dreams of youth in the eyes of Bella! "

The old woman meanwhile had been turning over the card in her withered palm, looking from the card to the visitor's face, and then to the card again, and mumbling to herself. At length she spoke:

"You, Mr. Losely! you! —Jasper Losely! how you be changed! what ha' ye done to yourself? where's your comeliness? where's the look that stole ladies' hearts? you, Jasper Losely! you are his goblin! "

"Hold your peace, old hussey! " said the visitor, evidently annoyed at remarks so disparaging. "I am Jasper Losely, more bronzed of cheek, more iron of hand. " He raised his switch with a threatening gesture, that might be in play, for the lips wore smiles, or might be in earnest, for the brows were bent; and pushing into the passage, and shutting the door, said, "Is your mistress up stairs? show me to her room, or—"

The old crone gave him one angry glance, which sank frightened beneath the cruel gleam of his eyes, and hastening up the stairs with a quicker stride than her age seemed to warrant, cried out, "Mistress, mistress! here is Mr. Losely! Jasper Losely himself! " By the time the visitor had reached the landing-place of the first floor, a female form had emerged from a room above, a female face peered over the banisters. Losely looked up and started as he saw it. A haggard face, —the face of one over whose life there has passed a blight. When last seen by him it had possessed beauty, though of a masculine rather than womanly character. Now of that beauty not a trace! the cheeks shrunk and hollow left the nose sharp, long, beaked as a bird of prey. The hair, once glossy in its ebon hue, now grizzled, harsh, neglected, hung in tortured, tangled meshes, —a study for an artist who would paint a fury. But the eyes were bright, —brighter than ever; bright now with a glare that lighted up the whole face bending over the man. In those burning eyes was there love? was there hate? was there welcome? was there menace? Impossible to distinguish; but at least one might perceive that there was joy.

"So, " said the voice from above, "so we do meet at last, Jasper Losely! you are come! "

Drawing a loose kind of dressing-robe more closely round her, the mistress of the house now descended the stairs, rapidly, flittingly, with a step noiseless as a spectre's, and, grasping Losely firmly by the hand, led him into a chill, dank, sunless drawing-room, gazing into his face fixedly all the while.

He winced and writhed. "There, there, let us sit down, my dear Mrs. Crane. "

"And once I was called Bella. "

"Ages ago! Basta! All things have their end. Do take those eyes of yours off my face; they were always so bright! and—really—now they are perfect burning-glasses! How close it is! Peuh! I am dead tired. May I ask for a glass of water; a drop of wine in it—or—brandy will do as well. "

"Ho! you have come to brandy and morning drams, eh, Jasper? " said Mrs. Crane, with a strange, dreary accent. "I, too, once tried if fire could burn up thought, but it did not succeed with me; that is years ago; and—there—see the bottles are full still! "

While thus speaking, she had unlocked a chiffonniere of the shape usually found in "genteel lodgings, " and taken out a leathern spirit-case containing four bottles, with a couple of wine-glasses. This case she placed on the table before Mr., Losely, and contemplated him at leisure while he helped himself to the raw spirits.

As she thus stood, an acute student of Lavater might have recognized, in her harsh and wasted countenance, signs of an original nature superior to that of her visitor; on her knitted brow, a sense higher in quality than on his smooth low forehead; on her straight stern lip, less cause for distrust than in the false good-humour which curved his handsome mouth into that smile of the fickle, which, responding to mirth but not to affection, is often lighted and never warmed. It is true that in that set pressure of her lip there might be cruelty, and, still more, the secretiveness which can harbour deceit; and yet, by the nervous workings of that lip, when relieved from such pressure, you would judge the woman to be rather by natural temperament passionate and impulsive than systematically cruel or deliberately-false, —false or cruel only as some predominating passion became the soul's absolute tyrant, and adopted the tyrant's vices. Above all, in those very lines destructive to beauty that had been ploughed, not by time, over her sallow cheeks, there was written the susceptibility to grief, to shame, to the sense of fall, which was not visible in the unreflective, reckless aspect of the sleek human animal before her.

In the room, too, there were some evidences of a cultivated taste. On the walls, book-shelves, containing volumes of a decorous and severe literature, such as careful parents allow to studious daughters, —the stately masterpieces of Fenelon and Racine; selections approved by boarding-schools from Tasso, Dante, Metastasio; amongst English authors, Addison, Johnson, Blair (his lectures as well as sermons); elementary works on such sciences as admit female neophytes into their porticos, if not into their penetralia, —botany, chemistry, astronomy. Prim as soldiers on parade stood the books, —not a gap in their ranks, —evidently never now displaced for recreation; well bound, yet faded, dusty; relics of a bygone life. Some of them might perhaps have been prizes at school, or birthday gifts from proud relations. There, too, on the table, near the spirit-case, lay open a once handsome workbox, —no silks now on the skeleton reels; discoloured, but not by use, in its nest of tarnished silk slept the golden thimble. There, too, in the corner, near a music-stand piled high with musical compositions of various schools and graduated complexity from "lessons for beginners" to the most arduous gamut of a German oratorio, slunk pathetically a poor lute-harp, the strings long since broken. There, too, by the window, hung a wire bird-cage, the bird long since dead. In a word, round the woman gazing on Jasper Losely, as he complacently drank his brandy, grouped the forlorn tokens of an early state, —the lost golden age of happy girlish studies, of harmless girlish tastes.

"Basta, eno', " said Mr. Losely, pushing aside the glass which he had twice filled and twice drained, "to business. Let me see the child: I feel up to it now. "

A darker shade fell over Arabella Crane's face, as she said, "The child! she is not here! I have disposed of her long ago. "

"Eh! —disposed of her! what do you mean? "

"Do you ask as if you feared I had put her out of the world? No! Well, then, —you come to England to see the child? You miss—you love, the child of that—of that—" She paused, checked herself, and added in an altered voice, "of that honest, high-minded gentlewoman whose memory must be so dear to me, —you love that child; very natural, Jasper. "

"Love her! a child I have scarcely seen since she was born! do talk common-sense. No. But have I not told you that she ought to be money's worth to me; ay, and she shall be yet, despite that proud man's disdainful insolence. "

"That proud man! what, you have ventured to address him—visit him—since your return to England? "

"Of course. That's what brought me over. I imagined the man would rejoice at what I told him, open his pursestrings, lavish blessings and bank-notes. And the brute would not even believe me; all because—"

"Because you had sold the right to be believed before. I told you, when I took the child, that you would never succeed there, that—I would never encourage you in the attempt. But you had sold the future as you sold your past, —too cheaply, it seems, Jasper. "

"Too cheaply, indeed. Who could ever have supposed that I should have been fobbed off with such a pittance? "

"Who, indeed, Jasper! You were made to spend fortunes, and call them pittances when spent, Jasper! You should have been a prince, Jasper; such princely tastes! Trinkets and dress, horses and dice, and plenty of ladies to look and die! Such princely spirit too! bounding all return for loyal sacrifice to the honour you vouchsafed in accepting it! "

Uttering this embittered irony, which nevertheless seemed rather to please than to offend her guest, she kept moving about the room, and (whether from some drawer in the furniture, or from her own person, Losely's careless eye did not observe) she suddenly drew forth a miniature, and, placing it before him, exclaimed, "Ah, but you are altered from those days; see what you then were! "

Losely's gaze, thus abruptly invited, fixed itself on the effigies of a youth eminently handsome, and of that kind of beauty which, without being effeminate, approaches to the fineness and brilliancy of the female countenance, —a beauty which renders its possessor inconveniently conspicuous, and too often, by winning that ready admiration which it costs no effort to obtain, withdraws the desire of applause from successes to be achieved by labour, and hardens egotism by the excuses it lends to self-esteem. It is true that this handsome face had not the elevation bestowed by thoughtful expression but thoughtful expression is not the attribute a painter seeks to give to the abstract comeliness of early youth; and it is seldom to be acquired without that constitutional wear and tear which is injurious to mere physical beauty. And over the whole countenance was diffused a sunny light, the freshness of buxom health, of luxuriant vigour; so that even that arrogant vanity which an acute observer might have detected as the prevailing mental characteristic seemed but a glad exultation in the gifts of benignant Nature. Not there the look which, in the matured man gazing on the bright ghost of his former self, might have daunted the timid and warned the wise. "And I was like this! True! I remember well when it was taken, and no one called it flattering, " said Mr. Losely, with pathetic self-condolence. "But I can't be very much changed, " he added, with a half laugh. "At my age one may have a manlier look, yet—"

"Yet still be handsome, Jasper, " said Mrs. Crane. "You are so. But look at me; what am I? "

"Oh, a very fine woman, my dear Crane, —always were. But you neglect yourself: you should not do that; keep it up to the last. Well, but to return to the child. You have disposed of her without my consent, without letting me know? "

"Letting you know! How many years is it since you even gave me your address! Never fear: she is in good hands. "

"Whose? At all events I must see her. "

"See her! What for? "

"What for! Hang it, it is natural that, now I am in England, I should at least wish to know what she is like. And I think it very strange that you should send her away, and then make all these difficulties. What's your object? I don't understand it. "

"My object? What could be my object but to serve you? At your request I took, fed, reared a child, whom you could not expect me to love, at my own cost. Did I ever ask you for a shilling? Did I ever suffer you to give me one? Never! At last, hearing no more from you, and what little I heard of you making me think that, if anything happened to me (and I was very ill at the time), you could only find her a burden, —at last I say, the old man came to me, —you had given him my address, —and he offered to take her, and I consented. She is with him. "

"The old man! She is with him! And where is he? "

"I don't know. "

"Humph; how does he live? Can he have got any money? "

"I don't know. "

"Did any old friends take him up? "

"Would he go to old friends? "

Mr. Losely tossed off two fresh glasses of brandy, one after the other, and, rising, walked to and fro the room, his hands buried in his pockets, and in no comfortable vein of reflection. At length he paused and said, "Well, upon the whole, I don't see what I could do with the girl just at present, though, of course, I ought to know where she is, and with whom. Tell me, Mrs. Crane, what is she like, —pretty or plain? "

"I suppose the chit would be called pretty, —by some persons at least. "

"Very pretty? handsome? " asked Losely, abruptly. "Handsome or not, what does it signify? what good comes of beauty? You had beauty enough; what have you done with it? "

At that question, Losely drew himself up with a sudden loftiness of look and gesture, which, though prompted but by offended vanity, improved the expression of the countenance, and restored to it much of its earlier character. Mrs. Crane gazed on him, startled into admiration, and it was in an altered voice, half reproachful, half bitter, that she continued,

"And now that you are satisfied about her, have you no questions to ask about me? —what I do? how I live? " "My dear Mrs. Crane, I know that you are comfortably off, and were never of a mercenary temper. I trust you are happy, and so forth: I wish I were; things don't prosper with me. If you could conveniently lend me a five-pound note—"

"You would borrow of me, Jasper? Ah! you come to me in your troubles. You shall have the money, —five pounds, ten pounds, what you please, but you will call again for it: you need me now; you will not utterly desert me now? "

"Best of creatures! —never! " He seized her hand and kissed it. She withdrew it quickly from his clasp, and, glancing over him from head to foot, said, "But are you really in want? —you are well-dressed, Jasper; that you always were. "

"Not always; three days ago very much the reverse: but I have had a trifling aid, and—"

"Aid in England? from whom? where? Not from him whom you say you had the courage to seek? "

"From whom else? Have I no claim? A miserable alms flung to me. Curse him! I tell you that man's look and language so galled me, — so galled, " echoed Losely, shifting his hold from the top of his switch to the centre, and bringing the murderous weight of the lead down on the palm of his other hand, "that, if his eye had quitted mine for a moment, I think I must have brained him, and been—"

"Hanged! " said Mrs. Crane.

"Of course, hanged, " returned Losely, resuming the reckless voice and manner in which there was that peculiar levity which comes from hardness of heart, as from the steel's hardness comes the blade's play. "But if a man did not sometimes forget consequences, there would be an end of the gallows. I am glad that his eye never left mine. " And the leaden head of the switch fell with a dull dumb sound on the floor.

Mrs. Crane made no immediate rejoinder, but fixed on her lawless visitor a gaze in which there was no womanly fear (though Losely's aspect and gesture might have sent a thrill through the nerves of many a hardy man), but which was not without womanly compassion, her countenance gradually softening more and more, as if under the influence of recollections mournful but not hostile. At length she said in a low voice, "Poor Jasper! Is all the vain ambition that made you so false shrunk into a ferocity that finds you so powerless? Would your existence, after all, have been harder, poorer, meaner, if your faith had been kept to me? "

Evidently disliking that turn in the conversation, but checking a reply which might have been rude had no visions of five pounds, ten pounds, loomed in the distance, Mr. Losely said, "Pshaw! Bella, pshaw! I was a fool, I dare say, and a sad dog, a very sad dog; but I had always the greatest regard for you, and always shall! Hillo, what's that? A knock at the door! Oh, by the by, a queer-looking man, in a white hat, called at the same time I did, to see you on private business, gave way to me, said he should come again; may I ask who he is? "

"I cannot guess; no one ever calls here on business except the tax-gatherer. "

The old woman-servant now entered. "A gentleman, ma'am; says his name is Rugge. "

"Rugge, —Rugge; let me think. "

"I am here, Mrs. Crane, " said the manager, striding in. "You don't, perhaps, call me to mind by name; but—oho! not gone, sir! Do I intrude prematurely? "

"No, I have done; good-day, my dear Mrs. Crane. "

"Stay, Jasper. I remember you now, Mr. Rugge; take a chair. "

She whispered a few words into Losely's ear, then turned to the manager, and said aloud, "I saw you at Mr. Waife's lodging, at the time he had that bad accident. "

"And I had the honour to accompany you home, ma'am, and—but shall I speak out before this gentleman? "

"Certainly; you see he is listening to you with attention. This gentleman and I have no secrets from each other. What has become of that person? This gentleman wishes to know. "

LOSELY. —"Yes, sir, I wish to know-particularly. "

RUGGE. —"So do I; that is partly what I came about. You are aware, I think, ma'am, that I engaged him and Juliet Araminta, that is, Sophy. "

LOSELY. —"Sophy? engaged them, sir, —how? "

RUGGE. —"Theatrical line, sir, —Rugge's Exhibition; he was a great actor once, that fellow Waife. "

LOSELY. —"Oh, actor! well, sir, go on. "

RUGGE (who in the course of his address turns from the lady to the gentleman, from the gentleman to the lady, with appropriate gesture and appealing look). —"But he became a wreck, a block of a man; lost an eye and his voice too. How ever, to serve him, I took his grandchild and him too. He left me—shamefully, and ran off with his grandchild, sir. Now, ma'am, to be plain with you, that little girl I looked upon as my property, —a very valuable property. She is worth a great deal to me, and I have been done out of her. If you can help me to get her back, articled and engaged say for three years, I am willing and happy, ma'am, to pay something handsome, — uncommon handsome. "

MRS. CRANE (loftily). —"Speak to that gentleman; he may treat with you. "

LOSELY. —"What do you call uncommon handsome, Mr. —Mr. Tugge? "

RUGGE. —"Rugge! Sir; we sha'n't disagree, I hope, provided you have the power to get Waife to bind the girl to me. "

LOSELY. —"I may have the power to transfer the young lady to your care—young lady is a more respectful phrase than girl—and possibly to dispense with Mr. Waife's consent to such arrangement. But excuse me if I say that I must know a little more of yourself, before I could promise to exert such a power on your behalf. "

RUGGE. —"Sir, I shall be proud to improve our acquaintance. As to Waife, the old vagabond, he has injured and affronted me, sir. I don't bear malice, but I have a spirit: Britons have a spirit, sir. And you will remember, ma'am, that when I accompanied you home, I observed that Mr. Waife was a mysterious man, and had apparently known better days, and that when a man is mysterious, and falls into the sear and yellow leaf, ma'am, without that which should accompany old age, sir, one has a right to suspect that some time or other, he has done something or other, ma'am, which makes him fear lest the very stones prate of his whereabout, sir. And you did not deny, ma'am, that the mystery was suspicious; but you said, with uncommon good sense, that it was nothing to me what Mr. Waife had once been, so long as he was of use to me at that particular season. Since then, sir, he has ceased to be of use, — ceased, too, in the unhandsomest manner. And if you would, ma'am, from a sense of justice, just unravel the mystery, put me in possession of the secret, it might make that base man of use to me again, give me a handle over him, sir, so that I might awe him into restoring my property, as, morally speaking, Juliet Araminta most undoubtedly is. That's why I call, —leaving my company, to which I am a father, orphans for the present. But I have missed that little girl, —that young lady, sir. I called her a phenomenon, ma'am; missed her much: it is natural, sir, I appeal to you. No man can be done out of a valuable property and not feel it, if he has a heart in his bosom. And if I had her back safe, I should indulge ambition. I have always had ambition. The theatre at York, sir, —that is my ambition; I had it from a child, sir; dreamed of it three tunes, ma'am. If I had back my property in that phenomenon, I would go at the thing, slap-bang, take the York, and bring out the phenomenon with A CLAW! "

LOSELY (musingly). —"You say the young lady is a phenomenon, and for this phenomenon you are willing to pay something handsome, —a vague expression. Put it into L. s. d. "

RUGGE. —"Sir, if she can be bound to me legally for three years, I would give L100. I did offer to Waife L50, —to you, sir, L100. "

Losely's eyes flashed, and his hands opened restlessly. "But, confound it, where is she? Have you no clew? "

RUGGE. —"No, but we can easily find one; it was not worth my while to hunt them up before I was quite sure that, if I regained my property in that phenomenon, the law would protect it. "

MRS. CRANE (moving to the door). —"Well, Jasper Losely, you will sell the young lady, I doubt not; and when you have sold her, let me know. " She came back and whispered, "You will not perhaps now want money from me, but I shall see you again; for, if you would find the child, you will need my aid. "

"Certainly, my dear friend, I will call again; honour bright. "

Mrs. Crane here bowed to the gentlemen, and swept out of the room.

Thus left alone, Losely and Rugge looked at each other with a shy and yet cunning gaze, —Rugge's hands in his trouser's pockets, his head thrown back; Losely's hands in voluntarily expanded, his head bewitchingly bent forward, and a little on one side.

"Sir, " said Rugge, at length, "what do you say to a chop and a pint of wine? Perhaps we could talk more at our ease elsewhere. I am only in town for a day; left my company thirty miles off, —orphans, as I said before. "

"Mr. Rugge, " said Losely, "I have no desire to stay in London, or indeed in England; and the sooner we can settle this matter the better. Grant that we find the young lady, you provide for her board and lodging; teach her your honourable profession; behave, of course, kindly to her. "

"Like a father. "

"And give to me the sum of L100? "

"That is, if you can legally make her over to me. But, sir, may I inquire by what authority you would act in this matter? "

"On that head it will be easy to satisfy you; meanwhile I accept your proposal of an early dinner. Let us adjourn; is it to your house? "

"I have no exact private house in London; but I know a public one, —commodious. "

"Be it so. After you, sir. "

As they descended the stairs, the old woman-servant stood at the street door. Rugge went out first; the woman detained Losely. "Do you find her altered? "

"Whom? Mrs. Crane? —why, years will tell. But you seem to have known me; I don't remember you. "

"Not Bridget Greggs? "

"Is it possible? I left you a middle-aged, rosy-faced woman. True, I recognize you now. There's a crown for you. I wish I had more to spare! "

Bridget pushed back the silver.

"No; I dare not! Take money from you, Jasper Losely! Mistress would not forgive me! "

Losely, not unreluctantly, restored the crown to his pocket; and, with a snort rather than sigh of relief, stepped into open daylight. As he crossed the street to join Rugge, who was waiting for him on the shady side, he mechanically turned to look back at the house, and, at the open window of an upper story, he beheld again those shining eyes which had glared down on him from the stairs. He tried to smile, and waved his hand feebly. The eyes seemed to return the smile; and as he walked down the street, arm-in-arm with the ruffian manager, slowly recovering his springy step, and in the gloss of the new garments that set forth his still symmetrical proportions, the eyes followed him watchfully, steadfastly, till his form had vanished, and the dull street was once more a solitude.

Then Arabella Crane turned from the window. Putting her hand to her heart, "How it beats! " she muttered; "if in love or in hate, in scorn or in pity, beats once more with a human emotion. He will come again; whether for money or for woman's wit, what care I? — he will come. I will hold, I will cling to him, no more to part; for better for worse, as it should have been once at the altar. And the child? " she paused; was it in compunction? "The child! " she continued fiercely, and as if lashing herself into rage, "the child of that treacherous, hateful mother, —yes! I will help him to sell her back as a stage-show, —help him in all that does not lift her to a state from which she may look down with disdain on me. Revenge on her, on that cruel house: revenge is sweet. Oh! that it were revenge alone that bids me cling to him who deserves revenge the most. " She closed her burning eyes, and sat down droopingly, rocking herself to and fro like one in pain.

CHAPTER XVII.

In life it is difficult to say who do you the most mischief—enemies with the worst intentions, or friends with the best.

The conference between Mr. Rugge and Mr. Losely terminated in an appointment to meet, the next day, at the village in which this story opened. Meanwhile Mr. Rugge would return to his "orphans, " and arrange performances in which for some days they might dispense with a father's part. Losely, on his side, undertook to devote the intervening hours to consultation with a solicitor to whom Mr. Rugge recommended him as to the prompt obtaining of legal powers to enforce the authority he asserted himself to possess. He would also persuade Mrs. Crane to accompany him to the village and aid in the requisite investigations; entertaining a tacit but instinctive belief in the superiority of her acuteness. "Set a female to catch a female, " quoth Mr. Rugge.

On the day and in the place thus fixed the three hunters opened their chase. They threw off at the Cobbler's stall. They soon caught the same scent which had been followed by the lawyer's clerk. They arrived at Mrs. Saunders's; there the two men would have been at fault like their predecessor. But the female was more astute. To drop the metaphor Mrs. Saunders could not stand the sharp cross-examination of one of her own sex. "That woman deceives us, " said Mrs. Crane on leaving the house. " They have not gone to London. What could they do there? Any man with a few stage juggling tricks can get on in country villages but would be lost in cities. Perhaps, as it seems he has got a dog, —we have found out that from Mrs. Saunders, —he will make use of it for an itinerant puppet-show. "

"Punch! " said Mr. Rugge; "not a doubt of it. "

"In that case, " observed Mrs. Crane, "they are probably not far off. Let us print handbills, offering a reward for their clew, and luring the old man himself by an assurance that the inquiry is made in order that he may learn of something to his advantage. "

In the course of the evening the handbills were printed. The next day they were posted up on the walls, not only of that village, but on those of the small towns and hamlets for some miles round. The handbills ran invitingly thus, "If William Waife, who left—on the

20th ult., will apply at the Red Lion Inn at — — —-, for X. X., he will learn of something greatly to his advantage. A reward of L5 will be given to any one who will furnish information where the said William Waife and the little girl who accompanies him may be found. The said William Waife is about sixty years of age, of middle stature, strongly built, has lost one eye, and is lame of one leg. The little girl, called Sophy, is twelve years old, but looks younger; has blue eyes and light brown hair. They had with them a white French poodle dog. This bill is printed by the friends of the missing party. " The next day passed; no information: but on the day following, a young gentleman of good mien, dressed in black, rode into the town, stopped at the Red Lion Inn, and asked to see X. X. The two men were out on their researches; Mrs. Crane stayed at home to answer inquiries.

The gentleman was requested to dismount, and walk in. Mrs. Crane received him in the inn parlour, which swarmed with flies. She stood in the centre, —vigilant, grim spider of the place.

"I c-ca-call, " said the gentleman, stammering fearfully, in con—consequence of a b-b-bill—I—ch-chanced to see in my ri-ri-ri-ride yesterday—on a wa-wa-wall. You-you, I—sup-sup—"

"Am X. X., " put in Mrs. Crane, growing impatient, "one of the friends of Mr. Waife, by whom the handbill has been circulated; it will indeed be a great relief to us to know where they are, —the little girl more especially. "

Mrs. Crane was respectably dressed, —in silk iron-gray; she had crisped her flaky tresses into stiff hard ringlets, that fell like long screws from under a black velvet band. Mrs. Crane never wore a cap, nor could you fancy her in a cap; but the velvet band looked as rigid as if gummed to a hoop of steel. Her manner and tone of voice were those of an educated person, not unused to some society above the vulgar; and yet the visitor, in whom the reader recognizes the piscatorial Oxonian, with whom Waife had interchanged philosophy on the marge of the running brooklet, drew back as she advanced and spoke; and, bent on an errand of kindness, he was seized with a vague misgiving.

MRS. CRANE (blandly). —"I fear they must be badly off. I hope they are not wanting the necessaries of life. But pray be seated, sir. " She looked at him again, and with more respect in her address than she had before thrown into it, added, with a half courtesy, as she seated herself by his side, "A clergyman of the Established Church, I presume, sir? "

OXONIAN (stammer, as on a former occasion, respectfully omitted). —"With this defect, ma'am! —But to the point. Some days ago I happened to fall in with an elderly person, such as is described, with a very pretty female child and a French dog. The man—gentleman, perhaps I may call him, judging from his conversation—interested me much; so did the little girl. And if I could be the means of directing real friends anxious to serve them—"

Mrs. CRANE. —"You would indeed be a benefactor. And where are they now, sir? "

OXONIAN. —"That I cannot positively tell you. But before I say more, will you kindly satisfy my curiosity? He is perhaps an eccentric person, —this Mr. Waife? —a little—" The Oxonian stopped, and touched his forehead. Mrs. Crane made no prompt reply: she was musing. Unwarily the scholar continued: "Because, in that case, I should not like to interfere. "

MRS. CRANE. —"Quite right, sir. His own friends would not interfere with his roving ways, his little whims on any account. Poor man, why should they? He has no property for them to covet. But it is a long story. I had the care of that dear little girl from her infancy, sweet child! "

OXONIAN. —"So she seems. "

MRS. CRANE. —"And now she has a most comfortable home provided for her; and a young girl, with good friends, ought not to be tramping about the country, whatever an old man may do. You must allow that, sir? "

OXONIAN. —"Well, —yes, I allow that; it occurred to me. But what is the man? —the gentleman? "

MRS. CRANE. —"Very 'eccentric, ' as you say, and inconsiderate, perhaps, as to the little girl. We will not call it insane, sir. But—are you married? "

OXONIAN (blushing). —"No, ma'am. "

MRS. CRANE. —"But you have a sister, perhaps? "

OXONIAN. —"Yes; I have one sister. "

MRS. CRANE. —"Would you like your sister to be running about the country in that way, —carried off from her home, kindred, and friends? "

OXONIAN. —"Ah! I understand. The poor little girl is fond of the old man, —a relation, grandfather perhaps? and he has taken her from her home; and though not actually insane, he is still —"

MRS. CRANE. —"An unsafe guide for a female child, delicately reared. I reared her; of good prospects, too. O sir, let us save the child! Look—" She drew from a sidepocket in her stiff iron-gray apron a folded paper; she placed it in the Oxonian's hand; he glanced over and returned it.

"I see, ma'am. I cannot hesitate after this. It is a good many miles off where I met the persons whom I have no doubt that you seek; and two or three days ago my father received a letter from a very worthy, excellent man, with whom he is often brought into communication upon benevolent objects, —a Mr. Hartopp, the Mayor of Gatesboro', in which, among other matters, the Mayor mentioned briefly that the Literary Institute of that town had been much delighted by the performance of a very remarkable man with one eye, about whom there seemed some mystery, with a little girl and a learned dog; and I can't help thinking that the man, the girl, and the dog, must be those whom I saw and you seek. "

MRS. CRANE. —"At Gatesboro'? is that far? "

OXONIAN. —"Some way; but you can get a cross train from this village. I hope that the old man will not be separated from the little girl; they seemed very fond of each other. "

MRS. CRANE. —"No doubt of it; very fond: it would be cruel to separate them. A comfortable home for both. I don't know, sir, if I dare offer to a gentleman of your evident rank the reward, —but for the poor of your parish. "

OXONIAN. —"Oh, ma'am, our poor want for nothing: my father is rich. But if you would oblige me by a line after you have found these interesting persons; I am going to a distant part of the country to-morrow, — to Montfort Court, in — — —-shire. "

MRS. CRANE. —"To Lord Montfort, the head of the noble family of Vipont? "

OXONIAN. —"Yes; do you know any of the family, ma'am? If you could refer me to one of them, I should feel more satisfied as to—"

MRS. CRANE (hastily). —"Indeed, sir, every one must know that great family by name and repute. I know no more. So you are going to Lord Montfort's! The Marchioness, they say, is very beautiful. "

OXONIAN. —"And good as beautiful. I have the honour to be connected both with her and Lord Montfort; they are cousins, and my grandfather was a Vipont. I should have told you my name, — Morley; George Vipont Morley. "

Mrs. Crane made a profound courtesy, and, with an unmistakable smile of satisfaction, said, as if half in soliloquy, "So it is to one of that noble family—to a Vipont—that the dear child will owe her restoration to my embrace! Bless you, sir! "

"I hope I have done right, " said George Vipont Morley, as he mounted his horse. "I must have done right, surely! " he said again, when he was on the high road. "I fear I have not done right, " he said a third time, as the face of Mrs. Crane began to haunt him; and when at sunset he reached his home, tired out, horse and man, with an unusually long ride, and the green water-bank on which he had overheard poor Waife's simple grace and joyous babble came in sight, "After all, " he said dolefully, "it was no business of mine. "

"I meant well; but—" His little sister ran to the gate to greet him. "Yes, I did quite right. How should I like my sister to be roving the country, and acting at Literary Institutes 'with a poodle dog? Quite right; kiss me, Jane! "

CHAPTER XVIII.

Let a king and a beggar converse freely together, and it is the beggar's fault if he does not say something which makes the king lift his hat to him.

The scene shifts back to Gatesboro', the forenoon of the day succeeding the memorable exhibition at the Institute of that learned town. Mr. Hartopp was in the little parlour behind his country-house, his hours of business much broken into by those intruders who deem no time unseasonable for the indulgence of curiosity, the interchange of thought, or the interests of general humanity and of national enlightenment. The excitement produced on the previous evening by Mr. Chapman, Sophy, and Sir Isaac was greatly on the increase. Persons who had seen them naturally called on the Mayor to talk over the exhibition. Persons who had not seen them, still more naturally dropped in just to learn what was really Mr. Mayor's private opinion. The little parlour was thronged by a regular levee There was the proprietor of a dismal building, still called "The Theatre, " which was seldom let except at election time, when it was hired by the popular candidate for the delivery of those harangues upon liberty and conscience, tyranny and oppression, which furnish the staple of declamation equally to the dramatist and the orator. There was also the landlord of the Royal Hotel, who had lately built to his house "The City Concert-Room, "—a superb apartment, but a losing speculation. There, too, were three highly respectable persons, of a serious turn of mind, who came to suggest doubts whether an entertainment of so frivolous a nature was not injurious to the morality of Gatesboro'. Besides these notables, there were loungers and gossips, with no particular object except that of ascertaining who Mr. Chapman was by birth and parentage, and suggesting the expediency of a deputation, ostensibly for the purpose of asking him to repeat his performance, but charged with private instructions to cross-examine him as to his pedigree. The gentle Mayor kept his eyes fixed on a mighty ledger-book, pen in hand. The attitude was a rebuke on intruders, and in ordinary times would have been so considered. But mildness, however majestic, is not always effective in periods of civic commotion. The room was animated by hubbub. You caught broken sentences here and there crossing each other, like the sounds that had been frozen in the air, and set free by a thaw, according to the veracious narrative of Baron Munchausen.

PLAYHOUSE PROPRIETOR. — "The theatre is the —"

SERIOUS GENTLEMAN. — "Plausible snare by which a population, at present grave and well-disposed, is decoyed into becoming —"

EXCITED ADMIRER. — "A French poodle, sir, that plays at dominos like a —"

CREDULOUS CONJECTURER. — "Benevolent philanthropist, condescending to act for the benefit of some distressed brother who is —"

PROPRIETOR of CITY CONCERT-ROOM. — "One hundred and twenty feet long by forty, Mr. Mayor! Talk of that damp theatre, sir, you might as well talk of the —"

Suddenly the door flew open, and pushing aside a clerk who designed to announce him, in burst Mr. Chapman himself.

He had evidently expected to find the Mayor alone, for at the sight of that throng he checked himself, and stood mute at the threshold. The levee for a moment was no less surprised, and no less mute. But the good folks soon recovered themselves. To many it was a pleasure to accost and congratulate the man who the night before had occasioned to them emotions so agreeable. Cordial smiles broke out; friendly hands were thrust forth. Brief but hearty compliments, mingled with entreaties to renew the performance to a larger audience, were showered round. The Comedian stood hat in hand, mechanically passing his sleeve over its nap, muttering half inaudibly, "You see before you a man, " and turning his single eye from one face to the other, as if struggling to guess what was meant, or where he was. The Mayor rose and came forward, — "My dear friends, " said he, mildly, "Mr. Chapman calls by appointment. Perhaps he may have something to say to me confidentially. "

The three serious gentlemen, who had hitherto remained aloof, eying Mr. Chapman much as three inquisitors might have eyed a Jew, shook three solemn heads, and set the example of retreat. The last to linger were the rival proprietors of the theatre and the city concert-room. Each whispered the stranger, — one the left ear, one the right. Each thrust into his hand a printed paper. As the door closed on them the Comedian let fall the papers: his arm drooped to his side; his whole frame seemed to collapse. Hartopp took him by the hand,

and led him gently to his own armchair beside the table. The Comedian dropped on the chair, still without speaking.

MR. HARTOPP. —"What is the matter? What has happened? "

WAIFE. —"She is very ill, —in a bad way; the doctor says so, —Dr. Gill. "

MR. HARTOPP (feelingly). —"Your little girl in a bad way! Oh, no; doctors always exaggerate in order to get more credit for the cure. Not that I would disparage Dr. Gill, fellow-townsman, first-rate man. Still 't is the way with doctors to talk cheerfully if one is in danger, and to look solemn if there is nothing to fear. "

WAIFE. —"DO you think so: you have children of your own, sir? — of her age, too? —Eh! eh! "

MR. HARTOPP. —"Yes; I know all about children, —better, I think, than Mrs. H. does. What is the complaint? "

WAIFE. —"The doctor says it is low fever. "

MR. HARTOPP. —"Caused by nervous excitement, perhaps. "

WAIFE (looking up). —"Yes: that's what he says, —nervous excitement. "

MR. HARTOPP. —"Clever sensitive children, subjected precociously to emulation and emotion, are always liable to such maladies. My third girl, Anna Maria, fell, into a low fever, caused by nervous excitement in trying for school prizes. "

WATFE. —"Did she die of it, sir? "

MR. HARTOPP (shuddering). —"Die! no! I removed her from school, set her to take care of the poultry, forbade all French exercises, made her take English exercises instead, and ride on a donkey. She's quite another thing now, cheeks as red as an apple, and as firm as a cricket-ball. "

WAIFE. —"I will keep poultry; I will buy a donkey. Oh, sir! you don't think she will go to heaven yet, and leave me here? "

MR. HARTOPP. —"Not if you give her rest and quiet. But no excitement, no exhibitions. "

WAIFE (emptying his pockets on the table). —"Will you kindly count that money, sir? Don't you think that would be enough to find her some pretty lodgings hereabouts till she gets quite strong again? With green fields, —she's fond of green fields and a farm-yard with poultry, —though we were lodging a few days ago with a good woman who kept hens, and Sophy did not seem to take to them much. A canary bird is more of a companion, and—"

HARTOPP (interrupting). —"Ay—ay—and you! what would you do? "

WAIFE. —"Why, I and the dog would go away for a little while about the country. "

HARTOPP. —"Exhibiting? "

WAIFE. —"That money will not last forever, and what can we do, I and the dog, in order to get more for her? "

HARTOPP (pressing his hand warmly). —"You are a good man, sir. I am sure of it; you cannot have done things which you should be afraid to tell me. Make me your confidant, and I may then find some employment fit for you, and you need not separate yourself from your little girl. "

WAIFE. —"Separate from her! I should only leave her for a few days at a time till she gets well. This money would keep her, —how long? Two months? three? how long? the doctor would not charge much. "

HARTOPP. —"YOU will not confide in me then? At your age, — have you no friends, —no one to speak a good word for you? "

WAIFE (jerking up his head with a haughty air). —"So—so! Who talks to you about me, sir? I am speaking of my innocent child. Does she want a good word spoken for her? Heaven has written it in her face. "

Hartopp persisted no more; the excellent man was sincerely grieved at his visitor's obstinate avoidance of the true question at issue; for the Mayor could have found employment for a man of Waife's evident education and talent. But such employment would entail responsibilities and trust. How recommend to it a man of whose life and circumstances nothing could be known, —a man without a character? And Waife interested him deeply. We have all felt that there are some persons towards whom we are attracted by a peculiar sympathy not to be explained, —a something in the manner, the cut of the face, the tone of the voice. If there are fifty applicants for a benefit in our gift, one of the fifty wins his way to our preference at first sight, though with no better right to it than his fellows. We can no more say why we like the man than we can say why we fall in love with a woman in whom no one else would discover a charm. "There is, " says a Latin love-poet, "no why or wherefore in liking. " Hartopp, therefore, had taken, from the first moment, to Waife, —the staid, respectable, thriving man, all muffled up from head to foot in the whitest lawn of reputation, —to the wandering, shifty, tricksome scatterling, who had not seemingly secured, through the course of a life bordering upon age, a single certificate for good conduct. On his hearthstone, beside his ledger-book, stood the Mayor, looking with a respectful admiration that puzzled himself upon the forlorn creature, who could give no reason why he should not be rather in the Gatesboro' parish stocks than in its chief magistrate's easy-chair. Yet, were the Mayor's sympathetic liking and respectful admiration wholly unaccountable? Runs there not between one warm human heart and another the electric chain of a secret understanding? In that maimed outcast, so stubbornly hard to himself, so tremulously sensitive for his sick child, was there not the majesty to which they who have learned that Nature has her nobles, reverently bow the head! A man true to man's grave religion can no more despise a life wrecked in all else, while a hallowing affection stands out sublime through the rents and chinks of fortune, than he can profane with rude mockery a temple in ruins, —if still left there the altar.

CHAPTER XIX.

Very well so far as it goes.

MR. HARTOPP. —"I cannot presume to question you further, Mr. Chapman. But to one of your knowledge of the world, I need not say that your silence deprives me of the power to assist yourself. We'll talk no more of that. "

WAIFE. —"Thank you, gratefully, Mr. Mayor. "

MR. HARTOPP. —"But for the little girl, make your mind easy, —at least for the present. I will place her at my farm cottage. My bailiff's wife, a kind woman, will take care of her, while you pursue your calling elsewhere. As for this money, you will want it yourself; your poor little child shall cost you nothing. So that's settled. Let me come up and see her. I am a bit of a doctor myself. Every man blest with a large family, in whose house there is always some interesting case of small-pox, measles, whooping-cough, scarlatina, etc., has a good private practice of his own. I'm not brilliant in book-learning, Mr. Chapman. But as to children's complaints in a practical way, " added Hartopp, with a glow of pride, "Mrs. H. says she'd rather trust the little ones to me than to Dr. Gill. I'll see your child, and set her up I'll be bound. But now I think of it, " continued Hartopp, softening more and more, "if exhibit you must, why not stay at Gatesboro' for a time? More may be made in this town than elsewhere. "

"No, no; I could not have the heart to act here again without her. I feel at present as if I can never again act at all! "

"Something else will turn up. Providence is so kind to me, Mr. Mayor. "

Waife turned to the door. "You will come soon? " he said anxiously.

The Mayor, who had been locking up his ledgers and papers, replied, "I will but stay to give some orders; in a quarter of an hour I shall be at your hotel. "

CHAPTER XX.

Sophy hides heart and shows temper.

The child was lying on a sofa drawn near the window in her own room, and on her lap was the doll Lionel had given to her. Carried with her in her wanderings, she had never played with it; never altered a ribbon in its yellow tresses; but at least once a day she had taken it forth and looked at it in secret. And all that morning, left much to herself, it had been her companion. She was smoothing down its frock, which she fancied had got ruffled, —smoothing it down with a sort of fearful tenderness, the doll all the while staring her full in the face with its blue bead eyes. Waife, seated near her, was trying to talk gayly; to invent fairy tales blithe with sport and fancy: but his invention flagged, and the fairies prosed awfully. He had placed the dominos before Sir Isaac, but Sophy had scarcely looked at them, from the languid heavy eyes on which the doll so stupidly fixed its own. Sir Isaac himself seemed spiritless; he was aware that something was wrong. Now and then he got up restlessly, sniffed the dominos, and placed a paw gently, very gently, on Sophy's knee. Not being encouraged, he lay down again uneasily, often shifting his position as if the floor was grown too hard for him. Thus the Mayor found the three. He approached Sophy with the step of a man accustomed to sick-rooms and ailing children, —step light as if shod with felt, —put his hand on her shoulder, kissed her forehead, and then took the doll. Sophy started, and took it back from him quickly, but without a word; then she hid it behind her pillow. The Mayor smiled. "My dear child, do you think I should hurt your doll? "

Sophy coloured and said murmuringly, "No, sir, not hurt it, but—" she stopped short.

"I have been talking to your grandpapa about you, my dear, and we both wish to give you a little holiday. Dolls are well enough for the winter, but green fields and daisy chains for the summer. "

Sophy glanced from the Mayor to her grandfather, and back again to the Mayor, shook her curls from her eyes, and looked seriously inquisitive.

The Mayor, observing her quietly, stole her hand into his own, feeling the pulse as if merely caressing the slender wrist. Then he began to describe his bailiff's cottage, with woodbine round the porch, the farm-yard, the bee-hives, the pretty duck-pond with an osier island, and the great China gander who had a pompous strut, which made him the droll est creature possible. And Sophy should go there in a day or two, and be as happy as one of the bees, but not so busy. Sophy listened very earnestly, very gravely, and then sliding her hand from the Mayor, caught hold of her grandfather's arm firmly, and said, "And you, Grandy, —will you like it? won't it be dull for you, Grandy dear? "

"Why, my darling, " said Waife, "I and Sir Isaac will go and take a stroll about the country for a few weeks, and—"

SOPHY (passionately). —"I thought so; I thought he meant that. I tried not to believe it; go away, —you? and who's to take care of you? who'll understand you? I want care! I! I! No, no, it is you, —you who want care. I shall be well to-morrow, —quite well, don't fear. He shall not be sent away from me; he shall not, sir. Oh, Grandfather, Grandfather, how could you? " She flung herself on his breast, clinging there, —clinging as if infancy and age were but parts of the same whole.

"But, " said the Mayor, "it is not as if you were going to school, my dear; you are going for a holiday. And your grandfather must leave you, —must travel about; 'tis his calling. If you fell ill and were with him, think how much you would be in his way. Do you know, " he added, smiling, "I shall begin to fear that you are selfish. "

"Selfish! " exclaimed Waife, angrily.

"Selfish! " echoed Sophy, with a melancholy scorn that came from a sentiment so deep that mortal eye could scarce fathom it. "Oh, no, sir! can you say it is for his good, not for what he supposes mine that you want us to part? The pretty cottage, and all for me; and what for him? —tramp, tramp along the hot dusty roads. Do you see that he is lame? Oh, Sir, I know him; you don't. Selfish! he would have no merry ways that make you laugh without me; would you, Grandy dear? Go away, you are a naughty man, —go, or I shall hate you as much as that dreadful Mr. Rugge. "

"Rugge, —who is he? " said the Mayor, curiously, catching at any clew.

"Hush, my darling! —hush! " said Waife, fondling her on his breast. "Hush! What is to be done, sir? "

Hartopp made a sly sign to him to say no more before Sophy, and then replied, addressing himself to her, "What is to be done? Nothing shall be done, my dear child, that you dislike. I don't wish to part you two. Don't hate me; lie down again; that's a dear. There, I have smoothed your pillow for you. Oh, here's your pretty doll again. " Sophy snatched at the doll petulantly, and made what the French call a moue at the good man as she suffered her grandfather to replace her on the sofa.

"She has a strong temper of her own, " muttered the Mayor; "so has Anna Maria a strong temper! "

Now, if I were anyway master of my own pen, and could write as I pleased, without being hurried along helter-skelter by the tyrannical exactions of that "young Rapid" in buskins and chiton called "THE HISTORIC MUSE, " I would break off this chapter, open my window, rest my eyes on the green lawn without, and indulge in a rhapsodical digression upon that beautifier of the moral life which is called "Good Temper. " Ha! the Historic Muse is dozing. By her leave! —Softly.

CHAPTER XXI.

Being an essay on temper in general, and a hazardous experiment on the reader's in particular.

There, the window is open! how instinctively the eye rests upon the green! How the calm colour lures and soothes it! But is there to the green only a single hue? See how infinite the variety of its tints! What sombre gravity in yon cedar, yon motionless pine-tree! What lively but unvarying laugh in yon glossy laurels! Do those tints charm us like the play in the young leaves of the lilac, —lighter here, darker there, as the breeze (and so slight the breeze!) stirs them into checker, —into ripple? Oh, sweet green, to the world what sweet temper is to man's life! Who would reduce into one dye all thy lovely varieties? who exclude the dark steadfast verdure that lives on through the winter day; or the mutinous caprice of the gentler, younger tint that came fresh through the tears of April, and will shadow with sportive tremor the blooms of luxuriant June?

Happy the man on whose marriage-hearth temper smiles kind from the eyes of woman! "No deity present, " saith the heathen proverb, "where absent Prudence; " no joy long a guest where Peace is not a dweller, —peace, so like Faith that they may be taken for each other, and poets have clad them with the same veil. But in childhood, in early youth, expect not the changeless green of the cedar. Wouldst thou distinguish fine temper from spiritless dulness, from cold simulation, —ask less what the temper than what the disposition.

Is the nature sweet and trustful; is it free from the morbid self-love which calls itself "sensitive feeling" and frets at imaginary offences; is the tendency to be grateful for kindness, yet take kindness meekly, and accept as a benefit what the vain call a due? From dispositions thus blessed, sweet temper will come forth to gladden thee, spontaneous and free. Quick with some, with some slow, word and look emerge out of the heart. Be thy first question, "Is the heart itself generous and tender? " If it be so, self-control comes with deepening affection. Call not that a good heart which, hastening to sting if a fibre be ruffled, cries, "I am no hypocrite. " Accept that excuse, and revenge becomes virtue. But where the heart, if it give the offence, pines till it win back the pardon; if offended itself, bounds forth to forgive, ever longing to soothe, ever grieved if it wound; then be sure that its nobleness will need but few trials of pain in each outbreak to refine and chastise its expression. Fear not then; be but noble thyself, thou art safe!

Yet what in childhood is often called, rebukingly, "temper" is but the cordial and puissant vitality which contains all the elements that make temper the sweetest at last. Who amongst us, how wise soever, can construe a child's heart? who conjecture all the springs that secretly vibrate within, to a touch on the surface of feeling? Each child, but especially the girl-child, would task the whole lore of a sage deep as Shakspeare to distinguish those subtle emotions which we grown folks have outlived.

"She has a strong temper, " said the Mayor, when Soppy snatched the doll from his hand a second time, and pouted at him, spoiled child, looking so divinely cross, so petulantly pretty! And how on earth could the Mayor know what associations with that stupid doll made her think it profaned by the touch of a stranger? Was it to her eyes as to his, —mere waxwork and frippery; or a symbol of holy remembrances, of gleams into a fairer world, of "devotion to something afar from the sphere of her sorrow? " Was not the evidence of "strong temper" the very sign of affectionate depth of heart? Poor little Sophy! Hide it again, —safe out of sight, close, inscrutable, unguessed, as childhood's first treasures of sentiment ever are!

CHAPTER XXII.

The object of civilization being always to settle people one way or the other, the Mayor of Gatesboro' entertains a statesmanlike ambition to settle Gentleman Waife; no doubt a wise conception, and in accordance with the genius of the Nation. Every session of Parliament England is employed in settling folks, whether at home or at the Antipodes, who ignorantly object to be settled in her way; in short, "I'll settle them, " has become a vulgar idiom, tantamount to a threat of uttermost extermination or smash; therefore the Mayor of Gatesboro' harbouring that benignant idea with reference to "Gentleman Waife, " all kindly readers will exclaim, "Dii meliora! What will he do with it? "

The doll once more safe behind the pillow, Sophy's face gradually softened; she bent forward, touched the Mayor's hand timidly, and looked at him with pleading, penitent eyes, still wet with tears, — eyes that said, though the lips were silent, "I'll not hate you. I was ungrateful and peevish; may I beg pardon? "

"I forgive you with all my heart, " cried the Mayor, interpreting the look aright. "And now try and compose yourself and sleep while I talk with your grandpapa below. "

"I don't see how it is possible that I can leave her, " said Waife, when the two men had adjourned to the sitting-room. "I am sure, " quoth the Mayor, seriously, "that it is the best thing for her: her pulse has much nervous excitability; she wants a complete rest; she ought not to move about with you on any account. But come: though I must not know, it seems, who and what you are, Mr. Chapman, I don't think you will run off with my cow; and if you like to stay at the bailiff's cottage for a week or two with your grandchild, you shall be left in peace, and asked no questions. I will own to you a weakness of mine: I value myself on being seldom or never taken in. I don't think I could forgive the man who did take me in. But taken in I certainly shall be, if, despite all your mystery, you are not as honest a fellow as ever stood upon shoe-leather! So come to the cottage. "

Waife was very much affected by this confiding kindness; but he shook his head despondently, and that same abject, almost cringing humility of mien and manner which had pained at times Lionel and Vance crept over the whole man, so that he seemed to cower and shrink as a Pariah before a Brahmin. "No, sir; thank you most humbly. No, sir; that must not be. I must work for my daily bread; if what a poor vagabond like me may do can be called work. I have made it a rule for years not to force myself to the hearth and home of any kind man, who, not knowing my past, has a right to suspect me. Where I lodge, I pay as a lodger; or whatever favour shown me spares my purse, I try to return in some useful humble way. Why, sir, how could I make free and easy with another man's board and roof-tree for days or weeks together, when I would not even come to your hearthstone for a cup of tea? " The Mayor remembered, and was startled. Waife hurried on. "But for my poor child I have no such scruples, —no shame, no false pride. I take what you offer her gratefully, —gratefully. Ah, sir, she is not in her right place with me; but there's no use kicking against the pricks. Where was I? Oh! well, I tell you what we will do, sir. I will take her to the cottage in a day or two, —as soon as she is well enough to go, —and spend the day with her, and deceive her, sir! yes, deceive, cheat her, sir! I am a cheat, a player, and she'll think I'm going to stay with her; and at night, when she's asleep, I'll creep off, I and the other dog. But I'll leave a letter for her: it will soothe her, and she'll be patient and wait. I will come back again to see her in a week, and once every week, till she's well again. "

"And what will you do? "

"I don't know; but, " said the actor, forcing a laugh, "I 'm not a man likely to starve. Oh, never fear, sir. "

So the Mayor went away, and strolled across the fields to his bailiff's cottage, to prepare for the guest it would receive. "It is all very well that the poor man should be away for some days, " thought Mr. Hartopp. "Before he comes again, I shall have hit on some plan to serve him; and I can learn more about him from the child in his absence, and see what he is really fit for. There's a schoolmaster wanted in Morley's village. Old Morley wrote to me to recommend him one. Good salary, —pretty house. But it would be wrong to set over young children—recommend to a respectable proprietor and his parson—a man whom I know nothing about. Impossible! that will not do. If there was any place of light service which did not require trust or responsibility, —but there is no such place in Great Britain. Suppose I were to set him up in some easy way of business, —a little shop, eh? I don't know. What would Williams say? If, indeed, I were taken in! if the man I am thus credulously trusting turned out a rogue, "—the Mayor paused and actually shivered at that thought, —"why then, I should be fallen indeed. My wife would not let me have half-a-crown in my pockets; and I could, not walk a hundred yards but Williams would be at my heels to protect me from being stolen by gypsies. Taken in by him! No, impossible! But if it turn out as I suspect, —that, contrary to vulgar prudence, I am divining a really great and good man in difficulties, aha, what a triumph I shall then gain over them all! How Williams will revere me! " The good man laughed aloud at that thought, and walked on with a prouder step.

CHAPTER, XXIII.

A pretty trifle in its way, no doubt, is the love between youth and youth, —gay varieties of the bauble spread the counter of the great toy-shop; but thou, courteous dame Nature, raise thine arm to yon shelf, somewhat out of every-day reach, and bring me down that obsolete, neglected, unconsidered thing, the love between age and childhood.

The next day Sophy was better; the day after, improvement was more visible; and on the third day Waife paid his bill, and conducted her to the rural abode to which, credulous at last of his promises to share it with her for a time, he enticed her fated steps. It was little more than a mile beyond the suburbs of the town; and, though the walk tired her, she concealed fatigue, and would not suffer him to carry her. The cottage now smiled out before them, —thatched gable roof, with fancy barge board; half Swiss, half what is called Elizabethan; all the fences and sheds round it, as only your rich traders, condescending to turn farmers, construct and maintain, — sheds and fences, trim and neat, as if models in waxwork. The breezy air came fresh from the new haystacks; from the woodbine round the porch; from the breath of the lazy kine, as they stood knee-deep in the pool, that, belted with weeds and broad-leaved water-lilies, lay calm and gleaming amidst level pastures.

Involuntarily they arrested their steps, to gaze on the cheerful landscape and inhale the balmy air. Meanwhile the Mayor came out from the cottage porch, his wife leaning on his arm, and two of his younger children bounding on before, with joyous faces, giving chase to a gaudy butterfly which they had started from the woodbine.

Mrs. Hartopp had conceived a lively curiosity to see and judge for herself of the objects of her liege lord's benevolent interest. She shared, of course, the anxiety which formed the standing excitement of all those who lived but for one godlike purpose, that of preserving Josiah Hartopp from being taken in. But whenever the Mayor specially wished to secure his wife's countenance to any pet project of his own, and convince her either that he was not taken in, or that to be discreetly taken in is in this world a very popular and sure mode of getting up, he never failed to attain his end. That man was the cunningest creature! As full of wiles and stratagems in order to get his own way—in benevolent objects—as men who set up to be clever are for selfish ones. Mrs. Hartopp was certainly a good woman, but a made good woman. Married to another man, I suspect that she would have been a shrew. Petruchio would never have tamed her, I'll swear. But she, poor lady, had been gradually, but completely, subdued, subjugated, absolutely cowed beneath the weight of her spouse's despotic mildness; for in Hartopp there was a weight of soft quietude, of placid oppression, wholly irresistible. It would have buried a Titaness under a Pelion of moral feather-beds. Mass upon mass of downy influence descended upon you, seemingly yielding as it fell, enveloping, overbearing, stifling you; not presenting a single hard point of contact; giving in as you pushed against it; supplying itself seductively round you, softer and softer, heavier and heavier, —till, I assure you, ma'am, no matter how high your natural wifely spirit, you would have had it smothered out of you, your last rebellious murmur dying languidly away under the descending fleeces.

"So kind in you to come with me, Mary, " said Hartopp. "I could not have been happy without your approval: look at the child; something about her like Mary Anne, and Mary Anne is the picture of you! "

Waife advanced, uncovering; the two children, having lost trace of the butterfly, had run up towards Sophy. But her shy look made themselves shy, —shyness is so contagious, and they stood a little aloof, gazing at her. Sir Isaac stalked direct to the Mayor, sniffed at him, and wagged his tail.

Mrs. Hartopp now bent over Sophy, and acknowledging that the face was singularly pretty, glanced graciously towards the husband, and said, "I see the likeness! " then to Sophy, "I fear you are tired, my dear: you must not overfatigue yourself; and you must take milk fresh from the cow every morning. " And now the bailiff's wife came briskly out, a tidy, fresh-coloured, kind-faced woman, fond of children; the more so because she had none of her own.

So they entered the farm-yard, Mrs. Hartopp being the chief talker; and she, having pointed out to Sophy the cows and the turkeys, the hen-coops, and the great China gander, led her by the one hand— while Sophy's other hand clung firmly to Waife's'—across the little garden, with its patent bee-hives, into the house, took off her bonnet, and kissed her. "Very like Mary Anne! —Mary Anne, dear. " One of the two children owning that name approached, —snub-nosed, black-eyed, with cheeks like peonies. "This little girl, my Mary Anne, was as pale as you, —over-study; and now, my dear child, you must try and steal a little of her colour. Don't you think my Mary Anne is like her papa, Mr. Chapman? "

"Like me! " exclaimed the Mayor, whispering Waife, "image of her mother! the same intellectual look! "

Said the artful actor, "Indeed, ma'am, the young lady has her father's mouth and eyebrows, but that acute, sensible expression is yours, — quite yours. Sir Isaac, make a bow to the young lady, and then, sir, go through the sword exercise! "

The dog, put upon his tricks, delighted the children; and the poor actor, though his heart lay in his breast like lead, did his best to repay benevolence by mirth. Finally, much pleased, Mrs. Hartopp took her husband's arm to depart. The children, on being separated from Sir Isaac, began to cry. The Mayor interrupted his wife, —who, if left to herself, would have scolded them into worse crying, —told Mary Anne that he relied on her strong intellect to console her brother Tom; observed to Tom that it was not like his manly nature to set an example of weeping to his sister; and contrived thus to flatter their tears away in a trice, and sent them forward in a race to the turnstile.

Waife and Sophy were alone in the cottage parlour, Mrs. Gooch, the bailiff's wife, walking part of the way back with the good couple, in order to show the Mayor a heifer who had lost appetite and taken to moping. "Let us steal out into the back garden, my darling, " said Waife. "I see an arbour there, where I will compose myself with a pipe, —a liberty I should not like to take indoors. " They stepped across the threshold, and gained the arbour, which stood at the extreme end of the small kitchen-garden, and commanded a pleasant view of pastures and cornfields, backed by the blue outline of distant hills. Afar were faintly heard the laugh of the Mayor's happy children, now and then a tinkling sheep-bell, or the tap of the woodpecker, unrepressed by the hush of the. Midmost summer, which stills the more tuneful choristers amidst their coverts. Waife lighted his pipe, and smoked silently; Sophy, resting her head on his bosom, silent also. She was exquisitely sensitive to nature: the quiet beauty of all round her was soothing a spirit lately troubled, and health came stealing gently back through frame and through heart.

At length she said softly, "We could be so happy here, Grandfather! It cannot last, can it? "

"It is no use in this life, my dear, " returned Waife, philosophizing, "no use at all disturbing present happiness by asking, 'Can it last? ' To-day is man's, to-morrow his Maker's. But tell me frankly, do you really dislike so much the idea of exhibiting? I don't mean as we did in Mr. Rugge's show. I know you hate that; but in a genteel private way, as the other night. You sigh! Out with it. "

"I like what you like, Grandy. "

"That's not true. I like to smoke; you don't. Come, you do dislike acting? Why? you do it so well, —wonderfully. Generally speaking, people like what they do well. "

"It is not the acting itself, Grandy dear, that I don't like. When I am in some part, I am carried away; I am not myself. I am some one else!"

"And the applause? "

"I don't feel it. I dare say I should miss it if it did not come; but it does not seem to me as if I were applauded. If I felt that, I should stop short, and get frightened. It is as if that somebody else into whom I was changed was making friends with the audience; and all my feeling is for that somebody, —just as, Grandy dear, when it is over, and we two are alone together, all my feeling is for you, —at least (hanging her head) it used to be; but lately, somehow, I am ashamed to think how I have been feeling for myself more than for you. Is it—is it that I am growing selfish? as Mr. Mayor said. Oh, no! Now we are here, —not in those noisy towns, —not in the inns and on the highways; now here, here, I do feel again for you, —all for you! "

"You are my little angel, you are, " said Waife, tremulously. "Selfish! you! a good joke that! Now you see, I am not what is called Demonstrative, —a long word, Sophy, which means, that I don't show to you always how fond I am of you; and, indeed, " he added ingenuously, "I am not al ways aware of it myself. I like acting, —I like the applause, and the lights, and the excitement, and the illusion, —the make-belief of the whole thing: it takes me out of memory and thought; it is a world that has neither past, present, nor future, an interlude in time, -an escape from space. I suppose it is the same with poets when they are making verses. Yes, I like all this; and, when I think of it, I forget you too much. And I never observed, Heaven forgive me! that you were pale and drooping till it was pointed out to me. Well, take away your arms. Let us consult! As soon as you get quite, quite well, how shall we live? what shall we do? You are as wise as a little woman, and such a careful, prudent housekeeper; and I'm such a harumscarum old fellow, without a sound idea in my head. What shall we do if we give up acting altogether? "

"Give up acting altogether, when you like it so! No, no. I will like it too, Grandy. But—but—" she stopped short, afraid to imply blame or to give pain.

"But what? let us make clean breasts, one to the other; tell truth, and shame the Father of Lies. "

"Tell truth, " said Sophy, lifting up to him her pure eyes with such heavenly, loving kindness that, if the words did imply reproof, the eyes stole it away. "Could we but manage to tell truth off the stage, I should not dislike acting! Oh, Grandfather, when that kind gentleman and his lady and those merry children come up and speak to us, don't you feel ready to creep into the earth? —I do. Are we telling truth? are we living truth? one name to-day, another name to morrow? I should not mind acting on a stage or in a room, for the time, but always acting, always, —we ourselves 'make beliefs! ' Grandfather, must that be? They don't do it; I mean by they, all who are good and looked up to and respected, as—as—oh, Grandy! Grandy! what am I saying? I have pained you. "

Waife indeed was striving hard to keep down emotion; but his lips were set firmly and the blood had left them, and his hands were trembling.

"We must, hide ourselves, " he said in a very low voice; "we must take false names; I—because—because of reasons I can't tell even to you; and you, because I failed to get you a proper home, where you ought to be; and there is one who, if he pleases, and he may please it any day, could take you away from me, if he found you out; and so—and so—" He paused abruptly, looked at her fearful wondering soft face, and, rising, drew himself up with one of those rare outbreaks of dignity which elevated the whole character of his person. "But as for me, " said he, "if I have lost all name; if, while I live, I must be this wandering, skulking outcast, —look above, Sophy, —look up above: there all secrets will be known, all hearts read; and there my best hope to find a place in which I may wait your coming is in what has lost me all birthright here. Not to exalt myself do I say this, —no; but that you may have comfort, darling, if ever hereafter you are pained by what men say to you of me. "

As he spoke, the expression of his face, at first solemn and lofty, relaxed into melancholy submission. Then passing his arm into hers, and leaning on it as if sunk once more into the broken cripple needing her frail support, he drew her forth from the arbour, and paced the little garden slowly, painfully. At length he seemed to recover himself, and said in his ordinary cheerful tone, "But to the point in question, suppose we have done with acting and roaming, and keep to one name and settle somewhere like plain folks, again I ask, How shall we live? "

"I have been thinking of that, " answered Sophy. "You remember that those good Miss Burtons taught me all kinds of needlework, and I know people can make money by needlework. And then, Grandy dear, what can't you do? Do you forget Mrs. Saunders's books that you bound, and her cups and saucers that you mended? So we would both work, and have a little cottage and a garden, that we could take care of, and sell the herbs and vegetables. Oh, I have thought over it all, the last fortnight, a hundred hundred times, only I did not dare to speak first. "

Waife listened very attentively. "I can make very good baskets, " said he, rubbing his chin, "famous baskets (if one could hire a bit of osier ground), and, as you say, there might be other fancy articles I could turn out prettily enough, and you could work samplers, and urn-rugs, and doileys, and pincushions, and so forth; and what with a rood or two of garden ground, and poultry (the Mayor says poultry is healthy for children), upon my word, if we could find a safe place, and people would not trouble us with their gossip, and we could save a little money for you when I am—"

"Bees too, —honey? " interrupted Sophy, growing more and more interested and excited.

"Yes, bees, —certainly. A cottage of that kind in a village would not be above L6 a year, and L20 spent on materials for fancy-works would set us up. Ah but furniture, beds and tables, —monstrous dear! "

"Oh, no! very little would do at first. "

"Let us count the money we have left, " said Waife, throwing himself down on a piece of sward that encircled a shady mulberry-tree. Old man and child counted the money, bit by bit, gayly yet anxiously, — babbling, interrupting each other, —scheme upon scheme: they forgot past and present as much as in acting plays; they were absorbed in the future, —innocent simple future, —innocent as the future planned by two infants fresh from "Robinson Crusoe" or fairy tales.

"I remember, I remember, just the place for us, " cried Waife, suddenly. "It is many, many, many years since I was there; I was courting my Lizzy at the time, —alas! alas. But no sad thoughts now! —just the place, near a large town, but in a pretty village quite retired from it. 'T was there I learned to make baskets. I had broken my leg; fall from a horse; nothing to do. I lodged with an old basketmaker; he had a capital trade. Rivulet at the back of his house; reeds, osiers, plentiful. I see them now, as I saw them from my little casement while my leg was setting. And Lizzy used to write to me such dear letters; my baskets were all for her. We had baskets enough to have furnished a house with bask'ts; could have dined in baskets, sat in baskets, slept in baskets. With a few lessons I could soon recover the knack of the work. I should like to see the place again; it would be shaking hands with my youth once more. None who could possibly recognize me could be now living. Saw no one but the surgeon, the basketmaker, and his wife; all so old they must be long since gathered to their fathers. Perhaps no one carries on the basket trade now. I may revive it and have it all to myself; perhaps the cottage itself may be easily hired. " Thus, ever disposed to be sanguine, the vagabond chattered on, Sophy listening fondly, and smiling up in his face. "And a fine large park close by: the owners, great lords, deserted it then; perhaps it is deserted still. You might wander over it as if it were your own, Sophy. Such wonderful trees, —such green solitudes; and pretty shy hares running across the vistas, —stately deer too! We will make friends with the lodge-keepers, and we will call the park yours, Sophy; and I shall be a genius who weaves magical baskets, and you shall be the enchanted princess concealed from all evil eyes, knitting doileys of pearl under leaves of emerald, and catching no sound from the world of perishable life, except as the boughs whisper and the birds sing. "

"Dear me, here you are; we thought you were lost, " said the bailiff's wife; "tea is waiting for you, and there's husband, sir, coming up from his work; he'll be proud and glad to know you, sir, and you too, my dear; we have no children of our own. "

It is past eleven. Sophy, worn out, but with emotions far more pleasurable than she has long known, is fast asleep. Waife kneels by her side, looking at her. He touches her hand, so cool and soft; all fever gone: he rises on tiptoe; he bends over her forehead, —a kiss there, and a tear; he steals away, down, down the stairs. At the porch is the bailiff holding Sir Isaac.

"We'll take all care of her, " said Mr. Gooch. "You'll not know her again when you come back. "

Waife pressed the hand of his grandchild's host, but did not speak.

"You are sure you will find your way, —no, that's the wrong turn, — straight onto the town. They'll be sitting up for you at the Saracen's Head, I suppose, of course, sir? It seems not hospitable like, your going away at the dead of night thus. But I understand you don't like crying, sir, we men don't; and your sweet little girl I dare say would sob ready to break her heart if she knew. Fine moonlight night, sir, —straight on. And I say, don't fret about her: wife loves children dearly, —so do I. Good-night. "

On went Waife, —lamely, slowly, —Sir Isaac's white coat gleaming in the moon, ghostlike. On he went, his bundle strapped across his shoulder, leaning on his staff, along by the folded sheep and the sleeping cattle. But when he got into the high road, Gatesboro' full before him, with all its roofs and spires, he turned his back on the town, and tramped once more along the desert thoroughfare, —more slowly and more, more lamely and more, till several milestones were passed; and then he crept through the gap of a hedgerow to the sheltering eaves of a haystack; and under that roof-tree he and Sir Isaac lay down to rest.

CHAPTER XXIV.

Laugh at forebodings of evil, but tremble after day-dreams of happiness.

Waife left behind him at the cottage two letters, —one entrusted to the bailiff, with a sealed bag, for Mr. Hartopp; one for Sophy, placed on a chair beside her bed.

The first letter was as follows: —

"I trust, dear and honoured sir, that I shall come back safely; and when I do, I may have found perhaps a home for her, and some way of life such as you would not blame. But, in case of accident, I have left with Mr. Gooch, sealed up, the money we made at Gatesboro', after paying the inn bill, doctor, etc., and retaining the mere trifle I need in case I and Sir Isaac fail to support ourselves. You will kindly take care of it. I should not feel safe with more money about me, an old man.

"I might be robbed; besides, I am careless. I never can keep money; it slips out of my hands like an eel. Heaven bless you, sir; your kindness seems like a miracle vouchsafed to me for that child's dear sake. No evil can chance to her with you; and if I should fall ill and die, even then you, who would have aided the tricksome vagrant, will not grudge the saving hand to the harmless child. "

The letter to Sophy ran thus: —

"Darling, forgive me; I have stolen away from you, but only for a few days, and only in order to see if we cannot gain the magic home where I am to be the Genius, and you the Princess. I go forth with such a light heart, Sophy dear, I shall be walking thirty miles a day, and not feel an ache in the lame leg: you could not keep up with me; you know you could not. So think over the cottage and the basket-work, and practise at samplers and pincushions, when it is too hot to play; and be stout and strong against I come back. That, I trust, will be this day week, —-'t is but seven days; and then we will only act fairy dramas to nodding trees, with linnets for the orchestra; and even Sir Isaac shall not be demeaned by mercenary tricks, but shall employ his arithmetical talents in casting up the weekly bills, and he shall never stand on his hind legs except on sunny days, when he shall carry a parasol to shade an enchanted princess. Laugh; darling, —let me fancy I see you laughing; but don't fret, —don't fancy I desert you. Do try and get well, —quite, quite well; I ask it of you on my knees. "

The letter and the bag were taken over at sunrise to Mr. Hartopp's villa. Mr. Hartopp was an early man. Sophy overslept herself: her room was to the west; the morning beams did not reach its windows; and the cottage without children woke up to labour noiseless and still. So when at last she shook off sleep, and tossing her hair from her blue eyes, looked round and became conscious of the strange place, she still fancied the hour early. But she got up, drew the curtain from the window, saw the sun high in the heavens, and, ashamed of her laziness, turned, and lo! the letter on the chair! Her heart at once misgave her; the truth flashed upon a reason prematurely quick in the intuition which belongs to the union of sensitive affection and active thought. She drew a long breath, and turned deadly pale. It was some minutes before she could take up the letter, before she could break the seal. When she did, she read on noiselessly, her tears dropping over the page, without effort or sob. She had no egotistical sorrow, no grief in being left alone with strangers: it was the pathos of the old man's lonely wanderings, of his bereavement, of his counterfeit glee, and genuine self-sacrifice; this it was that suffused her whole heart with unutterable yearnings of tenderness, gratitude, pity, veneration. But when she had wept silently for some time, she kissed the letter with devout passion, and turned to that Heaven to which the outcast had taught her first to pray.

Afterwards she stood still, musing a little while, and the sorrowful shade gradually left her face. Yes; she would obey him: she would not fret; she would try and get well and strong. He would feel, at the distance, that she was true to his wishes; that she was fitting herself to be again his companion: seven days would soon pass. Hope, that can never long quit the heart of childhood, brightened over her meditations, as the morning sun over a landscape that just before had lain sad amidst twilight and under rains.

When she came downstairs, Mrs. Gooch was pleased and surprised to observe the placid smile upon her face, and the quiet activity with which, after the morning meal, she moved about by the good woman's side assisting her in her dairywork and other housewife tasks, talking little, comprehending quickly, —composed, cheerful.

"I am so glad to see you don't pine after your good grandpapa, as we feared you would. "

"He told me not to pine, " answered Sophy, simply, but with a quivering lip.

When the noon deepened, and it became too warm for exercise, Sophy timidly asked if Mrs. Gooch had any worsted and knitting-needles, and being accommodated with those implements and materials, she withdrew to the arbour, and seated herself to work, — solitary and tranquil.

What made, perhaps, the chief strength in this poor child's nature was its intense trustfulness, —a part, perhaps, of its instinctive appreciation of truth. She trusted in Waife, in the future, in Providence, in her own childish, not helpless, self.

Already, as her slight fingers sorted the worsteds and her graceful taste shaded their hues into blended harmony, her mind was weaving, not less harmoniously, the hues in the woof of dreams, — the cottage home, the harmless tasks, Waife with his pipe in the armchair under some porch, covered like that one yonder, —why not? —with fragrant woodbine, and life if humble, honest, truthful, not shrinking from the day, so that if Lionel met her again she should not blush, nor he be shocked. And if their ways were so different as her grandfather said, still they might cross, as they had crossed before, and—the work slid from her hand—the sweet lips parted, smiling: a picture came before her eyes, —her grandfather, Lionel, herself; all three, friends, and happy; a stream, fair as the Thames had seemed; green trees all bathed in summer; the boat gliding by; in that boat they three, borne softly on, —away, away, — what matters whither? —by her side the old man; facing her, the boy's bright kind eyes. She started. She heard noises, —a swing ing gate, footsteps. She started, —she rose, —voices; one strange to her, —a man's voice, —then the Mayor's. A third voice, —shrill, stern; a terrible voice, -heard in infancy, associated with images of cruelty, misery, woe. It could not be! impossible! Near, nearer, came the footsteps. Seized with the impulse of flight, she sprang to the mouth of the arbour. Fronting her glared two dark, baleful eyes. She stood, —arrested, spellbound, as a bird fixed rigid by the gaze of a serpent.

"Yes, Mr. Mayor; all right! it is our little girl, —our dear Sophy. This way, Mr. Losely. Such a pleasant surprise for you, Sophy, my love! " said Mrs. Crane.

BOOK IV.

CHAPTER I.

In the kindliest natures there is a certain sensitiveness, which, when wounded, occasions the same pain, and bequeaths the same resentment, as mortified vanity or galled self-love.

It is exactly that day week, towards the hour of five in the evening, Mr. Hartopp, alone in the parlour behind his warehouse, is locking up his books and ledgers preparatory to the return to his villa. There is a certain change in the expression of his countenance since we saw it last. If it be possible for Mr. Hartopp to look sullen, —sullen he looks; if it be possible for the Mayor of Gatesboro' to be crestfallen, crestfallen he is. That smooth existence has surely received some fatal concussion, and has not yet recovered the shock. But if you will glance beyond the parlour at Mr. Williams giving orders in the warehouse, at the warehousemen themselves, at the rough faces in the tan-yard, -nay, at Mike Callaghan, who has just brought a parcel from the railway, all of them have evidently shared in the effects of the concussion; all of them wear a look more or less sullen; all seem crestfallen. Could you carry your gaze farther on, could you peep into the shops in the High Street, or at the loungers in the city reading-room; could you extend the vision farther still, —to Mr. Hartopp's villa, behold his wife, his little ones, his men-servants, and his maid-servants, more and more impressively general would become the tokens of disturbance occasioned by that infamous concussion. Everywhere a sullen look, —everywhere that ineffable aspect of crestfallenness! What can have happened? is the good man bankrupt? No, rich as ever! What can it be? Reader! that fatal event which they who love Josiah Hartopp are ever at watch to prevent, despite all their vigilance, has occurred! Josiah Hartopp has been TAKEN IN! Other men may be occasionally taken in, and no one mourns; perhaps they deserve it! they are not especially benevolent, or they set up to be specially wise. But to take in that lamb! And it was not only the Mayor's heart that was wounded, but his pride, his self-esteem, his sense of dignity, were terribly humiliated. For as we know, though all the world considered Mr. Hartopp the very man born to be taken in, and therefore combined to protect him, yet in his secret soul Mr. Hartopp considered that no man less needed such protection; that he was never taken in, unless he meant to be so. Thus the cruelty and ingratitude of the base action under which his crest was so fallen jarred on his whole system. Nay, more, he could not but feel that the event would long affect his personal comfort and independence; he would be more than ever under the affectionate tyranny of Mr. Williams, more than ever be an object of universal surveillance and espionage. There would be one thought paramount throughout Gatesboro'. "The Mayor, God bless him! has been taken in: this must not occur again, or Gatesboro' is dishonoured, and Virtue indeed a name! " Mr. Hartopp felt not only mortified but subjugated, —he who had hitherto been the soft subjugator of the hardest. He felt not only subjugated, but indignant at the consciousness of being so. He was too meekly convinced of Heaven's unerring justice not to feel assured that the man who had taken him in would come to a tragic end. He would not have hung that man with his own hands: he was too mild for vengeance. But if he had seen that man hanging he would have said piously, "Fitting retribution, " and passed on his way soothed and comforted. Taken in! —taken in at last! —he, Josiah Hartopp, taken in by a fellow with one eye!

CHAPTER II.

The Mayor is so protected that he cannot help himself.

A commotion without, —a kind of howl, a kind of hoot. Mr. Williams, the warehousemen, the tanners, Mike Callaghan, share between them the howl and the hoot. The Mayor started: is it possible! His door is burst open, and, scattering all who sought to hold him back, —scattering them to the right and left from his massive torso in rushed the man who had taken in the Mayor, —the fellow with one eye, and with that fellow, shaggy and travel-soiled, the other dog!

"What have you done with the charge I intrusted to you? My child! my child! where is she? "

Waife's face was wild with the agony of his emotions, and his voice was so sharply terrible that it went like a knife into the heart of the men, who, thrust aside for the moment, now followed him, fearful, into the room.

"Mr. —Mr. Chapman, sir, " faltered the Mayor, striving hard to recover dignity and self-possession, "I am astonished at your— your—"

"Audacity! " interposed Mr. Williams.

"My child! my Sophy! my child! answer me, man! " "Sir, " said the Mayor, drawing himself up, "have you not got the note which I left at my bailiff's cottage in case you called there? "

"Your note! this thing! " said Waife, striking a crumpled paper with his hand, and running his eye over its contents. "You have rendered up, you say, the child to her lawful protector? Gracious heavens! did I trust her to you, or not? "

"Leave the room all of you, " said the Mayor, with a sudden return of his usual calm vigour.

"You go, —you, sirs; what the deuce do you do here? " growled Williams to the meaner throng. "Out! I stay, never fear, men, I'll take care of him! "

The bystanders surlily slunk off: but none returned to their work; they stood within reach of call by the shut door. Williams tucked up his coat-sleeves, clenched his fists, hung his head doggedly on one side, and looked altogether so pugnacious and minatory that Sir Isaac, who, though in a state of great excitement, had hitherto retained self-control, peered at him under his curls, stiffened his back, showed his teeth, and growled formidably.

"My good Williams, leave us, " said the Mayor; "I would be alone with this person. "

"Alone, —you! out of the question. Now you have been once taken in, and you own it, —it is my duty to protect you henceforth; and I will to the end of my days. "

The Mayor sighed heavily. "Well, Williams, well! —take a chair, and be quiet. Now, Mr. Chapman, so to call you still; you have deceived me. "

"I? how? "

The Mayor was puzzled. "Deceived me, " he said at last, "in my knowledge of human nature. I thought you an honest man, sir. And you are—but no matter. "

WAIFE (impatiently). —"My child! my child! you have given her up to—to—"

MAYOR. —"Her own father, sir. "

WAIFE (echoing the words as he staggers back). —"I thought so! I thought it! "

MAYOR. —"In so doing I obeyed the law: he had legal power to enforce his demand. " The Mayor's voice was almost apologetic in its tone; for he was affected by Waife's anguish, and not able to silence a pang of remorse. After all, he had been trusted; and he had, excusably perhaps, necessarily perhaps, but still he had failed to fulfil the trust. "But, " added the Mayor, as if reassuring himself, "but I refused at first to give her up even to her own father; at first insisted upon waiting till your return; and it was only when I was informed what you yourself were that my scruples gave Way. "

Waife remained long silent, breathing very hard, passing his hand several times over his forehead; at last he said more quietly than he had yet spoken, "Will you tell me where they have gone? "

"I do not know; and, if I did know, I would not tell you! Are they not right when they say that that innocent child should not be tempted away by—by—a—in short by you, sir? "

"They said! Her father—said that! —he said that! —Did he—did he say it? Had he the heart? "

MAYOR. —"No, I don't think he said it. Eh, Mr. Williams? He spoke little to me! "

MR. WILLIAMS. —"Of course he would not expose that person. But the woman, —the lady, I mean. "

WAIFE. —"Woman! Ah, yes. The bailiff's wife said there was a woman. What woman? What's her name? "

MAYOR. —"Really you must excuse me. I can say no more. I have consented to see you thus, because whatever you might have been, or may be, still it was due to myself to explain how I came to give up the child; and, besides, you left money with me, and that, at least, I can give to your own hand. "

The Mayor turned to his desk, unlocked it, and drew forth the bag which Waife had sent to him.

As he extended it towards the Comedian, his hand trembled, and his cheek flushed. For Waife's one bright eye had in it such depth of reproach, that again the Mayor's conscience was sorely troubled; and he would have given ten times the contents of that bag to have been alone with the vagrant, and to have said the soothing things he did not dare to say before Williams, who sat there mute and grim, guarding him from being once more "taken in. " "If you had confided in me at first, Mr. Chapman, " he said, pathetically, "or even if now, I could aid you in an honest way of life! "

"Aid him—now! " said Williams, with a snort. "At it again! you're not a man: you're an angel! "

"But if he is penitent, Williams. "

"So! so! so! " murmured Waife. "Thank Heaven it was not he who spoke against me: it was but a strange woman. Oh! " he suddenly broke off with a groan. "Oh—but that strange woman, —who, what can she be? and Sophy with her and him. Distraction! Yes, yes, I take the money. I shall want it all. Sir Isaac, pick up that bag. Gentlemen, good day to you! " He bowed; such a failure that bow! Nothing ducal in it! bowed and turned towards the door; then, when he gained the threshold, as if some meeker, holier thought restored to him dignity of bearing, his form rose, though his face softened, and stretching his right hand towards the Mayor, he said, "You did but as all perhaps would have done on the evidence before you. You meant to be kind to her. "

"If you knew all, how you would repent! I do not blame, —I forgive you. "

He was gone: the Mayor stood transfixed. Even Williams felt a cold comfortless thrill. "He does not look like it, " said the foreman. "Cheer up, sir, no wonder you were taken in: who would not have been? "

"Hark! that hoot again. Go, Williams, don't let the men insult him. Go, do, —I shall be grateful. "

But before Williams got to the door, the cripple and his dog had vanished; vanished down a dark narrow alley on the opposite side of the street. The rude workmen had followed him to the mouth of the alley, mocking him. Of the exact charge against the Comedian's good name they were not informed; that knowledge was confined to the Mayor and Mr. Williams. But the latter had dropped such harsh expressions, that bad as the charge might really be, all in Mr. Hartopp's employment probably deemed it worse, if possible, than it really was. And wretch indeed must be the man by whom the Mayor had been confessedly taken in, and whom the Mayor had indignantly given up to the reproaches of his own conscience. But the cripple was now out of sight, lost amidst those labyrinths of squalid homes which, in great towns, are thrust beyond view, branching off abruptly behind High Streets and Market Places, so that strangers passing only along the broad thoroughfares, with glittering shops and gaslit causeways, exclaim, "Ah here do the poor live? "

CHAPTER III.

Ecce iterum Crispinus!

It was by no calculation, but by involuntary impulse, that Waife, thus escaping from the harsh looks and taunting murmurs of the gossips round the Mayor's door, dived into those sordid devious lanes. Vaguely he felt that a ban was upon him; that the covering he had thrown over his brand of outcast was lifted up; that a sentence of expulsion from the High Streets and Market Places of decorous life was passed against him. He had been robbed of his child, and Society, speaking in the voice of the Mayor of Gatesboro', said, "Rightly! thou art not fit companion for the innocent! "

At length he found himself out of the town, beyond its straggling suburbs, and once more on the solitary road. He had already walked far that day. He was thoroughly exhausted. He sat himself down in a dry ditch by the hedgerow, and taking his head between his hands, strove to recollect his thoughts and rearrange his plans.

Waife had returned that day to the bailiff's cottage joyous and elated. He had spent the week in travelling; partly, though not all the way, on foot, to the distant village, in which he had learned in youth the basketmaker's art! He had found the very cottage wherein he had then lodged vacant and to be let. There seemed a ready opening for the humble but pleasant craft to which he had diverted his ambition.

The bailiff intrusted with the letting of the cottage and osier-ground had, it is true, requested some reference; not, of course, as to all a tenant's antecedents, but as to the reasonable probability that the tenant would be a quiet sober man, who would pay his rent and abstain from poaching. Waife thought he might safely presume that the Mayor of Gatesboro' would not, so far as that went, object to take his past upon trust, and give him a good word towards securing so harmless and obscure a future. Waife had never before asked such a favour of any man; he shrank from doing so now; but for his grandchild's sake, he would waive his scruples or humble his pride.

Thus, then, he had come back, full of Elysian dreams, to his Sophy, —his Enchanted Princess. Gone, taken away, and with the Mayor's consent, —the consent of the very man upon whom he had been relying to secure a livelihood and a shelter! Little more had he learned at the cottage, for Mr. and Mrs. Gooch had been cautioned to be as brief as possible, and give him no clew to regain his lost treasure, beyond the note which informed him it was with a lawful possessor. And, indeed, the worthy pair were now prejudiced against the vagrant, and were rude to him. But he had not tarried to cross-examine and inquire. He had rushed at once to the Mayor. Sophy was with one whose legal right to dispose of her he could not question. But where that person would take her, where he resided, what he would do with her, he had no means to conjecture. Most probably (he thought and guessed) she would be carried abroad, was already out of the country. But the woman with Losely, he had not heard her described; his guesses did not turn towards Mrs. Crane: the woman was evidently hostile to him; it was the woman who had spoken against him, —not Losely; the woman whose tongue had poisoned Hartopp's mind, and turned into scorn all that admiring respect which had before greeted the great Comedian. Why was that woman his enemy? Who could she be? What had she to do with Sophy? He was half beside himself with terror. It was to save her less even from Losely than from such direful women as Losely made his confidants and associates that Waife had taken Sophy to himself. As for Mrs. Crane, she had never seemed a foe to him; she had ceded the child to him willingly: he had no reason to believe, from the way in which she had spoken of Losely when he last saw her, that she could henceforth aid the interests or share the schemes of the man whose perfidies she then denounced; and as to Rugge, he had not appeared at Gatesboro'. Mrs. Crane had prudently suggested that his presence would not be propitiatory or discreet, and that all reference to him, or to the contract with him, should be suppressed. Thus Waife was wholly without one guiding evidence, one groundwork for conjecture, that might enable him to track the lost; all he knew was, that she had been given up to a man whose whereabouts it was difficult to discover, —a vagrant, of life darker and more hidden than his own.

But how had the hunters discovered the place where he had treasured up his Sophy? how dogged that retreat? Perhaps from the village in which we first saw him. Ay, doubtless, learned from Mrs. Saunders of the dog he had purchased, and the dog would have served to direct them on his path. At that thought he pushed away Sir Isaac, who had been resting his head on the old man's knee, — pushed him away angrily; the poor dog slunk off in sorrowful surprise, and whined.

"Ungrateful wretch that I am! " cried Waife, and he opened his arms to the brute, who bounded forgivingly to his breast.

"Come, come, we will go back to the village in Surrey. Tramp, tramp! " said the cripple, rousing himself. And at that moment, just as he gained his feet, a friendly hand was laid on his shoulder, and a friendly voice said,

"I have found you! the crystal said so! Marbellous! "

"Merle, " faltered out the vagrant, "Merle, you here! Oh, perhaps you come to tell me good news: you have seen Sophy; you know where she is! "

The Cobbler shook his head. "Can't see her just at present. Crystal says nout about her. But I know she was taken from you—and—and—you shake tremenjous! Lean on me, Mr. Waite, and call off that big animal. He's a suspicating my calves and circumtittyvating them. Thank ye, sir. You see I was born with sinister aspects in my Twelfth House, which appertains to big animals and enemies; and dogs of that size about one's calves are—malefics! "

As Merle now slowly led the cripple, and Sir Isaac, relinquishing his first suspicions, walked droopingly beside them, the Cobbler began a long story, much encumbered by astrological illustrations and moralizing comments. The substance of his narrative is thus epitomized: Rugge, in pursuing Waife's track, had naturally called on Merle in company with Losely and Mrs. Crane. The Cobbler had no clew to give, and no mind to give it if clew he had possessed. But his curiosity being roused, he had smothered the inclination to dismiss the inquirers with more speed than good breeding, and even refreshed his slight acquaintance with Mr. Rugge in so well simulated a courtesy that that gentleman, when left behind by Losely and Mrs. Crane in their journey to Gatesboro', condescended, for want of other company, to drink tea with Mr. Merle; and tea being succeeded by stronger potations, he fairly unbosomed himself of his hopes of recovering Sophy and his ambition of hiring the York theatre.

The day afterwards Rugge went away seemingly in high spirits, and the Cobbler had no doubt, from some words he let fall in passing Merle's stall towards the railway, that Sophy was recaptured, and that Rugge was summoned to take possession of her. Ascertaining from the manager that Losely and Mrs. Crane had gone to Gatesboro', the Cobbler called to mind that he had a sister living there, married to a green-grocer in a very small way, whom he had not seen for many years; and finding his business slack just then, he resolved to pay this relative a, visit, with the benevolent intention of looking up Waife, whom he expected from Rugge's account to find there, and offering him any consolation or aid in his power, should Sophy have been taken from him against his will. A consultation with his crystal, which showed him the face of Mr. Waife alone and much dejected, and a horary scheme which promised success to his journey, decided his movements. He had arrived at Gatesboro' the day before, had heard a confused story about a Mr. Chapman, with his dog and his child, whom the Mayor had first taken up, but who afterwards, in some mysterious manner, had taken in the Mayor. Happily, the darker gossip in the High Street had not penetrated the back lane in which Merle's sister resided. There, little more was known than the fact that this mysterious stranger had imposed on the wisdom of Gatesboro's learned Institute and enlightened Mayor. Merle, at no loss to identify Waife with Chapman, could only suppose that he had been discovered to be a strolling player in Rugge's exhibition, after pretending to be some much greater man. Such an offence the Cobbler was not disposed to consider heinous. But Mr. Chapman was gone from Gatesboro' none knew whither; and Merle had not yet ventured to call himself on the chief magistrate of the place, to inquire after a man by whom that august personage had been deceived. "Howsomever, " quoth Merle, in conclusion, "I was just standing at my sister's door, with her last babby in my arms, in Scrob Lane, when I saw you pass by like a shot. You were gone while I ran in to give up the babby, who is teething, with malefics in square, —gone, clean out of sight. You took one turn; I took another: but you see we meet at last, as good men always do in this world or the other, which is the same thing in the long run."

Waife, who had listened to his friend without other interruption than an occasional nod of the head or interjectional expletive, was now restored to much of his constitutional mood of sanguine cheerfulness. He recognized Mrs. Crane in the woman described; and, if surprised, he was rejoiced. For, much as he disliked that gentlewoman, he thought Sophy might be in worse female hands. Without much need of sagacity, he divined the gist of the truth. Losely had somehow or other become acquainted with Rugge, and sold Sophy to the manager. Where Rugge was, there would Sophy be. It could not be very difficult to find out the place in which Rugge was now exhibiting; and then—ah then! Waife whistled to Sir Isaac, tapped his forehead, and smiled triumphantly. Meanwhile the Cobbler had led him back into the suburb, with the kind intention of offering him food and bed for the night at his sister's house. But Waife had already formed his plan; in London, and in London alone, could he be sure to learn where Rugge was now exhibiting; in London there were places at which that information could be gleaned at once. The last train to the metropolis was not gone. He would slink round the town to the station: he and Sir Isaac at that hour might secure places unnoticed.

When Merle found it was in vain to press him to stay over the night, the good-hearted Cobbler accompanied him to the train, and, while Waife shrank into a dark corner, bought the tickets for dog and master. As he was paying for these, he overheard two citizens talking of Mr. Chapman. It was indeed Mr. Williams explaining to a fellow-burgess just returned to Gatesboro', after a week's absence, how and by what manner of man Mr. Hartopp had been taken in. At what Williams said, the Cobbler's cheek paled. When he joined the Comedian his manner was greatly altered; he gave the tickets without speaking, but looked hard into Waife's face, as the latter repaid him the fares. "No, " said the Cobbler, suddenly, "I don't believe it. "

"Believe what? " asked Waife, startled. "That you are—"

The Cobbler paused, bent forward, whispered the rest of the sentence close in the vagrant's ear. Waife's head fell on his bosom, but he made no answer.

"Speak, " cried Merle; "say 't is a lie. " The poor cripple's lip writhed, but he still spoke not.

Merle looked aghast at that obstinate silence. At length, but very slowly, as the warning bell summoned him and Sir Isaac to their several places in the train, Waife found voice. "So you too, you too desert and despise me! God's will be done! " He moved away, — spiritless, limping, hiding his face as well as he could. The porter took the dog from him, to thrust it into one of the boxes reserved for such four-footed passengers.

Waife thus parted from his last friend — I mean the dog — looked after Sir Isaac wistfully, and crept into a third-class carriage, in which luckily there was no one else. Suddenly Merle jumped in, snatched his hand, and pressed it tightly.

"I don't despise, I don't turn my back on you: whenever you and the little one want a home and a friend, come to Kit Merle as before, and I'll bite my tongue out if I ask any more questions of you; I'll ask the stars instead. "

The Cobbler had but just time to splutter out these comforting words and redescend the carriage, when the train put itself into movement, and the lifelike iron miracle, fuming, hissing, and screeching, bore off to London its motley convoy of human beings, each passenger's heart a mystery to the other, all bound the same road, all wedged close within the same whirling mechanism; what a separate and distinct world in each! Such is Civilization! How like we are one to the other in the mass! how strangely dissimilar in the abstract!

CHAPTER IV.

"If, " says a great thinker (Degerando, *"Du Perfectionment Moral, "* chapter ix., "On the Difficulties we encounter in Self-Study")—"if one concentrates reflection too much on one's self, one ends by no longer seeing anything, or seeing only what one wishes. By the very act, as it were, of capturing one's self, the personage we believe we have seized escapes, disappears. Nor is it only the complexity of our inner being which obstructs our examination, but its exceeding variability. The investigator's regard should embrace all the sides of the subject, and perseveringly pursue all its phases. "

It is the race-week in Humberston, a county town far from Gatesboro', and in the north of England. The races last three days: the first day is over; it has been a brilliant spectacle; the course crowded with the carriages of provincial magnates, with equestrian betters of note from the metropolis; blacklegs in great muster; there have been gaming-booths on the ground, and gypsies telling fortunes; much champagne imbibed by the well-bred, much soda-water and brandy by the vulgar. Thousands and tens of thousands have been lost and won: some paupers have been for the time enriched; some rich men made poor for life. Horses have won fame; some of their owners lost character. Din and uproar, and coarse oaths, and rude passions, —all have had their hour. The amateurs of the higher classes have gone back to dignified country-houses, as courteous hosts or favoured guests. The professional speculators of a lower grade have poured back into the county town, and inns and taverns are crowded. Drink is hotly called for at reeking bars; waiters and chambermaids pass to and fro, with dishes and tankards and bottles in their hands. All is noise and bustle, and eating and swilling, and disputation and slang, wild glee, and wilder despair, amongst those who come back from the race-course to the inns in the county town. At one of these taverns, neither the best nor the worst, and in a small narrow slice of a room that seemed robbed from the landing-place, sat Mrs. Crane, in her iron-gray silk gown. She was seated close by the open window, as carriages, chaises, flies, carts, vans, and horsemen succeeded each other thick and fast, watching the scene with a soured, scornful look. For human joy, as for human grief, she had little sympathy. Life had no Saturnalian holidays left for her. Some memory in her past had poisoned the well-springs of her social being. Hopes and objects she had still, but out of the wrecks of the natural and healthful existence of womanhood, those objects and hopes stood forth exaggerated, intense, as are the ruling passions in monomania. A bad woman is popularly said to be worse than a wicked man. If so, partly because women, being more solitary, brood more unceasingly over cherished ideas, whether good or evil; partly also, for the same reason that makes a wicked gentleman, who has lost caste and character, more irreclaimable than a wicked clown, low-born and lowbred, namely, that in proportion to the loss of shame is the gain in recklessness: but principally, perhaps, because in extreme wickedness there is necessarily a distortion of the reasoning faculty; and man, accustomed from the cradle rather to reason than to feel, has that faculty more firm against abrupt twists and lesions than it is in woman; where virtue may have left him, logic may still linger; and he may decline to push evil to a point at which it is clear to his understanding that profit vanishes and punishment rests; while woman, once abandoned to ill, finds sufficient charm in its mere excitement, and, regardless of consequences, where the man asks, "Can I? " raves out, "I will! " Thus man may be criminal through cupidity, vanity, love, jealousy, fear, ambition; rarely in civilized, that is, reasoning life, through hate and revenge; for hate is a profitless investment, and revenge a ruinous speculation. But when women are thoroughly depraved and hardened, nine times out of ten it is hatred or revenge that makes them so. Arabella Crane had not, however, attained to that last state of wickedness, which, consistent in evil, is callous to remorse; she was not yet unsexed. In her nature was still that essence, "varying and mutable, " which distinguishes woman while womanhood is left to her. And now, as she sat gazing on the throng below, her haggard mind recoiled perhaps from the conscious shadow of the Evil Principle which, invoked as an ally, remains as a destroyer. Her dark front relaxed; she moved in her seat uneasily. "Must it be always thus? " she muttered, —"always this hell here! Even now, if in one large pardon I could include the undoer, the earth, myself, and again be human, —human, even as those slight triflers or coarse brawlers that pass yonder! Oh, for something in common with common life! "

Her lips closed, and her eyes again fell upon the crowded street. At that moment three or four heavy vans or wagons filled with operatives or labourers and their wives, coming back from the race-course, obstructed the way; two outriders in satin jackets were expostulating, cracking their whips, and seeking to clear space for an open carriage with four thoroughbred impatient horses. Towards that carriage every gazer from the windows was directing eager eyes; each foot-passenger on the pavement lifted his hat: evidently in that carriage some great person! Like all who are at war with the world as it is, Arabella Crane abhorred the great, and despised the small for worshipping the great. But still her own fierce dark eyes mechanically followed those of the vulgar. The carriage bore a marquess's coronet on its panels, and was filled with ladies; two other carriages bearing a similar coronet, and evidently belonging to the same party, were in the rear. Mrs. Crane started. In that first carriage, as it now slowly moved under her very window, and paused a minute or more till the obstructing vehicles in front were marshalled into order, there flashed upon her eyes a face radiant with female beauty in its most glorious prime. Amongst the crowd at that moment was a blind man, adding to the various discords of the street by a miserable hurdy-gurdy. In the movement of the throng to get nearer to a sight of the ladies in the carriage, this poor creature was thrown forward; the dog that led him, an ugly brute, on his own account or his master's took fright, broke from the string, and ran under the horses' hoofs, snarling. The horses became restive; the blind man made a plunge after his dog, and was all but run over. The lady in the first carriage, alarmed for his safety, rose up from her seat, and made her outriders dismount, lead away the poor blind man, and restore to him his dog. Thus engaged, her face shone full upon Arabella Crane; and with that face rushed a tide of earlier memories. Long, very long, since she had seen that face, —seen it in those years when she herself, Arabella Crane, was young and handsome.

The poor man, —who seemed not to realize the idea of the danger he had escaped, —once more safe, the lady resumed her seat; and now that the momentary animation of humane fear and womanly compassion passed from her countenance, its expression altered; it took the calm, almost the coldness, of a Greek statue. But with the calm there was a listless melancholy which Greek sculpture never gives to the Parian stone: stone cannot convey that melancholy; it is the shadow which needs for its substance a living, mortal heart.

Crack went the whips: the horses bounded on; the equipage rolled fast down the street, followed by its satellites. "Well! " said a voice in the street below, "I never saw Lady Montfort in such beauty. Ah, here comes my lord! "

Mrs. Crane heard and looked forth again. A dozen or more gentlemen on horseback rode slowly up the street; which of these was Lord Montfort? —not difficult to distinguish. As the bystanders lifted their hats to the cavalcade, the horsemen generally returned their salutation by simply touching their own: one horseman uncovered wholly. That one must be the Marquess, the greatest man in those parts, with lands stretching away on either side that town for miles and miles, —a territory which in feudal times might have alarmed a king. He, the civilest, must be the greatest. A man still young, decidedly good-looking, wonderfully well-dressed, wonderfully well-mounted, the careless ease of high rank in his air and gesture. To the superficial gaze, just what the great Lord of Montfort should be. Look again! In that fair face is there not something that puts you in mind of a florid period which contains a feeble platitude? —something in its very prettiness that betrays a weak nature and a sterile mind?

The cavalcade passed away; the vans and the wagons again usurped the thoroughfare. Arabella Crane left the window, and approached the little looking-glass over the mantelpiece. She gazed upon her own face bitterly; she was comparing it with the features of the dazzling marchioness.

The door was flung open, and Jasper Losely sauntered in, whistling a French air, and flapping the dust from his boots with his kid glove.

"All right, " said he, gayly. "A famous day of it! "

"You have won, " said Mrs. Crane, in a tone rather of disappointment than congratulation.

"Yes. That L100 of Rugge's has been the making of me. "

"I only wanted a capital just to start with! " He flung himself into a chair, opened his pocket-book, and scrutinized its contents. "Guess, " said he, suddenly, "on whose horse I won these two rouleaux? Lord Montfort's! Ay, and I saw my lady! "

"So did I see her from this window. She did not look happy! "

"Not happy! —with such an equipage, —neatest turn-out I ever set eyes on; not happy, indeed! I had half a mind to ride up to her carriage and advance a claim to her gratitude. "

"Gratitude? Oh, for your part in that miserable affair of which you told me? "

"Not a miserable affair for her; but certainly I never got any good from it. Trouble for nothing! *Basta!* No use looking back. "

"No use; but who can help it? " said Arabella Crane, sighing heavily; then, as if eager to change the subject, she added abruptly, "Mr. Rugge has been here twice this morning, highly excited the child will not act. He says you are bound to make her do so! "

"Nonsense. That is his look-out. I see after children, indeed! "

MRS. CRANE (with a visible effort). —"Listen to me, Jasper Losely. I have no reason to love that child, as you may suppose. But now that you so desert her, I think I feel compassion for her; and when this morning I raised my hand to strike her for her stubborn spirit, and saw her eyes unflinching, and her pale, pale, but fearless face, my arm fell to my side powerless. She will not take to this life without the old man. She will waste away and die. "

LOSELY. —"How you bother me! Are you serious? What am I to do?"

MRS. CRANE. —"You have won money you say; revoke the contract; pay Rugge back his L100. He is disappointed in his bargain; he will take the money. "

LOSELY. —"I dare say he will indeed! No: I have won to-day, it is true, but I may lose to-morrow; and besides I am in want of so many things: when one gets a little money, one has an immediate necessity for more—ha! ha! Still I would not have the child die; and she may grow up to be of use. I tell you what I will do; if, when the races are over, I find I have gained enough to afford it, I will see about buying her off. But L100 is too much! Rugge ought to take half the money, or a quarter, because, if she don't act, I suppose she does eat. "

Odious as the man's words were, he said them with a laugh that seemed to render them less revolting, —the laugh of a very handsome mouth, showing teeth still brilliantly white. More comely than usual that day, for he was in great good-humour, it was difficult to conceive that a man with so healthful and fair an exterior was really quite rotten at heart.

"Your own young laugh, " said Arabella Crane, almost tenderly. "I know not how it is, but this day I feel as if I were less old, —altered though I be in face and mind. I have allowed myself to pity that child; while I speak, I can pity you. Yes! pity, —when I think of what you were. Must you go on thus? To what! Jasper Losely, " she continued, sharply, eagerly, clasping her hands, "hear me: I have an income, not large, it is true, but assured; you have nothing but what, as you say, you may lose to-morrow; share my income! Fulfil your solemn promises: marry me. I will forget whose daughter that girl is; I will be a mother to her. And for yourself, give me the right to feel for you again as I once did, and I may find a way to raise you yet, — higher than you can raise yourself. I have some wit, Jasper, as you know. At the worst you shall have the pastime, I the toil. In your illness I will nurse you: in your joys I will intrude no share. Whom else can you marry? to whom else could you confide? who else could—"

She stopped short as if an adder had stung her, uttering a shriek of rage, of pain; for Jasper Losely, who had hitherto listened to her, stupefied, astounded, here burst into a fit of merriment, in which there was such undisguised contempt, such an enjoyment of the ludicrous, provoked by the idea of the marriage pressed upon him, that the insult pierced the woman to her very soul.

Continuing his laugh, despite that cry of wrathful agony it had caused, Jasper rose, holding his sides, and surveying himself in the glass, with very different feelings at the sight from those that had made his companion's gaze there a few minutes before so mournful.

"My dear good friend, " he said, composing himself at last, and wiping his eyes, "excuse me, but really when you said whom else could I marry—ha! ha! —it did seem such a capital joke! Marry you, my fair Crane! No: put that idea out of your head; we know each other too well for conjugal felicity. You love me now: you always did, and always will; that is, while we are not tied to each other. Women who once love me, always love me; can't help themselves. I am sure I don't know why, except that I am what they call a villain! Ha! the clock striking seven: I dine with a set of fellows I have picked up on the race-ground; they don't know me, nor I them; we shall be better acquainted after the third bottle. Cheer up, Crane: go and scold Sophy, and make her act if you can; if not, scold Rugge into letting her alone. Scold somebody; nothing like it, to keep other folks quiet, and one's self busy. Adieu! and pray, no more matrimonial solicitations: they frighten me! Gad, " added Losely, as he banged the door, "such overtures would frighten Old Nick himself! "

Did Arabella Crane hear those last words, —or had she not heard enough? If Losely had turned and beheld her face, would it have startled back his trivial laugh? Possibly; but it would have caused only a momentary uneasiness. If Alecto herself had reared over him her brow horrent with vipers, Jasper Losely would have thought he had only to look handsome and say coaxingly, "Alecto, my dear, " and the Fury would have pawned her head-dress to pay his washing-bill.

After all, in the face of the grim woman he had thus so wantonly incensed, there was not so much menace as resolve. And that resolve was yet more shown in the movement of the hands than in the aspect of the countenance; those hands—lean, firm, nervous hands— slowly expanded, then as slowly clenched, as if her own thought had taken substance, and she was locking it in a clasp—tightly, tightly— never to be loosened till the pulse was still.

CHAPTER V.

The most submissive where they love may be the most stubborn where they do not love. —Sophy is stubborn to Mr. Rugge. —That injured man summons to his side Mrs. Crane, imitating the policy of those potentates who would retrieve the failures of force by the successes of diplomacy.

Mr. Rugge has obtained his object. But now comes the question, "What will he do with it? " Question with as many heads as the Hydra; and no sooner does an author dispose of one head than up springs another.

Sophy has been bought and paid for: she is now, legally, Mr. Rugge's property. But there was a wise peer who once bought Punch: Punch became his property, and was brought in triumph to his lordship's house. To my lord's great dismay, Punch would not talk. To Rugge's great dismay, Sophy would not act.

Rendered up to Jasper Losely and Mrs. Crane, they had lost not an hour in removing her from Gatesboro' and its neighbourhood. They did not, however, go back to the village in which they had left Rugge, but returned straight to London, and wrote to the manager to join them there.

Sophy, once captured, seemed stupefied: she evinced no noisy passion; she made no violent resistance. When she was told to love and obey a father in Jasper Losely, she lifted her eyes to his face; then turned them away, and shook her head mute and credulous. That man her father! she, did not believe it. Indeed, Jasper took no pains to convince her of the relationship or win her attachment. He was not unkindly rough: he seemed wholly indifferent; probably he was so. For the ruling vice of the man was in his egotism. It was not so much that he had bad principles and bad feelings, as that he had no principles and no feelings at all, except as they began, continued, and ended in that system of centralization which not more paralyzes healthful action in a State than it does in the individual man. Self-indulgence with him was absolute. He was not without power of keen calculation, not without much cunning. He could conceive a project for some gain far off in the future, and concoct, for its realization, schemes subtly woven, astutely guarded. But he could not secure their success by any long-sustained sacrifices of the caprice of one hour or the indolence of the next. If it had been a great object to him for life to win Sophy's filial affection, he would not have bored himself for five minutes each day to gain that object. Besides, he had just enough of shame to render him uneasy at the sight of the child he had deliberately sold. So after chucking her under the chin, and telling her to be a good girl and be grateful for all that Mrs. Crane had done for her and meant still to do, he consigned her almost solely to that lady's care.

When Rugge arrived, and Sophy was informed of her intended destination, she broke silence, —her colour went and came quickly, —she declared, folding her arms upon her breast, that she would never act if separated from her grandfather. Mrs. Crane, struck by her manner, suggested to Rugge that it might be as well, now that she was legally secured to the manager, to humour her wish and re-engage Waife. Whatever the tale with which, in order to obtain Sophy from the Mayor, she had turned that worthy magistrate's mind against the Comedian, she had not gratified Mr. Rugge by a similar confidence to him. To him she said nothing which might operate against renewing engagements with Waife, if he were so disposed. But Rugge had no faith in a child's firmness, and he had a strong spite against Waife, so he obstinately refused. He insisted, however, as a peremptory condition of the bargain, that Mr. Losely and Mrs. Crane should accompany him to the town to which he had transferred his troupe, both in order by their presence to confirm his authority over Sophy, and to sanction his claim to her, should Waife reappear and dispute it. For Rugge's profession being scarcely legitimate and decidedly equivocal, his right to bring up a female child to the same calling might be called into question before a magistrate, and necessitate the production of her father in order to substantiate the special contract. In return, the manager handsomely offered to Mr. Losely and Mrs. Crane to pay their expenses in the excursion, —a liberality haughtily rejected by Mrs. Crane for herself, though she agreed at her own charge to accompany Losely if he decided on complying with the manager's request. Losely at first raised objections, but hearing that there would be races in the neighbourhood, and having a peculiar passion for betting and all kinds of gambling, as well as an ardent desire to enjoy his L100 in so fashionable a manner, he consented to delay his return to the Continent, and attend Arabella Crane to the provincial Elis. Rugge, carried off Sophy to her fellow "orphans. "

AND SOPHY WOULD NOT ACT!

In vain she was coaxed; in vain she was threatened; in vain she was deprived of food; in vain shut up in a dark hole; in vain was the lash held over her. Rugge, tyrant though he was, did not suffer the lash to fall. His self-restraint there might be humanity, —might be fear of the consequences; for the state of her health began to alarm him. She might die; there might be an inquest. He wished now that he had taken Mrs. Crane's suggestion, and re-engaged Waife. But where was Waife? Meanwhile he had advertised the young Phenomenon; placarded the walls with the name of Juliet Araminta; got up the piece of the Remorseless Baron, with a new rock-scene. Waife had had nothing to say in that drama, so any one could act his part.

The first performance was announced for that night: there would be such an audience! the best seats even now pre-engaged; first night of the race-week. The clock had struck seven; the performance began at eight. AND SOPHY WOULD NOT ACT!

The child was seated in a space that served for the greenroom, behind the scenes. The whole company had been convened to persuade or shame her out of her obstinacy. The king's lieutenant, the seductive personage of the troupe, was on one knee to her, like a lover. He was accustomed to lovers' parts, both on the stage and off it. Off it, he had one favoured phrase, hackneyed, but effective. "You are too pretty to be so cruel. " Thrice he now repeated that phrase, with a simper between each repetition that might have melted a heart of stone. Behind Sophy's chair, and sticking calico-flowers into the child's tresses, stood the senior matron of the establishment, — not a bad sort of woman, —who kept the dresses, nursed the sick, revered Rugge, told fortunes on a pack of cards which she always kept in her pocket, and acted occasionally in parts where age was no drawback and ugliness desirable, —such as a witch, or duenna, or whatever in the dialogue was poetically called "Hag. " Indeed, Hag was the name she usually took from Rugge; that which she bore from her defunct husband was Gormerick. This lady, as she braided the garland, was also bent on the soothing system, saying, with great sweetness, considering that her mouth was full of pins, "Now, deary, now, dovey, look at ooself in the glass; we could beat oo, and pinch oo, and stick pins into oo, dovey, but we won't. Dovey will be good, I know; " and a great patch of rouge came on the child's pale cheeks. The clown therewith, squatting before her with his hands on his knees, grinned lustily, and shrieked out, "My eyes, what a beauty! "

Rugge, meanwhile, one hand thrust in his bosom, contemplated the diplomatic efforts of his ministers, and saw, by Sophy's compressed lips and unwinking eyes, that their cajoleries were unsuccessful. He approached and hissed into her ear, "Don't madden me! don't! you will act, eh? "

"No, " said Sophy, suddenly rising; and tearing the wreath from her hair, she set her small foot on it with force. "No, not if you kill me! "

"Gods! " faltered Rugge. "And the sum I have paid! I am diddled! Who has gone for Mrs. Crane? "

"Tom, " said the clown.

The word was scarcely out of the clown's mouth ere Mrs. Crane herself emerged from a side scene, and, putting off her bonnet, laid both hands on the child's shoulders, and looked her in the face without speaking. The child as firmly returned the gaze. Give that child a martyr's cause, and in that frail body there would have been a martyr's soul. Arabella Crane, not inexperienced in children, recognized a power of will stronger than the power of brute force, in that tranquillity of eye, the spark of calm light in its tender blue, blue, pure as the sky; light, steadfast as the star.

"Leave her to me, all of you, " said Mrs. Crane. "I will take her to your private room, Mr. Rugge; " and she led the child away to a sort of recess, room it could not be rightly called, fenced round with boxes and crates, and containing the manager's desk and two stools.

"Sophy, " then said Mrs. Crane, "you say you will not act unless your grandfather be with you. Now, hear me. You know that I have been always stern and hard with you. I never professed to love you, —nor do I. But you have not found me untruthful. When I say a thing seriously, as I am speaking now, you may believe me. Act to-night, and I will promise you faithfully that I will either bring your grandfather here, or I will order it so that you shall be restored to him. If you refuse, I make no threat, but I shall leave this place; and my belief is that you will be your grandfather's death. "

"His death! his death! I! "

"By first dying yourself. Oh, you smile; you think it would be happiness to die. What matter that the old man you profess to care for is broken-hearted! Brat, leave selfishness to boys: you are a girl! suffer! "

"Selfish! " murmured Sophy, "selfish! that was said of me before. Selfish! ah, I understand. No, I ought not to wish to die: what would become of him? " She fell on her knees, and raising both her clasped hands, prayed inly, silently, an instant, not more. She rose. "If I do act, then, —it is a promise: you will keep it. I shall see him: he shall know where I am; we shall meet! "

"A promise, —sacred. I will keep it. Oh, girl, how much you will love some day! how your heart will ache! and when you are my age, look at that heart, then at your glass; perhaps you may be, within and without, like me. "

Sophy, innocent Sophy, stared, awe-stricken, but uncomprehending; Mrs. Crane led her back passive.

"There, she will act. Put on the wreath. Trick her out. Hark ye, Mr. Rugge. This is for one night. I have made conditions with her: either you must take back her grandfather, or—she must return to him. "

"And my L100? "

"In the latter case ought to be repaid to you. "

"Am I never to have the Royal York Theatre? Ambition of my life, ma'am. Dreamed of it thrice! Ha! but she will act; and succeed. But to take back the old vagabond, —a bitter pill. He shall halve it with me! Ma'am, I'm your grateful—"

CHAPTER VI.

Threadbare is the simile which compares the world to a stage. Schiller, less complimentary than Shakspeare, lowers the illustration from a stage to a puppet-show. But ever between realities and shows there is a secret communication, an undetected interchange, — sometimes a stern reality in the heart of the ostensible actor, a fantastic stage-play in the brain of the unnoticed spectator. The bandit's child on the proscenium is still poor little Sophy, in spite of garlands and rouge. But that honest rough-looking fellow to whom, in respect for services to sovereign and country, the apprentice yields way, may he not be—the crafty Comedian?

TARAN-TARANTARA! rub-a-dub-dub! play up horn! roll drum! a quarter to eight; and the crowd already thick before Rugge's Grand Exhibition, —" Remorseless Baron and Bandit's Child! Young Phenomenon, —Juliet Araminta, —Patronized by the Nobility in general, and expecting daily to be summoned to perform before the Queen, —*Vivat Regina!* "—Ruba-dub-dub! The company issue from the curtain, range in front of the proscenuim. Splendid dresses. The Phenomenon! —'t is she!

"My eyes, there's a beauty! " cries the clown.

The days have already grown somewhat shorter; but it is not yet dusk. How charmingly pretty she still is, despite that horrid paint; but how wasted those poor bare snowy arms!

A most doleful lugubrious dirge mingles with the drum and horn. A man has forced his way close by the stage, —a man with a confounded cracked hurdy-gurdy. Whine! whine! creaks the hurdy-gurdy. "Stop that! stop that mu-zeek! " cries a delicate apprentice, clapping his hands to his ears. "Pity a poor blind—" answers the man with the hurdygurdy.

"Oh, you are blind, are you? but we are not deaf. There's a penny not to play. What black thing have you got there by a string? "

"My dog, sir! "

"Deuced ugly one; not like a dog; more like a bear with horns! "

"I say, master, " cries the clown, "here's a blind man come to see the Phenomenon! "

The crowd laugh; they make way for the blind man's black dog. They suspect, from the clown's address, that the blind man has something to do with the company.

You never saw two uglier specimens of their several species than the blind man and his black dog. He had rough red hair and a red beard, his face had a sort of twist that made every feature seem crooked. His eyes were not bandaged, but the lids were closed, and he lifted them up piteously as if seeking for light. He did not seem, however, like a common beggar: had rather the appearance of a reduced sailor. Yes, you would have bet ten to one he had been a sailor; not that his dress belonged to that noble calling, but his build, the roll of his walk, the tie of his cravat, a blue anchor tattooed on that great brown hand: certainly a sailor; a British tar! poor man.

The dog was hideous enough to have been exhibited as a *lusus naturae*; evidently very aged, —for its face and ears were gray, the rest of it a rusty reddish black; it had immensely long ears, pricked up like horns; it was a dog that must have been brought from foreign parts; it might have come from Acheron, sire by Cerberus, so portentous, and (if not irreverent the epithet) so infernal was its aspect, with that gray face, those antlered ears, and its ineffably weird demeanour altogether. A big dog, too, and evidently a strong one. All prudent folks would have made way for a man led by that dog. Whine creaked the hurdy-gurdy, and bow-wow all of a sudden barked the dog. Sophy stifled a cry, pressed her hand to her breast, and such a ray of joy flashed over her face that it would have warmed your heart for a month to have seen it.

But do you mean to say, Mr. Author, that that British tar (gallant, no doubt, but hideous) is Gentleman Waife, or that Stygian animal the snowy-curled Sir Isaac?

Upon my word, when I look at them myself, I, the Historian, am puzzled. If it had not been for that bow-bow, I am sure Sophy would not have suspected. Taratarantara! Walk in, ladies and gentlemen, walk in; the performance is about to commence! Sophy lingers last.

"Yes, sir, " said the blind man, who had been talking to the apprentice, "yes, sir, " said he, loud and emphatically, as if his word had been questioned. "The child was snowed up, but luckily the window of the hut was left open: exactly at two o'clock in the morning, that dog came to the window, set up a howl, and —"

Soppy could hear no more—led away behind the curtain by the King's Lieutenant. But she had heard enough to stir her heart with an emotion that set all the dimples round her lip into undulating play.

CHAPTER VII.

A sham carries off a reality.

And she did act, and how charmingly! with what glee and what gusto! Rugge was beside himself with pride and rapture. He could hardly perform his own Baronial part for admiration. The audience, a far choicer and more fastidious one than that in the Surrey village, was amazed, enthusiastic. "I shall live to see my dream come true! I shall have the great York theatre! " said Rugge, as he took off his wig and laid his head on his pillow. "Restore her for the L100! not for thousands! "

Alas, my sweet Sophy, alas! Has not the joy that made thee perform so well undone thee? Ah, hadst thou but had the wit to act horribly, and be hissed!

"Uprose the sun and uprose Baron Rugge. "

Not that ordinarily he was a very early man; but his excitement broke his slumbers. He had taken up his quarters on the ground-floor of a small lodging-house close to his exhibition; in the same house lodged his senior matron, and Sophy herself. Mrs. Gormerick, being ordered to watch the child and never lose sight of her, slept in the same room with Sophy, in the upper story of the house. The old woman served Rugge for housekeeper, made his tea, grilled his chop, and for company's sake shared his meals. Excitement as often sharpens the appetite as takes it away. Rugge had supped on hope, and he felt a craving for a more substantial breakfast. Accordingly, when he had dressed, he thrust his head into the passage, and seeing there the maid-of-all-work unbarring the street-door, bade her go upstairs and wake the Hag, that is, Mrs. Gormerick. Saying this he extended a key; for he ever took the precaution, before retiring to rest, to lock the door of the room to which Sophy was consigned on the outside, and guard the key till the next morning.

The maid nodded, and ascended the stairs. Less time than he expected passed away before Mrs. Gormerick made her appearance, her gray hair streaming under her nightcap, her form indued in a loose wrapper, —her very face a tragedy.

"Powers above! What has happened? " exclaimed Rugge, prophetically.

"She is gone, " sobbed Mrs. Gormerick; and, seeing the lifted arm and clenched fist of the manager, prudently fainted away.

CHAPTER VIII.

Corollaries from the problems suggested in chapters VI. and VII.

Broad daylight, nearly nine o'clock indeed, and Jasper Losely is walking back to his inn from the place at which he had dined the evening before. He has spent the night drinking, gambling, and though he looks heated, there is no sign of fatigue. Nature, in wasting on this man many of her most glorious elements of happiness, had not forgotten an herculean constitution, —always restless and never tired, always drinking and never drunk. Certainly it is some consolation to delicate invalids that it seldom happens that the sickly are very wicked. Criminals are generally athletic; constitution and conscience equally tough; large backs to their heads; strong suspensorial muscles; digestions that save them from the over-fine nerves of the virtuous. The native animal must be vigorous in the human being, when the moral safeguards are daringly overleapt. Jasper was not alone, but with an acquaintance he had made at the dinner, and whom he invited to his inn to breakfast; they were walking familiarly arm-in-arm. Very unlike the brilliant Losely, —a young man under thirty, who seemed to have washed out all the colours of youth in dirty water. His eyes dull, their whites yellow; his complexion sodden. His form was thickset and heavy; his features pug, with a cross of the bull-dog. In dress, a specimen of the flash style of sporting man, as exhibited on the Turf, or more often perhaps in the Ring; Belcher neckcloth, with an immense pin representing a jockey at full gallop; cut-away coat, corduroy breeches, and boots with tops of a chalky white. Yet, withal, not the air and walk of a genuine born and bred sporting man, even of the vulgar order. Something about him which reveals the pretender. A would-be hawk with a pigeon's liver, —a would-be sportsman with a Cockney's nurture.

Samuel Adolphus Poole is an orphan of respectable connections. His future expectations chiefly rest on an uncle from whom, as godfather, he takes the loathed name of Samuel. He prefers to sign himself Adolphus; he is popularly styled Dolly. For his present existence he relies ostensibly on his salary as an assistant in the house of a London tradesman in a fashionable way of business. Mr. Latham, his employer, has made a considerable fortune, less by his shop than by discounting the bills of his customers, or of other borrowers whom the loan draws into the net of the custom. Mr.

Latham connives at the sporting tastes of Dolly Poole. Dolly has often thus been enabled to pick up useful pieces of information as to the names and repute of such denizens of the sporting world as might apply to Mr. Latham for temporary accommodation. Dolly Poole has many sporting friends; he has also many debts. He has been a dupe, he is now a rogue; but he wants decision of character to put into practice many valuable ideas that his experience of dupe and his development into rogue suggest to his ambition. Still, however, now and then, wherever a shabby trick can be safely done, he is what he calls "lucky. " He has conceived a prodigious admiration for Jasper Losely, one cause for which will be explained in the dialogue about to be recorded; another cause for which is analogous to that loving submission with which some ill-conditioned brute acknowledges a master in the hand that has thrashed it. For at Losely's first appearance at the convivial meeting just concluded, being nettled at the imperious airs of superiority which that roysterer assumed, mistaking for effeminacy Jasper's elaborate dandyism, and not recognizing in the bravo's elegant proportions the tiger-like strength of which, in truth, that tiger-like suppleness should have warned him, Dolly Poole provoked a quarrel, and being himself a stout fellow, nor unaccustomed to athletic exercises, began to spar; the next moment he was at the other end of the room full sprawl on the floor; and two minutes afterwards, the quarrel made up by conciliating banqueters, with every bone in his skin seeming still to rattle, he was generously blubbering out that he never bore malice, and shaking hands with Jasper Losely as if he had found a benefactor. But now to the dialogue.

JASPER. —"Yes, Poole, my hearty, as you say, that fellow trumping my best club lost me the last rubber. There's no certainty in whist, if one has a spoon for a partner. "

POOLE. —"No certainty in every rubber, but next to certainty in the long run, when a man plays as well as you do, Mr. Losely. Your winnings to-night must have been pretty large, though you had a bad partner almost every hand; pretty large, eh? "

JASPER (carelessly). —"Nothing to talk of, —a few ponies! "

POOLE. —"More than a few; I should know. "

JASPER. —"Why? You did not play after the first rubber. "

POOLE. —"No, when I saw your play on that first rubber, I cut out, and bet on you; and very grateful to you I am. Still you would win more with a partner who understood your game. "

The shrewd Dolly paused a moment, and leaning significantly on Jasper's arm, added, in a half whisper, "I do; it is a French one. "

Jasper did not change colour, but a quick rise of the eyebrow, and a slight jerk of the neck, betrayed some little surprise or uneasiness: however, he rejoined without hesitation, "French, ay! In France there is more dash in playing out trumps than there is with English players. "

"And with a player like you, " said Poole, still in a half whisper, "more trumps to play out. "

Jasper turned round sharp and short; the hard, cruel expression of his mouth, little seen of late, came back to it. Poole recoiled, and his bones began again to ache. "I did not mean to offend you, Mr. Losely, but to caution. "

"Caution! "

"There were two knowing coves, who, if they had not been so drunk, would not have lost their money without a row, and they would have seen how they lost it; they are sharpers: you served them right; don't be angry with me. You want a partner; so do I: you play better than I do, but I play well; you shall have two-thirds of our winnings, and when you come to town I'll introduce you to a pleasant set of young fellows—green. "

Jasper mused a moment. "You know a thing or two, I see, Master Poole, and we'll discuss the whole subject after breakfast. Ar'n't you hungry? No! I am! Hillo! who 's that? "

His arm was seized by Mr. Rugge. "She's gone, —fled, " gasped the manager, breathless. "Out of the lattice; fifteen feet high; not dashed to pieces; vanished. "

"Go on and order breakfast, " said Losely to Mr. Poole, who was listening too inquisitively. He drew the manager away. "Can't you keep your tongue in your head before strangers? The girl is gone? "

"Out of the lattice, and fifteen feet high! "

"Any sheets left hanging out of the lattice? "

"Sheets! No. "

"'Then she did not go without help: somebody must have thrown up to her a rope-ladder; nothing so easy; done it myself scores of times for the descent of 'maids who love the moon, ' Mr. Rugge. But at her age there is not a moon; at least there is not a man in the moon: one must dismiss, then, the idea of a rope-ladder, —too precocious. But are you quite sure she is gone? not hiding in some cupboard? Sacre! very odd. Have you seen Mrs. Crane about it? "

"Yes, just come from her; she thinks that villain Waife must have stolen her. But I want you, sir, to come with me to a magistrate. "

"Magistrate! I! why? nonsense; set the police to work. "

"Your deposition that she is your lawful child, lawfully made over to me, is necessary for the inquisition; I mean police. "

"Hang it, what a bother! I hate magistrates, and all belonging to them. Well, I must breakfast! I'll see to it afterwards. Oblige me by not calling Mr. Waife a villain; good old fellow in his way. "

"Good! Powers above! "

"But if he took her off, how did he get at her? It must have been preconcerted. "

"Ha! true. But she has not been suffered to speak to a soul not in the company, Mrs. Crane excepted. "

"Perhaps at the performance last night some signal was given? "

"But if Waife had been there I should have seen him; my troupe would have known him: such a remarkable face; one eye too. "

"Well, well, do what you think best. I'll call on you after breakfast; let me go now. Basta! Basta! "

Losely wrenched himself from the manager, and strode off to the inn; then, ere joining Poole, he sought Mrs. Crane. "This going before a magistrate, " said Losely, "to depose that I have made over my child to that blackguard showman—in this town too, after such luck as I have had and where bright prospects are opening on me—is most disagreeable. And supposing, when we have traced Sophy, she should be really with the old man; awkward! In short, my dear friend, my dear Bella, " (Losely could be very coaxing when it was worth his while) "you just manage this for me. I have a fellow in the next room waiting to breakfast: as soon as breakfast is over I shall be off to the race-ground, and so shirk that ranting old bore; you'll call on him instead, and settle it somehow. " He was out of the room before she could answer.

Mrs. Crane found it no easy matter to soothe the infuriate manager when he heard Losely was gone to amuse himself at the race-course. Nor did she give herself much trouble to pacify Mr. Rugge's anger or assist his investigations. Her interest in the whole affair seemed over. Left thus to his own devices, Rugge, however, began to institute a sharp, and what promised to be an effective, investigation. He ascertained that the fugitive certainly had not left by the railway or by any of the public conveyances; he sent scoots over all the neighbourhood: he enlisted the sympathy of the police, who confidently assured him that they had "a network over the three kingdoms. " Rugge's suspicions were directed to Waife: he could collect, however, no evidence to confirm them. No person answering to Waife's description had been seen in the town. Once, indeed, Rugge was close on the right scent; for, insisting upon Waife's one eye, and his possession of a white dog, he was told by several witnesses that a man blind of two eyes, and led by a black dog, had been close before the stage, just previous to the performance. But then the clown had spoken to that very man; all the Thespian company had observed him; all of them had known Waife familiarly for years; and all deposed that any creature more unlike to Waife than the blind man could not be turned out of Nature's workshop. But where was that blind man? They found out the wayside inn in which he had taken a lodging for the night; and there it was ascertained that he had paid for his room beforehand, stating that he should start for the race-course early in the morning. Rugge himself set out to the racecourse to kill two birds with one stone, —catch Mr. Losely, examine the blind man himself.

He did catch Mr. Losely, and very nearly caught something else; for that gentleman was in a ring of noisy horsemen, mounted on a hired hack, and loud as the noisiest. When Rugge came up to his stirrup, and began his harangue, Losely turned his hack round with so sudden an appliance of bit and spur, that the animal lashed out, and its heel went within an inch of the manager's cheek-bone. Before Rugge could recover, Losely was in a hand-gallop. But the blind man! Of course Rugge did not find him? You are mistaken: he did. The blind man was there, dog and all. The manager spoke to him, and did not know him from Adam.

Nor have you or I, my venerated readers, any right whatsoever to doubt whether Mr. Rugge could be so stolidly obtuse. Granting that blind sailor to be the veritable William Waife, William Waife was a man of genius, taking pains to appear an ordinary mortal. And the anecdotes of Munden, or of Bamfylde Moore Carew, suffice to tell us how Protean is the power of transformation in a man whose genius is mimetic. But how often does it happen to us, venerated readers, not to recognize a man of genius, even when he takes no particular pains to escape detection! A man of genius may be for ten years our next-door neighbour; he may dine in company with us twice a week; his face may be as familiar to our eyes as our armchair; his voice to our ears as the click of our parlour-clock: yet we are never more astonished than when all of a sudden, some bright day, it is discovered that our next-door neighbour is—a man of genius. Did you ever hear tell of the life of a man of genius but what there were numerous witnesses who deposed to the fact, that until, perfidious dissembler! he flared up and set the Thames on fire they had never seen anything in him; an odd creature, perhaps a good creature, — probably a poor creature, —but a MAN of GENIUS! They would as soon have suspected him of being the Khann of Tartary! Nay, candid readers, are there not some of you who refuse to the last to recognize the maa of genius, till he has paid his penny to Charon, and his passport to immortality has been duly examined by the customhouse officers of Styx! When one half the world drag forth that same next-door neighbour, place him on a pedestal, and have him cried, "Oyez! Oyez! Found a man of genius! Public property! open to inspection! " does not the other half the world put on its spectacles, turn up its nose, and cry, "That a man of genius, indeed! Pelt him! —pelt him! " Then of course there is a clatter, what the vulgar call "a shindy, " round the pedestal. Squeezed by his believers, shied at by his scoffers, the poor man gets horribly mauled about, and drops from the perch in the midst of the row. Then they shovel him over, clap a great stone on his relics, wipe their foreheads, shake hands, compromise the dispute, the one half the world admitting that though he was a genius he was still an ordinary man; the other half allowing that though he was an ordinary man he was still a genius. And so on to the next pedestal with its "Hic stet, " and the next great stone with its "Hic jacet. "

The manager of the Grand Theatrical Exhibition gazed on the blind sailor, and did not know him from Adam!

CHAPTER IX.

The aboriginal man-eater, or pocket-cannibal, is susceptible of the refining influences of Civilization. He decorates his lair with the skins of his victims; he adorns his person with the spoils of those whom he devours. Mr. Losely, introduced to Mr. Poole's friends, dresses for dinner; and, combining elegance with appetite, eats them up.

Elated with the success which had rewarded his talents for pecuniary speculation, and dismissing from his mind all thoughts of the fugitive Sophy and the spoliated Rugge, Jasper Losely returned to London in company with his new friend, Mr. Poole. He left Arabella Crane to perform the same journey unattended; but that grim lady, carefully concealing any resentment at such want of gallantry, felt assured that she should not be long in London without being honoured by his visits.

In renewing their old acquaintance, Mrs. Crane had contrived to establish over Jasper that kind of influence which a vain man, full of schemes that are not to be told to all the world, but which it is convenient to discuss with some confidential friend who admires himself too highly not to respect his secrets, mechanically yields to a woman whose wits are superior to his own.

It is true that Jasper, on his return to the metropolis, was not magnetically attracted towards Podden Place; nay, days and even weeks elapsed, and Mrs. Crane was not gladdened by his presence. But she knew that her influence was only suspended, —not extinct. The body attracted was for the moment kept from the body attracting by the abnormal weights that had dropped into its pockets. Restore the body thus temporarily counterpoised to its former lightness, and it would turn to Podden Place as the needle to the Pole. Meanwhile, oblivious of all such natural laws, the disloyal Jasper had fixed himself as far from the reach of the magnet as from Bloomsbury's remotest verge in St. James's animated centre. The apartment he engaged was showy and commodious. He added largely to his wardrobe, his dressing-case, his trinket box. Nor, be it here observed, was Mr. Losely one of those beauish brigands who wear tawdry scarves over soiled linen, and paste rings upon unwashed digitals. To do him justice, the man, so stony-hearted to others, loved and cherished his own person with exquisite tenderness, lavished upon it delicate attentions, and gave to it the very best he could afford. He was no coarse debauchee, smelling of bad cigars and ardent spirits. Cigars, indeed, were not among his vices (at worst the rare peccadillo of a cigarette): spirit-drinking was; but the monster's digestion was still so strong that he could have drunk out a gin-palace, and you would only have sniffed the jasmine or heliotrope on the dainty cambric that wiped the last drop from his lips. Had his soul been a tenth part as clean as the form that belied it, Jasper Losely had been a saint! His apartments secured, his appearance thus revised and embellished, Jasper's next care was an equipage in keeping; he hired a smart cabriolet with a high-stepping horse, and, to go behind it, a groom whose size had been stunted in infancy by provident parents designing him to earn his bread in the stables as a light-weight, and therefore mingling his mother's milk with heavy liquors. In short, Jasper Losely set up to be a buck about town: in that capacity Dolly Poole introduced him to several young gentlemen who combined commercial vocations with sporting tastes; they could not but participate in Poole's admiring and somewhat envious respect for Jasper Losely. There was indeed about the vigorous miscreant a great deal of false brilliancy. Deteriorated from earlier youth though the beauty of his countenance might be, it was still undeniably handsome; and as force of muscle is beauty in itself in the eyes of young sporting men, so Jasper dazzled many a *gracilis puer*, who had the ambition to become an athlete, with the rare personal strength which, as if in the exuberance of animal spirits, he would sometimes condescend to display, by feats that astonished the curious and frightened the timid, —such as bending a poker or horseshoe between hands elegantly white, nor unadorned with rings, —or lifting the weight of Samuel Dolly by the waistband, and holding him at arm's length, with a playful bet of ten to one that he could stand by the fireplace and pitch the said Samuel Dolly out of the open window. To know so strong a man, so fine an animal, was something to boast of. Then, too, if Jasper had a false brilliancy, he had also a false bonhommie: it was true that he was somewhat imperious, swaggering, bullying; but he was also off-hand and jocund; and as you knew him, that sidelong look, that defying gait (look and gait of the man whom the world cuts), wore away. In fact, he had got into a world which did not cut him, and his exterior was improved by the atmosphere.

Mr. Losely professed to dislike general society. Drawing rooms were insipid; clubs full of old fogies. "I am for life, my boys, " said Mr. Losely,

"'Can sorrow from the goblet flow,
Or pain from Beauty's eye?'"

Mr. Losely, therefore, his hat on one side, lounged into the saloons of theatres, accompanied by a cohort of juvenile admirers, their hats on one side also, and returned to the pleasantest little suppers in his own apartment. There "the goblet" flowed; and after the goblet, cigars for some, and a rubber for all.

So puissant Losely's vitality, and so blest by the stars his luck, that his form seemed to wax stronger and his purse fuller by this "life. " No wonder he was all for a life of that kind; but the slight beings who tried to keep up with him grew thinner and thinner, and poorer and poorer; a few weeks made their cheeks spectral and their pockets a dismal void. Then as some dropped off from sheer inanition, others whom they had decoyed by their praises of "Life" and its hero came into the magic circle to fade and vanish in their turn.

In a space of time incredibly brief, not a whist-player was left upon the field: the victorious Losely had trumped out the last; some few whom Nature had endowed more liberally than Fortune still retained strength enough to sup—if asked;

"But none who came to sup remained to play. "

"Plague on it, " said Losely to Poole, as one afternoon they were dividing the final spoils, "your friends are mightily soon cleaned out: could not even get up double dummy last night; and we must hit on some new plan for replenishing the coffers. You have rich relations; can't I help you to make them more useful? "

Said Dolly Poole, who was looking exceedingly bilious, and had become a martyr to chronic headache,

"My relations are prigs! Some of them give me the cold shoulder, others—a great deal of jaw. But as for tin, I might as well scrape a flint for it. My uncle Sam is more anxious about my sins than the other codgers, because he is my godfather, and responsible for my sins, I suppose; and he says he will put me in the way of being respectable. My head's splitting —"

"Wood does split till it is seasoned, " answered Losely. "Good fellow, uncle Sam! He'll put you in the way of tin; nothing else makes a man respectable. "

"Yes, —so he says; a girl with money—"

"A wife, —tin canister! Introduce me to her, and she shall be tied to you. "

Samuel Dolly did not appear to relish the idea of such an introduction. "I have not been introduced to her myself, " said he. "But if you advise me to be spliced, why don't you get spliced yourself? a handsome fellow like you can be at no loss for an heiress."

"Heiresses are the most horrid cheats in the world, " said Losely: "there is always some father, or uncle, or fusty Lord Chancellor whose consent is essential, and not to be had. Heiresses in scores have been over head and ears in love with me. Before I left Paris, I sold their locks of hair to a wig maker, —three great trunksful. Honour bright. But there were only two whom I could have safely allowed to run away with me; and they were so closely watched, poor things, that I was forced to leave them to their fate, —early graves! Don't talk to me of heiresses, Dolly; I have been the victim of heiresses. But a rich widow is an estimable creature. Against widows, if rich, I have not a word to say; and to tell you the truth, there is a widow whom I suspect I have fascinated, and whose connection I have a particular private reason for deeming desirable! She has a whelp of a son, who is a spoke in my wheel: were I his father-in-law, would not I be a spoke in his? I'd teach the boy 'life, ' Dolly. " Here all trace of beauty vanished from Jasper's face, and Poole, staring at him, pushed away his chair. "But, " continued Losely, regaining his more usual expression of levity and boldness, "but I am not yet quite sure what the widow has, besides her son, in her own possession; we shall see. Meanwhile, is there—no chance of a rubber to-night? "

"None; unless you will let Brown and Smith play upon tick. "

"Pooh! but there's Robinson, he has an aunt he can borrow from? "

"Robinson! spitting blood, with an attack of delirium tremens! You have done for him. "

"'Can sorrow from the goblet flow? '" said Losely. "Well, I suppose it can—when a man has no coats to his stomach; but you and I, Dolly Poole, have stomachs thick as peajackets, and proof as gutta-percha."

Poole forced a ghastly smile, while Losely, gayly springing up, swept his share of booty into his pockets, slapped his comrade on the back, and said, "Then, if the mountain will not come to Mahomet, Mahomet must go to the mountain! Hang whist, and up with rouge-et-noir! I have an infallible method of winning; only it requires capital. You will club your cash with mine, and I 'll play for both. Sup here to night, and we'll go to the Hell afterwards. "

Samuel Dolly had the most perfect confidence in his friend's science in the art of gambling, and he did not, therefore, dissent from the proposal made. Jasper gave a fresh touch to his toilet, and stepped into his cabriolet. Poole cast on him a look of envy, and crawled to his lodging, —too ill for his desk, and with a strong desire to take to his bed.

CHAPTER X.

"Is there a heart that never loved,
Nor felt soft woman's sigh?"

If there be such a heart, it is not in the breast of a pocket- cannibal. Your true man-eater is usually of an amorous temperament: he can be indeed sufficiently fond of a lady to eat her up. Mr. Losely makes the acquaintance of a widow. For further particulars inquire within.

The dignified serenity of Gloucester Place, Portman Square, is agitated by the intrusion of a new inhabitant. A house in that favoured locality, which had for several months maintained "the solemn stillness and the dread repose" which appertain to dwellings that are to be let upon lease, unfurnished, suddenly started into that exuberant and aggressive life which irritates the nerves of its peaceful neighbours. The bills have been removed from the windows; the walls have been cleaned down and pointed; the street-door repainted a lively green; workmen have gone in and out. The observant ladies (single ones) in the house opposite, discover, by the help of a telescope, that the drawing-rooms have been new papered, canary-coloured ground, festoon borders; and that the mouldings of the shutters have been gilded. Gilt shutters! that looks ominous of an ostentatious and party-giving tenant. Then carts full of furniture have stopped at the door; carpets, tables, chairs, beds, wardrobes, — all seemingly new, and in no inelegant taste, —have been disgorged into the hall. It has been noticed, too, that every day a lady of slight figure and genteel habiliments has come, seemingly to inspect progress; evidently the new tenant. Sometimes she comes alone; sometimes with a dark-eyed, handsome lad, probably her son. Who can she be? what is she? what is her name? her history? has she a right to settle in Gloucester Place, Portman Square? The detective police of London is not peculiarly vigilant; but its defects are supplied by the voluntary efforts of unmarried ladies. The new comer was a widow; her husband had been in the army; of good family; but a *mauvais sujet*; she had been left in straitened circumstances with an only son. It was supposed that she had unexpectedly come into a fortune, on the strength of which she had removed from Pimlico into Gloucester Place. At length, the preparations completed, one Monday afternoon the widow, accompanied by her son, came to settle. The next day a footman, in genteel livery (brown and orange), appeared at the door. Then, for the rest of the week, the baker and butcher called regularly. On the following Sunday, the lady and her son appeared at church.

No reader will be at a loss to discover in the new tenant of No. — Gloucester Place the widowed mother of Lionel Haughton. The letter for that lady which Darrell had entrusted to his young cousin had, in complimentary and cordial language, claimed the right to provide for her comfortable and honourable subsistence; and announced that henceforth L800 a year would be placed quarterly to her account at Mr. Darrell's banker, and that an additional sum of L1200 was already there deposited in her name, in order to enable her to furnish any residence to which she might be inclined to remove. Mrs. Haughton therewith had removed to Gloucester Place.

She is seated by the window in her front drawing-room, surveying with proud though grateful heart the elegances by which she is surrounded. A very winning countenance: lively eyes, that in themselves may be over-quick and petulant; but their expression is chastened by a gentle kindly mouth. And over the whole face, the attitude, the air, even the dress itself, is diffused the unmistakable simplicity of a sincere natural character. No doubt Mrs. Haughton has her tempers and her vanities, and her little harmless feminine weaknesses; but you could not help feeling in her presence that you were with an affectionate, warm-hearted, honest, good woman. She might not have the refinements of tone and manner which stamp the high-bred gentlewoman of convention; she might evince the deficiencies of an imperfect third-rate education: but she was saved from vulgarity by a certain undefinable grace or person and music of voice, —even when she said or did things that well-bred people do not say or do; and there was an engaging intelligence in those quick hazel eyes that made you sure that she was sensible, even when she uttered what was silly.

Mrs. Haughton turned from the interior of the room to the open window. She is on the look-out for her son, who has gone to call on Colonel Morley, and who ought to be returned by this time. She begins to get a little fidgety, somewhat cross. While thus standing and thus watchful, there comes thundering down the street a high-stepping horse, bay, with white legs; it whirls on a cabriolet, —blue, with vermilion wheels; two hands, in yellow kid gloves, are just seen under the hood. Mrs. Haughton suddenly blushes and draws in her head. Too late! the cabriolet has stopped; a gentleman leans forward, takes off his hat, bows respectfully. "Dear, dear! " murmurs Mrs. Haughton, "I do think he is going to call: some people are born to be tempted; my temptations have been immense! He is getting out; he knocks; I can't say, now, that I am not at home, —very awkward! I wish Lionel were here! What does he mean, neglecting his own mother, and leaving her a prey to tempters? "

While the footman is responding to the smart knock of the visitor, we will explain how Mrs. Haughton had incurred that gentleman's acquaintance. In one of her walks to her new house while it was in the hands of the decorators, her mind being much absorbed in the consideration whether her drawing-room curtains should be chintz or tabouret, —just as she was crossing the street, she was all but run over by a gentleman's cabriolet. The horse was hard-mouthed, going at full speed. The driver pulled up just in time; but the wheel grazed her dress, and though she ran back instinctively, yet when she was safe on the pavement, the fright overpowered her nerves, and she clung to the street-post almost fainting. Two or three passers-by humanely gathered round her; and the driver, looking back, and muttering to himself, "Not bad-looking; neatly dressed; lady-like; French shawl; may have tin; worth while perhaps! " gallantly descended and hastened to offer apologies, with a respectful hope that she was not injured.

Mrs. Haughton answered somewhat tartly, but being one of those good-hearted women who, apt to be rude, are extremely sorry for it the moment afterwards, she wished to repair any hurt to his feelings occasioned by her first impulse; and when, renewing his excuses, he offered his arm over the crossing, she did not like to refuse. On gaining the side of the way on which her house was situated, she had recovered sufficiently to blush for having accepted such familiar assistance from a perfect stranger, and somewhat to falter in returning thanks for his politeness.

Our gentleman, whose estimate of his attractions was not humble, ascribed the blushing cheek and faltering voice to the natural effect produced by his appearance; and he himself admiring very much a handsome bracelet on her wrist, which he deemed a favourable prognostic of "tin, " watched her to her door, and sent his groom in the course of the evening to make discreet inquiries in the neighbourhood. The result of the inquiries induced him to resolve upon prosecuting the acquaintance thus begun. He contrived to learn the hours at which Mrs. Haughton usually visited the house, and to pass by Gloucester Place at the very nick of time. His bow was recognizing, respectful, interrogative, —a bow that asked "How much farther? " But Mrs. Haughton's bow respondent seemed to declare, "Not at all! " The stranger did not venture more that day; but a day or two afterwards he came again into Gloucester Place on foot. On that occasion Mrs. Haughton was with her son, and the gentleman would not seem to perceive her. The next day he returned; she was then alone, and just as she gained her door, he advanced. "I beg you ten thousand pardons, madam; but if I am rightly informed, I have the honour to address Mrs. Charles Haughton! "

The lady bowed in surprise.

"Ah, madam, your lamented husband was one of my most particular friends. "

"You don't say so! " cried Mrs. Haughton. And looking more attentively at the stranger, there was in his dress and appearance something that she thought very stylish; a particular friend of Charles Haughton's was sure to be stylish, to be a man of the first water. And she loved the poor Captain's memory; her heart warmed to any "particular friend of his. "

"Yes, " resumed the gentleman, noting the advantage he had gained, "though I was considerably his junior, we were great cronies; excuse that familiar expression; in the Hussars together —"

"The Captain was not in the Hussars, sir; he was in the Guards. "

"Of course he was; but I was saying—in the Hussars, together with the Guards, there were some very fine fellows; very fine; he was one of them. I could not resist paying my respects to the widowed lady of so fine a fellow. I know it is a liberty, ma'am, but 't is my way. People who know me well—and I have a large acquaintance—are kind enough to excuse my way. And to think that villanous horse, which I had just bought out of Lord Bolton's stud (200 guineas, ma'am, and cheap), should have nearly taken the life of Charles Haughton's lovely relict! If anybody else had been driving that brute, I shudder to think what might have been the consequences; but I have a wrist of iron. Strength is a vulgar qualification, —very vulgar; but when it saves a lady from perishing, how can one be ashamed of it? But I am detaining you. Your own house, Mrs. Haughton? "

"Yes, sir, I have just taken it, but the workmen have not finished. I am not yet settled here. "

"Charming situation! My friend left a son, I believe? In the army already? "

"No, sir, but he wishes it very much. "

"Mr. Darrell, I think, could gratify that wish. "

"What! you know Mr. Darrell, that most excellent generous man. All we have we owe to him. "

The gentleman abruptly turned aside, — wisely; for his expression of face at that praise might have startled Mrs.

Haughton. "Yes, I knew him once. He has had many a fee out of my family. Goodish lawyer; cleverish man; and rich as a Jew. I should like to see my old friend's son, ma'am. He must be monstrous handsome with such parents! "

"Oh, sir, very like his father. I shall be proud to present him to you. "

"Ma'am, I thank you. I will have the honour to call—"

And thus is explained how Jasper Losely has knocked at Mrs. Haughton's door; has walked up her stairs; has seated himself in her drawing-room, and is now edging his chair somewhat nearer to her, and throwing into his voice and looks a degree of admiration which has been sincerely kindled by the aspect of her elegant apartments.

Jessica Haughton was not one of those women, if such there be, who do not know when a gentleman is making up to them. She knew perfectly well that with a very little encouragement her visitor would declare himself a suitor. Nor, to speak truth, was she quite insensible to his handsome person, nor quite unmoved by his flatteries. She had her weak points, and vanity was one of them. Nor conceived she, poor lady, the slightest suspicion that Jasper Losely was not a personage whose attentions might flatter any woman. Though lie had not even announced a name, but, pushing aside the footman, had sauntered in with as familiar an ease as if he had been a first cousin; though he had not uttered a syllable that could define his station, or attest his boasted friendship with the dear defunct, still Mrs. Haughton implicitly believed that she was with one of those gay chiefs of ton who had glittered round her Charlie in that earlier morning of his life, ere he had sold out of the Guards, and bought himself out of jail; a lord, or an honourable at least; and she was even (I shudder to say) revolving in her mind whether it might not be an excellent thing for her dear Lionel if she could prevail on herself to procure for him the prop and guidance of a distinguished and brilliant father-in-law, —rich, noble, evidently good-natured, sensible, attractive. Oh! but the temptation was growing more and more IMMENSE! when suddenly the door opened, and in sprang Lionel crying out, "Mother dear, the Colonel has come with me on purpose to—"

He stopped short, staring hard at Jasper Losely. That gentleman advanced a few steps, extending his hand, but came to an abrupt halt on seeing Colonel Morley's figure now filling up the doorway. Not that he feared recognition: the Colonel did not know him by sight, but he knew by sight the Colonel. In his own younger day, when lolling over the rails of Rotten Row, he had enviously noted the leaders of fashion pass by, and Colonel Morley had not escaped his observation. Colonel Morley, indeed, was one of those men who by name and repute are sure to be known to all who, like Jasper Losely in his youth, would fain learn something about that gaudy, babbling, and remorseless world which, like the sun, either vivifies or corrupts, according to the properties of the object on which it shines. Strange to say, it was the mere sight of the real fine gentleman that made the mock fine gentleman shrink and collapse. Though Jasper Losely knew himself to be still called a magnificent man, —one of royal Nature's Lifeguardsmen; though confident that from top to toe his habiliments could defy the criticism of the strictest martinet in polite costume, no sooner did that figure, by no means handsome and clad in garments innocent of buckram but guilty of wrinkles, appear on the threshold than Jasper Losely felt small and shabby, as if he had been suddenly reduced to five feet two, and had bought his coat out of an old clothesman's bag.

Without appearing even to see Mr. Losely, the Colonel, in his turn, as he glided past him towards Mrs. Haughton, had, with what is proverbially called the corner of the eye, taken the whole of that impostor's superb personnel into calm survey, had read him through and through, and decided on these two points without the slightest hesitation, —"a lady-killer and a sharper. "

Quick as breathing had been the effect thus severally produced on Mrs. Haughton's visitors, which it has cost so many words to describe, —so quick that the Colonel, without any apparent pause of dialogue, has already taken up the sentence Lionel left uncompleted, and says, as he bows over Mrs. Haughton's hand, "Come on purpose to claim acquaintance with an old friend's widow, a young friend's mother. "

MRS. HAUGHTON. —"I am sure, Colonel Morley, I am very much flattered. And you, too, knew the poor dear Captain; 't is so pleasant to think that his old friends come round us now. This gentleman, also, was a particular friend of dear Charles's. "

The Colonel had somewhat small eyes, which moved with habitual slowness. He lifted those eyes, let them drop upon Jasper (who still stood in the middle of the room, with one hand still half-extended towards Lionel), and letting the eyes rest there while he spoke, repeated,

"Particular friend of Charles Haughton, —the only one of his particular friends whom I never had the honour to see before. "

Jasper, who, whatever his deficiency in other virtues, certainly did not lack courage, made a strong effort at self-possession, and without replying to the Colonel, whose remark had not been directly addressed to himself, said in his most rollicking tone, "Yes, Mrs. Haughton, Charles was my particular friend, but, " lifting his eyeglass, "but this gentleman was, " dropping the eyeglass negligently, "not in our set, I suppose. " Then advancing to Lionel, and seizing his hand, "I must introduce myself, —the image of your father, I declare! I was saying to Mrs. Haughton how much I should like to see you; proposing to her, just as you came in, that we should go to the play together. Oh, ma'am, you may trust him to me safely. Young men should see Life! " Here Jasper tipped Lionel one of those knowing winks with which he was accustomed to delight and ensnare the young friends of Mr. Poole, and hurried on: "But in an innocent way, ma'am, such as mothers would approve. We'll fix an evening for it when I have the honour to call again. Good morning, Mrs. Haughton. Your hand again, sir (to Lionel). Ah, we shall be great friends, I guess! You must let me take you out in my cab; teach you to handle the ribbons, eh? 'Gad, my old friend Charles was a whip. Ha! Ha! Goodday, good-day! "

Not a muscle had moved in the Colonel's face during Mr. Losely's jovial monologue. But when Jasper had bowed himself out, Mrs. Haughton, courtesying, and ringing the bell for the footman to open the street-door, the man of the world (and, as a man of the world, Colonel Morley was consummate) again raised those small slow eyes, —this time towards her face, —and dropped the words,

"My old friend's particular friend is—not bad looking, Mrs. Haughton! "

"And so lively and pleasant, " returned Mrs. Haughton, with a slight rise of colour, but no other sign of embarrassment. "It may be a nice acquaintance for Lionel. "

"Mother! " cried that ungrateful boy, "you are not speaking seriously? I think the man is odious. If he were not my father's friend, I should say he was—"

"What, Lionel? " asked the Colonel, blandly, "was what? "

"Snobbish, sir. "

"Lionel, how dare you? " exclaimed Mrs. Haughton. "What vulgar words boys do pick up at school, Colonel Morley. "

"We must be careful that they do not pick up worse than words when they leave school, my dear madam. You will forgive me, but Mr. Darrell has so expressly—of course, with your permission—commended this young gentleman to my responsible care and guidance; so openly confided to me his views and intentions, —that perhaps you would do me the very great favour not to force upon him, against his own wishes, the acquaintance of—that very good-looking person. "

Mrs. Haughton pouted, and kept down her rising temper. The Colonel began to awe her.

"By the by, " continued the man of the world, "may I inquire the name of my old friend's particular friend? "

"His name? upon my word I really don't know it. Perhaps he left his card; ring the bell, Lionel. "

"You don't know his name, yet you know him, ma'am, and would allow your son to see LIFE under his auspices! I beg you ten thousand pardons; but even ladies the most cautious, mothers the most watchful, are exposed to—"

"Immense temptations, —that is—to—to—"

"I understand perfectly, my dear Mrs. Haughton. "

The footman appeared. "Did that gentleman leave a card? "

"No, ma'am. "

"Did not you ask his name when he entered? "

"Yes, ma'am, but he said he would announce himself. " When the footman had withdrawn, Mrs. Haughton exclaimed piteously, "I have been to blame, Colonel; I see it. But Lionel will tell you how I came to know the gentleman, —the gentleman who nearly ran over me, Lionel, and then spoke so kindly about your dear father. "

"Oh, that is the person! —I supposed so, " cried Lionel, kissing his mother, who was inclined to burst into tears. "I can explain it all now, Colonel Morley. Any one who says a kind word about my father warms my mother's heart to him at once; is it not so, Mother dear? "

"And long be it so, " said Colonel Morley, with grateful earnestness; "and may such be my passport to your confidence, Mrs. Haughton. Charles was my old schoolfellow, —a little boy when I and Darrell were in the sixth form; and, pardon me, when I add, that if that gentleman were ever Charles Haughton's particular friend, he could scarcely have been a very wise one. For unless his appearance greatly belies his years he must have been little more than a boy when Charles Haughton left Lionel fatherless. "

Here, in the delicacy of tact, seeing that Mrs. Haughton looked ashamed of the subject, and seemed aware of her imprudence, the Colonel rose, with a request—cheerfully granted—that Lionel might be allowed to come to breakfast with him the next morning.

CHAPTER XI.

A man of the world, having accepted a troublesome charge, considers "what he will do with it; " and, having promptly decided, is sure, first, that he could not have done better; and, secondly, that much may be said to prove that he could not have done worse.

Reserving to a later occasion anymore detailed description of Colonel Morley, it suffices for the present to say that he was a man of a very fine understanding as applied to the special world in which he lived. Though no one had a more numerous circle of friends, and though with many of those friends he was on that footing of familiar intimacy which Darrell's active career once, and his rigid seclusion of late, could not have established with any idle denizen of that brilliant society in which Colonel Morley moved and had his being, yet to Alban Morley's heart (a heart not easily reached) no friend was so dear as Guy Darrell. They had entered Eton on the same day, left it the same day, lodged while there in the same house; and though of very different characters, formed one of those strong, imperishable, brotherly affections which the Fates weave into the very woof of existence.

Darrell's recommendation would have secured to any young protege Colonel Morley's gracious welcome and invaluable advice. But, both as Darrell's acknowledged kinsman and as Charles Haughton's son, Lionel called forth his kindliest sentiments and obtained his most sagacious deliberations. He had already seen the boy several times before waiting on Mrs. Haughton, deeming it would please her to defer his visit until she could receive him in all the glories of Gloucester Place; and he had taken Lionel into high favour and deemed him worthy of a conspicuous place in the world. Though Darrell in his letter to Colonel Morley had emphatically distinguished the position of Lionel, as a favoured kinsman, from that of a presumptive or even a probable heir, yet the rich man had also added: "But I wish him to take rank as the representative to the Haughtons; and, whatever I may do with the bulk of my fortune, I shall insure to him a liberal independence. The completion of his education, the adequate allowance to him, the choice of a profession, are matters in which I entreat you to act for yourself, as if you were his guardian. I am leaving England: I may be abroad for years. " Colonel Morley, in accepting the responsibilities thus pressed on him, brought to bear upon his charge subtle discrimination, as well as conscientious anxiety.

He saw that Lionel's heart was set upon the military profession, and that his power of application seemed lukewarm and desultory when not cheered and concentred by enthusiasm, and would, therefore, fail him if directed to studies which had no immediate reference to the objects of his ambition. The Colonel, accordingly, dismissed the idea of sending him for three years to a university. Alban Morley summed up his theories on the collegiate ordeal in these succinct aphorisms: "Nothing so good as a university education, nor worse than a university without its education. Better throw a youth at once into the wider sphere of a capital—provided you there secure to his social life the ordinary checks of good company, the restraints imposed by the presence of decorous women, and men of grave years and dignified repute—than confine him to the exclusive society of youths of his own age, the age of wild spirits and unreflecting imitation, unless he cling to the safeguard which is found in hard reading, less by the book-knowledge it bestows than by the serious and preoccupied mind which it abstracts from the coarser temptations. "

But Lionel, younger in character than in years, was too boyish as yet to be safely consigned to those trials of tact and temper which await the neophyte who enters on life through the doors of a mess-room. His pride was too morbid, too much on the alert for offence; his frankness too crude, his spirit too untamed by the insensible discipline of social commerce.

Quoth the observant man of the world: "Place his honour in his own keeping, and he will carry it about with him on full cock, to blow off a friend's head or his own before the end of the first month. Huffy! decidedly huffy! and of all causes that disturb regiments, and induce courts-martial, the commonest cause is a huffy lad! Pity! for that youngster has in him the right metal, —spirit and talent that should make him a first-rate soldier. It would be time well spent that should join professional studies with that degree of polite culture which gives dignity and cures dulness. I must get him out of London, out of England; cut him off from his mother's apron-strings, and the particular friends of his poor father who prowl unannounced into the widow's drawing-room. He shall go to Paris; no better place to learn military theories, and be civilized out of huffy dispositions. No doubt my old friend, the chevalier, who has the art strategic at his fingerends, might be induced to take him en pension, direct his studies, and keep him out of harm's way. I can secure to him the entree into the circles of the rigid old Faubourg St. Germain, where manners are best bred, and household ties most respected. Besides, as I am so often at Paris myself, I shall have him under my eye, and a few years there, spent in completing him as man, may bring him nearer to that marshal's baton which every recruit should have in his eye, than if I started him at once a raw boy, unable to take care of himself as an ensign, and unfitted, save by mechanical routine, to take care of others, should he live to buy the grade of a colonel. "

The plans thus promptly formed Alban Morley briefly explained to Lionel when the boy came to breakfast in Curzon Street; requesting him to obtain Mrs. Haughton's acquiesence in that exercise of the discretionary powers with which he had been invested by Mr. Darrell. To Lionel the proposition that commended the very studies to which his tastes directed his ambition, and placed his initiation into responsible manhood among scenes bright to his fancy, because new to his experience, seemed of course the perfection of wisdom. Less readily pleased was poor Mrs. Haughton, when her son returned to communicate the arrangement, backing a polite and well-worded letter from the Colonel with his own more artless eloquence. Instantly she flew off on the wing of her "little tempers. " "What! her only son taken from her; sent to that horrid Continent, just when she was so respectably settled! What was the good of money if she was to be parted from her boy! Mr. Darrell might take the money back if he pleased; she would write and tell him so. Colonel Morley had no feeling; and she was shocked to think Lionel was in such unnatural hands. She saw very plainly that he no longer cared for her, —a serpent's tooth, " etc. But as soon as the burst was over, the sky cleared and Mrs. Haughton became penitent and sensible. Then her grief for Lionel's loss was diverted by preparations for his departure. There was his wardrobe to see to; a patent portmanteau to purchase and to fill. And, all done, the last evening mother and son spent together, though painful at the moment, it would be happiness for both hereafter to recall! Their hands clasped in each other, her head leaning on his young shoulder, her tears kissed so soothingly away, and soft words of kindly motherly counsel, sweet promises of filial performances. Happy, thrice happy, as an after remembrance, be the final parting between hopeful son and fearful parent at the foot of that mystic bridge, which starts from the threshold of home, —lost in the dimness of the far-opposing shore! —bridge over which goes the boy who will never return but as the man.

CHAPTER XII.

The pocket-cannibal baits his woman's trap with love-letters, and a widow allured steals timidly towards it from under the weeds.

Jasper Losely is beginning to be hard up! The infallible calculation at rouge-et-noir has carried off all that capital which had accumulated from the savings of the young gentlemen whom Dolly Poole had contributed to his exchequer. Poole himself is beset by duns, and pathetically observes "that he has lost three stone in weight, and that he believes the calves to his legs are gone to enlarge his liver. "

Jasper is compelled to put down his cabriolet, to discharge his groom, to retire from his fashionable lodgings; and just when the prospect even of a dinner becomes dim, he bethinks himself of Arabella Crane, and remembers that she promised him L5, nay L10, which are still due from her. He calls; he is received like the prodigal son. Nay, to his own surprise, he finds Mrs. Crane has made her house much more inviting: the drawing-rooms are cleaned up; the addition of a few easy articles of furniture gives them quite a comfortable air. She herself has improved in costume, though her favourite colour still remains iron gray. She informs Jasper that she fully expected him; that these preparations are in his honour; that she has engaged a very good cook; that she hopes he will dine with her when not better engaged; in short, lets him feel himself at home in Podden Place.

Jasper at first suspected a sinister design, under civilities that his conscience told him were unmerited, —a design to entrap him into that matrimonial alliance which he had so ungallantly scouted, and from which he still recoiled with an abhorrence which man is not justified in feeling for any connubial partner less preternaturally terrific than the Witch of Endor or the Bleeding Nun!

But Mrs. Crane quickly and candidly hastened to dispel his ungenerous apprehensions. She had given up, she said, all ideas so preposterous; love and wedlock were equally out of her mind. But ill as he had behaved to her, she could not but feel a sincere regard for him, —a deep interest in his fate. He ought still to make a brilliant marriage: did that idea not occur to him? She might help him there with her woman's wit. "In short, " said Mrs. Crane, pinching her lips, "In short, Jasper, I feel for you as a mother. Look on me as such!"

The pure and affectionate notion wonderfully tickled and egregiously delighted Jasper Losely. "Look on you as a mother! I will, " said he, with emphasis. "Best of creatures! " And though in his own mind he had not a doubt that she still adored him (not as a mother), he believed it was a disinterested, devoted adoration, such as the beautiful brute really had inspired more than once in his abominable life. Accordingly, he moved into the neighbourhood of Podden Place, contenting himself with a second-floor bedroom in a house recommended to him by Mrs. Crane, and taking his meals at his adopted mother's with filial familiarity. She expressed a desire to make Mr. Poole's acquaintance; Jasper hastened to present that worthy. Mrs. Crane invited Samuel Dolly to dine one day, to sup the next; she lent him L3 to redeem his dress-coat from pawn, and she gave him medicaments for the relief of his headache.

Samuel Dolly venerated her as a most superior woman; envied Jasper such a "mother. " Thus easily did Arabella Crane possess herself of the existence of Jasper Losely. Lightly her fingers closed over it, —lightly as the fisherman's over the captivated trout. And whatever her generosity, it was not carried to imprudence. She just gave to Jasper enough to bring him within her power; she had no idea of ruining herself by larger supplies: she concealed from him the extent of her income (which was in chief part derived from house-rents), the amount of her savings, even the name of her banker. And if he carried off to the rouge-et-noir table the coins he obtained from her, and came for more, Mrs. Crane put on the look of a mother incensed, —mild but awful, —and scolded as mothers sometimes can scold. Jasper Losely began to be frightened at Mrs. Crane's scoldings. And he had not that power over her which, though arrogated by a lover, is denied to an adopted son. His mind, relieved from the habitual distraction of the gaming-table for which the resource was wanting, settled with redoubled ardour on the image of Mrs. Haughton. He had called at her house several times since the fatal day on which he had met there Colonel Morley, but Mrs. Haughton was never at home. And as when the answer was given to him by the footman, he had more than once, on crossing the street, seen herself through the window, it was clear that his acquaintance was not courted. Jasper Losely, by habit, was the reverse of a pertinacious and troublesome suitor; not, Heaven knows, from want of audacity, but from excess of self-love. Where a

Lovelace so superb condescended to make overtures, a Clarissa so tasteless as to decline them deserved and experienced his contempt. Besides, steadfast and prolonged pursuit of any object, however important and attractive, was alien to the levity and fickleness of his temper. But in this instance he had other motives than those on the surface for unusual perseverance.

A man like Jasper Losely never reposes implicit confidence in any one. He is garrulous, indiscreet; lets out much that Machiavel would have advised him not to disclose: but he invariably has nooks and corners in his mind which he keeps to himself. Jasper did not confide to his adopted mother his designs upon his intended bride. But she knew them through Poole, to whom he was more frank; and when she saw him looking over her select and severe library, taking therefrom the "Polite Letter-Writer" and the "Elegant Extracts, " Mrs. Crane divined at once that Jasper Losely was meditating the effect of epistolary seduction upon the widow of Gloucester Place.

Jasper did not write a bad love-letter in the florid style. He had at his command, in especial, certain poetical quotations, the effect of which repeated experience had assured him to be as potent upon the female breast as the incantations or carmina of the ancient sorcery. The following in particular,

"Had I a heart for falsehood framed,
I neer could injure you."

Another, generally to be applied when confessing that his career had been interestingly wild, and would, if pity were denied him, be pathetically short,

"When he who adores thee has left but the name
Of his faults and his follies behind."

Armed with these quotations, many a sentence from the "Polite Letter-Writer" or the "Elegant Extracts, " and a quire of rose-edged paper, Losely sat down to Ovidian composition.

But as he approached the close of epistle the first, it occurred to him that a signature and address were necessary. The address was not difficult. He could give Poole's (hence his confidence to that gentleman): Poole had a lodging in Bury Street, St. James's, a fashionable locality for single men. But the name required more consideration. There were insuperable objections against signing his own to any person who might be in communication with Mr. Darrell; a pity, for there was a good old family of the name of Losely. A name of aristocratic sound might indeed be readily borrowed from any lordly proprietor thereof without asking a formal consent. But this loan was exposed to danger. Mrs. Haughton might very naturally mention such name, as borne by her husband's friend, to Colonel Morley; and Colonel Morley would most probably know enough of the connections and relations of any peer so honoured to say, "There is no such Greville, Cavendish, or Talbot. " But Jasper Losely was not without fertility of invention and readiness of resource. A grand idea, worthy of a master, and proving that, if the man had not been a rogue in grain, he could have been reared into a very clever politician, flashed across him. He would sign himself "SMITH. " Nobody could say there is no such Smith; nobody could say that a Smith might not be a most respectable, fashionable, highly-connected man. There are Smiths who are millionaires; Smiths who are large-acred squires; substantial baronets; peers of England, and pillars of the State. You can no more question a man's right to be a Smith than his right to be a Briton; and wide as the diversity of rank, lineage, virtue, and genius in Britons is the diversity in Smiths. But still a name so generic often affects a definitive precursor. Jasper signed himself "J. COURTENAY SMITH. " He called, and left epistle the first with his own kid-gloved hand, inquiring first if Mrs. Haughton were at home, and, responded to in the negative this time, he asked for her son. "Her son was gone abroad with Colonel Morley. " Jasper, though sorry to lose present hold over the boy, was consoled at learning that the Colonel was off the ground. Afore sanguine of success, he glanced up at the window, and, sure that Mrs. Haughton was there, though he saw her not, lifted his hat with as melancholy an expression of reproach as he could throw into his face.

The villain could not have found a moment in Mrs. Haughton's widowed life so propitious to his chance of success. In her lodging-house at Pimlico, the good lady had been too incessantly occupied for that idle train of revery, in which the poets assure us that Cupid finds leisure to whet his arrows and take his aim. Had Lionel still been by her side, had even Colonel Morley been in town, her affection for the one, her awe of the other, would have been her safeguards. But alone in that fine new house, no friends, no acquaintances as yet, no dear visiting circle on which to expend the desire of talk and the zest for innocent excitement that are natural to ladies of an active mind and a nervous temperament, the sudden obtrusion of a suitor so respectfully ardent, —oh, it is not to be denied that the temptation was IMMENSE.

And when that note, so neatly folded, so elegantly sealed, lay in her irresolute hand, the widow could not but feel that she was still young, still pretty; and her heart flew back to the day when the linendraper's fair daughter had been the cynosure of the provincial High Street; when young officers had lounged to and fro the pavement, looking in at her window; when ogles and notes had alike beset her, and the dark eyes of the irresistible Charlie Haughton had first taught her pulse to tremble. And in her hand lies the letter of Charlie Haughton's particular friend. She breaks the seal. She reads—a declaration!

Five letters in five days did Jasper write. In the course of those letters, he explains away the causes for suspicion which Colonel Morley had so ungenerously suggested. He is no longer anonymous; he is J. Courtenay Smith. He alludes incidentally to the precocious age in which he had become "lord of himself, that heritage of woe. " This accounts for his friendship with a man so much his senior as the late Charlie. He confesses that in the vortex of dissipation his hereditary estates have disappeared; but he has still a genteel independence; and with the woman of his heart, etc. He had never before known what real love was, etc. "Pleasure had fired his maddening soul; " "but the heart, —the heart been lonely still. " He entreated only a personal interview, even though to be rejected, — scorned. Still, when "he who adored her had left but the name, " etc. Alas! alas! as Mrs. Haughton put down epistle the fifth, she hesitated; and the woman who hesitates in such a case, is sure, at least—to write a civil answer.

Mrs. Haughton wrote but three lines, —still they were civil; and conceded an interview for the next day, though implying that it was but for the purpose of assuring Mr. J. Courtenay Smith, in person, of her unalterable fidelity to the shade of his lamented friend.

In high glee Jasper showed Mrs. Haughton's answer to Dolly Poole, and began seriously to speculate on the probable amount of the widow's income, and the value of her movables in Gloucester Place. Thence he repaired to Mrs. Crane; and, emboldened by the hope forever to escape from her maternal tutelage, braved her scoldings and asked for a couple of sovereigns. He was sure that he should be in luck that night. She gave to him the sum, and spared the scoldings. But, as soon as he was gone, conjecturing from the bravado of his manner what had really occurred, Mrs. Crane put on her bonnet and went out.

CHAPTER XIII.

Unhappy is the man who puts his trust in a woman.

Late that evening a lady, in a black veil, knocked at No. —Gloucester Place, and asked to see Mrs. Haughton on urgent business. She was admitted. She remained but five minutes.

The next day when, "gay as a bridegroom prancing to his bride, " Jasper Losely presented himself at the widow's door, the servant placed in his hand a packet, and informed him bluffly that Mrs. Haughton had gone out of town. Jasper with difficulty suppressed his rage, opened the packet, —his own letters returned, with these words, "Sir, your name is not Courtenay Smith. If you trouble me again, I shall apply to the police. " Never from female hand had Jasper Losely's pride received such a slap on its face. He was literally stunned. Mechanically he hastened to Arabella Crane; and having no longer any object in concealment, but, on the contrary, a most urgent craving for sympathy, he poured forth his indignation and wrongs. No mother could be more consolatory than Mrs. Crane. She soothed, she flattered, she gave him an excellent dinner; after which, she made him so comfortable, what with an easy-chair and complimentary converse, that, when Jasper rose late to return to his lodging, he said, "After all, if I had been ugly and stupid, and of a weakly constitution, I should have been of a very domestic turn of mind. "

CHAPTER XIV.

No author ever drew a character consistent to human nature, but what he was forced to ascribe to it many inconsistencies.

Whether moved by that pathetic speech of Jasper's, or by some other impulse not less feminine, Arabella Crane seemed suddenly to conceive the laudable and arduous design of reforming that portentous sinner. She had some distant relations in London, whom she very rarely troubled with a visit, and who, had she wanted anything from them, would have shut their doors in her face; but as, on the contrary, she was well off, single, and might leave her money to whom she pleased, the distant relations were always warm in manner, and prodigal in their offers of service. The next day she repaired to one of these kinsfolk, —a person in a large way of business, —and returned home with two great books in white sheepskin. And when Losely looked in to dine, she said, in the suavest tones a tender mother can address to an amiable truant, "Jasper, you have great abilities; at the gaming-table abilities are evidently useless: your forte is calculation; you were always very quick at that. I have been fortunate enough to procure you an easy piece of task-work, for which you will be liberally remunerated. A friend of mine wishes to submit these books to a regular accountant: he suspects that a clerk has cheated him; but he cannot tell how or where. You know accounts thoroughly, —no one better, —and the pay will be ten guineas. "

Jasper, though his early life had rendered familiar and facile to him the science of book-keeping and double-entry, made a grimace at the revolting idea of any honest labour, however light and well paid. But ten guineas were an immense temptation, and in the evening Mrs. Crane coaxed him into the task.

Neglecting no feminine art to make the lawless nomad feel at home under her roof, she had provided for his ease and comfort morocco slippers and a superb dressing-robe, in material rich, in colour becoming. Men, single or marital, are accustomed to connect the idea of home with dressing-gown and slippers, especially if, after dinner, they apply (as Jasper Losely now applied) to occupations in which the brain is active, the form in repose. What achievement, literary or scientific, was ever accomplished by a student strapped to unyielding boots, and "cabined, cribbed, confined, " in a, coat that fits him like wax? As robed in the cozy garment which is consecrated to the sacred familiar Lares, the relaxing, handsome ruffian sat in the quiet room, bending his still regular profile over the sheepskin books, the harmless pen in that strong well-shaped hand, Mrs. Crane watched him with a softening countenance. To bear him company, she had actively taken, herself, to work, —the gold thimble dragged from its long repose, —marking and hemming, with nimble artistic fingers, new cravats for the adopted son! Strange creature is woman! Ungrateful and perfidious as that sleek tiger before her had often proved himself, though no man could less deserve one kindly sentiment in a female heart, though she knew that he cared nothing for her, still it was pleasing to know that he cared for nobody else, that he was sitting in the same room; and Arabella Crane felt that, if that existence could continue, she could forget the past and look contented towards the future. Again I say, strange creature is woman; and in this instance, creature more strange, because so grim! But as her eyes soften, and her fingers work, and her mind revolves schemes for making that lawless wild beast an innocuous tame animal, who can help feeling for and with grim Arabella Crane?

Poor woman! And will not the experiment succeed? Three evenings does Jasper Losely devote to this sinless life and its peaceful occupation. He completes his task; he receives the ten guineas. (How much of that fee came out of Mrs. Crane's privy purse?) He detects three mistakes, which justify suspicion of the book-keeper's integrity. Set a thief to catch a thief! He is praised for acuteness, and promised a still lighter employment, to be still better paid. He departs, declaring that he will come the next day, earlier than usual; he volunteers an eulogium upon work in general; he vows that evenings so happy he has not spent for years; he leaves Mrs. Crane so much impressed by the hope of his improvement that, if a good clergyman had found her just at that moment, she might almost have been induced to pray. But

> "Heu quoties fidem
> Mutatosque deos flebit!"

Jasper Losely returns not, neither to Podden place or his lodging in the neighborhood. Days elapse and still he comes not; even Poole does not know where he has gone; even Poole has not seen him! But that worthy is now laid up with a serious rheumatic fever—confined to his room and a water gruel. And Jasper Losely is not the man to intrude himself on the privacy of a sick chamber. Mrs. Crane, more benevolent, visits Poole cheers him up—gets him a nurse—writes to Uncle Sam. Poole blesses her. He hopes that Uncle Sam, moved by the spectacle of the sick-bed will say, "Don't let your debts fret you: I will pay them! " Whatever her disappointment or resentment at Jasper's thankless and mysterious evasion, Arabella Crane is calmly confident of his return. To her servant, Bridget Greggs, who was perhaps the sole person in the world who entertained affection for the lone gaunt woman, and who held Jasper Losely in profound detestation, she said, with tranquil sternness, "That man has crossed my life, and darkened it. He passed away, and left Night behind him. He has dared to return. He shall never escape me again till the grave yawn for one of us. "

"But, Lor' love you, miss, you would not put yourself in the power of such a black-hearted villing? "

"In his power! No, Bridget; fear not, he must be in mine, sooner or later in mine, hand and foot. Patience! " As she was thus speaking, —a knock at the door! "It is he; I told you so; quick! "

But it was not Jasper Losely. It was Mr. Rugge.

CHAPTER XV.

"When God wills, all winds bring rain. " — Ancient Proverb.

The manager had not submitted to the loss of his property in Sophy and L100 without taking much vain trouble to recover the one or the other. He had visited Jasper while that gentleman lodged in St. James's; but the moment he hinted at the return of the L100, Mr. Losely opened both door and window, and requested the manager to make his immediate choice of the two. Taking the more usual mode of exit, Mr. Rugge vented his just indignation in a lawyer's letter, threatening Mr. Losely with an action for conspiracy and fraud. He had also more than once visited Mrs. Crane, who somewhat soothed him by allowing that he had been very badly used, that he ought at least to be repaid his money, and promising to do her best to persuade Mr. Losely "to behave like a gentleman. " With regard to Sophy herself, Mrs. Crane appeared to feel a profound indifference. In fact, the hatred which Mrs. Crane had unquestionably conceived for Sophy while under her charge was much diminished by Losely's unnatural conduct towards the child. To her it was probably a matter of no interest whether Sophy was in Rugge's hands or Waife's; enough for her that the daughter of a woman against whose memory her fiercest passions were enlisted was, in either case, so far below herself in the grades of the social ladder.

Perhaps of the two protectors for Sophy, Rugge and Waife, her spite alone would have given the preference to Waife. He was on a still lower step of the ladder than the itinerant manager. Nor, though she had so mortally injured the forlorn cripple in the eyes of Mr. Hartopp, had she any deliberate purpose of revenge to gratify against him! On the contrary, if she viewed him with contempt, it was a contempt not unmixed with pity. It was necessary to make to the Mayor the communications she had made, or that worthy magistrate would not have surrendered the child intrusted to him, at least until Waife's return. And really it was a kindness to the old man to save him both from an agonizing scene with Jasper, and from the more public opprobrium which any resistance on his part to Jasper's authority or any altercation between the two would occasion. And as her main object then was to secure Losely's allegiance to her, by proving her power to be useful to him, so Waifes and Sophys and Mayors and Managers were to her but as pawns to be moved and sacrificed, according to the leading strategy of her game.

Rugge came now, agitated and breathless, to inform Mrs. Crane that Waife had been seen in London. Mr. Rugge's clown had seen him, not far from the Tower; but the cripple had disappeared before the clown, who was on the top of an omnibus, had time to descend. "And even if he had actually caught hold of Mr. Waife, " observed Mrs. Crane, "what then? You have no claim on Mr. Waife. "

"But the Phenomenon must be with that ravishing marauder, " said Rugge. "However, I have set a minister of justice—that is, ma'am, a detective police—at work; and what I now ask of you is simply this: should it be necessary for Mr. Losely to appear with me before the senate—that is to say, ma'am, a metropolitan police-court—in order to prove my legal property in my own bought and paid for Phenomenon, will you induce that bold bad man not again to return the poisoned chalice to my lips? "

"I do not even know where Mr. Losely is; perhaps not in London. "

"Ma'am, I saw him last night at the theatre, —Princess's. I was in the shilling gallery. He who owes me L100, ma'am, —he in a private box! "

"Ah! you are sure; by himself? "

"With a lady, ma'am, —a lady in a shawl from Ingee. I know them shawls. My father taught me to know them in early childhood, for he was an ornament to British commerce, —a broker, ma'am, —pawn! And, " continued Rugge, with a withering smile, "that man in a private box, which at the Princess's costs two pounds two, and with the spoils of Ingee by his side, lifted his eyeglass and beheld me, — me in the shilling gallery! and his conscience did not say, 'Should we not change places if I paid that gentleman L100? ' Can such things be, and overcome us, ma'am, like a summer cloud, without our special—I put it to you, ma'am—wonder? "

"Oh, with a lady, was he? " exclaimed Arabella Crane, her wrath, which, while the manager spoke, gathered fast and full, bursting now into words. "His ladies shall know the man who sells his own child for a show; only find out where the girl is, then come here again before you stir further. Oh, with a lady! Go to your detective policeman, or rather send him to me; we will first discover Mr. Losely's address. I will pay all the expenses. Rely on my zeal, Mr. Rugge. "

Much comforted, the manager went his way. He had not been long gone before Jasper himself appeared. The traitor entered with a more than customary bravado of manner, as if he apprehended a scolding, and was prepared to face it; but Mrs. Crane neither reproached him for his prolonged absence, nor expressed surprise at his return. With true feminine duplicity, she received him as if nothing had happened. Jasper, thus relieved, became of his own accord apologetic and explanatory; evidently he wanted something of Mrs. Crane. "The fact is, my dear friend, " said he, sinking into a chair, "that the day after I last saw you I happened to go to the General Post Office to see if there were any letters for me. You smile: you don't believe me. Honour bright, here they are; " and Jasper took from the side pocket of his coat a pocket-book, a new pocket-book, a brilliant pocket-book, fragrant Russian leather, delicately embossed, golden clasps, silken linings, jewelled pencil-case, malachite pen-knife, —an arsenal of knickknacks stored in neat recesses; such a pocket-book as no man ever gives to himself. Sardanapalus would not have given that pocket-book to himself! Such a pocket-book never comes to you, O enviable Lotharios, save as tributary keepsakes from the charmers who adore you! Grimly the Adopted Mother eyed that pocket-book. Never had she seen it before. Grimly she pinched her lips. Out of this dainty volume—which would have been of cumbrous size to a slim thread-paper exquisite, but scarcely bulged into ripple the Atlantic expanse of Jasper Losely's magnificent chest—the monster drew forth two letters on French paper, —foreign post-marks. He replaced them quickly, only suffering her eye to glance at the address, and continued, "Fancy! that purse-proud Grand Turk of an infidel, though he would not believe me, has been to France, —yes, actually to — —- making inquiries evidently with reference to Sophy. The woman who ought to have thoroughly converted him took flight, however, and missed seeing him. Confound her! "

"I ought to have been there. So I have no doubt for the present the Pagan remains stubborn. Gone on into Italy I hear; doing me, violating the laws of Nature, and roving about the world, with his own solitary hands in his bottomless pockets, —like the wandering Jew! But, as some slight set-off in my run of ill-luck, I find at the post-office a pleasanter letter than the one which brings me this news. A rich elderly lady, who has no family, wants to adopt a nice child; will take Sophy, —make it worth my while to let her have Sophy. 'T is convenient in a thousand ways to settle one's child comfortably in a rich house; establishes rights, subject, of course, to cheques which would not affront me, —a father! But the first thing requisite is to catch Sophy: 't is in that I ask your help; you are so clever. Best of creatures! what could I do without you? As you say, whenever I want a friend I come to you, —Bella! "

Mrs. Crane surveyed Jasper's face deliberately. It is strange how much more readily women read the thoughts of men than men detect those of women. "You know where the child is, " said she, slowly.

"Well, I take it for granted she is with the old man; and I have seen him, —seen him yesterday. "

"Go on; you saw him, —where? "

"Near London Bridge. "

"What business could you possibly have in that direction? Ah! I guess, the railway station to Dover: you are going abroad? "

"No such thing; you are so horribly suspicious. But it is true I had been to the station inquiring after some luggage or parcels which a friend of mine had ordered to be left there; now, don't interrupt me. At the foot of the bridge I caught a sudden glimpse of the old man, —changed, altered, aged, one eye lost. You had said I should not know him again, but I did; I should never have recognized his face. I knew him by the build of the shoulder, a certain turn of the arms, I don't know what; one knows a man familiar to one from birth without seeing his face. Oh, Bella; I declare that I felt as soft, —as soft as the silliest muff who ever—" Jasper did not complete his comparison, but paused a moment, breathing hard, and then broke into another sentence. "He was selling something in a basket, — matches, boot-straps, deuce knows what. He! a clever man too! I should have liked to drop into that d——d basket all the money I had about me. "

"Why did not you? "

"Why? How could I? He would have recognized me. There would have been a scene, —a row, a flare up, a mob round us, I dare say. I had no idea it would so upset me; to see him selling matches too; glad we did not meet at Gatesboro'. Not even for that L100 do I think I could have faced him. No; as he said when we last parted, 'The world is wide enough for both. ' Give me some brandy; thank you. "

"You did not speak to the old man; he did not see you: but you wanted to get back the child; you felt sure she must be with him; you followed him home? "

"I? No; I should have had to wait for hours. A man like me, loitering about London Bridge! I should have been too conspicuous; he would have soon caught sight of me, though I kept on his blind side. I employed a ragged boy to watch and follow him, and here is the address. Now, will you get Sophy back for me without any trouble to me, without my appearing? I would rather charge a regiment of horse-guards than bully that old man. "

"Yet you would rob him of the child, —his sole comfort? "

"Bother! " cried Losely, impatiently; "the child can be only a burden to him; well out of his way; 't is for the sake of that child he is selling matches! It would be the greatest charity we could do him to set him free from that child sponging on him, dragging him down; without her he'd find a way to shift for himself. Why, he's even cleverer than I am! And there—there; give him this money, but don't say it came from me. "

He thrust, without counting, several sovereigns—at least twelve or fourteen—into Mrs. Crane's palm; and so powerful a charm has goodness the very least, even in natures the most evil, that that unusual, eccentric, inconsistent gleam of human pity in Jasper Losely's benighted soul shed its relenting influence over the angry, wrathful, and vindictive feelings with which Mrs. Crane the moment before regarded the perfidious miscreant; and she gazed at him with a sort of melancholy wonder. What! though so little sympathizing with affection that he could not comprehend that he was about to rob the old man of a comfort which no gold could repay; what though so contemptuously callous to his own child, —yet there in her hand lay the unmistakable token that a something of humanity, compunction, compassion, still lingered in the breast of the greedy cynic; and at that thought all that was softest in her own human nature moved towards him, indulgent, gentle. But in the rapid changes of the heart feminine, the very sentiment that touched upon love brought back the jealousy that bordered upon hate. How came he by so much money? more than days ago he, the insatiate spendthrift, had received for his task-work? And that POCKETBOOK!

"You have suddenly grown rich, Jasper. "

For a moment he looked confused, but replied as he rehelped himself to the brandy, "Yes, rouge-et-noir, —luck. Now, do go and see after this affair, that's a dear good woman. Get the child to-day if you can; I will call here in the evening. "

"Should you take her, then, abroad at once to this worthy lady who will adopt her? If so, we shall meet, I suppose, no, more; and I am assisting you to forget that I live still. "

"Abroad, —that crotchet of yours again! You are quite mistaken; in fact, the lady is in London. It was for her effects that I went to the station. Oh, don't be jealous; quite elderly. "

"Jealous, my dear Jasper! you forget. I am as your mother. One of your letters, then, announced this lady's intended arrival; you were in correspondence with this—elderly lady. "

"Why, not exactly in correspondence. But when I left Paris I gave the General Post Office as my address to a few friends in France. And this lady, who took an interest in my affairs (ladies, whether old or young, who have once known me, always do), was aware that I had expectations with respect to the child. So some days ago, when I was so badly off, I wrote a line to tell her that Sophy had been no go, and that, but for a dear friend (that is you), I might be on the pave. In her answer, she said she should be in London as soon as I received her letter; and gave me an address here at which to learn where to find her when arrived, —a good old soul, but strange to London. I have been very busy, helping her to find a house, recommending tradesmen, and so forth. She likes style, and can afford it. A pleasant house enough, but our quiet evenings here spoil me for anything else. Now get on your bonnet, and let me see you off. "

"On one condition, my dear Jasper, —that you stay here till I return."

Jasper made a wry face. But, as it was near dinner-time and he never wanted for appetite, he at length agreed to employ the interval of her absence in discussing a meal, which experience had told him Mrs. Crane's new cook would, not unskilfully, though hastily, prepare. Mrs. Crane left him to order the dinner, and put on her shawl and bonnet. But, gaining her own room, she rang for Bridget Greggs, and when that confidential servant appeared, she said, "In the side pocket of Mr. Losely's coat there is a POCKET-BOOK; in it there are some letters which I must see. I shall appear to go out; leave the street-door ajar, that I may slip in again unobserved. You will serve dinner as soon as possible. And when Mr. Losely, as usual, exchanges his coat for the dressing-gown, contrive to take out that pocket-book unobserved by him. Bring it to me here, in this room: you can as easily replace it afterwards. A moment will suffice to my purpose. "

Bridget nodded, and understood. Jasper, standing by the window, saw Mrs. Crane leave the house, walking briskly. He then threw himself on the sofa, and began to doze: the doze deepened, and became sleep. Bridget, entering to lay the cloth, so found him. She approached on tiptoe, sniffed the perfume of the pocket-book, saw its gilded corners peep forth from its lair. She hesitated; she trembled; she was in mortal fear of that truculent slumberer; but sleep lessens the awe thieves feel or heroes inspire. She has taken the pocketbook; she has fled with the booty; she is in Mrs. Crane's apartment not five minutes after Mrs. Crane has regained its threshold.

Rapidly the jealous woman ransacked the pocket-book; started to see, elegantly worked with gold threads, in the lining, the words, "SOUVIENS TOI DE TA GABRIELLE; " no other letters, save the two, of which Jasper had vouchsafed to her but the glimpse. Over these she hurried her glittering eyes; and when she restored them to their place, and gave back the book to Bridget, who stood by breathless and listening, lest Jasper should awake, her face was colourless, and a kind of shudder seemed to come over her. Left alone, she rested her face on, her hand, her lips moving as if in self-commune. Then noiselessly she glided down the stairs, regained the street, and hurried fast upon her way.

Bridget was not in time to restore the book to Jasper's pocket, for when she re-entered he was turning round and stretching himself between sleep and waking. But she dropped the book skilfully on the floor, close beside the sofa: it would seem to him, on waking, to have fallen out of the pocket in the natural movements of sleep.

And, in fact, when he rose, dinner now on the table, he picked up the pocket-book without suspicion. But it was lucky that Bridget had not waited for the opportunity suggested by her mistress. For when Jasper put on the dressing-gown, he observed that his coat wanted brushing; and, in giving it to the servant for that purpose, he used the precaution of taking out the pocket-book, and placing it in some other receptacle of his dress.

Mrs. Crane returned in less than two hours, —returned with a disappointed look, which at once prepared Jasper for the intelligence that the birds to be entrapped had flown.

"They went away this afternoon, " said Mrs. Crane, tossing Jasper's sovereigns on the table as if they burned her fingers. "But leave the fugitives to me. I will find them. "

Jasper relieved his angry mind by a series of guilty but meaningless expletives; and then, seeing no further use to which Mrs. Crane's wish could be applied at present, finished the remainder of her brandy, and wished her good-night, with a promise to call again, but without any intimation of his own address. As soon as he was gone, Mrs. Crane once more summoned Bridget.

"You told me last week that your brother-in-law, Simpson, wished to go to America, that he had the offer of employment there, but that he could not afford the fare of the voyage. I promised I would help him if it was a service to you. "

"You are a hangel, miss! " exclaimed Bridget, dropping a low courtesy, —so low that it seemed as if she was going on her knees. "And may you have your deserts in the next blessed world, where there are no black-hearted villings. "

"Enough, enough, " said Mrs. Crane, recoiling perhaps from that grateful benediction. "You have been faithful to me, as none else have ever been; but this time I do not serve you in return so much as I meant to do. The service is reciprocal, if your brother-in-law will do me a favour. He takes with him his daughter, a mere child. Bridget, let them enter their names on the steam-vessel as William and Sophy Waife; they can, of course, resume their own name when the voyage is over. There is the fare for them, and something more. Pooh, no thanks. I can spare the money. See your brother-in-law the first thing in the morning; and remember that they go by the next vessel, which sails from Liverpool on Thursday. "

CHAPTER XVI.

Those poor pocket-cannibals, how society does persecute them! Even a menial servant would give warning if disturbed at his meals. But your man-eater is the meekest of creatures; he will never give warning, and — not often take it.

Whatever the source that had supplied Jasper Losely with the money from which he had so generously extracted the sovereigns intended to console Waife for the loss of Sophy, that source either dried up or became wholly inadequate to his wants; for elasticity was the felicitous peculiarity of Mr. Losely's wants. They accommodated themselves to the state of his finances with mathematical precision, always requiring exactly five times the amount of the means placed at his disposal. From a shilling to a million, multiply his wants by five times the total of his means, and you arrived at a just conclusion. Jasper called upon Poole, who was slowly recovering, but unable to leave his room; and finding that gentleman in a more melancholy state of mind than usual, occasioned by Uncle Sam's brutal declaration that "if responsible for his godson's sins he was not responsible for his debts, " and that he really thought "the best thing Samuel Dolly could do, was to go to prison for a short time and get whitewashed, " Jasper began to lament his own hard fate: "And just when one of the finest women in Paris has come here on purpose to see me, " said the lady-killer, —"a lady who keeps her carriage, Dolly! Would have introduced you, if you had been well enough to go out. One can't be always borrowing of her. I wish one could. There's mother Crane would sell her gown off her back for me; but 'Gad, sir, she snubs, and positively frightens me. Besides, she lays traps to demean me; set me to work like a clerk! —not that I would hurt your feelings, Dolly: if you are a clerk, or something of that sort, you are a gentleman at heart. Well, then, we are both done up and cleaned out; and my decided opinion is, that nothing is left but a bold stroke. "

"I have no objection to bold strokes, but I don't see any; and Uncle Sam's bold stroke of the Fleet prison is not at all to my taste. "

"Fleet prison! Fleet fiddlestick! No. You have never been in Russia. Why should we not go there both? My Paris friend, Madame Caumartin, was going to Italy, but her plans are changed, and she is now all for St. Petersburg. She will wait a few days for you to get well. We will all go together and enjoy ourselves. The Russians dote upon whist. We shall get into their swell sets and live like princes. " Therewith Jasper launched forth on the text of Russian existence in such glowing terms that Dolly Poole shut his aching eyes and fancied himself sledging down the Neva, covered with furs; a countess waiting for him at dinner, and counts in dozens ready to offer bets to a fabulous amount that Jasper Losely lost the rubber.

Having lifted his friend into this region of aerial castles, Jasper then, descending into the practical world, wound up with the mournful fact that one could not get to St. Petersburg, nor when there into swell sets, without having some little capital on hand.

"I tell you what we will do. Madame Caumartin lives in prime style. Get old Latham, your employer, to discount her bill at three months' date for L500, and we will be all off in a crack. " Poole shook his head. "Old Latham is too knowing a file for that. A foreigner! He'd want security. "

"I'll be security. "

Dolly shook his head a second time, still more emphatically than the first.

"But you say he does discount paper, —gets rich on it? "

"Yes, gets rich on 'it, which he might not do if he discounted the paper you propose. No offence. "

"Oh, no offence among friends! You have taken him bills which he has discounted? "

"Yes, —good paper. "

"Any paper signed by good names is good paper. We can sign good names if we know their handwritings. "

Dolly started, and turned white. Knave he was, —cheat at cards, blackleg on the turf, —but forgery! that crime was new to him. The very notion of it brought on a return of fever; and while Jasper was increasing his malady by arguing with his apprehensions, luckily for Poole, Uncle Sam came in. Uncle Sam, a sagacious old tradesman, no sooner clapped eyes on the brilliant Losely than he conceived for him a distrustful repugnance, similar to that with which an experienced gander may regard a fox in colloquy with its gosling. He had already learned enough of his godson's ways and chosen society to be assured that Samuel Dolly had indulged in very anti-commercial tastes, and been sadly contaminated by very anti-commercial friends. He felt persuaded that Dolly's sole chance of redemption was in working on his mind while his body was still suffering, so that Poole might, on recovery, break with all former associations. On seeing Jasper in the dress of an exquisite, with the thrws of a prize-fighter, Uncle Sam saw the stalwart incarnation of all the sins which a godfather had vowed that a godson should renounce. Accordingly, he made himself so disagreeable that Losely, in great disgust, took a hasty departure. And Uncle Sam, as he helped the nurse to plunge Dolly into his bed, had the brutality to tell his nephew, in very plain terms, that if ever he found that Brummagem gent in Poole's rooms again, Poole would never again see the colour of Uncle Sam's money. Dolly beginning to blubber, the good man relenting patted him on the back, and said, "But as soon as you are well, I'll carry you with me to my country-box, and keep you out of harm's way till I find you a wife, who will comb your head for you; " at which cheering prospect Poole blubbered more dolefully than before. On retiring to his own lodging in the Gloucester Coffee-house, Uncle Sam, to make all sure, gave positive orders to Poole's landlady, who respected in Uncle Sam the man who might pay what Poole owed to her, on no account to let in any of Dolly's profligate friends, but especially the chap he had found there; adding, "'T is as much as my nephew's life is worth; and, what is more to the purpose, as much as your bill is. " Accordingly, when Jasper presented himself at Poole's door again that very evening, the landlady apprised him of her orders; and, proof to his insinuating remonstrances, closed the door in his face. But a French chronicler has recorded that when Henry IV. was besieging Paris, though not a loaf of bread could enter the walls, love-letters passed between city and camp as easily as if there had been no siege at all. And does not Mercury preside over money as well as Love? Jasper, spurred on by Madame Caumartin, who was exceedingly anxious to exchange London for St. Petersburg as soon as possible, maintained a close and frequent correspondence with Poole by the agency of the nurse, who luckily was not above being bribed by shillings. Poole continued to reject the villany proposed by Jasper; but, in course of the correspondence, he threw out rather incoherently—for his mind began somewhat to wander—a scheme equally flagitious, which Jasper, aided perhaps by Madame Caumartin's yet keener wit, caught up, and quickly reduced to deliberate method. Old Mr. Latham, amongst the bills he discounted, kept those of such more bashful customers as stipulated that their resort to temporary accommodation should be maintained a profound secret in his own safe. Amongst these bills Poole knew that there was one for L1,000 given by a young nobleman of immense estates, but so entailed that he could neither sell nor mortgage, and, therefore, often in need of a few hundreds for pocket money. The nobleman's name stood high. His fortune was universally known; his honour unimpeachable. A bill of his any one would cash at sight. Could Poole but obtain that bill! It had, he believed, only a few weeks yet to run. Jasper or Madame Caumartin might get it discounted even by Lord — — —-'s own banker; and if that were too bold, by any professional bill-broker, and all three be off before a suspicion could arise. But to get at that safe, a false key might be necessary. Poole suggested a waxen impression of the lock. Jasper sent him a readier contrivance, —a queer-looking tool, that looked an instrument of torture. All now necessary was for Poole to recover sufficiently to return to business, and to get rid of Uncle Sam by a promise to run down to the country the moment Poole had conscientiously cleared some necessary arrears of work. While this correspondence went on, Jasper Losely shunned Mrs. Crane, and took his meals and spent his leisure hours with Madame Caumartin. He needed no dressing-gown and slippers to feel himself at home there. Madame Canmartin had really taken a showy house in a genteel street. Her own appearance was eminently what the French call *distingue*; dressed to perfection from head to foot; neat and finished as an epigram; her face in shape like a thoroughbred cobra-capella, —low smooth frontal widening at the summit, chin tapering but jaw strong, teeth marvellously white, small, and with points sharp as those in the maw of the fish called the "Sea Devil; " eyes like dark emeralds, of which the pupils, when she was angry or when she was scheming, retreated upward towards the temples, emitting a luminous green ray that shot through space like the gleam that escapes from a dark-lantern; complexion superlatively feminine (call it not pale but white, as if she lived on blanched almonds, peach-stones, and arsenic); hands so fine and so bloodless, with fingers so pointedly taper there seemed stings at their tips; manners of one who had ranged all ranks of society from highest to lowest, and duped the most wary in each of them. Did she please it, a crown prince might have thought her youth must have passed in the chambers of porphyry! Did she please it, an old soldier would have sworn the creature had been a vivandiere, —in age, perhaps, bordering on forty. She looked younger, but had she been a hundred and twenty, she could not have been more wicked. Ah, happy indeed for Sophy, if it were to save her youth from ever being fostered in elegant boudoirs by those bloodless hands, that the crippled vagabond had borne her away from Arabella's less cruel unkindness; better far even Rugge's village stage; better far stealthy by-lanes, feigned names, and the erudite tricks of Sir Isaac!

But still it is due even to Jasper to state here that, in Losely's recent design to transfer Sophy from Mr. Waife's care to that of Madame Caumartin, the Sharper harboured no idea of a villany so execrable as the character of the Parisienne led the jealous Arabella to suspect. His real object in getting the child at that time once more into his power was (whatever its nature) harmless compared with the mildest of Arabella's dark doubts. But still if Sophy had been regained, and the object, on regaining her, foiled (as it probably would have been), what then might have become of her, —lost, perhaps, forever, to Waife, —in a foreign land and under such guardianship? Grave question, which Jasper Losely, who exercised so little foresight in the paramount question, namely, what some day or other would become of himself? was not likely to rack his brains by conjecturing!

Meanwhile Mrs. Crane was vigilant. The detective police-officer sent to her by Mr. Rugge could not give her the information which Rugge desired, and which she did not longer need. She gave the detective some information respecting Madame Caumartin. One day towards the evening she was surprised by a visit from Uncle Sam. He called ostensibly to thank her for her kindness to his godson and nephew; and to beg her not to be offended if he had been rude to Mr. Losely, who, he understood from Dolly, was a particular friend of hers. "You see, ma'am, Samuel Dolly is a weak young man, and easily led astray; but, luckily for himself, he has no money and no stomach. So he may repent in time; and if I could find a wife to manage him, he has not a bad head for the main chance, and may become a practical man. Repeatedly I have told him he should go to prison, but that was only to frighten him; fact is, I want to get him safe down into the country, and he don't take to that. So I am forced to say, 'My box, home-brewed and South-down, Samuel Dolly, or a Lunnon jail and debtors' allowance. ' Must give a young man his choice, my dear lady. "

Mrs. Crane observing that what he said was extremely sensible, Uncle Sam warmed in his confidence.

"And I thought I had him, till I found Mr. Losely in his sick-room; but ever since that day, I don't know how it is, the lad has had something on his mind, which I don't half like, —cracky, I think, my dear lady, —cracky. I suspect that old nurse passes letters. I taxed her with it, and she immediately wanted to take her Bible-oath, and smelt of gin, two things which, taken together, look guilty. "

"But, " said Mrs. Crane, growing much interested, "if Mr. Losely and Mr. Poole do correspond, what then? "

"That's what I want to know, ma'am. Excuse me; I don't wish to disparage Mr. Losely, —a dashing gent, and nothing worse, I dare say. But certain sure I am that he has put into Samuel Dolly's head something which has cracked it! There is the lad now up and dressed, when he ought to be in bed, and swearing he'll go to old Latham's to-morrow, and that long arrears of work are on his conscience! Never heard him talk of conscience before: that looks guilty! And it does not frighten him any longer when I say he shall go to prison for his debts; and he's very anxious to get me out of Lunnon; and when I threw in a word about Mr. Losely (slyly, my good lady, —just to see its effect), he grew as white as that paper; and then he began strutting and swelling, and saying that Mr. Losely would be a great man, and he should be a great man, and that he did not care for my money; he could get as much money as he liked. That looks guilty, my dear lady. And oh, " cried Uncle Sam, clasping his hands, "I do fear that he's thinking of something worse than he has ever done before, and his brain can't stand it. And, ma'am, he has a great respect for you; and you've a friendship for Mr. Losely. Now, just suppose that Mr. Losely should have been thinking of what your flash sporting gents call a harmless spree, and my sister's son should, being cracky, construe into something criminal. Oh, Mrs. Crane, do go and see Mr. Losely, and tell him that Samuel Dolly is not safe, —is not safe! "

"Much better that I should go to your nephew, " said Mrs. Crane; "and with your leave I will do so at once. Let me see him alone. Where shall I find you afterwards? "

"At the Gloucester Coffee-house. Oh, my dear lady, how can I thank you enough? The boy can be nothing to you; but to me, he's my sister's son, —the blackguard! "

CHAPTER XVII.

"Dices laborantes in uno
Penelopen vitreamque Circen." —HORAT.

Mrs. Crane found Poole in his little sitting-room, hung round with prints of opera-dancers, prize-fighters, race-horses, and the dog Billy. Samuel Dolly was in full dress. His cheeks, usually so pale, seemed much flushed. He was evidently in a state of high excitement, bowed extremely low to Mrs. Crane, called her Countess, asked if she had been lately on the Continent and if she knew Madame Caumartin, and whether the nobility at St. Petersburg were jolly, or stuck-up fellows, who gave themselves airs, —not waiting for her answer. In fact his mind was unquestionably disordered.

Arabella Crane abruptly laid her hand on his shoulder. "You are going to the gallows, " she said suddenly. "Down on your knees, and tell me all, and I will keep your secret, and save you; lie, and you are lost! "

Poole burst into tears, and dropped on his knees as he was told.

In ten minutes Mrs. Crane knew all that she cared to know, possessed herself of Losely's letters, and, leaving Poole less light-headed and more light-hearted, she hastened to Uncle Sam at the Gloucester Coffee-house. "Take your nephew, out of town this evening, and do not let him from your sight for the next six months. Hark you, he will never be a good man; but you may save him from the hulks. Do so. Take my advice. " She was gone before Uncle Sam could answer. She next proceeded to the private house of the detective with whom she had before conferred; this time less to give than to receive information. Not half an hour after her interview with him, Arabella Crane stood in the street wherein was placed the showy house of Madame Caumartin. The lamps in the street were now lighted; the street, even at day a quiet one, was comparatively deserted. All the windows in the Frenchwoman's house were closed with shutters and curtains, except on the drawing-room floor. From those the lights within streamed over a balcony filled with gay plants; one of the casements was partially open. And now and then, where the watcher stood, she could just catch the glimpse of a passing form behind the muslin draperies, or hear the sound of some louder laugh. In her dark-gray dress and still darker mantle,

Arabella Crane stood motionless, her eyes fixed on those windows. The rare foot-passenger who brushed by her turned involuntarily to glance at the countenance of one so still, and then as involuntarily to survey the house to which that countenance was lifted. No such observer so incurious as not to hazard conjecture what evil to that house was boded by the dark lurid eyes that watched it with so fixed a menace. Thus she remained, sometimes, indeed, moving from her post, as a sentry moves from his, slowly pacing a few steps to and fro, returning to the same place, and again motionless; thus she remained for hours. Evening deepened into night; night grew near to dawn: she was still there in that street, and still her eyes were on that house. At length the door opened noiselessly; a tall man tripped forth with a gay light step, and humming the tune of a gay French chanson. As he came straight towards the spot where Arabella Crane was at watch, from her dark mantle stretched forth her long arm and lean hand and seized him. He started and recognized her.

"You here! " he exclaimed, "you! —at such an hour, —you! "

"Ay, Jasper Losely, here to warn you. To-morrow the officers of justice will be in that accursed house. To-morrow that woman—not for her worst crimes, they elude the law, but for her least by which the law hunts her down—will be a prisoner, —no, you shall not return to warn her as I warn you" (for Jasper here broke away, and retreated some steps towards the house); "or, if you do, share her fate. I cast you off. "

"What do you mean? " said Jasper, halting, till with slow steps she regained his side. "Speak more plainly: if poor Madame Caumartin has got into a scrape, which I don't think likely, what have I to do with it? "

"The woman you call Caumartin fled from Paris to escape its tribunals. She has been tracked; the French government have claimed her—ho! —you smile. This does not touch you? "

"Certainly not. "

"But there are charges against her from English tradesmen; and if it be proved that you knew her in her proper name, —the infamous Gabrielle Desmarets; if it be proved that you have passed off the French billets de banque that she stole; if you were her accomplice in obtaining goods under her false name; if you, enriched by her robberies, were aiding and abetting her as a swindler here, —though you may be safe from the French law, will you be safe from the English? You may be innocent, Jasper Losely; if so, fear nothing. You may be guilty: if so, hide, or follow me! "

Jasper paused. His first impulse was to trust implicitly to Mrs. Crane, and lose not a moment in profiting by such counsels of concealment or flight as an intelligence so superior to his own could suggest. But suddenly remembering that Poole had undertaken to get the bill for L1,000 by the next day, —that if flight were necessary, there was yet a chance of flight with booty, —his constitutional hardihood, and the grasping cupidity by which it was accompanied, made him resolve at least to hazard the delay of a few hours. And, after all, might not Mrs. Crane exaggerate? Was not this the counsel of a jealous woman? "Pray, " said he, moving on, and fixing quick keen eyes on her as she walked by his side, "pray, how did you learn all these particulars? "

"From a detective policeman employed to discover Sophy. In conferring with him, the name of Jasper Losely as her legal protector was of course stated; that name was already coupled with the name of the false Caumartin. Thus, indirectly, the child you would have consigned to that woman saves you from sharing that woman's ignominy and doom. "

"Stuff! " said Jasper, stubbornly, though he winced at her words: "I don't, on reflection, see that anything can be proved against me. I am not bound to know why a lady changes her name, nor how she comes by her money. And as to her credit with tradesmen, —nothing to speak of: most of what she has got is paid for; what is not paid for is less than the worth of her goods. Pooh! I am not so easily frightened; much obliged to you all the same. Go home now; 't is horridly late. Good-night, or rather good-morning. "

"Jasper, mark me, if you see that woman again; if you attempt to save or screen her, —I shall know, and you lose in me your last friend, last hope, last plank in a devouring sea! "

These words were so solemnly uttered that they thrilled the heart of the reckless man. "I have no wish to screen or save her, " he said, with selfish sincerity. "And after what you have said I would as soon enter a fireship as that house. But let me have some hours to consider what is best to be done. "

"Yes, consider—I shall expect you to-morrow. "

He went his way up the twilight streets towards a new lodging he had hired not far from the showy house. She drew her mantle close round her gaunt figure, and, taking the opposite direction, threaded thoroughfares yet lonelier, till she gained the door, and was welcomed back by the faithful Bridget.

CHAPTER XVIII.

Hope, tells a flattering tale to Mr. Rugge. He is undeceived by a solicitor; and left to mourn; but in turn, though unconsciously, Mr. Rugge deceives the solicitor, and the solicitor deceives his client, — which is 6s. 8d. in the solicitor's pocket.

The next morning Arabella Crane was scarcely dressed before Mr. Rugge knocked at her door. On the previous day the detective had informed him that William and Sophy Waife were discovered to have sailed for America. Frantic, the unhappy manager hurried away to the steam-packet office, and was favoured by an inspection of the books, which confirmed the hateful tidings. As if in mockery of his bereaved and defrauded state, on returning home he found a polite note from Mr. Gotobed, requesting him to call at the office of that eminent solicitor, with reference to a young actress, named Sophy Waife, and hinting "that the visit might prove to his advantage! " Dreaming for a wild moment that Mr. Losely, conscience-stricken, might through his solicitor pay back his L100, he rushed incontinent to Mr. Gotobed's office, and was at once admitted into the presence of that stately practitioner.

"I beg your pardon, sir, " said Mr. Gotobed, with formal politeness, "but I heard a day or two ago accidentally from my head clerk, who had learned it also accidentally from a sporting friend, that you were exhibiting at Humberston, during the race-week, a young actress, named on the play-bills (here is one) 'Juliet Araminta, ' and whom, as I am informed, you had previously exhibited in Surrey and elsewhere; but she was supposed to have relinquished that earlier engagement, and left your stage with her grandfather, William Waife. I am instructed by a distinguished client, who is wealthy, and who from motives of mere benevolence interests himself in the said William and Sophy Waife, to discover their residence. Please, therefore, to render up the child to my charge, apprising me also of the address of her grandfather, if he be not with you; and without waiting for further instructions from my client, who is abroad, I will venture to say that any sacrifice in the loss of your juvenile actress will be most liberally compensated. "

"Sir, " cried the miserable and imprudent Rugge, "I paid L100 for that fiendish child, —a three years' engagement, —and I have been

351

robbed. Restore me the L100, and I will tell you where she is, and her vile grandfather also. "

At hearing so bad a character lavished upon objects recommended to his client's disinterested charity, the wary solicitor drew in his pecuniary horns.

"Mr. Rugge, " said he, "I understand from your words that you cannot place the child Sophy, alias Juliet Araminta, in my hands. You ask L100 to inform me where she is. Have you a lawful claim on her? "

"Certainly, sir: she is my property. "

"Then it is quite clear that though you may know where she is, you cannot get at her yourself, and cannot, therefore, place her in my hands. Perhaps she 's—in Heaven! "

"Confound her, sir! no—in America! or on the seas to it. "

"Are you sure? "

"I have just come from the steam-packet office, and seen the names in their book. William and Sophy Waife sailed from Liverpool last Thursday week. "

"And they formed an engagement with you, received your money; broke the one, absconded with the other. Bad characters indeed! "

"Bad! you may well say that, —a set of swindling scoundrels, the whole kit and kin. And the ingratitude! " continued Rugge; "I was more than a father to that child" (he began to whimper); "I had a babe of my own once; died of convulsions in teething. I thought that child would have supplied its place, and I dreamed of the York Theatre; but"—here his voice was lost in the folds of a marvellously dirty red pocket-handkerchief.

Mr. Gotobed having now, however, learned all that he cared to learn, and not being a soft-hearted man (first-rate solicitors rarely are), here pulled out his watch, and said,

"Sir, you have been very ill-treated, I perceive. I must wish you good-day; I have an engagement in the City. I cannot help you back to your L100, but accept this trifle (a L5 note) for your loss of time in calling" (ringing the bell violently). "Door, —show out this gentleman. "

That evening Mr. Gotobed wrote at length to Guy Darrell, informing him that, after great pains and prolonged research, he had been so fortunate as to ascertain that the strolling player and the little girl whom Mr. Darrell had so benevolently requested him to look up were very bad characters, and had left the country for the United States, as happily for England bad characters were wont to do.

That letter reached Guy Darrell when he was far away, amidst the forlorn pomp of some old Italian city, and Lionel's tale of the little girl not very fresh in his gloomy thoughts. Naturally, he supposed that the boy had been duped by a pretty face and his own inexperienced kindly heart. And so, and so, —why, so end all the efforts of men who entrust to others the troublesome execution of humane intentions! The scales of earthly justice are poised in their quivering equilibrium, not by huge hundred-weights, but by infinitesimal grains, needing the most wary caution, the most considerate patience, the most delicate touch, to arrange or readjust. Few of our errors, national or individual, come from the design to be unjust; most of them from sloth, or incapacity to grapple with the difficulties of being just. Sins of commission may not, perhaps, shock the retrospect of conscience. Large and obtrusive to view we have confessed, mourned, repented, possibly atoned them. Sins of omission so veiled amidst our hourly emotions, blent, confused, unseen, in the conventional routine of existence, —alas! could these suddenly emerge from their shadow, group together in serried mass and accusing order, —alas, alas! would not the best of us then start in dismay, and would not the proudest humble himself at the Throne of Mercy?

CHAPTER XIX.

Joy, nevertheless, does return to Mr. Rugge: and hope now inflicts herself on Mrs. Crane; a very fine-looking hope too, —six feet one, —strong as Achilles, and as fleet of foot!

Buy we have left Mr. Rugge at Mrs. Crane's door; admit him. He bursts into her drawing-room wiping his brows. "Ma'am, they're off to America! "

"So I have heard. You are fairly entitled to the return of your money—"

"Entitled, of course, but—"

"There it is; restore to me the contract for the child's services. "

Rugge gazed on a roll of bank-notes, and could scarcely believe his eyes. He darted forth his hand, —the notes receded like the dagger in Macbeth. "First the contract, " said Mrs. Crane. Rugge drew out his greasy pocket-book, and extracted the worthless engagement.

"Henceforth, then, " said Mrs. Crane, "you have no right to complain; and whether or not the girl ever again fall in your way, your claim over her ceases. "

"The gods be praised! it does, ma'am, I have had quite enough of her. But you are every inch a lady, and allow me to add that I put you on my free list for life. "

Rugge gone, Arabella Crane summoned Bridget to her presence.

"Lor', miss, " cried Bridget, impulsively, "who'd think you'd been up all night raking! I have not seen you look so well this many a year. "

"Ah, " said Arabella Crane, "I will tell you why. I have done what for many a year I never thought I should do again, —a good action. That child, —that Sophy, —do you remember how cruelly I used her? "

"Oh, miss, don't go for to blame yourself; you fed her, you clothed her, when her own father, the villing, sent her away from hisself to you, —you of all people, you. How could you be caressing and fawning on his child, —their child? "

Mrs. Crane hung her head gloomily. "What is past is past. I have lived to save that child, and a curse seems lifted from my soul. Now listen. I shall leave London—England—probably this evening. You will keep this house; it will be ready for me any moment I return. The agent who collects my house-rents will give you money as you want it. Stint not yourself, Bridget. I have been saving and saving and saving for dreary years, —nothing else to interest me, and I am richer than I seem. "

"But where are you going, miss? " said Bridget, slowly recovering from the stupefaction occasioned by her mistress's announcement.

"I don't know; I don't care. "

"Oh, gracious stars! is it with that dreadful Jasper Losely? —it is, it is. You are crazed, you are bewitched, miss! "

"Possibly I am crazed, —possibly bewitched; but I take that man's life to mine as a penance for all the evil mine has ever known; and a day or two since I should have said, with rage and shame, 'I cannot help it; I loathe myself that I can care what becomes of him. ' Now, without rage, without shame, I say, 'The man whom I once so loved shall not die on a gibbet if I can help it' and, please Heaven, help it I will. "

The grim woman folded her arms on her breast, and raising her head to its full height, there was in her face and air a stern gloomy grandeur, which could not have been seen without a mixed sensation of compassion and awe.

"Go now, Bridget; I have said all. He will be here soon: he will come; he must come; he has no choice; and then—and then—" she closed her eyes, bowed her head, and shivered.

Arabella Crane was, as usual, right in her predictions. Before noon Jasper came, —came, not with his jocund swagger, but with that sidelong sinister look—of the man whom the world cuts— triumphantly restored to its former place in his visage. Madame

Caumartin had been arrested; Poole had gone into the country with Uncle Sam; Jasper had seen a police-officer at the door of his own lodgings. He slunk away from the fashionable thoroughfares, slunk to the recesses of Podden Place, slunk into Arabella Crane's prim drawing-room, and said sullenly, "All is up; here I am! "

Three days afterwards, in a quiet street in a quiet town of Belgium, —wherein a sharper, striving to live by his profession, would soon become a skeleton, —in a commodious airy apartment, looking upon a magnificent street, the reverse of noisy, Jasper Losely sat secure, innocuous, and profoundly miserable. In another house, the windows of which—facing those of Jasper's sitting-room, from an upper story-commanded so good a view therein that it placed him under a surveillance akin to that designed by Mr. Bentham's reformatory Panopticon, sat Arabella Crane. Whatever her real feelings towards Jasper Losely (and what those feelings were no virile pen can presume authoritatively to define; for lived there ever a man who thoroughly understood a woman?), or whatever in earlier life might have been their reciprocated vows of eternal love, —not only from the day that Jasper, on his return to his native shores, presented himself in Podden Place, had their intimacy been restricted to the austerest bonds of friendship, but after Jasper had so rudely declined the hand which now fed him, Arabella Crane had probably perceived that her sole chance of retaining intellectual power over his lawless being necessitated the utter relinquishment of every hope or project that could expose her again to his contempt. Suiting appearances to reality, the decorum of a separate house was essential to the maintenance of that authority with which the rigid nature of their intercourse invested her. The additional cost strained her pecuniary resources, but she saved in her own accommodation in order to leave Jasper no cause to complain of any stinting in his. There, then, she sat by her window, herself unseen, eying him in his opposite solitude, accepting for her own life a barren sacrifice, but a jealous sentinel on his. Meditating as she sat and as she eyed him, — meditating what employment she could invent, with the bribe of emoluments to be paid furtively by her, for those strong hands that could have felled an ox, but were nerveless in turning an honest penny, and for that restless mind hungering for occupation, and with the digestion of an ostrich for dice and debauch, riot and fraud, but queasy as an exhausted dyspeptic at the reception of one innocent amusement, one honourable toil. But while that woman still schemes how to rescue from hulks or halter that execrable man, who shall say

that he is without a chance? A chance he has: WHAT WILL HE DO
WITH IT?

BOOK V.

CHAPTER I.

Envy will be a science when it learns the use of the microscope.

When leaves fall and flowers fade, great people are found in their country-seats. Look! —that is Montfort Court, —a place of regal magnificence, so far as extent of pile and amplitude of domain could satisfy the pride of ownership, or inspire the visitor with the respect due to wealth and power. An artist could have made nothing of it. The Sumptuous everywhere; the Picturesque nowhere. The house was built in the reign of George I., when first commenced that horror of the beautiful, as something in bad taste, which, agreeably to our natural love of progress, progressively advanced through the reigns of succeeding Georges. An enormous fafade, in dull brown brick; two wings and a centre, with double flights of steps to the hall-door from the carriage-sweep. No trees allowed to grow too near the house; in front, a stately flat with stone balustrades. But wherever the eye turned, there was nothing to be seen but park, miles upon miles of park; not a cornfield in sight, not a roof-tree, not a spire, only those *lata silentia*, —still widths of turf, and, somewhat thinly scattered and afar, those groves of giant trees. The whole prospect so vast and so monotonous that it never tempted you to take a walk. No close-neighbouring poetic thicket into which to plunge, uncertain whither you would emerge; no devious stream to follow. The very deer, fat and heavy, seemed bored by pastures it would take them a week to traverse. People of moderate wishes and modest fortunes never envied Montfort Court: they admired it; they were proud to say they had seen it. But never did they say—

"Oh, that for me some home like this would smile! "

Not so, very, very great people! —they rather coveted than admired. Those oak trees so large, yet so undecayed; that park, eighteen miles at least in circumference; that solid palace which, without inconvenience, could entertain and stow away a king and his whole court; in short, all that evidence of a princely territory and a weighty rent-roll made English dukes respectfully envious, and foreign potentates gratifyingly jealous.

But turn from the front. Open the gate in that stone balustrade. Come southward to the garden side of the house. Lady Montfort's flower-garden. Yes; not so dull! —flowers, even autumnal flowers, enliven any sward. Still, on so large a scale, and so little relief; so little mystery about those broad gravel-walks; not a winding alley anywhere. Oh, for a vulgar summer-house; for some alcove, all honeysuckle and ivy! But the dahlias are splendid! Very true; only, dahlias, at the best, are such uninteresting prosy things. What poet ever wrote upon a dahlia! Surely Lady Montfort might have introduced a little more taste here, shown a little more fancy! Lady Montfort! I should like to see my lord's face if Lady Montfort took any such liberty. But there is Lady Montfort walking slowly along that broad, broad, broad gravel-walk; those splendid dahlias, on either side, in their set parterres. There she walks, in full evidence from all those sixty remorseless windows on the garden front, each window exactly like the other. There she walks, looking wistfully to the far end ('t is a long way off), where, happily, there is a wicket that carries a persevering pedestrian out of sight of the sixty windows into shady walks, towards the banks of that immense piece of water, two miles from the house. My lord has not returned from his moor in Scotland; my lady is alone. No company in the house: it is like saying, "No acquaintance in a city. " But the retinue is full. Though she dined alone she might, had she pleased, have had almost as many servants to gaze upon her as there were windows now staring at her lonely walk with their glassy spectral eyes.

Just as Lady Montfort gains the wicket she is overtaken by a visitor, walking fast from the gravel sweep by the front door, where he has dismounted, where he has caught sight of her: any one so dismounting might have caught sight of her; could not help it. Gardens so fine were made on purpose for fine persons walking in them to be seen.

"Ah, Lady Montfort, " said the visitor, stammering painfully, "I am so glad to find you at home. "

"At home, George! " said the lady, extending her hand; "where else is it likely that I should be found? But how pale you are! What has happened? "

She seated herself on a bench, under a cedar-tree, just without the wicket; and George Morley, our old friend the Oxonian, seated himself by her side familiarly, but with a certain reverence. Lady

Montfort was a few years older than himself, his cousin: he had known her from his childhood.

"What has happened! " he repeated; "nothing new. I have just come from visiting the good bishop. "

"He does not hesitate to ordain you? " "No; but I shall never ask him to do so. "

"My dear cousin, are you not over-scrupulous? You would be an ornament to the Church, sufficient in all else to justify your compulsory omission of one duty, which a curate could perform for you. "

Morley shook his head sadly. "One duty omitted! " said he. "But is it not that duty which distinguishes the priest from the layman? and how far extends that duty? Whereever there needs a voice to speak the word, —not in the pulpit only, but at the hearth, by the sick-bed, —there should be the Pastor! No: I cannot, I ought not, I dare not! Incompetent as the labourer, how can I be worthy of the hire? " It took him long to bring out these words: his emotion increased his infirmity. Lady Montfort listened with an exquisite respect visible in her compassion, and paused long before she answered.

George Morley was the younger son of a country gentleman, with a good estate settled upon the elder son. George's father had been an intimate friend of his kinsman, the Marquess of Montfort (predecessor and grandsire of the present lord); and the marquess had, as he thought, amply provided for George in undertaking to secure to him, when of fitting age, the living of Humberston, the most lucrative preferment in his gift. The living had been held for the last fifteen years by an incumbent, now very old, upon the honourable understanding that it was to be resigned in favour of George, should George take orders. The young man, from his earliest childhood thus destined to the Church, devoted to the prospect of that profession all his studies, all his thoughts. Not till he was sixteen did his infirmity of speech make itself seriously perceptible: and then elocution masters undertook to cure it; they failed. But George's mind continued in the direction towards which it had been so systematically biased. Entering Oxford, he became absorbed in its academical shades. Amidst his books he almost forgot the impediment of his speech. Shy, taciturn, and solitary, he mixed too little with others to have it much brought before his own notice. He carried off prizes; he took high honours. On leaving the University, a profound theologian, an enthusiastic Churchman, filled with the most earnest sense of the pastor's solemn calling, —he was thus complimentarily accosted by the Archimandrite of his college, "What a pity you cannot go into the Church! "

"Cannot; but I am going into the Church. "

"You! is it possible? But, perhaps, you are sure of a living —"

"Yes, —Humberston. "

"An immense living, but a very large population. Certainly it is in the bishop's own discretionary power to ordain you, and for all the duties you can keep a curate. " But the Don stopped short, and took snuff.

That "but" said as plainly as words could say, "It may be a good thing for you; but is it fair for the Church? "

So George Morley at least thought that "but" implied.

His conscience took alarm. He was a thoroughly noble-hearted man, likely to be the more tender of conscience where tempted by worldly interests. With that living he was rich, without it very poor. But to give up a calling, to the idea of which he had attached himself with all the force of a powerful and zealous nature, was to give up the whole scheme and dream of his existence. He remained irresolute for some time; at last he wrote to the present Lord Montfort, intimating his doubts, and relieving the Marquess from the engagement which his lordship's predecessor had made. The present Marquess was not a man capable of understanding such scruples. But, luckily perhaps for George and for the Church, the larger affairs of the great House of Montfort were not administered by the Marquess. The parliamentary influences, the ecclesiastical preferments, together with the practical direction of minor agents to the vast and complicated estates attached to the title, were at that time under the direction of Mr. Carr Vipont, a powerful member of Parliament, and husband to that Lady Selina whose condescension had so disturbed the nerves of Frank Vance the artist. Mr. Carr Vipont governed this vice-royalty according to the rules and traditions by which the House of Montfort had become great and prosperous. For not only every state, but every great seignorial House has its hereditary maxims of policy, —not less the House of Montfort than the House of Hapsburg. Now the House of Montfort made it a rule that all admitted to be members of the family should help each other; that the head of the House should never, if it could be avoided, suffer any of its branches to decay and wither into poverty. The House of Montfort also held it a duty to foster and make the most of every species of talent that could swell the influence or adorn the annals of the family. Having rank, having wealth, it sought also to secure intellect, and to knit together into solid union, throughout all ramifications of kinship and cousinhood, each variety of repute and power that could root the ancient tree more firmly in the land. Agreeably to this traditional policy, Mr. Carr Vipont not only desired that a Vipont Morley should not lose a very good thing, but that a very good thing should not lose a Vipont Morley of high academical distinction, -a Vipont Morley who might be a bishop. He therefore drew up an admirable letter, which the Marquess signed, —that the Marquess should take the trouble of copying it was out of the question, —wherein Lord Montfort was made to express great admiration of the disinterested delicacy of sentiment, which proved George Vipont Morley to be still more fitted to the cure of souls; and, placing rooms at Montfort Court at his service (the Marquess not being himself there at the moment), suggested that George should talk the matter over with the present incumbent of Humberston (that town was not many miles distant from Montfort Court), who, though he had no impediment in his speech, still never himself preached nor read prayers, owing to an affection of the trachea, and who was, nevertheless, a most efficient clergy man. George Morley, therefore, had gone down to Montfort Court some months ago, just after his interview with Mrs. Crane. He had then accepted an invitation to spend a week or two with the Rev. Mr. Allsop, the Rector of Humberston; a clergyman of the old school, a fair scholar, a perfect gentleman, a man of the highest honour, good-natured, charitable, but who took pastoral duties much more easily than good clergymen of the new school—be they high or low-are disposed to do. Mr. Allsop, who was then in his eightieth year, a bachelor with a very good fortune of his own, was perfectly willing to fulfil the engagement on which he held his living, and render it up to George; but he was touched by the earnestness with which George assured him that at all events he would not consent to displace the venerable incumbent from a tenure he had so long and honourably held, and would wait till the living was vacated in the ordinary course of nature. Mr. Allsop conceived a warm affection for the young scholar. He had a grand-niece staying with him on a visit, who less openly, but not less warmly, shared that affection; and with her George Morley fell shyly and timorously in love. With that living he would be rich enough to marry; without it, no. Without it he had nothing but a fellowship, which matrimony would forfeit, and the scanty portion of a country squire's younger son. The young lady herself was dowerless, for Allsop's fortune was so settled that no share of it would come to his grand-niece, —another reason for conscience to gulp down that unhappy impediment of speech. Certainly, during this visit, Morley's scruples relaxed; but when he returned home they came back with greater force than ever, —with greater force, because he felt that now not only a spiritual ambition, but a human love was a casuist in favour of self-interest. He had returned on a visit to Humberston Rectory about a week previous to the date of this chapter; the niece was not there. Sternly he had forced himself to examine a little more closely into the condition of the flock which (if he accepted the charge) he would have to guide, and the duties that devolved upon a chief pastor in a populous trading town. He became appalled. Humberston, like most towns under the political influence of a great House, was rent by parties, —one party, who succeeded in returning one of the two members for Parliament, all for the House of Montfort; the other party, who returned also their member, all against it. By one half the town, whatever came from Montfort Court was sure to be regarded with a most malignant and distorted vision. Meanwhile, though Mr. Allsop was popular with the higher classes and with such of the extreme poor as his charity relieved, his pastoral influence generally was a dead letter. His curate, who preached for him—a good young man, but extremely dull-was not one of those preachers who fill a church. Tradesmen wanted an excuse to stay away or choose another place of worship; and they contrived to hear some passages in the sermons—over which, while the curate mumbled, they habitually slept—that they declared to be "Puseyite. " The church became deserted; and about the same time a very eloquent Dissenting minister appeared at Humberston, and even professed Church folks went to hear him. George Morley, alas! perceived that at Humberston, if the Church there were to hold her own, a powerful and popular preacher was essentially required. His mind was now made up. At Carr Vipont's suggestion the bishop of the diocese, being then at his palace, had sent to see him; and, while granting the force of his scruples, had yet said, "Mine is the main responsibility. But if you ask me to ordain you, I will do so without hesitation; for if the Church wants preachers, it also wants deep scholars and virtuous pastors. " Fresh from this interview, George Morley came to announce to Lady

Montfort that his resolve was unshaken. She, I have said, paused long before she answered. "George, " she began at last, in a voice so touchingly sweet that its very sound was balm to a wounded spirit, "I must not argue with you: I bow before the grandeur of your motives, and I will not say that you are not right. One thing I do feel, that if you thus sacrifice your inclinations and interests from scruples so pure and holy, you will never be to be pitied; you will never know regret. Poor or rich, single or wedded, a soul that so seeks to reflect heaven will be serene and blessed. " Thus she continued to address him for some time, he all the while inexpressibly soothed and comforted; then gradually she insinuated hopes even of a worldly and temporal kind, —literature was left to him, —the scholar's pen, if not the preacher's voice. In literature he might make a career that would lead on to fortune. There were places also in the public service to which a defect in speech was no obstacle. She knew his secret, modest attachment; she alluded to it just enough to encourage constancy and rebuke despair. As she ceased, his admiring and grateful consciousness of his cousin's rare qualities changed the tide of his emotions towards her from himself, and he exclaimed with an earnestness that almost wholly subdued his stutter,

"What a counsellor you are! what a soother! If Montfort were but less prosperous or more ambitious, what a treasure, either to console or to sustain, in a mind like yours! "

As those words were said, you might have seen at once why Lady Montfort was called haughty and reserved. Her lip seemed suddenly to snatch back its sweet smile; her dark eye, before so purely, softly friend-like, became coldly distant; the tones of her voice were not the same as she answered, —

"Lord Montfort values me, as it is, far beyond my merits: far, " she added with a different intonation, gravely mournful.

"Forgive me; I have displeased you. I did not mean it. Heaven forbid that I should presume either to disparage Lord Montfort—or—or to—" he stopped short, saving the hiatus by a convenient stammer. "Only, " he continued, after a pause, "only forgive me this once. Recollect I was a little boy when you were a young lady, and I have pelted you with snowballs, and called you 'Caroline'. " Lady Montfort suppressed a sigh, and gave the young scholar back her gracious smile, but not a smile that would have permitted him to call her "Caroline" again. She remained, indeed, a little more distant than usual during the rest of their interview, which was not much prolonged; for Morley felt annoyed with himself that he had so indiscreetly offended her, and seized an excuse to escape. "By the by, " said he, "I have a letter from Mr. Carr Vipont, asking me to give him a sketch for a Gothic bridge to the water yonder. I will, with your leave, walk down and look at the proposed site. Only do say that you forgive me. "

"Forgive you, cousin George, oh, yes! One word only: it is true you were a child still when I fancied I was a woman, and you have a right to talk to me upon all things, except those that relate to me and Lord Montfort; unless, indeed, " she added with a bewitching half laugh, "unless you ever see cause to scold me, there. Good-by, my cousin, and in turn forgive me, if I was so petulant. The Caroline you pelted with snowballs was always a wayward, impulsive creature, quick to take offence, to misunderstand, and—to repent. "

Back into the broad, broad gravel-walk, walked, more slowly than before, Lady Montfort. Again the sixty ghastly windows stared at her with all their eyes; back from the gravelwalk, through a side-door into the pompous solitude of the stately house; across long chambers, where the mirrors reflected her form, and the huge chairs, in their flaunting damask and flaring gold, stood stiff on desolate floors; into her own private room, —neither large nor splendid that; plain chintzes, quiet book shelves. She need not have been the Marchioness of Montfort to inhabit a room as pleasant and as luxurious. And the rooms that she could only have owned as marchioness, what were those worth to her happiness? I know not. "Nothing, " fine ladies will perhaps answer. Yet those same fine ladies will contrive to dispose their daughters to answer, "All. " In her own room Lady Montfort sank on her chair; wearily, wearily she looked at the clock; wearily at the books on the shelves, at the harp near the window. Then she leaned her face on her hand, and that face was so sad, and so humbly sad, that you would have wondered how any one could call Lady Montfort proud.

"Treasure! I! I! worthless, fickle, credulous fool! I! I! "

The groom of the chambers entered with the letters by the afternoon post. That great house contrived to worry itself with two posts a day. A royal command to Windsor—

"I shall be more alone in a court than here, " murmured Lady Montfort.

CHAPTER II.

Truly saith the proverb, "Much corn lies under the straw that is not seen. "

Meanwhile George Morley followed the long shady walk, — very handsome walk, full of prize roses and rare exotics, artificially winding too, — walk so well kept that it took thirty-four men to keep it, — noble walk, tiresome walk, till it brought him to the great piece of water, which, perhaps, four times in the year was visited by the great folks in the Great House. And being thus out of the immediate patronage of fashion, the great piece of water really looked natural, companionable, refreshing: you began to breathe; to unbutton your waistcoat, loosen your neckcloth, quote Chaucer, if you could recollect him, or Cowper, or Shakspeare, or Thomson's "Seasons; " in short, any scraps of verse that came into your head, — as your feet grew joyously entangled with fern; as the trees grouped forest-like before and round you; trees which there, being out of sight, were allowed to grow too old to be worth five shillings a piece, moss-grown, hollow-trunked, some pollarded, — trees invaluable! Ha, the hare! How she scuds! See, the deer marching down to the water side. What groves of bulrushes! islands of water-lily! And to throw a Gothic bridge there, bring a great gravel road over the bridge! Oh, shame, shame!

So would have said the scholar, for he had a true sentiment for Nature, if the bridge had not clean gone out of his head. Wandering alone, he came at last to the most umbrageous and sequestered bank of the wide water, closed round on every side by brushwood, or still, patriarchal trees. Suddenly he arrested his steps; an idea struck him, — one of those old, whimsical, grotesque ideas which often when we are alone come across us, even in our quietest or most anxious moods. Was his infirmity really incurable? Elocution masters had said certainly not; but they had done him no good. Yet had not the greatest orator the world ever knew a defect in utterance? He, too, Demosthenes, had, no doubt, paid fees to elocution masters, the best in Athens, where elocution masters must have studied their art ad unguem, and the defect had baffled them. But did Demosthenes despair? No, he resolved to cure himself, — how? Was it not one of his methods to fill his mouth with pebbles, and practise, manfully to the roaring sea? George Morley had never tried the effect of pebbles. Was there any virtue in them? Why not try? No sea there, it is true;

but a sea was only useful as representing the noise of a stormy democratic audience. To represent a peaceful congregation that still sheet of water would do as well. Pebbles there were in plenty just by that gravelly cove, near which a young pike lay sunning his green back. Half in jest, half in earnest, the scholar picked up a handful of pebbles, wiped them from sand and mould, inserted them between his teeth cautiously, and, looking round to assure himself that none were by, began an extempore discourse. So interested did he become in that classical experiment, that he might have tortured the air and astonished the magpies (three of whom from a neighbouring thicket listened perfectly spell-bound) for more than half an hour, when seized with shame at the ludicrous impotence of his exertions, with despair that so wretched a barrier should stand between his mind and its expression, he flung away the pebbles, and sinking on the ground, he fairly wept, wept like a baffled child.

The fact was, that Morley had really the temperament of an orator; he had the orator's gifts in warmth of passion, rush of thought, logical arrangement; there was in him the genius of a great preacher. He felt it, —he knew it; and in that despair which only genius knows when some pitiful cause obstructs its energies and strikes down its powers, making a confidant of Solitude he wept loud and freely.

"Do not despond, sir, I undertake to cure you, " said a voice behind.

George started up in confusion; a man, elderly, but fresh and vigorous, stood beside him, in a light fustian jacket, a blue apron, and with rushes in his hands, which he continued to plait together nimbly and deftly as he bowed to the startled scholar.

"I was in the shade of the thicket yonder, sir; pardon me, I could not help hearing you. "

The Oxonian rubbed his eyes, and stared at the man with a vague impression that he had seen him before; —when? where?

"You can cure me, " he stuttered out; "what of? —the folly of trying to speak in public? Thank you, I am cured. "

"Nay, sir, you see before you a man who can make you a very good speaker. Your voice is naturally fine. I repeat, I can cure a defect which is not in the organ, but in the management! "

"You can! you—who and what are you? "

"A basketmaker, sir; I hope for your custom. " "Surely this is not the first time I have seen you? "

"True, you once kindly suffered me to borrow a resting-place on your father's land. One good turn deserves another. "

At that moment Sir Isaac peered through the brambles, and restored to his original whiteness, and relieved from his false, horned ears, marched gravely towards the water, sniffed at the scholar, slightly wagged his tail, and buried himself amongst the reeds in search of a water-rat he had therein disturbed a week before, and always expected to find again.

The sight of the dog immediately cleared up the cloud in the scholar's memory; but with recognition came back a keen curiosity and a sharp pang of remorse.

"And your little girl? " he asked, looking down abashed.

"Better than she was when we last met. Providence is so kind to us. "

Poor Waife! He never guessed that to the person he thus revealed himself he owed the grief for Sophy's abduction. He divined no reason for the scholar's flushing cheek and embarrassed manner.

"Yes, sir, we have just settled in this neighbourhood. I have a pretty cottage yonder at the outskirts of the village, and near the park pales. I recognized you at once; and as I heard you just now, I called to mind that when we met before, you said your calling should be the Church, were it not for your difficulty in utterance; and I said to myself, 'No bad thing those pebbles, if his utterance were thick, which is it not; ' and I have not a doubt, sir, that the true fault of Demosthenes, whom I presume you are imitating, was that he spoke through his nose. "

"Eh! " said the scholar, "through his nose? I never knew that? —and I—"

"And you are trying to speak without lungs; that is without air in them. You don't smoke, I presume? "

"No; certainly not. "

"You must learn; speak between each slow puff of your pipe. All you want is time, —time to quiet the nerves, time to think, time to breathe. The moment you begin to stammer, stop, fill the lungs thus, then try again! It is only a clever man who can learn to write, —that is, to compose; but any fool can be taught to speak. Courage! "

"If you really can teach me, " cried the learned man, forgetting all self-reproach for his betrayal of Waife to Mrs. Crane in the absorbing interest of the hope that sprang up within him, "if you can teach me; if I can but con-con-con—conq—"

"Slowly, slowly, breath and time; take a whiff from my pipe; that's right. Yes, you can conquer the impediment. "

"Then I will be the best friend to you that man ever had. There's my hand on it. "

"I take it, but I ask leave to change the parties in the contract. I don't want a friend: I don't deserve one. You'll be a friend to my little girl instead; and if ever I ask you to help me in aught for her welfare and happiness—"

"I will help, heart and soul! slight indeed any service to her or to you compared with such service to me. Free this wretched tongue from its stammer, and thought and zeal will not stammer whenever you say, 'Keep your promise. ' I am so glad your little girl is still with you. "

Waife looked surprised, "Is still with me! —why not? " The scholar bit his tongue. That was not the moment to confess; it might destroy all Waife's confidence in him. He would do so later. "When shall I begin my lesson? "

"Now, if you like. But have you a book in your pocket? "

"I always have. "

"Not Greek, I hope, sir? "

"No, a volume of Barrow's Sermons. Lord Chatham recommended those sermons to his great son as a study for eloquence. "

"Good! Will you lend me the volume, sir? and now for it. Listen to me; one sentence at a time; draw your breath when I do. "

The three magpies pricked up their ears again, and, as they listened, marvelled much.

CHAPTER III.

Could we know by what strange circumstances a man's genius became prepared for practical success, we should discover that the most serviceable items in his education were never entered in the bills which his father paid for it.

At the end of the very first lesson George Morley saw that all the elocution masters to whose skill he had been consigned were blunderers in comparison with the basketmaker.

Waife did not puzzle him with scientific theories. All that the great comedian required of him was to observe and to imitate. Observation, imitation, lo! the groundwork of all art! the primal elements of all genius! Not there, indeed to halt, but there ever to commence. What remains to carry on the intellect to mastery? Two steps, —to reflect, to reproduce. Observation, imitation, reflection, reproduction. In these stands a mind complete and consummate, fit to cope with all labour, achieve all success.

At the end of the first lesson George Morley felt that his cure was possible. Making an appointment for the next day at the same place, he came thither stealthily and so on day by day. At the end of a week he felt that the cure was nearly certain; at the end of a month the cure was self-evident. He should live to preach the Word. True, that he practised incessantly in private. Not a moment in his waking hours that the one thought, one object, was absent from his mind! True, that with all his patience, all his toil, the obstacle was yet serious, might never be entirely overcome. Nervous hurry, rapidity of action, vehemence of feeling, brought back, might at unguarded moments always bring back, the gasping breath, the emptied lungs, the struggling utterance. But the relapse, rarer and rarer now with each trial, would be at last scarce a drawback. "Nay, " quoth Waife, "instead of a drawback, become but an orator, and you will convert a defect into a beauty. "

Thus justly sanguine of the accomplishment of his life's chosen object, the scholar's gratitude to Waife was unspeakable. And seeing the man daily at last in his own cottage, —Sophy's health restored to her cheeks, smiles to her lip, and cheered at her light fancy-work beside her grandsire's elbow-chair, with fairy legends instilling perhaps golden truths, —seeing Waife thus, the scholar mingled with gratitude a strange tenderness of respect. He knew nought of the vagrant's past, his reason might admit that in a position of life so at variance with the gifts natural and acquired of the singular basketmaker, there was something mysterious and suspicious. But he blushed to think that he had ever ascribed to a flawed or wandering intellect the eccentricities of glorious Humour, —abetted an attempt to separate an old age so innocent and genial from a childhood so fostered and so fostering. And sure I am that if the whole world had risen up to point the finger of scorn at the one-eyed cripple, George Morley—the well-born gentleman, the refined scholar, the spotless Churchman—would have given him his arm to lean upon, and walked by his side unashamed.

CHAPTER IV.

To judge human character rightly, a man may sometimes have very small experience, provided he has a very large heart.

Numa Pimpilius did not more conceal from notice the lessons he received from Egeria than did George Morley those which he received from the basketmaker. Natural, indeed, must be his wish for secrecy; pretty story it would be for Humberston, its future rector learning how to preach a sermon from an old basketmaker! But he had a nobler and more imperious motive for discretion: his honour was engaged to it. Waife exacted a promise that he would regard the intercourse between them as strictly private and confidential.

"It is for my sake I ask this, " said Waife, frankly, "though I might say it was for yours; " the Oxonian promised, and was bound. Fortunately Lady Montfort quitted the great house the very day after George had first encountered the basketmaker, and writing word that she should not return to it for some weeks, George was at liberty to avail himself of her lord's general invitation to make use of Montfort Court as his lodgings when in the neighbourhood; which the proprieties of the world would not have allowed him to do while Lady Montfort was there without either host or female guests. Accordingly, he took up his abode in a corner of the vast palace, and was easily enabled, when he pleased, to traverse unobserved the solitudes of the park, gain the waterside, or stroll thence through the thick copse leading to Waife's cottage, which bordered the park pales, solitary, sequestered, beyond sight of the neighbouring village. The great house all to himself, George was brought in contact with no one to whom, in unguarded moments, he could even have let out a hint of his new acquaintance, except the clergyman of the parish, a worthy man, who lived in strict retirement upon a scanty stipend. For the Marquess was the lay impropriator; the living was therefore but a very poor vicarage, below the acceptance of a Vipont or a Vipont's tutor, sure to go to a worthy man forced to live in strict retirement. George saw too little of this clergyman, either to let out secrets or pick up information. From him, however, George did incidentally learn that Waife had some months previously visited the village, and proposed to the bailiff to take the cottage and osier land, which he now rented; that he represented himself as having known an old basketmaker who had dwelt there many years ago, and as having learned the basket craft of that long deceased operative. As he offered a higher rent than the bailiff could elsewhere obtain, and as the bailiff was desirous to get credit with Mr. Carr Vipont for improving the property, by reviving thereon an art which had fallen into desuetude, the bargain was struck, provided the candidate, being a stranger to the place, could furnish the bailiff with any satisfactory reference. Waife had gone away, saying he should shortly return with the requisite testimonial. In fact, poor man, as we know, he was then counting on a good word from Mr. Hartopp. He had not, however, returned for some months. The cottage, having been meanwhile wanted for the temporary occupation of an under-gamekeeper, while his own was under repair, fortunately remained unlet. Waife, on returning, accompanied by his little girl, had referred the bailiff to a respectable house-agent and collector of street rents in Bloomsbury, who wrote word that a lady, then abroad, had authorized him, as the agent employed in the management of a house property from which much of her income was derived, not only to state that Waife was a very intelligent man, likely to do well whatever he undertook, but also to guarantee, if required, the punctual payment of the rent for any holding of which he became the occupier. On this the agreement was concluded, the basketmaker installed. In the immediate neighbourhood there was no custom for basket-work, but Waife's performances were so neat, and some so elegant and fanciful, that he had no difficulty in contracting with a large tradesman (not at Humberston, but a more distant and yet more thriving town about twenty miles off) for as much of such work as he could supply. Each week the carrier took his goods and brought back the payments; the profits amply sufficed for Waife's and Sophy's daily bread, with even more than the surplus set aside for the rent. For the rest, the basketmaker's cottage being at the farthest outskirts of the straggling village inhabited by a labouring peasantry, his way of life was not much known nor much inquired into. He seemed a harmless, hard-working man; never seen at the beer-house; always seen with his neatly-dressed little grandchild in his quiet corner at church on Sundays; a civil, well-behaved man too; who touched his hat to the bailiff and took it off to the vicar.

An idea prevailed that the basketmaker had spent much of his life in foreign countries, favoured partly by a sobriety of habits which is not altogether national, partly by something in his appearance, which, without being above his lowly calling, did not seem quite in keeping with it, —outlandish in short, —but principally by the fact that he had received since his arrival two letters with a foreign postmark. The idea befriended the old man, —allowing it to be inferred that he had probably outlived the friends he had formerly left behind him in England, and, on his return, been sufficiently fatigued with his rambles to drop contented in any corner of his native soil wherein he could find a quiet home, and earn by light toil a decent livelihood.

George, though naturally curious to know what had been the result of his communication to Mrs. Crane, —whether it had led to Waife's discovery or caused him annoyance, —had hitherto, however, shrunk from touching upon a topic which subjected himself to an awkward confession of officious intermeddling, and to which any indirect allusion might appear an indelicate attempt to pry into painful family affairs. But one day he received a letter from his father which disturbed him greatly, and induced him to break ground and speak to his preceptor frankly. In this letter, the elder Mr. Morley mentioned incidentally, amongst other scraps of local news, that he had seen Mr. Hartopp, who was rather out of sorts, his good heart not having recovered the shock of having been abominably "taken in" by an impostor for whom he had conceived a great fancy, and to whose discovery George himself had providentially led (the father referred here to what George had told him of his first meeting with Waife, and his visit to Mrs. Crane); the impostor, it seemed, from what Mr. Hartopp let fall, not being a little queer in the head, as George had been led to surmise, but a very bad character. "In fact, " added the elder Morley, "a character so bad that Mr. Hartopp was too glad to give up to her lawful protectors the child, whom the man appears to have abducted; and I suspect, from what Hartopp said, though he does not like to own that he was taken in to so gross a degree, that he had been actually introducing to his fellow-townsfolk and conferring familiarly with a regular jail-bird, —perhaps a burglar. How lucky for that poor, soft-headed, excellent Jos Hartopp, whom it is positively as inhuman to take in as it would be to defraud a born natural, that the lady you saw arrived in time to expose the snares laid for his benevolent credulity. But for that, Jos might have taken the fellow into his own house (just like him!), and been robbed by this time, perhaps murdered, —Heaven knows! "

Incredulous and indignant, and longing to be empowered to vindicate his friend's fair name, George seized his hat, and strode quick along the path towards the basketmaker's cottage. As he gained the water-side, he perceived Waife himself, seated on a mossy bank, under a gnarled fantastic thorntree, watching a deer as it came to drink, and whistling a soft mellow tune, —the tune of an old English border-song. The deer lifted his antlers from the water, and turned his large bright eyes towards the opposite bank, whence the note came, listening and wistful. As George's step crushed the wild thyme, which the thorn-tree shadowed, "Hush! " said Waife, "and mark how the rudest musical sound can affect the brute creation. " He resumed the whistle, —a clearer, louder, wilder tune, —that of a lively hunting-song. The deer turned quickly round, — uneasy, restless, tossed its antlers, and bounded through the fern. Waife again changed the key of his primitive music, —a melancholy belliny note, like the belling itself of a melancholy hart, but more modulated into sweetness. The deer arrested its flight, and, lured by the mimic sound, returned towards the water-side, slowly and statelily.

"I don't think the story of Orpheus charming the brutes was a fable; do you, sir? " said Waife. "The rabbits about here know me already; and, if I had but a fiddle, I would undertake to make friends with that reserved and unsocial water-rat, on whom Sir Isaac in vain endeavours at present to force his acquaintance. Man commits a great mistake in not cultivating more intimate and amicable relations with the other branches of earth's great family. Few of them not more amusing than we are; naturally, for they have not our cares. And such variety of character too, where you would least expect it! "

GEORGE MORLEY. —"Very true. Cowper noticed marked differences of character in his favourite hares. "

WAIFE. —"Hares! I am sure that there are not two house-flies on a window-pane, two minnows in that water, that would not present to us interesting points of contrast as to temper and disposition. If house-flies and minnows could but coin money, or set up a manufacture, —contrive something, in short, to buy or sell attractive to Anglo-Saxon enterprise and intelligence, —of course we should soon have diplomatic relations with them; and our despatches and newspapers would instruct us to a T in the characters and propensities of their leading personages. But, where man has no pecuniary nor ambitious interests at stake in his commerce with any class of his fellow-creatures, his information about them is extremely confused and superficial. The best naturalists are mere generalizers, and think they have done a vast deal when they classify a species. What should we know about mankind if we had only a naturalist's definition of man? We only know mankind by knocking classification on the head, and studying each man as a class in himself. Compare Buffon and Shakspeare! Alas, sir! can we never have a Shakspeare for house-flies and minnows? "

GEORGE MORLEY. —"With all respect for minnows and house-flies, if we found another Shakspeare, he might be better employed, like his predecessor, in selecting individualities from the classifications of man. "

WAIFE. —"Being yourself a man, you think so: a housefly might be of a different opinion. But permit me, at least, to doubt whether such an investigator would be better employed in reference to his own happiness, though I grant that he would be so in reference to your intellectual amusement and social interests. Poor Shakspeare! How much he must have suffered! "

GEORGE MORLEY. —"You mean that he must have been racked by the passions he describes, —bruised by collision with the hearts he dissects. That is not necessary to genius. The judge on his bench, summing up evidence and charging the jury, has no need to have shared the temptations or been privy to the acts of the prisoner at the bar. Yet how consummate may be his analysis! "

"No, " cried Waife, roughly. "No! Your illustration destroys your argument. The judge knows nothing of the prisoner. There are the circumstances; there is the law. By these he generalizes, by these he judges, —right or wrong. But of the individual at the bar, of the world—the tremendous world—within that individual heart, I repeat, he knows nothing. Did he know, law and circumstances might vanish, human justice would be paralyzed. Ho, there! place that swart-visaged, ill-looking foreigner in the dock, and let counsel open the case; hear the witnesses depose! Oh, horrible wretch! a murderer! unmanly murderer! —a defenceless woman smothered by caitiff hands! Hang him up! hang him up! 'Softly, ' whispers the POET, and lifts the veil from the assassin's heart. 'Lo! it is Othello the Moor! ' What jury now dare find that criminal guilty? what judge now put on the black cap? who now says, 'Hang him up! hang him up! "

With such lifelike force did the Comedian vent this passionate outburst that he thrilled his listener with an awe akin to that which the convicted Moor gathers round himself at the close of the sublime drama. Even Sir Isaac was startled; and leaving his hopeless pursuit of the water-rat, uttered a low bark, came to his master, and looked into his face with solemn curiosity.

WAIFE (relapsing into colloquial accents). —"Why do we sympathize with those above us more than with those below? why with the sorrows of a king rather than those of a beggar? why does Sir Isaac sympathize with me more than (let that water-rat vex him ever so much) I can possibly sympathize with him? Whatever be the cause, see at least, Mr. Morley, one reason why a poor creature like myself finds it better employment to cultivate the intimacy of brutes than to prosecute the study of men. Among men, all are too high to sympathize with me; but I have known two friends who never injured nor betrayed. Sir Isaac is one; Wamba was another. Wamba, sir, the native of a remote district of the globe (two friends civilized Europe is not large enough to afford any one man), Wamba, sir, was less gifted by nature, less refined by education, than Sir Isaac; but he was a safe and trustworthy companion: Wamba, sir, was—an opossum. "

GEORGE MORLEY. —"Alas, my dear Mr. Waife, I fear that men must have behaved very ill to you. "

WAIFE. —"I have no right to complain. I have behaved very ill to myself. When a man is his own enemy, he is very unreasonable if he expect other men to be his benefactors. "

GEORGE MORLEY (with emotion). —"Listen, I have a confession to make to you. I fear I have done you an injury, where, officiously, I meant to do a kindness. " The scholar hurried on to narrate the particulars of his visit to Mrs. Crane. On concluding the recital, he added, "When again I met you here, and learned that your Sophy was with you, I felt inexpressibly relieved. It was clear then, I thought, that your grandchild had been left to your care unmolested, either that you had proved not to be the person of whom the parties were in search, or family affairs had been so explained and reconciled that my interference had occasioned you no harm. But to-day I have a letter from my father which disquiets me much. It seems that the persons in question did visit Gatesboro', and have maligned you to Mr. Hartopp. Understand me, I ask for no confidence which you may be unwilling to give; but if you will arm me with the power to vindicate your character from aspersions which I need not your assurance to hold unjust and false, I will not rest till that task be triumphantly accomplished. "

WAIFE (in a tone calm but dejected). —"I thank you with all my heart. But there is nothing to be done. I am glad that the subject did not start up between us until such little service as I could render you, Mr. Morley, was pretty well over. It would have been a pity if you had been compelled to drop all communication with a man of attainted character, before you had learned how to manage the powers that will enable you hereafter to exhort sinners worse than I have been. Hush, sir! you feel that, at least now, I am an inoffensive old man, labouring for a humble livelihood. You will not repeat here what you may have heard, or yet hear, to the discredit of my former life. You will not send me and my grandchild forth from our obscure refuge to confront a world with which we have no strength to cope. And, believing this, it only remains for me to say, Fare-you-well, sir."

"I should deserve to lose spe-spe-speech altogether, " cried the Oxonian, gasping and stammering fearfully as he caught Waife firmly by the arm, "if I suffered—suff-suff-suff—"

"One, two! take time, sir! " said the Comedian, softly. And with a sweet patience he reseated himself on the bank. The Oxonian threw himself at length by the outcast's side; and, with the noble tenderness of a nature as chivalrously Christian as Heaven ever gave to priest, he rested his folded hands upon Waife's shoulder, and looking him full and close in the face, said thus, slowly, deliberately, not a stammer, "You do not guess what you have done for me; you have secured to me a home and a career; the wife of whom I must otherwise have despaired; the Divine Vocation on which all my earthly hopes were set, and which I was on the eve of renouncing: do not think these are obligations which can be lightly shaken off. If there are circumstances which forbid me to disabuse others of impressions which wrong you, imagine not that their false notions will affect my own gratitude, —my own respect for you! "

"Nay, sir! they ought; they must. Perhaps not your exaggerated gratitude for a service which you should not, however, measure by its effects on yourself, but by the slightness of the trouble it gave to me; not perhaps your gratitude, but your respect, yes. "

"I tell you no! Do you fancy that I cannot judge of a man's nature without calling on him to trust me with all the secrets—all the errors, if you will—of his past life? Will not the calling to which I may now hold myself destined give me power and commandment to absolve all those who truly repent and unfeignedly believe? Oh, Mr. Waife! if in earlier days you have sinned, do you not repent? and how often, in many a lovely gentle sentence dropped unawares from your lips, have I had cause to know that you unfeignedly believe! Were I now clothed with sacred authority, could I not absolve you as a priest? Think you that, in the meanwhile, I dare judge you as a man? I, — Life's new recruit, guarded hitherto from temptation by careful parents and favouring fortune, —I presume to judge, and judge harshly, the gray-haired veteran, wearied by the march, wounded in the battle! "

"You are a noble-hearted human being, " said Waife, greatly affected. "And, mark my words, a mantle of charity so large you will live to wear as a robe of honour. But hear me, sir! Mr. Hartopp also is a man infinitely charitable, benevolent, kindly, and, through all his simplicity, acutely shrewd; Mr. Hartopp, on hearing what was said against me, deemed me unfit to retain my grandchild, resigned the trust I had confided to him, and would have given me alms, no doubt, had I asked them, but not his hand. Take your hands, sir, from my shoulder, lest the touch sully you. "

George did take his hands from the vagrant's shoulder, but it was to grasp the hand that waived them off and struggled to escape the pressure. "You are innocent! you are innocent! forgive me that I spoke to you of repentance as if you had been guilty. I feel you are innocent, —feel it by my own heart. You turn away. I defy you to say that you are guilty of what has been laid to your charge, of what has darkened your good name, of what Mr. Hartopp believed to your prejudice. Look me in the face and say, 'I am not innocent; I have not been belied. '"

Waife remained voiceless, motionless.

The young man, in whose nature lay yet unproved all those grand qualities of heart, without which never was there a grand orator, a grand preacher, —qualities which grasp the results of argument, and arrive at the end of elaborate reasoning by sudden impulse, —here released Waife's hand, rose to his feet, and, facing Waife, as the old man sat with face averted, eyes downcast, breast heaving, said loftily,

"Forget that I may soon be the Christian minister whose duty bows his ear to the lips of Shame and Guilt; whose hand, when it points to

Heaven, no mortal touch can sully; whose sublimest post is by the sinner's side. Look on me but as man and gentleman. See, I now extend this hand to you. If, as man and gentleman, you have done that which, could all hearts be read, all secrets known, human judgment reversed by Divine omniscience, forbids you to take this hand, —then reject it, go hence: we part! But if no such act be on your conscience, however you submit to its imputation, —THEN, in the name of Truth, as man and gentleman to man and gentleman, I command you to take this right hand, and, in the name of that Honour which bears no paltering, I forbid you to disobey. "

The vagabond rose, like the Dead at the spell of a Magician, —took, as if irresistibly, the hand held out to him. And the scholar, overjoyed, fell on his breast, embracing him as a son.

"You know, " said George, in trembling accents, "that the hand you have taken will never betray, never desert; but is it—is it really powerless to raise and to restore you to your place? "

"Powerless amongst your kind for that indeed, " answered Waife, in accents still more tremulous. "All the kings of the earth are not strong enough to raise a name that has once been trampled into the mire. Learn that it is not only impossible for me to clear myself, but that it is equally impossible for me to confide to mortal being a single plea in defence if I am innocent, in extenuation if I am guilty. And saying this, and entreating you to hold it more merciful to condemn than to question me, —for question is torture, —I cannot reject your pity; but it would be mockery to offer me respect! "

"What! not respect the fortitude which calumny cannot crush? Would that fortitude be possible if you were not calm in the knowledge that no false witnesses can mislead the Eternal Judge? Respect you! yes, —because I have seen you happy in despite of men, and therefore I know that the cloud around you is not the frown of Heaven. "

"Oh, " cried Waife, the tears rolling down his cheeks, "and not an hour ago I was jesting at human friendship, venting graceless spleen on my fellow-men! And now—now—ah, sir! Providence is so kind to me! And, " said he, brushing away his tears, as the old arch smile began to play round the corner of his mouth, "and kind to me in the very quarter in which unkindness had so sorely smitten me. True, you directed towards me the woman who took from me my grandchild, who destroyed me in the esteem of good Mr. Hartopp. Well, you see, I have my sweet Sophy back again; we are in the home of all others I most longed for; and that woman, yes, I can, at least, thus far, confide to you my secrets, so that you may not blame yourself for sending her to Gatesboro', —that very woman knows of my shelter; furnished me with the very reference necessary to obtain it; has freed my grandchild from a loathsome bondage, which I could not have legally resisted; and should new persecutions chase us will watch and warn and help us. And if you ask me how this change in her was effected; how, when we had abandoned all hope of green fields, and deemed that only in the crowd of a city we could escape those who pursued us when discovered there, though I fancied myself an adept in disguise, and the child and the dog were never seen out of the four garret walls in which I hid them, —if you ask me, I say, to explain how that very woman was suddenly converted from a remorseless foe into a saving guardian, I can only answer 'By no wit, no device, no persuasive art of mine. Providence softened her heart, and made it kind, just at a moment when no other agency on earth could have rescued us from—from—"

"Say no more: I guess! the paper this woman showed me was a legal form authorizing your poor little Sophy to be given up to the care of a father. I guess! of that father you would not speak ill to me; yet from that father you would save your grandchild. Say no more. And yon quiet home, your humble employment, really content you? "

"Oh, if such a life can but last! Sophy is so well, so cheerful, so happy. Did not you bear her singing the other day? She never used to sing! But we had not been here a week when song broke out from her, —untaught, as from a bird. But if any ill report of me travel hither from Gatesboro' or elsewhere, we should be sent away, and the bird would be mute in my thorn-tree: Sophy would sing no more. "

"Do not fear that slander shall drive you hence. Lady Montfort, you know, is my cousin, but you know not—few do—how thoroughly generous and gentle-hearted she is. I will speak of you to her, —oh! do not look alarmed. She will take my word when I tell her, 'That is a good man; ' and if she ask more, it will be enough to say, 'Those who have known better days are loth to speak to strangers of the past. '"

"I thank you earnestly, sincerely, " said Waife, brightening up. "One favour more: if you saw in the formal document shown to you, or retain on your memory, the name of—of the person authorized to claim Sophy as his child, you will not mention it to Lady Montfort. I am hot sure if ever she heard that name, but she may have done so, and—and—" he paused a moment, and seemed to muse; then went on, not concluding his sentence. "You are so good to me, Mr. Morley, that I wish to confide in you as far as I can. Now, you see, I am already an old man, and my chief object is to raise up a friend for Sophy when I am gone, —a friend in her own sex, sir. Oh, you cannot guess how I long, how I yearn, to view that child under the holy fostering eyes of a woman. Perhaps if Lady Montfort saw my pretty Sophy she might take a fancy to her. Oh, if she did! if she did! And Sophy, " added Waife, proudly, "has a right to respect. She is not like me, —any hovel is good enough for me; but for her! Do you know that I conceived that hope, that the hope helped to lead me back here when, months ago, I was at Humberston, intent upon rescuing Sophy; and saw—though, " observed Waife, with a sly twitch of the muscles round his mouth, "I had no right at that precise moment to be seeing anything—Lady Montfort's humane fear for a blind old impostor, who was trying to save his dog—a black dog, sir, who had dyed his hair—from her carriage wheels. And the hope became stronger still, when, the first Sunday I attended yon village church, I again saw that fair—wondrously fair—face at the far end, —fair as moonlight and as melancholy. Strange it is, sir, that I— naturally a boisterous, mirthful man, and now a shy, skulking fugitive—feel more attracted, more allured towards a countenance, in proportion as I read there the trace of sadness. I feel less abased by my own nothingness, more emboldened to approach and say, 'Not so far apart from me: thou too hast suffered. ' Why is this? "

GEORGE MORLEY. —"'The fool hath said in his heart that there is no God; ' but the fool hath not said in his heart that there is no sorrow, —pithy and most profound sentence; intimating the irrefragable claim that binds men to the Father. And when the chain tightens, the children are closer drawn together. But to your wish: I will remember it. And when my cousin returns, she shall see your Sophy. "

CHAPTER V.

Mr. Waife, being by nature unlucky, considers that, in proportion as fortune brings him good luck, nature converts it into bad. He suffers Mr. George Morley to go away in his debt, and Sophy fears that he will be dull in consequence.

George Morley, a few weeks after the conversation last recorded, took his departure from Montfort Court, prepared, without a scruple, to present himself for ordination to the friendly bishop. From Waife he derived more than the cure of a disabling infirmity; he received those hints which, to a man who has the natural temperament of an orator, so rarely united with that of the scholar, expedite the mastery of the art that makes the fleeting human voice an abiding, imperishable power. The grateful teacher exhausted all his lore upon the pupil whose genius he had freed, whose heart had subdued himself. Before leaving, George was much perplexed how to offer to Waife any other remuneration than that which, in Waife's estimate, had already overpaid all the benefits he had received; namely, unquestioning friendship and pledged protection. It need scarcely be said that George thought the man to whom he owed fortune and happiness was entitled to something beyond that moral recompense. But he found, at the first delicate hint, that Waife would not hear of money, though the ex-Comedian did not affect any very Quixotic notion on that practical subject. "To tell you the truth, sir, I have rather a superstition against having more money in my hands than I know what to do with. It has always brought me bad luck. And what is very hard, —the bad luck stays, but the money goes. There was that splendid sum I made at Gatesboro'. You should have seen me counting it over. I could not have had a prouder or more swelling heart if I had been, that great man Mr. Elwes the miser. And what bad luck it brought me, and how it all frittered itself away! Nothing to show for it but a silk ladder and an old hurdy-gurdy, and I sold them at half price. Then when I had the accident, which cost me this eye, the railway people behaved so generously, gave me L120, —think of that! And before three days the money "

"How was that? " said George, half-amused, half-pained, —"stolen perhaps? "

"Not so, " answered Waife, somewhat gloomily, "but restored. A poor dear old man, who thought very ill of me, and I don't wonder

385

at it, —was reduced from great wealth to great poverty. While I was laid up, my landlady read a newspaper to me, and in that newspaper was an account of his reverse and destitution. But I was accountable to him for the balance of an old debt, and that, with the doctor's bills, quite covered my L120. I hope he does not think quite so ill of me now. But the money brought good luck to him, rather than to me. Well, sir, if you were now to give me money, I should be on the look-out for some mournful calamity. Gold is not natural to me. Some day, however, by and by, when you are inducted into your living, and have become a renowned preacher, and have plenty to spare, with an idea that you will feel more comfortable in your mind if you had done something royal for the basketmaker, I will ask you to help me to make up a sum, which I am trying by degrees to save, —an enormous sum, almost as much as I paid away from my railway compensation: I owe it to the lady who lent it to release Sophy from an engagement which I—certainly without any remorse of conscience—made the child break. "

"Oh, yes! What is the amount? Let me at least repay that debt. "

"Not yet. The lady can wait; and she would be pleased to wait, because she deserves to wait: it would be unkind to her to pay it off at once. But in the meanwhile if you could send me a few good books for Sophy, —instructive, yet not very, very dry, -and a French dictionary, I can teach her French when the winter days close in. You see I am not above being paid, sir. But, Mr. Morley, there is a great favour you can do me. "

"What is it? Speak. "

"Cautiously refrain from doing me a great disservice! You are going back to your friends and relations. Never speak of me to them. Never describe me and my odd ways. Name not the lady, nor—nor—nor— the man who claimed Sophy.

"Your friends might not hurt me; others might. Talk travels. The hare is not long in its form when it has a friend in a hound that gives tongue. Promise what I ask. Promise it as 'man and gentleman. '"

"Certainly. Yet I have one relation to whom I should like, with your permission, to speak of you, with whom I could wish you acquainted. He is so thorough a man of the world, that he might suggest some method to clear your good name, which you yourself would approve. My uncle, Colonel Morley—"

"On no account! " cried Waife, almost fiercely, and he evinced so much anger and uneasiness that it was long before George could pacify him by the most earnest assurances that his secret should be inviolably kept, and his injunctions faithfully obeyed. No men of the world consulted how to force him back to the world of men that he fled from! No colonels to scan him with martinet eyes, and hint how to pipeclay a tarnish! Waife's apprehensions gradually allayed and his confidence restored, one fine morning George took leave of his eccentric benefactor.

Waife and Sophy stood gazing after him from their garden-gate, the cripple leaning lightly on the child's arm. She looked with anxious fondness into the old man's thoughtful face, and clung to him more closely as she looked.

"Will you not be dull, poor Grandy? will you not miss him? "

"A little at first, " said Waife, rousing himself. "Education is a great thing. An educated mind, provided that it does us no mischief, — which is not always the case, —cannot be withdrawn from our existence without leaving a blank behind. Sophy, we must seriously set to work and educate ourselves! "

"We will, Grandy dear, " said Sophy, with decision; and a few minutes afterwards, "If I can become very, very clever, you will not pine so much after that gentleman, —will you, Grandy? "

CHAPTER VI.

Being a chapter that comes to an untimely end.

Winter was far advanced when Montfort Court was again brightened by the presence of its lady. A polite letter from Mr. Carr Vipont had reached her before leaving Windsor, suggesting how much it would be for the advantage of the Vipont interest if she would consent to visit for a month or two the seat in Ireland, which had been too long neglected, and at which my lord would join her on his departure from his Highland moors. So to Ireland went Lady Montfort. My lord did not join her there; but Mr. Carr Vipont deemed it desirable for the Vipont interest that the wedded pair should reunite at Montfort Court, where all the Vipont family were invited to witness their felicity or mitigate their ennui.

But before proceeding another stage in this history, it becomes a just tribute of respect to the great House of Vipont to pause and place its past records and present grandeur in fuller display before the reverential reader. The House of Vipont! —what am I about? The House of Vipont requires a chapter to itself.

CHAPTER VII.

The House of Vipont, —"*Majora canamus.* "

The House of Vipont! Looking back through ages, it seems as if the House of Vipont were one continuous living idiosyncrasy, having in its progressive development a connected unity of thought and action, so that through all the changes of its outward form it had been moved and guided by the same single spirit, —"*Le roi est mort; vive le roi!* "—A Vipont dies; live the Vipont! Despite its high-sounding Norman name, the House of Vipont was no House at all for some generations after the Conquest. The first Vipont who emerged from the obscurity of time was a rude soldier of Gascon origin, in the reign of Henry II., —one of the thousand fighting-men who sailed from Milford Haven with the stout Earl of Pembroke, on that strange expedition which ended in the conquest of Ireland. This gallant man obtained large grants of land in that fertile island; some Mac or some O' — —- vanished, and the House of Vipont rose.

During the reign of Richard I., the House of Vipont, though recalled to England (leaving its Irish acquisitions in charge of a fierce cadet, who served as middleman), excused itself from the Crusade, and, by marriage with a rich goldsmith's daughter, was enabled to lend moneys to those who indulged in that exciting but costly pilgrimage. In the reign of John, the House of Vipont foreclosed its mortgages on lands thus pledged, and became possessed of a very fair property in England, as well as its fiefs in the sister isle.

The House of Vipont took no part in the troublesome politics of that day. Discreetly obscure, it attended to its own fortunes, and felt small interest in Magna Charta. During the reigns of the Plantagenet Edwards, who were great encouragers of mercantile adventure, the House of Vipont, shunning Crecy, Bannockburn, and such profitless brawls, intermarried with London traders, and got many a good thing out of the Genoese. In the reign of Henry IV. the House of Vipont reaped the benefit of its past forbearance and modesty. Now, for the first time, the Viponts appear as belted knights; they have armorial bearings; they are Lancasterian to the backbone; they are exceedingly indignant against heretics; they burn the Lollards; they have places in the household of Queen Joan, who was called a witch, —but a witch is a very good friend when she wields a sceptre instead of a broomstick. And in proof of its growing importance, the

House of Vipont marries a daughter of the then mighty House of Darrell. In the reign of Henry V., during the invasion of France, the House of Vipont—being afraid of the dysentery which carried off more brave fellows than the field of Agincourt—contrived to be a minor. The Wars of the Roses puzzled the House of Vipont sadly. But it went through that perilous ordeal with singular tact and success. The manner in which it changed sides, each change safe, and most changes lucrative, is beyond all praise.

On the whole, it preferred the Yorkists; it was impossible to be actively Lancasterian with Henry VI. of Lancaster always in prison. And thus, at the death of Edward IV., the House of Vipont was Baron Vipont of Vipont, with twenty manors. Richard III. counted on the House of Vipont, when he left London to meet Richmond at Bosworth: he counted without his host. The House of Vipont became again intensely Lancasterian, and was amongst the first to crowd round the litter in which Henry VII. entered the metropolis. In that reign it married a relation of Empson's, did the great House of Vipont! and as nobles of elder date had become scarce and poor, Henry VII. was pleased to make the House of Vipont an Earl, —the Earl of Montfort. In the reign of Henry VIII., instead of burning Lollards, the House of Vipont was all for the Reformation: it obtained the lands of two priories and one abbey. Gorged with that spoil, the House of Vipont, like an anaconda in the process of digestion, slept long. But no, it slept not. Though it kept itself still as a mouse during the reign of Bloody Queen Mary (only letting it be known at Court that the House of Vipont had strong papal leanings); though during the reigns of Elizabeth and James it made no noise, the House of Vipont was silently inflating its lungs and improving its constitution. Slept, indeed! it was wide awake. Then it was that it began systematically its grand policy of alliances; then was it sedulously grafting its olive branches on the stems of those fruitful New Houses that had sprung up with the Tudors; then, alive to the spirit of the day, provident of the wants of the morrow, over the length and breadth of the land it wove the interlacing network of useful cousinhood! Then, too, it began to build palaces, to enclose parks; it travelled, too, a little, did the House of Vipont! it visited Italy; it conceived a taste: a very elegant House became the House of Vipont! And in James's reign, for the first time, the House of Vipont got the Garter. The Civil Wars broke out: England was rent asunder. Peer and knight took part with one side or the other. The House of Vipont was again perplexed. Certainly at the commencement it, was all for King Charles. But when King Charles took to fighting, the

House of Vipont shook its sagacious head, and went about, like Lord Falkland, sighing, "Peace, peace! " Finally, it remembered its neglected estates in Ireland: its duties called it thither. To Ireland it went, discreetly sad, and, marrying a kinswoman of Lord Fauconberg, —the connection least exposed to Fortune's caprice of all the alliances formed by the Lord Protector's family, —it was safe when Cromwell visited Ireland; and no less safe when Charles II. was restored to England. During the reign of the merry monarch the House of Vipont was a courtier, married a beauty, got the Garter again, and, for the first time, became the fashion. Fashion began to be a power. In the reign of James II. the House of Vipont again contrived to be a minor, who came of age just in time to take the oaths of fealty to William and Mary. In case of accidents, the House of Vipont kept on friendly terms with the exiled Stuarts, but it wrote no letters, and got into no scrapes. It was not, however, till the Government, under Sir Robert Walpole, established the constitutional and parliamentary system which characterizes modern freedom, that the puissance accumulated through successive centuries by the House of Vipont became pre-eminently visible. By that time its lands were vast; its wealth enormous; its parliamentary influence, as "a Great House, " was a part of the British Constitution. At this period, the House of Vipont found it convenient to rend itself into two grand divisions, —the peer's branch and the commoner's. The House of Commons had become so important that it was necessary for the House of Vipont to be represented there by a great commoner. Thus arose the family of Carr Vipont. That division, owing to a marriage settlement favouring a younger son by the heiress of the Carrs, carried off a good slice from the estate of the earldom: *uno averso, non deficit alter*; the earldom mourned, but replaced the loss by two wealthy wedlocks of its own; and had long since seen cause to rejoice that its power in the Upper Chamber was strengthened by such aid in the Lower. For, thanks to its parliamentary influence, and the aid of the great commoner, in the reign of George III. the House of Vipont became a Marquess. From that time to the present day, the House of Vipont has gone on prospering and progressive. It was to the aristocracy what the "Times" newspaper is to the press. The same quick sympathy with public feeling, the same unity of tone and purpose, the same adaptability, and something of the same lofty tone of superiority to the petty interests of party. It may be conceded that the House of Vipont was less brilliant than the "Times" newspaper, but eloquence and wit, necessary to the duration of a newspaper, were not necessary to that of the House of Vipont. Had they been so, it would have had them.

The head of the House of Vipont rarely condescended to take office. With a rent-roll loosely estimated at about L170,000 a year, it is beneath a man to take from the public a paltry five or six thousand a year, and undergo all the undignified abuse of popular assemblies, and "a ribald press. " But it was a matter of course that the House of Vipont should be represented in any Cabinet that a constitutional monarch could be advised to form. Since the time of Walpole, a Vipont was always in the service of his country, except in those rare instances when the country was infamously misgoverned. The cadets of the House, or the senior member of the great commoner's branch of it, sacrificed their ease to fulfil that duty. The Montfort marquesses in general were contented with situations of honour in the household, as of Lord Steward, Lord Chamberlain, or Master of the Horse, etc., —not onerous dignities; and even these they only deigned to accept on those special occasions when danger threatened the star of Brunswick, and the sense of its exalted station forbade the House of Vipont to leave its country in the dark.

Great Houses like that of Vipont assist the work of civilization by the law of their existence. They are sure to have a spirited and wealthy tenantry, to whom, if but for the sake of that popular character which doubles political influence, they are liberal and kindly landlords. Under their sway fens and sands become fertile; agricultural experiments are tested on a large scale; cattle and sheep improve in breed; national capital augments, and, springing beneath the ploughshare, circulates indirectly to speed the ship and animate the loom. Had there been no Woburn, no Holkham, no Montfort Court, England would be the poorer by many a million. Our great Houses tend also to the refinement of national taste; they have their show places, their picture galleries, their beautiful grounds. The humblest drawing-rooms owe an elegance or comfort, the smallest garden a flower or esculent, to the importations which luxury borrowed from abroad, or the inventions it stimulated at home, for the original benefits of great Houses. Having a fair share of such merits, in common with other great Houses, the House of Vipont was not without good qualities peculiar to itself. Precisely because it was the most egotistical of Houses, filled with the sense of its own identity, and guided by the instincts of its own conservation, it was a very civil, good-natured House, —courteous, generous, hospitable; a House (I mean the head of it, not of course all its subordinate members, including even the august Lady Selina) that could bow graciously and shake hands with you. Even if you had no vote yourself, you might have a cousin who had a vote. And once admitted into the family, the House adopted you; you had only to marry one of its remotest relations and the House sent you a wedding present; and at every general election, invited you to rally round your connection, —the Marquess. Therefore, next only to the Established Church, the House of Vipont was that British institution the roots of which were the most widely spread.

Now the Viponts had for long generations been an energetic race. Whatever their defects, they had exhibited shrewdness and vigour. The late Marquess (grandfather to the present) had been perhaps the ablest (that is, done most for the House of Vipont) of them all. Of a grandiose and superb mode of living; of a majestic deportment; of princely manners; of a remarkable talent for the management of all business, whether private or public; a perfect enthusiast for the House of Vipont, and aided by a marchioness in all respects worthy of him, —he might be said to be the culminating flower of the venerable stem. But the present lord, succeeding to the title as a mere child, was a melancholy contrast, not only to his grandsire, but to the general character of his progenitors. Before his time, every Head of the House had done something for it; even the most frivolous had contributed one had collected the pictures, another the statues, a third the medals, a fourth had amassed the famous Vipont library; while others had at least married heiresses, or augmented, through ducal lines, the splendour of the interminable cousinhood. The present Marquess was literally nil. The pith of the Viponts was not in him. He looked well; he dressed well: if life were only the dumb show of a tableau, he would have been a paragon of a Marquess. But he was like the watches we give to little children, with a pretty gilt dial-plate, and no works in them. He was thoroughly inert; there was no winding him up: he could not manage his property; he could not answer his letters, —very few of them could he even read through. Politics did not interest him, nor literature, nor field-sports. He shot, it is true, but mechanically; wondering, perhaps, why he did shoot. He attended races, because the House of Vipont kept a racing stud. He bet on his own horses, but if they lost showed no vexation. Admirers (no Marquess of Montfort could be wholly without them) said, "What fine temper! what good breeding! " it was nothing but constitutional apathy. No one could call him a bad man: he was not a profligate, an oppressor, a miser, a spendthrift; he would not have taken the trouble to be a bad man on any account. Those who beheld his character at a distance would have called him an exemplary man. The more conspicuous duties of his station—subscriptions, charities, the maintenance of grand establishments, the encouragement of the fine arts—were virtues admirably performed for him by others. But the phlegm or nullity of his being was not, after all, so complete as I have made it, perhaps, appear. He had one susceptibility which is more common with women than with men, —the susceptibility to pique. His *amour propre* was unforgiving: pique that, and he could do a rash thing, a foolish thing, a spiteful thing; pique that, and, prodigious! the watch went! He had a rooted pique against his marchioness. Apparently he had conceived this pique from the very first. He showed it passively by supreme neglect; he showed it actively by removing her from all the spheres of power which naturally fall to the wife when the husband shuns the details of business. Evidently he had a dread lest any one should say, "Lady Montfort influences my lord. " Accordingly, not only the management of his estates fell to Carr Vipont, but even of his gardens, his household, his domestic arrangements. It was Carr Vipont or Lady Selina who said to Lady Montfort, "Give a ball; " "You should ask so and so to dinner; " "Montfort was much hurt to see the old lawn at the Twickenham villa broken up by those new bosquets. True, it is settled on you as a jointure-house, but for that very reason Montfort is sensitive, " etc. In fact, they were virtually as separated, my lord and my lady, as if legally disunited, and as if Carr Vipont and Lady Selina were trustees or intermediaries in any polite approach to each other. But, on the other hand, it is fair to say that where Lady Montfort's sphere of action did not interfere with her husband's plans, habits, likings, dislikings, jealous apprehensions that she should be supposed to have any ascendency over what exclusively belonged to himself as *Roi faineant* of the Viponts, she was left free as air. No attempt at masculine control or conjugal advice. At her disposal was wealth without stint, every luxury the soft could desire, every gewgaw the vain could covet. Had her pin-money, which in itself was the revenue of an ordinary peeress, failed to satisfy her wants; had she grown tired of wearing the family diamonds, and coveted new gems from Golconda, —a single word to Carr Vipont or Lady Selina would have been answered by a carte blanche on the Bank of England. But Lady Montfort had the misfortune not to be extravagant in her tastes. Strange to say, in the world Lord Montfort's marriage was called a love-match; he had married a portionless girl, daughter to one of his poorest and obscurest cousins, against the uniform policy of the House of Vipont, which did all it could for poor cousins except marrying them to its chief. But Lady Montfort's conduct in these trying circumstances was admirable and rare. Few affronts can humiliate us unless we resent them — and in vain. Lady Montfort had that exquisite dignity which gives to submission the grace of cheerful acquiescence. That in the gay world flatterers should gather round a young wife so eminently beautiful, and so wholly left by her husband to her own guidance, was inevitable. But at the very first insinuated compliment or pathetic condolence, Lady Montfort, so meek in her household, was haughty enough to have daunted Lovelace. She was thus very early felt to be beyond temptation, and the boldest passed on, nor presumed to tempt. She was unpopular; called "proud and freezing; " she did not extend the influence of "The House; " she did not confirm its fashion, — fashion which necessitates social ease, and which no rank, no wealth, no virtue, can of themselves suffice to give. And this failure on her part was a great offence in the eyes of the House of Vipont. "She does absolutely nothing for us, " said Lady Selina; but Lady Selina in her heart was well pleased that to her in reality thus fell, almost without a rival, the female representation, in the great world, of the Vipont honours. Lady Selina was fashion itself.

Lady Montfort's social peculiarity was in the eagerness with which she sought the society of persons who enjoyed a reputation for superior intellect, whether statesmen, lawyers, authors, philosophers, artists. Intellectual intercourse seemed as if it was her native atmosphere, from which she was habitually banished, to which she returned with an instinctive yearning and a new zest of life; yet was she called, even here, nor seemingly without justice, capricious and unsteady in her likings. These clever personages, after a little while, all seemed to disappoint her expectations of them; she sought the acquaintance of each with cordial earnestness; slid from the acquaintance with weary languor, — never, after all, less alone than when alone.

And so wondrous lovely! Nothing so rare as beauty of the high type: genius and beauty, indeed, are both rare; genius, which is the beauty of the mind, -beauty, which is the gen ius of the body. But, of the two, beauty is the rarer. All of us can count on our fingers some forty or fifty persons of undoubted and illustrious genius, including those famous in action, letters, art. But can any of us remember to have seen more than four or five specimens of first-rate ideal beauty? Whosoever had seen Lady Montfort would have ranked her amongst such four or five in his recollection. There was in her face that lustrous dazzle to which the Latin poet, perhaps, refers when he speaks of the —

> "Nitor
> Splendentis Pario marmore purius . . .
> Et voltus, niminm lubricus adspici,"

and which an English poet, with the less sensuous but more spiritual imagination of northern genius, has described in lines that an English reader may be pleased to see rescued from oblivion, —

> "Her face was like the milky way i' the sky,
> A meeting of gentle lights without a name."
> (Suckling)

The eyes so purely bright, the exquisite harmony of colouring between the dark (not too dark) hair and the ivory of the skin; such sweet radiance in the lip when it broke into a smile. And it was said that in her maiden day, before Caroline Lyndsay became Marchioness of Montfort, that smile was the most joyous thing imaginable. Absurd now; you would not think it, but that stately lady had been a wild, fanciful girl, with the merriest laugh and the quickest tear, filling the air round her with April sunshine. Certainly, no beings ever yet lived the life Nature intended them to live, nor had fair play for heart and mind, who contrived, by hook or by crook, to marry the wrong person!

CHAPTER VIII.

The interior of the great house. —The British Constitution at home in a family party.

Great was the family gathering that Christmas-tide at Montfort Court. Thither flocked the cousins of the House in all degrees and of various ranks. From dukes, who had nothing left to wish for that kings and cousinhoods can give, to briefless barristers and aspiring cornets, of equally good blood with the dukes, —the superb family united its motley scions. Such reunions were frequent: they belonged to the hereditary policy of the House of Vipont. On this occasion the muster of the clan was more significant than usual; there was a "CRISES" in the constitutional history of the British empire. A new Government had been suddenly formed within the last six weeks, which certainly portended some direful blow on our ancient institutions; for the House of Vipont had not been consulted in its arrangements, and was wholly unrepresented in the Ministry, even by a lordship of the Treasury. Carr Vipont had therefore summoned the patriotic and resentful kindred.

It is an hour or so after the conclusion of dinner. The gentlemen have joined the ladies in the state suite, a suite which the last Marquess had rearranged and redecorated in his old age, during the long illness that finally conducted him to his ancestors. During his earlier years that princely Marquess had deserted Montfort Court for a seat nearer to London, and therefore much more easily filled with that brilliant society of which he had been long the ornament and centre, —railways not then existing for the annihilation of time and space, and a journey to a northern county four days with posthorses making the invitations even of a Marquess of Montfort unalluring to languid beauties and gouty ministers. But nearing the end of his worldly career, this long neglect of the dwelling identified with his hereditary titles smote the conscience of the illustrious sinner. And other occupations beginning to pall, his lordship, accompanied and cheered by a chaplain, who had a fine taste in the decorative arts, came resolutely to Montfort Court; and there, surrounded with architects and gilders and upholsterers, redeemed his errors; and, soothed by the reflection of the palace provided for his successor, added to his vaults—a coffin.

The suite expands before the eye. You are in the grand drawing-room, copied from that of Versailles. That is the picture, full length, of the late Marquess in his robes; its pendant is the late Marchioness, his wife. That table of malachite is a present from the Russian Emperor Alexander; that vase of Sevres which rests on it was made for Marie Antoinette, —see her portrait enamelled in its centre. Through the open door at the far end your eye loses itself in a vista of other pompous chambers, —the music-room, the statue hall, the orangery; other rooms there are appertaining to the suite, a ballroom fit for Babylon, a library that might have adorned Alexandria, —but they are not lighted, nor required, on this occasion; it is strictly a family party, sixty guests and no more.

In the drawing-room three whist-tables carry off the more elderly and grave. The piano, in the music-room, attracts a younger group. Lady Selina Vipont's eldest daughter, Honoria, a young lady not yet brought out, but about to be brought out the next season, is threading a wonderfully intricate German piece,

"Link'd sweetness, long drawn out, "

with variations. Her science is consummate. No pains have been spared on her education; elaborately accomplished, she is formed to be the sympathizing spouse of a wealthy statesman. Lady Montfort is seated by an elderly duchess, who is good-natured and a great talker; near her are seated two middle-aged gentlemen, who had been conversing with her till the duchess, having cut in, turned dialogue into monologue.

The elder of these two gentlemen is Mr. Carr Vipont, bald, with clipped parliamentary whiskers; values himself on a likeness to Canning, but with a portlier presence; looks a large-acred man. Carr Vipont has about L40,000 a year; has often refused office for himself, while taking care that other Viponts should have it; is a great authority in committee business and the rules of the House of Commons; speaks very seldom, and at no great length, never arguing, merely stating his opinion, carries great weight with him, and as he votes vote fifteen other members of the House of Vipont, besides admiring satellites. He can therefore turn divisions, and has decided the fate of cabinets. A pleasant man, a little consequential, but the reverse of haughty, —unctuously overbearing. The other gentleman, to whom he is listening, is our old acquaintance Colonel Alban Vipont Morley, Darrell's friend, George's uncle, —a man of importance, not inferior, indeed, to that of his kinsman Carr; an authority in clubrooms, an oracle in drawing-rooms, a first-rate man of the beau monde. Alban Morley, a younger brother, had entered the Guards young; retired young also from the Guards with the rank of Colonel, and on receipt of a legacy from an old aunt, which, with the interest derived from the sum at which he sold his commission, allowed him a clear income of L1,000 a year. This modest income sufficed for all his wants, fine gentleman though he was. He had refused to go into Parliament, —refused a high place in a public department. Single himself, he showed his respect for wedlock by the interest he took in the marriages of other people; just as Earl Warwick, too wise to set up for a king, gratified his passion for royalty by becoming the king-maker. The Colonel was exceedingly accomplished, a very fair scholar, knew most modern languages. In painting an amateur, in music a connoisseur; witty at times, and with wit of a high quality, but thrifty in the expenditure of it; too wise to be known as a wit. Manly too, a daring rider, who had won many a fox's brush; a famous deer-stalker, and one of the few English gentlemen who still keep up the noble art of fencing, —twice a week to be seen, foil in hand, against all comers in Angelo's rooms. Thin, well-shaped, —not handsome, my dear young lady, far from it, but with an air so thoroughbred that, had you seen him in the day when the opera-house had a crushroom and a fops' alley, —seen him in either of those resorts, surrounded by elaborate dandies and showy beauty-men, dandies and beauty-men would have seemed to you secondrate and vulgar; and the eye, fascinated by that quiet form, — plain in manner, plain in dress, plain in feature, —you would have said, "How very distinguished it is to be so plain! " Knowing the great world from the core to the cuticle, and on that knowledge basing authority and position, Colonel Morley was not calculating, not cunning, not suspicious, —his sagacity the more quick because its movements were straightforward; intimate with the greatest, but sought, not seeking; not a flatterer nor a parasite, but when his advice was asked (even if advice necessitated reproof) giving it with military candour: in fine, a man of such social reputation as rendered him an ornament and prop to the House of Vipont; and with unsuspected depths of intelligence and feeling, which lay in the lower strata of his knowledge of this world to witness of some other one, and justified Darrell in commending a boy like Lionel Haughton to the Colonel's friendly care and admonitory counsels. The Colonel, like other men, had his weakness, if weakness it can be called: he believed that the House of Vipont was not merely the Corinthian capital, but the embattled keep—not merely the *dulce decus*, but the *praesidium columenque rerum*—of the British monarchy. He did not boast of his connection with the House; he did not provoke your spleen by enlarging on its manifold virtues; he would often have his harmless jest against its members, or even against its pretensions: but such seeming evidences of forbearance or candour were cunning devices to mitigate envy. His devotion to the House was not obtrusive: it was profound. He loved the House of Vipont for the sake of England: he loved England for the sake of the House of Vipont. Had it been possible, by some tremendous reversal of the ordinary laws of nature, to dissociate the cause of England from the cause of the House of Vipont, the Colonel would have said, "Save at least the Ark of the Constitution! and rally round the old House! "

The Colonel had none of Guy Darrell's infirmity of family pride; he cared not a rush for mere pedigrees, —much too liberal and enlightened for such obsolete prejudices. No! He knew the world too well not to be quite aware that old family and long pedigrees are of no use to a man if he has not some money or some merit. But it was of use to a man to be a cousin of the House of Vipont, though without any money, without any merit at all. It was of use to be part and parcel of a British institution; it was of use to have a legitimate indefeasible right to share in the administration and patronage of an empire, on which (to use a novel illustration) "the sun never sets. " You might want nothing for yourself; the Colonel and the Marquess equally wanted nothing for themselves but man is not to be a selfish egotist! Man has cousins: his cousins may want something. Demosthenes denounces, in words that inflame every manly breast, the ancient Greek who does not love his POLIS or State, even though he take nothing from it but barren honour, and contribute towards it—a great many disagreeable taxes. As the POLIS to the Greek, was the House of Vipont to Alban Vipont Morley. It was the most beautiful, touching affection imaginable! Whenever the House was in difficulties, whenever it was threatened by a CRISIS, the Colonel was by its side, sparing no pains, neglecting no means, to get the Ark of the Constitution back into smooth water. That duty done, he retired again into private life, and scorned all other reward than the still whisper of applauding conscience.

"Yes, " said Alban Morley, whose voice, though low and subdued in tone, was extremely distinct, with a perfect enunciation. "Yes, it is quite true, my nephew has taken orders, —his defect in speech, if not quite removed, has ceased to be any obstacle, even to eloquence; an occasional stammer may be effective, —it increases interest, and when the right word comes, there is the charm of surprise in it. I do not doubt that George will be a very distinguished clergyman. "

MR. CARR VIPONT. —"We want one; the House wants a very distinguished clergyman: we have none at this moment, —not a bishop, not even a dean! all mere parish parsons, and among them not one we could push. Very odd, with more than forty livings too. But the Viponts seldom take to the Church kindly: George must be pushed. The more I think of it, the more we want a bishop: a bishop would be useful in the present CRISIS. " (Looking round the rooms proudly, and softening his voice), "A numerous gathering, Morley! This demonstration will strike terror in Downing Street, eh! The old House stands firm, —never was a family so united: all here, I think, —that is, all worth naming, —all, except Sir James, whom Montfort chooses to dislike, and George—and George comes to-morrow. "

COLONEL MORLEY. —"You forget the most eminent of all our connections, —the one who could indeed strike terror into Downing Street, were his voice to be heard again! "

CARR VIPONT. —"Whom do you mean? Ah, I know! Guy Darrell. His wife was a Vipont; and he is not here. But he has long since ceased to communicate with any of us; the only connection that ever fell away from the House of Vipont, especially in a CRISIS like the present. Singular man! For all the use he is to us, he might as well be dead! But he has a fine fortune: what will he do with it? "

THE DUCHESS. —"My dear Lady Montfort, you have hurt yourself with that paper cutter. "

LADY MONTFORT. —"NO, indeed. Hush! we are disturbing Mr. Carr Vipont! "

The Duchess, in awe of Carr Vipont, sinks her voice, and gabbles on, whisperously.

CARR VIPONT (resuming the subject). —"A very fine fortune: what will he do with it? "

COLONEL MORLEY. —"I don't know; but I had a letter from him some months ago. "

CARR VIPONT. —"You had, and never told me! "

COLONEL MORLEY. —"Of no importance to you, my dear Carr. His letter merely introduced to me a charming young fellow, —a kinsman of his own (no Vipont), —Lionel Haughton, son of poor Charlie Haughton, whom you may remember. "

CARR VIPONT. —"Yes, a handsome scamp; went to the dogs. So Darrell takes up Charlie's son: what! as his heir? "

COLONEL MORLEY. —"In his letter to me he anticipated that question in the negative. "

CARR VIPONT. —"Has Darrell any nearer kinsman? "

COLONEL MORLEY. —"Not that I know of. "

CARR VIPONT. —"Perhaps he will select one of his wife's family for his heir, —a Vipont; I should not wonder. "

COLONEL MORLEY (dryly). —"I should. But why may not Darrell marry again? I always thought he would; I think so still. "

CARR VIPONT (glancing towards his own daughter Honoria). — "Well, a wife well chosen might restore him to society, and to us. Pity, indeed, that so great an intellect should be suspended, —a voice so eloquent hushed. You are right; in this CRISIS, Guy Darrell once more in the House of Commons, we should have all we require, —an orator, a debater! Very odd, but at this moment we have no speakers, —WE the Viponts! "

COLONEL MORLEY. —"Yourself! "

CARR VIPONT. —"You are too kind. I can speak on occasions; but regularly, no. Too much drudgery; not young enough to take to it now. So you think Darrell will marry again? A remarkably fine-looking fellow when I last saw him: not old yet; I dare say well preserved. I wish I had thought of asking him here—Montfort! " (Lord Montfort, with one or two male friends, was passing by towards a billiard-room, opening through a side-door from the regular suite) "Montfort! only think, we forgot to invite Guy Darrell. Is it too late before our party breaks up? "

LORD MONTFORT (sullenly). —"I don't choose Guy Darrell to be invited to my house. "

Carr Vipont was literally stunned by a reply so contumacious. Lord Montfort demur at what Carr Vipont suggested? He could not believe his senses.

"Not choose, my dear Montfort! you are joking. A monstrous clever fellow, Guy Darrell, and at this CRISIS—"

"I hate clever fellows; no such bores! " said Lord Montfort, breaking from the caressing clasp of Carr Vipont, and stalking away.

"Spare your regrets, my dear Carr, " said Colonel Morley. "Darrell is not in England: I rather believe he is in Verona. " Therewith the Colonel sauntered towards the group gathered round the piano. A little time afterwards Lady Montfort escaped from the Duchess, and, mingling courteously with her livelier guests, found herself close to Colonel Morley. "Will you give me my revenge at chess? " she asked, with her rare smile. The Colonel was charmed. As they sat down and ranged their men, Lady Montfort remarked carelessly,

"I overheard you say you had lately received a letter from Mr. Darrell. Does he write as if well, —cheerful? You remember that I was much with his daughter, much in his house, when I was a child. He was ever most kind to me. " Lady Montfort's voice here faltered.

"He writes with no reference to himself, his health, or his spirits. But his young kinsman described him to me as in good health, — wonderfully young-looking for his years. But cheerful, —no! Darrell and I entered the world together; we were friends as much as a man so busy and so eminent as he could be friends with a man like myself, indolent by habit and obscure out of Mayfair. I know his nature; we both know something of his family sorrows. He cannot be happy! Impossible! —alone, childless, secluded. Poor Darrell, abroad now; in Verona, too! —the dullest place! in mourning still for Romeo and Juliet! 'T is your turn to move. In his letter Darrell talked of going on to Greece, Asia, penetrating into the depths of Africa, —the wildest schemes! Dear County Guy, as we called him at Eton! what a career his might have been! Don't let us talk of him, it makes me mournful. Like Goethe, I avoid painful subjects upon principle. "

LADY MONTFORT. —"No; we will not talk of him. No; I take the Queen's pawn. No, we will not talk of him! no! " The game proceeded; the Colonel was within three moves of checkmating his adversary. Forgetting the resolution come to, he said, as she paused, and seemed despondently meditating a hopeless defence,

"Pray, my fair cousin, what makes Montfort dislike my old friend Darrell? "

"Dislike! Does he! I don't know. Vanquished again, Colonel Morley! " She rose; and as he restored the chessmen to their box, she leaned thoughtfully over the table.

"This young kinsman, will he not be a comfort to Mr. Darrell? "

"He would be a comfort and a pride to a father; but to Darrell, so distant a kinsman, —comfort! —why and how? Darrell will provide for him, that is all. A very gentlemanlike young man; gone to Paris by my advice; wants polish and knowledge of life. When he comes back he must enter society: I have put his name up at White's; may I introduce him to you? "

Lady Montfort hesitated, and, after a pause, said, almost rudely, "No. "

She left the Colonel, slightly shrugging his shoulders, and passed into the billiard-room with a quick step. Some ladies were already there looking at the players. Lord Montfort was chalking his cue. Lady Montfort walked straight up to him: her colour was heightened; her lip was quivering; she placed her hand on his shoulder with a wife-like boldness. It seemed as if she had come there to seek him from an impulse of affection. She asked with a hurried fluttering kindness of voice, if he had been successful, and called him by his Christian name. Lord Montfort's countenance, before merely apathetic, now assumed an expression of extreme distaste. "Come to teach me to make a cannon, I suppose! " he said mutteringly, and turning from her, contemplated the balls and missed the cannon.

"Rather in my way, Lady Montfort, " said he then, and, retiring to a corner, said no more.

Lady Montfort's countenance became still more flushed. She lingered a moment, returned to the drawing-room, and for the rest of the evening was unusually animated, gracious, fascinating. As she retired with her lady guests for the night she looked round, saw Colonel Morley, and held out her hand to him.

"Your nephew comes here to-morrow, " said she, "my old play-fellow; impossible quite to forget old friends; good night. "

CHAPTER IX.

"Les extremes se touchent. "

The next day the gentlemen were dispersed out of doors, a large shooting party. Those who did not shoot, walked forth to inspect the racing stud or the model farm. The ladies had taken their walk; some were in their own rooms, some in the reception-rooms, at work, or reading, or listening to the piano, —Honoria Carr Vipont again performing. Lady Montfort was absent; Lady Selina kindly supplied the hostess's place. Lady Selina was embroidering, with great skill and taste, a pair of slippers for her eldest boy, who was just entered at Oxford, having left Eton with a reputation of being the neatest dresser, and not the worst cricketer, of that renowned educational institute. It is a mistake to suppose that fine ladies are not sometimes very fond mothers and affectionate wives. Lady Selina, beyond her family circle, was trivial, unsympathizing, cold-hearted, supercilious by temperament, never kind but through policy, artificial as clock work. But in her own home, to her husband, her children, Lady Selina was a very good sort of woman, —devotedly attached to Carr Vipont, exaggerating his talents, thinking him the first man in England, careful of his honour, zealous for his interest, soothing in his cares, tender in his ailments; to her girls prudent and watchful, to her boys indulgent and caressing; minutely attentive to the education of the first, according to her high-bred ideas of education, —and they really were "superior" girls, with much instruction and well-balanced minds, —less authoritative with the last, because boys being not under her immediate control, her sense of responsibility allowed her to display more fondness and less dignity in her intercourse with them than with young ladies who must learn from her example, as well as her precepts, the patrician decorum which becomes the smooth result of impulse restrained and emotion checked: boys might make a noise in the world, girls should make none. Lady Selina, then, was working the slippers for her absent son, her heart being full of him at that moment. She was describing his character and expatiating on his promise to two or three attentive listeners, all interested, as being themselves of the Vipont blood, in the probable destiny of the heir to the Carr Viponts.

"In short, " said Lady Selina, winding up, "as soon as Reginald is of age we shall get him into Parliament. Carr has always lamented that he himself was not broken into office early; Reginald must be.

Nothing so requisite for public men as early training; makes them practical, and not too sensitive to what those horrid newspaper men say. That was Pitt's great advantage. Reginald has ambition; he should have occupation to keep him out of mischief. It is an anxious thing for a mother, when a son is good-looking: such danger of his being spoiled by the women. Yes, my dear, it is a small foot, very small, —his father's foot. "

"If Lord Montfort should have no family, " said a somewhat distant and subaltern Vipont, whisperingly and hesitating, "does not the title—"

"No, my dear, " interrupted Lady Selina; "no, the title does not come to us. It is a melancholy thought, but the marquisate, in that case, is extinct. No other heir-male from Gilbert, the first marquess. Carr says there is even likely to be some dispute about the earldom. The Barony, of course, is safe; goes with the Irish estates, and most of the English; and goes (don't you know?) to Sir James Vipont, the last person who ought to have it; the quietest, stupidest creature; not brought up to the sort of thing, —a mere gentleman-farmer on a small estate in Devonshire. "

"He is not here? "

"No. Lord Montfort does not like him. Very natural. Nobody likes his heir, if not his own child; and some people don't even like their own eldest sons! Shocking; but so it is. Montfort is the kindest, most tractable being that ever was, except where he takes a dislike. He dislikes two or three people very much. "

"True; how he did dislike poor Mrs. Lyndsay! " said one of the listeners, smiling.

"Mrs. Lyndsay, yes, —dear Lady Montfort's mother. I can't say I pitied her, though I was sorry for Lady Montfort. How Mrs. Lyndsay ever took in Montfort for Caroline I can't conceive! How she had the face to think of it! He, a mere youth at the time! Kept secret from all his family, even from his grandmother, —the darkest transaction. I don't wonder that he never forgave it. "

FIRST LISTENER. —"Caroline has beauty enough to—"

LADY SELINA (interrupting). —"Beauty, of course: no one can deny that. But not at all suited to such a position, not brought up to the sort of thing. Poor Montfort! he should have married a different kind of woman altogether, —a woman like his grandmother, the last Lady Montfort. Caroline does nothing for the House, —nothing; has not even a child, —most unfortunate affair. "

SECOND LISTENER. —"Mrs. Lyndsay was very poor, was not she? Caroline, I suppose, had no opportunity of forming those tastes and habits which are necessary for—for—"

LADY SELINA (helping the listener). —"For such a position and such a fortune. You are quite right, my dear. People brought up in one way cannot accommodate themselves to another; and it is odd, but I have observed that people brought up poor can accommodate themselves less to being very rich than people brought up rich can accommodate themselves to being very poor. As Carr says, in his pointed way, 'It is easier to stoop than to climb. ' Yes; Mrs. Lyndsay was, you know, a daughter of Seymour Vipont, who was for so many years in the Administration, with a fair income from his salary, and nothing out of it. She married one of the Scotch Lyndsays, — good family, of course, with a very moderate property. She was left a widow young, with an only child, Caroline. Came to town with a small jointure. The late Lady Montfort was very kind to her. So were we all; took her up; pretty woman; pretty manners; worldly, —oh, very! I don't like worldly people. Well, but all of a sudden a dreadful thing happened. The heir-at-law disputed the jointure, denied that Lyndsay had any right to make settlements on the Scotch property; very complicated business. But, luckily for her, Vipont Crooke's daughter, her cousin and intimate friend, had married Darrell, the famous Darrell, who was then at the bar. It is very useful to have cousins married to clever people. He was interested in her case, took it up. I believe it did not come on in the courts in which Darrell practised. But he arranged all the evidence, inspected the briefs, spent a great deal of his own money in getting up the case; and in fact he gained her cause, though he could not be her counsel. People did say that she was so grateful that after his wife's death she had set her heart on becoming Mrs. Darrell the second. But Darrell was then quite wrapped up in politics, —the last man to fall in love, and only looked bored when women fell in love with him, which a good many did. Grand-looking creature, my dear, and quite the rage for a year or two. However, Mrs. Lyndsay all of a sudden went off to Paris, and there Montfort saw Caroline, and was caught. Mrs. Lyndsay, no doubt, calculated on living with her daughter, having the run of Montfort House in town and Montfort Court in the country. But Montfort is deeper than people think for. No, he never forgave her. She was never asked here; took it to heart, went to Rome, and died. "

At this moment the door opened, and George Morley, now the Rev. George Morley, entered, just arrived to join his cousins.

Some knew him, some did not. Lady Selina, who made it a point to know all the cousins, rose graciously, put aside the slippers, and gave him two fingers. She was astonished to find him not nearly so shy as he used to be: wonderfully improved; at his ease, cheerful, animated. The man now was in his right place, and following hope on the bent of inclination. Few men are shy when in their right places. He asked after Lady Montfort. She was in her own small sitting-room, writing letters, —letters that Carr Vipont had entreated her to write, —correspondence useful to the House of Vipont. Before long, however, a servant entered, to say that Lady Montfort would be very happy to see Mr. Morley. George followed the servant into that unpretending sitting-room, with its simple chintzes and quiet bookshelves, —room that would not have been too fine for a cottage.

CHAPTER X.

In every life, go it fast, go it slow, there are critical pausing- places. When the journey is renewed the face of the country is changed.

How well she suited that simple room; herself so simply dressed, her marvellous beauty so exquisitely subdued! She looked at home there, as if all of home that the house could give were there collected.

She had finished and sealed the momentous letters, and had come, with a sense of relief, from the table at the farther end of the room, on which those letters, ceremonious and conventional, had been written, —come to the window, which, though mid-winter, was open, and the redbreast, with whom she had made friends, hopped boldly almost within reach, looking at her with bright eyes and head curiously aslant. By the window a single chair, and a small reading-desk, with the book lying open. The short day was not far from its close, but there was ample light still in the skies, and a serene if chilly stillness in the air without.

Though expecting the relation she had just summoned to her presence, I fear she had half forgotten him. She was standing by the window deep in revery as he entered, so deep that she started when his voice struck her ear and he stood before her. She recovered herself quickly, however, and said with even more than her ordinary kindliness of tone and manner towards the scholar, "I am so glad to see and congratulate you. "

"And I so glad to receive your congratulations, " answered the scholar in smooth, slow voice, without a stutter.

"But, George, how is this? " asked Lady Montfort. "Bring that chair, sit down here, and tell me all about it. You wrote me word you were cured, —at least sufficiently to re move your noble scruples. You did not say how. Your uncle tells me, by patient will and resolute practice. "

"Under good guidance. But I am going to confide to you a secret, if you will promise to keep it. "

"Oh, you may trust me: I have no female friends. "

The clergyman smiled, and spoke at once of the lessons he had received from the basketmaker.

"I have his permission, " he said in conclusion, "to confide the service he rendered me, the intimacy that has sprung up between us, but to you alone, —not a word to your guests. When you have once seen him, you will understand why an eccentric man, who has known better days, would shrink from the impertinent curiosity of idle customers. Contented with his humble livelihood, he asks but liberty and repose. "

"That I already comprehend, " said Lady Montfort, half sighing, half smiling. "But my curiosity shall not molest him, and when I visit the village, I will pass by his cottage. "

"Nay, my dear Lady Montfort, that would be to refuse the favour I am about to ask, which is that you would come with me to that very cottage. It would so please him. "

"Please him! why? "

"Because this poor man has a young female grandchild, and he is so anxious that you should see and be kind to her, and because, too, he seems most anxious to remain in his present residence. The cottage, of course, belongs to Lord Montfort, and is let to him by the bailiff, and if you deign to feel interest in him, his tenure is safe. "

Lady Montfort looked down, and coloured. She thought, perhaps, how false a security her protection, and how slight an influence her interest would be; but she did not say so. George went on; and so eloquently, and so touchingly did he describe both grandsire and grandchild, so skilfully did he intimate the mystery which hung over them, that Lady Montfort became much moved by his narrative; and willingly promised to accompany him across the park to the basketmaker's cottage the first opportunity. But when one has sixty guests in one's house, one has to wait for an opportunity to escape from them unremarked. And the opportunity, in fact, did not come for many days; not till the party broke up, save one or two dowager she-cousins who "gave no trouble, " and one or two bachelor he-cousins whom my lord retained to consummate the slaughter of pheasants, and play at billiards in the dreary intervals between sunset and dinner, dinner and bedtime.

411

Then one cheerful frosty noon George Morley and his fair cousin walked boldly *en evidence*, before the prying ghostly windows, across the broad gravel walks; gained the secluded shrubbery, the solitary deeps of park-land; skirted the wide sheet of water, and, passing through a private wicket in the paling, suddenly came upon the patch of osier-ground and humble garden, which were backed by the basketmaker's cottage.

As they entered those lowly precincts a child's laugh was borne to their ears, —a child's silvery, musical, mirthful laugh; it was long since the great lady had heard a laugh like that, —a happy child's natural laugh. She paused and listened with a strange pleasure. "Yes, " whispered George Morley, "stop—and hush! there they are. "

Waife was seated on the stump of a tree, materials for his handicraft lying beside neglected. Sophy was standing before him, —he raising his finger as if in reproof, and striving hard to frown. As the intruders listened, they overheard that he was striving to teach her the rudiments of French dialogue, and she was laughing merrily at her own blunders, and at the solemn affectation of the shocked schoolmaster. Lady Montfort noted with no unnatural surprise the purity of idiom and of accent with which this singular basketmaker was unconsciously displaying his perfect knowledge of a language which the best-educated English gentleman of that generation, nay, even of this, rarely speaks with accuracy and elegance. But her attention was diverted immediately from the teacher to the face of the sweet pupil. Women have a quick appreciation of beauty in their own sex; and women who are themselves beautiful, not the least. Irresistibly Lady Montfort felt attracted towards that innocent countenance so lively in its mirth, and yet so softly gay. Sir Isaac, who had hitherto lain *perdu*, watching the movements of a thrush amidst a holly-bush, now started up with a bark. Waife rose; Sophy turned half in flight. The visitors approached.

Here slowly, lingeringly, let fall the curtain. In the frank license of narrative, years will have rolled away ere the curtain rise again. Events that may influence a life often date from moments the most serene, from things that appear as trivial and unnoticeable as the great lady's visit to the basketmaker's cottage. Which of those lives will that visit influence hereafter, —the woman's, the child's, the vagrant's? Whose? Probably little that passes now would aid conjecture, or be a visible link in the chain of destiny. A few desultory questions; a few guarded answers; a look or so, a musical syllable or two, exchanged between the lady and the child; a basket bought, or a promise to call again. Nothing worth the telling. Be it then untold. View only the scene itself as the curtain drops reluctantly. The rustic cottage, its garden-door open, and open its old-fashioned lattice casements. You can see how neat and cleanly, how eloquent of healthful poverty, how remote from squalid penury, the whitewashed walls, the homely furniture within. Creepers lately trained around the doorway; Christmas holly, with berries red against the window-panes; the bee-hive yonder; a starling, too, outside the threshold, in its wicker cage; in the background (all the rest of the neighbouring hamlet out of sight), the church spire tapering away into the clear blue wintry sky. All has an air of repose, of safety. Close beside you is the Presence of HOME; that ineffable, sheltering, loving Presence, which amidst solitude murmurs "not solitary, " —a Presence unvouchsafed to the great lady in the palace she has left. And the lady herself? She is resting on the rude gnarled root-stump from which the vagrant had risen; she has drawn Sophy towards her; she has taken the child's hand; she is speaking now, now listening; and on her face kindness looks like happiness. Perhaps she is happy that moment. And Waife? he is turning aside his weatherbeaten mobile countenance with his hand anxiously trembling upon the young scholar's arm. The scholar whispers, "Are you satisfied with me? " and Waife answers in a voice as low but more broken, "God reward you! Oh, joy! if my pretty one has found at last a woman friend! " Poor vagabond, he has now a calm asylum, a fixed humble livelihood; more than that, he has just achieved an object fondly cherished. His past life, —alas! what has he done with it? His actual life, broken fragment though it be, is at rest now. But still the everlasting question, —mocking terrible question, with its phrasing of farce and its enigmas of tragical sense, —"WHAT WILL HE DO WITH IT? " Do with what? The all that remains to him, the all he holds! the all which man himself, betwixt Free-will and Pre-decree, is permitted to do. Ask not the vagrant alone: ask each of the four there assembled on that flying bridge called the Moment. Time before thee, —what wilt thou do with it? Ask thyself! ask the wisest! Out of effort to answer that question, what dream-schools have risen, never wholly to perish, — the science of seers on the Chaldee's Pur-Tor, or in the rock-caves of Delphi, gasped after and grasped at by horn-handed mechanics to-day in their lanes and alleys. To the heart of the populace sink down the blurred relics of what once was the law of the secretest sages, hieroglyphical tatters which the credulous vulgar attempt to interpret. "WHAT WILL HE DO WITH IT? " Ask Merle and his

Crystal! But the curtain descends! Yet a moment, there they are, — age and childhood, —poverty, wealth, station, vagabondage; the preacher's sacred learning and august ambition; fancies of dawning reason; hopes of intellect matured; memories of existence wrecked; household sorrows; untold regrets; elegy and epic in low, close, human sighs, to which Poetry never yet gave voice: all for the moment personified there before you, —a glimpse for the guess, no more. Lower and lower falls the curtain! All is blank!

BOOK VI.

CHAPTER I.

Etchings of Hyde Park in the month of June, which, if this history escapes those villains the trunk-makers, may be of inezstimable value to unborn antiquarians. —Characters, long absent, reappear and give some account of themselves.

Five years have passed away since this history opened. It is the month of June once more, —June, which clothes our London in all its glory, fills its languid ballrooms with living flowers, and its stony causeways with human butterflies. It is about the hour of six P. M. The lounge in Hyde Park is crowded; along the road that skirts the Serpentine crawl the carriages one after the other; congregate by the rails the lazy lookers-on, —lazy in attitude, but with active eyes, and tongues sharpened on the whetstone of scandal, —the Scaligers of club windows airing their vocabulary in the Park. Slowly saunter on foot idlers of all degrees in the hierarchy of London idlesse: dandies of established-fame; youthful tyros in their first season. Yonder in the Ride, forms less inanimate seem condemned to active exercise; young ladies doing penance in a canter; old beaux at hard labour in a trot. Sometimes, by a more thoughtful brow, a still brisker pace, you recognize a busy member of the Imperial Parliament, who, advised by physicians to be as much on horseback as possible, snatches an hour or so in the interval between the close of his Committee and the interest of the Debate, and shirks the opening speech of a well-known bore. Among such truant lawgivers (grief it is to say it) may be seen that once model member, Sir Gregory Stollhead. Grim dyspepsia seizing on him at last, "relaxation from his duties" becomes the adequate punishment for all his sins. Solitary he rides, and communing with himself, yawns at every second. Upon chairs beneficently located under the trees towards the north side of the walk are interspersed small knots and coteries in repose. There you might see the Ladies Prymme, still the Ladies Prymme, —Janet and Wilhelmina; Janet has grown fat, Wilhelmina thin. But thin or fat, they are no less Prymmes. They do not lack male attendants; they are girls of high fashion, with whom young men think it a distinction to be seen talking; of high principle, too, and high pretensions (unhappily for themselves, they are co-heiresses), by whom young men under the rank of earls need not fear to be artfully entrapped into "honourable intentions. " They coquet majestically, but they never flirt; they exact devotion, but they do not ask in each victim a sacrifice on the horns of the altar; they will never give their hands where they do not give their hearts; and being ever afraid that they are courted for their money, they will never give their hearts save to wooers who have much more money than themselves. Many young men stop to do passing homage to the Ladies Prymme: some linger to converse; safe young men, — they are all younger sons. Farther on, Lady Frost and Mr. Crampe, the wit, sit amicably side by side, pecking at each other with sarcastic beaks; occasionally desisting, in order to fasten nip and claw upon that common enemy, the passing friend! The Slowes, a numerous family, but taciturn, sit by themselves; bowed to much, accosted rarely.

Note that man of good presence, somewhere about thirty, or a year or two more, who, recognized by most of the loungers, seems not at home in the lounge. He has passed by the various coteries just described, made his obeisance to the Ladies Prymme, received an icy epigram from Lady Frost, and a laconic sneer from Mr. Crampe, and exchanged silent bows with seven silent Slowes. He has wandered on, looking high in the air, but still looking for some one not in the air, and evidently disappointed in his search, comes to a full stop at length, takes off his hat, wipes his brow, utters a petulant "Prr—r—pshaw! " and seeing, a little in the background, the chairless shade of a thin, emaciated, dusty tree, thither he retires, and seats himself with as little care whether there to seat himself be the right thing in the right place, as if in the honeysuckle arbour of a village inn. "It serves me right, " said he to himself: "a precocious villain bursts in upon me, breaks my day, makes an appointment to meet me here, in these very walks, ten minutes before six; decoys me with the promise of a dinner at Putney, —room looking on the river and fried flounders. I have the credulity to yield: I derange my habits; I leave my cool studio; I put off my easy blouse; I imprison my freeborn throat in a cravat invented by the Thugs; the dog-days are at hand, and I walk rashly over scorching pavements in a black frock-coat and a brimless hat; I annihilate 3s. 6d. in a pair of kid gloves; I arrive at this haunt of spleen; I run the gauntlet of Frosts, Slowes, and Prymmes: and my traitor fails me! Half-past six, —not a sign of him! and the dinner at Putney, —fried flounders? Dreams! Patience, five minutes more; if then he comes not, breach for life between him and me! Ah, voila! there he comes, the laggard! But how those fine folks are catching at him! Has he asked them also to dinner at Putney, and do they care for fried flounders? "

The soliloquist's eye is on a young man, much younger than himself, who is threading the motley crowd with a light quick step, but is compelled to stop at each moment to interchange a word of welcome, a shake of the hand. Evidently he has already a large acquaintance; evidently he is popular, on good terms with the world and himself. What free grace in his bearing! what gay good-humour in his smile! Powers above! Lady Wilhelmina surely blushes as she returns his bow. He has passed Lady Frost unblighted; the Slowes evince emotion, at least the female Slowes, as he shoots by them with that sliding bow. He looks from side to side, with the rapid glance of an eye in which light seems all dance and sparkle: he sees the soliloquist under the meagre tree; the pace quickens, the lips part half laughing.

"Don't scold, Vance. I am late, I know; but I did not make allowance for interceptions. "

"Body o' me, interceptions! For an absentee just arrived in London, you seem to have no lack of friends. "

"Friends made in Paris and found again here at every corner, like pleasant surprises, —but no friend so welcome and dear as Frank Vance. "

"Sensible of the honour, O Lionello the Magnificent. Verily you are *bon prince!* The Houses of Valois and of Medici were always kind to artists. But whither would you lead me? Back into that treadmill? Thank you, humbly; no. "

"A crowd in fine clothes is of all mobs the dullest. I can look undismayed on the many-headed monster, wild and rampant; but when the many-headed monster buys its hats in Bond Street, and has an eyeglass at each of its inquisitive eyes, I confess I take fright. Besides, it is near seven o'clock; Putney not visible, and the flounders not fried! "

"My cab is waiting yonder; we must walk to it: we can keep on the turf, and avoid the throng. But tell me honestly, Vance, do you really dislike to mix in crowds; you, with your fame, dislike the eyes that turn back to look again, and the lips that respectfully murmur, 'Vance the Painter'? Ah, I always said you would be a great painter, —and in five short years you have soared high. "

"Pooh! " answered Vance, indifferently. "Nothing is pure and unadulterated in London use; not cream, nor cayenne pepper; least of all Fame, —mixed up with the most deleterious ingredients. Fame! did you read the 'Times' critique on my pictures in the present Exhibition? Fame indeed Change the subject. Nothing so good as flounders. Ho! is that your cab? Superb! Car fit for the 'Grecian youth of talents rare, ' in Mr. Enfield's 'Speaker; ' horse that seems conjured out of the Elgin Marbles. Is he quiet? "

"Not very; but trust to my driving. You may well admire the horse, —present from Darrell, chosen by Colonel Morley. " When the young men had settled themselves into the vehicle, Lionel dismissed his groom, and, touching his horse, the animal trotted out briskly.

"Frank, " said Lionel, shaking his dark curls with a petulant gravity, "your cynical definitions are unworthy that masculine beard. You despise fame! what sheer affectation!

"'Pulverem Olympicum
Collegisse juvat; metaque fervidis
Evitata rotis— —-'"

"Take care, " cried Vance; "we shall be over. " For Lionel, growing excited, teased the horse with his whip; and the horse bolting, took the cab within an inch of a water-cart.

"Fame, fame! " cried Lionel, unheeding the interruption. "What would I not give to have and to hold it for an hour? " "Hold an eel, less slippery; a scorpion, less stinging! But—" added Vance, observing his companion's heightened colour—"but, " he added seriously, and with an honest compunction, "I forgot, you are a soldier, you follow the career of arms! Never heed what is said on the subject by a querulous painter! The desire of fame may be folly in civilians: in soldiers it is wisdom. Twin-born with the martial sense of honour, it cheers the march; it warms the bivouac; it gives music to the whir of the bullet, the roar of the ball; it plants hope in the thick of peril; knits rivals with the bond of brothers; comforts the survivor when the brother falls; takes from war its grim aspect of carnage; and from homicide itself extracts lessons that strengthen the safeguards to humanity, and perpetuate life to nations. Right: pant for fame; you are a soldier! "

This was one of those bursts of high sentiment from Vance, which, as they were very rare with him, had the dramatic effect of surprise. Lionel listened to him with a thrilling delight. He could not answer: he was too moved. The artist resumed, as the cabriolet now cleared the Park, and rolled safely and rapidly along the road. "I suppose, during the five years you have spent abroad completing your general education, you have made little study, or none, of what specially appertains to the profession you have so recently chosen. "

"You are mistaken there, my dear Vance. If a man's heart be set on a thing, he is always studying it. The books I loved best, and most pondered over, were such as, if they did not administer lessons, suggested hints that might turn to lessons hereafter. In social intercourse, I never was so pleased as when I could fasten myself to some practical veteran, —question and cross-examine him. One picks up more ideas in conversation than from books; at least I do. Besides, my idea of a soldier who is to succeed some day is not that of a mere mechanician-at-arms. See how accomplished most great captains have been. What observers of mankind! what diplomatists! what reasoners! what men of action, because men to whom reflection had been habitual before they acted! How many stores of idea must have gone to the judgment which hazards the sortie or decides on the retreat! "

"Gently, gently! " cried Vance. "We shall be into that omnibus! Give me the whip, —do; there, a little more to the left, —so. Yes; I am glad to see such enthusiasm in your profession: 't is half the battle. Hazlitt said a capital thing, 'The 'prentice who does not consider the Lord Mayor in his gilt coach the greatest man in the world will live to be hanged! '"

"Pish! " said Lionel, catching at the whip.

VANCE (holding it back). —"No. I apologize. I retract the Lord Mayor: comparisons are odious. I agree with you, nothing like leather. I mean nothing like a really great soldier, —Hannibal, and so forth. Cherish that conviction, my friend: meanwhile, respect human life; there is another omnibus! "

The danger past, the artist thought it prudent to divert the conversation into some channel less exciting.

"Mr. Darrell, of course, consents to your choice of a profession? "

"Consents! approves, encourages. Wrote me such a beautiful letter! what a comprehensive intelligence that man has! "

"Necessarily; since he agrees with you. Where is he now? "

"I have no notion: it is some months since I heard from him. He was then at Malta, on his return from Asia Minor. "

"So! you have never seen him since he bade you farewell at his old Manor-house? "

"Never. He has not, I believe, been in England. "

"Nor in Paris, where you seem to have chiefly resided. "

"Nor in Paris. Ah, Vance, could I but be of some comfort to him. Now that I am older, I think I understand in him much that perplexed me as a boy when we parted. Darrell is one of those men who require a home. Between the great world and solitude, he needs the intermediate filling-up which the life domestic alone supplies: a wife to realize the sweet word helpmate; children, with whose future he could knit his own toils and his ancestral remembrances. That intermediate space annihilated, the great world and the solitude are left, each frowning on the other. "

"My dear Lionel, you must have lived with very clever people: you are talking far above your years. "

"Am I? True; I have lived, if not with very clever people, with people far above my years. That is a secret I learned from Colonel Morley, to whom I must present you, —the subtlest intellect under the quietest manner. Once he said to me, 'Would you throughout life be up to the height of your century, —always in the prime of man's reason, without crudeness and without decline, —live habitually while young with persons older, and when old with persons younger, than yourself. '"

"Shrewdly said indeed. I felicitate you on the evident result of the maxim. And so Darrell has no home, —no wife and no children? "

"He has long been a widower; he lost his only son in boyhood, and his daughter—did you never hear? "

"No, what? "

"Married so ill—a runaway match—and died many years since, without issue. "

"Poor man! It was these afflictions, then, that soured his life, and made him the hermit or the wanderer? "

"There, " said Lionel, "I am puzzled; for I find that, even after his son's death and his daughter's unhappy marriage and estrangement from him, he was still in Parliament and in full activity of career. But certainly he did not long keep it up. It might have been an effort to which, strong as he is, he felt himself unequal; or, might he have known some fresh disappointment, some new sorrow, which the world never guesses? What I have said as to his family afflictions the world knows. But I think he will marry again. That idea seemed strong in his own mind when we parted; he brought it out bluntly, roughly. Colonel Morley is convinced that he will marry, if but for the sake of an heir. "

VANCE. —"And if so, my poor Lionel, you are ousted of—"

LIONEL (quickly interrupting). —"Hush! Do not say, my dear Vance, do not you say—you! —one of those low, mean things which, if said to me even by men for whom I have no esteem, make my ears tingle and my cheek blush. When I think of what Darrell has already done for me, —me who have no claim on him, —it seems to me as if I must hate the man who insinuates, 'Fear lest your benefactor find a smile at his own hearth, a child of his own blood; for you may be richer at his death in proportion as his life is desolate. '"

VANCE. —"You are a fine young fellow, and I beg your pardon. Take care of that milestone: thank you. But I suspect that at least two-thirds of those friendly hands that detained you on the way to me were stretched out less to Lionel Haughton, a subaltern in the Guards, than to Mr. Darrell's heir presumptive. "

LIONEL. —"That thought sometimes galls me, but it does me good; for it goads on my desire to make myself some one whom the most worldly would not disdain to know for his own sake. Oh for active service! Oh for a sharp campaign! Oh for fair trial how far a man in earnest can grapple Fortune to his breast with his own strong hands! You have done so, Vance; you had but your genius and your painter's brush. I have no genius; but I have a resolve, and resolve is perhaps as sure of its ends as genius. Genius and Resolve have three grand elements in common, —Patience, Hope, and Concentration. "

Vance, more and more surprised, looked hard at Lionel without speaking. Five years of that critical age, from seventeen to twenty-two, spent in the great capital of Europe; kept from its more dangerous vices partly by a proud sense of personal dignity, partly by a temperament which, regarding love as an ideal for all tender and sublime emotion, recoiled from low profligacy as being to love what the Yahoo of the mocking satirist was to man; absorbed much by the brooding ambition that takes youth out of the frivolous present into the serious future, and seeking companionship, not with contemporary idlers, but with the highest and maturest intellects that the free commonwealth of good society brought within his reach: five years so spent had developed a boy, nursing noble dreams, into a man fit for noble action, —retaining freshest youth in its enthusiasm, its elevation of sentiment, its daring, its energy, and divine credulity in its own unexhausted resources; but borrowing from maturity compactness and solidity of idea, —the link between speculation and practice, the power to impress on others a sense of the superiority which has been self-elaborated by unconscious culture.

"So! " said Vance, after a prolonged pause, "I don't know whether I have resolve or genius; but certainly if I have made my way to some small reputation, patience, hope, and concentration of purpose must have the credit of it; and prudence, too, which you have forgotten to name, and certainly don't evince as a charioteer. I hope, my dear fellow, you are not extravagant? No doubt, eh? —why do you laugh?"

"The question is so like you, Frank, —thrifty as ever. "

"Do you think I could have painted with a calm mind if I knew that at my door there was a dun whom I could not pay? Art needs serenity; and if an artist begin his career with as few shirts to his back as I had, he must place economy amongst the rules of perspective. "

Lionel laughed again, and made some comments on economy which were certainly, if smart, rather flippant, and tended not only to lower the favourable estimate of his intellectual improvement which Vance had just formed, but seriously disquieted the kindly artist. Vance knew the world, —knew the peculiar temptations to which a young man in Lionel's position would be exposed, —knew that contempt for economy belongs to that school of Peripatetics which reserves its last lessons for finished disciples in the sacred walks of the Queen's Bench.

However, that was no auspicious moment for didactic warnings.

"Here we are! " cried Lionel, —"Putney Bridge. "

They reached the little inn by the river-side, and while dinner was getting ready they hired a boat. Vance took the oars.

VANCE. —"Not so pretty here as by those green quiet banks along which we glided, at moonlight, five years ago. "

LIONEL. —"Ah, no! And that innocent, charming child, whose portrait you took, —you have never heard of her since? "

VANCE. —"Never! How should I? Have you? "

LIONEL. —"Only what Darrell repeated to me. His lawyer had ascertained that she and her grandfather had gone to America. Darrell gently implied that, from what he learned of them, they scarcely merited the interest I felt in their fate. But we were not deceived, were we, Vance? "

VANCE—"No; the little girl—what was her name? Sukey? Sally? Sophy, true—Sophy had something about her extremely prepossessing, besides her pretty face; and, in spite of that horrid cotton print, I shall never forget it. "

LIONEL—"Her face! Nor I. I see it still before me! "

VANCE—"Her cotton print! I see it still before me! But I must not be ungrateful. Would you believe it, —that little portrait, which cost me three pounds, has made, I don't say my fortune, but my fashion? "

LIONEL—"How! You had the heart to sell it? "

VANCE. —"No; I kept it as a study for young female heads—'with variations, ' as they say in music. It was by my female heads that I became the fashion; every order I have contains the condition, 'But be sure, one of your sweet female heads, Mr. Vance. ' My female heads are as necessary to my canvas as a white horse to Wouvermans'. Well, that child, who cost me three pounds, is the original of them all. Commencing as a Titania, she has been in turns a 'Psyche, ' a 'Beatrice-Cenci, ' a 'Minna, ' 'A Portrait of a Nobleman's Daughter, ' 'Burns's Mary in Heaven, ' 'The Young Gleaner, ' and 'Sabrina Fair, ' in Milton's 'Comus. ' I have led that child through all history, sacred and profane. I have painted her in all costumes (her own cotton print excepted). My female heads are my glory; even the 'Times' critic allows that! 'Mr. Vance, there, is inimitable! a type of childlike grace peculiarly his own, ' etc. I'll lend you the article. "

LIONEL. —"And shall we never again see the original darling Sophy? You will laugh, Vance, but I have been heartproof against all young ladies. If ever I marry, my wife must have Sophy's eyes! In America! "

VANCE. —"Let us hope by this time happily married to a Yankee! Yankees marry girls in their teens, and don't ask for dowries. Married to a Yankee! not a doubt of it! a Yankee who thaws, whittles, and keeps a 'store'! "

LIONEL. —"Monster! Hold your tongue. *A propos* of marriage, why are you still single? "

VANCE. —"Because I have no wish to be doubled up! Moreover, man is like a napkin, the more neatly the housewife doubles him, the more carefully she lays him on the shelf. Neither can a man once doubled know how often he may be doubled. Not only his wife folds him in two, but every child quarters him into a new double, till what was a wide and handsome substance, large enough for anything in reason, dwindles into a pitiful square that will not cover one platter, —all puckers and creases, smaller and smaller with every double, with every double a new crease. Then, my friend, comes the washing-bill! and, besides all the hurts one receives in the mangle, consider the hourly wear and tear of the linen-press! In short, Shakspeare vindicates the single life, and depicts the double in the famous line, which is no doubt intended to be allegorical of marriage,

"'Double, double, toil and trouble. '

Besides, no single man can be fairly called poor. What double man can with certainty be called rich? A single man can lodge in a garret, and dine on a herring: nobody knows; nobody cares. Let him marry, and he invites the world to witness where he lodges, and how he dines. The first necessary a wife demands is the most ruinous, the most indefinite superfluity; it is Gentility according to what her neighbours call genteel. Gentility commences with the honeymoon; it is its shadow, and lengthens as the moon declines. When the honey is all gone, your bride says, 'We can have our tea without sugar when quite alone, love; but, in case Gentility drop in, here's a bill for silver sugar-tongs! ' That's why I'm single. "

"Economy again, Vance. "

"Prudence, —dignity, " answered Vance, seriously; and sinking into a revery that seemed gloomy, he shot back to shore.

CHAPTER II.

Mr. Vance explains how he came to grind colours and save half-pence. — A sudden announcement.

The meal was over; the table had been spread by a window that looked upon the river. The moon was up: the young men asked for no other lights; conversation between them—often shifting, often pausing—had gradually become grave, as it usually does with two companions in youth; while yet long vistas in the Future stretch before them deep in shadow, and they fall into confiding talk on what they wish, —what they fear; making visionary maps in that limitless Obscure.

"There is so much power in faith, " said Lionel, "even when faith is applied but to things human and earthly, that let a man be but firmly persuaded that he is born to do, some day, what at the moment seems impossible, and it is fifty to one but what he does it before he dies. Surely, when you were a child at school, you felt convinced that there was something in your fate distinct from that of the other boys, whom the master might call quite as clever, —felt that faith in yourself which made you sure that you would be one day what you are. "

"Well, I suppose so; but vague aspirations and self-conceits must be bound together by some practical necessity—perhaps a very homely and a very vulgar one—or they scatter and evaporate. One would think that rich people in high life ought to do more than poor folks in humble life. More pains are taken with their education; they have more leisure for following the bent of their genius: yet it is the poor folks, often half self-educated, and with pinched bellies, that do three-fourths of the world's grand labour. Poverty is the keenest stimulant; and poverty made me say, not 'I will do, ' but 'I must. '"

"You knew real poverty in childhood, Frank? "

"Real poverty, covered over with sham affluence. My father was Genteel Poverty, and my mother was Poor Gentility. The sham affluence went when my father died. The real poverty then came out in all its ugliness. I was taken from a genteel school, at which, long afterwards, I genteelly paid the bills; and I had to support my mother somehow or other, —somehow or other I succeeded. Alas, I fear not genteelly! But before I lost her, which I did in a few years, she had some comforts which were not appearances; and she kindly allowed, dear soul, that gentility and shams do not go well together. Oh, beware of debt, Lionello mio; and never call that economy meanness which is but the safeguard from mean degradation. "

"I understand you at last, Vance; shake hands: I know why you are saving. "

"Habit now, " answered Vance, repressing praise of himself, as usual. "But I remember so well when twopence was a sum to be respected that to this day I would rather put it by than spend it. All our ideas—like orange-plants—spread out in proportion to the size of the box which imprisons the roots. Then I had a sister. " Vance paused a moment, as if in pain, but went on with seeming carelessness, leaning over the window-sill, and turning his face from his friend. "I had a sister older than myself, handsome, gentle. "

"I was so proud of her! Foolish girl! my love was not enough for her. Foolish girl! she could not wait to see what I might live to do for her. She married—oh! so genteelly! —a young man, very well born, who had wooed her before my father died. He had the villany to remain constant when she had not a farthing, and he was dependent on distant relations, and his own domains in Parnassus. The wretch was a poet! So they married. They spent their honeymoon genteelly, I dare say. His relations cut him. Parnassus paid no rents. He went abroad. Such heart-rending letters from her. They were destitute. How I worked! how I raged! But how could I maintain her and her husband too, mere child that I was? No matter. They are dead now, both; all dead for whose sake I first ground colours and saved halfpence. And Frank Vance is a stingy, selfish bachelor. Never revive this dull subject again, or I shall borrow a crown from you and cut you dead. Waiter, ho! —the bill. I'll just go round to the stables, and see the horse put to. "

As the friends re-entered London, Vance said, "Set me down anywhere in Piccadilly; I will walk home. You, I suppose, of course, are staying with your mother in Gloucester Place? "

"No, " said Lionel, rather embarrassed; "Colonel Morley, who acts for me as if he were my guardian, took a lodging for me in Chesterfield Street, Mayfair. My hours, I fear, would ill suit my dear mother. Only in town two days; and, thanks to Morley, my table is already covered with invitations. "

"Yet you gave me one day, generous friend! "

"You the second day, my mother the first. But there are three balls before me to-night. Come home with me, and smoke your cigar while I dress. "

"No; but I will at least light my cigar in your hall, prodigal! "

Lionel now stopped at his lodging. The groom, who served him also as valet, was in waiting at the door. "A note for you, sir, from Colonel Morley, —just come. " Lionel hastily opened it, and read,

MY DEAR HAUGHTON, —Mr. Darrell has suddenly arrived in London. Keep yourself free all to-morrow, when, no doubt, he will see you. I am hurrying off to him.

Yours in haste, A. V. M.

CHAPTER III.

Once more Guy Darrell.

Guy Darrell was alone: a lofty room in a large house on the first floor, —his own house in Carlton Gardens, which he had occupied during his brief and brilliant parliamentary career; since then, left contemptuously to the care of a house agent, to be let by year or by season, it had known various tenants of an opulence and station suitable to its space and site. Dinners and concerts, routs and balls, had assembled the friends and jaded the spirits of many a gracious host and smiling hostess. The tenure of one of these temporary occupants had recently expired; and, ere the agent had found another, the long absent owner dropped down into its silenced halls as from the clouds, without other establishment than his old servant Mills and the woman in charge of the house. There, as in a caravansery, the traveller took his rest, stately and desolate. Nothing so comfortless as one of those large London houses all to one's self. In long rows against the walls stood the empty fauteuils. Spectral from the gilded ceiling hung lightless chandeliers. —The furniture, pompous, but worn by use and faded by time, seemed mementos of departed revels. When you return to your house in the country—no matter how long the absence, no matter how decayed by neglect the friendly chambers may be, if it has only been deserted in the meanwhile (not let to new races, who, by their own shifting dynasties, have supplanted the rightful lord, and half-effaced his memorials)—the walls may still greet you forgivingly, the character of Home be still there. You take up again the thread of associations which had, been suspended, not snapped. But it is otherwise with a house in cities, especially in our fast-living London, where few houses descend from father to son, —where the title-deeds are rarely more than those of a purchased lease for a term of years, after which your property quits you. A house in London, which your father never entered, in which no elbow-chair, no old-fashioned work-table, recall to you the kind smile of a mother; a house that you have left as you leave an inn, let to people whose names you scarce know, with as little respect for your family records as you have for theirs, —when you return after a long interval of years to a house like that, you stand, as stood Darrell, a forlorn stranger under your own roof-tree. What cared he for those who had last gathered round those hearths with their chill steely grates, whose forms had reclined on those formal couches, whose feet had worn away the gloss from those costly carpets? Histories in the lives of many might be recorded within those walls. "Lovers there had breathed their first vows; bridal feasts had been held; babes had crowed in the arms of proud young mothers; politicians there had been raised into ministers; ministers there had fallen back into independent members; " through those doors corpses had been borne forth to relentless vaults. For these races and their records what cared the owner? Their writing was not on the walls. Sponged out, as from a slate, their reckonings with Time; leaving dim, here and there, some chance scratch of his own, blurred and bygone. Leaning against the mantelpiece, Darrell gazed round the room with a vague wistful look, as if seeking to conjure up associations that might link the present hour to that past life which had slipped away elsewhere; and his profile, reflected on the mirror behind, pale and mournful, seemed like that ghost of himself which his memory silently evoked.

The man is but little altered externally since we saw him last, however inly changed since he last stood on those unwelcoming floors; the form still retained the same vigour and symmetry, —the same unspeakable dignity of mien and bearing; the same thoughtful bend of the proud neck, —so distinct, in its elastic rebound, from the stoop of debility or age, thick as ever the rich mass of dark-brown hair, though, when in the impatience of some painful thought his hand swept the loose curls from his forehead, the silver threads might now be seen shooting here and there, —vanishing almost as soon as seen. No, whatever the baptismal register may say to the contrary, that man is not old, —not even elderly; in the deep of that clear gray eye light may be calm, but in calm it is vivid; not a ray, sent from brain or from heart, is yet flickering down. On the whole, however, there is less composure than of old in his mien and bearing; less of that resignation which seemed to say, "I have done with the substances of life. " Still there was gloom, but it was more broken and restless. Evidently that human breast was again admitting, or forcing itself to court, human hopes, human objects. Returning to the substances of life, their movement was seen in the shadows which, when they wrap us round at remoter distance, seem to lose their trouble as they gain their width. He broke from his musing attitude with an abrupt angry movement, as if shaking off thoughts which displeased him, and gathering his arms tightly to his breast, in a gesture peculiar to himself, walked to and fro the room, murmuring inaudibly. The door opened; he turned quickly, and with an evident sense of relief, for his face brightened. "Alban, my dear Alban! "

"Darrell! old friend! old school-friend! dear, dear Guy Darrell! " The two Englishmen stood, hands tightly clasped in each other, in true English greeting, their eyes moistening with remembrances that carried them back to boyhood.

Alban was the first to recover self-possession; and, when the friends had seated themselves, he surveyed Darrell's countenance deliberately, and said, "So little change! —wonderful! What is your secret? "

"Suspense from life, —hibernating. But you beat me; you have been spending life, yet seem as rich in it as when we parted. "

"No; I begin to decry the present and laud the past; to read with glasses, to decide from prejudice, to recoil from change, to find sense in twaddle, to know the value of health from the fear to lose it; to feel an interest in rheumatism, an awe of bronchitis; to tell anecdotes, and to wear flannel. To you in strict confidence I disclose the truth: I am no longer twenty-five. You laugh; this is civilized talk: does it not refresh you after the gibberish you must have chattered in Asia Minor? "

Darrell might have answered in the affirmative with truth. What man, after long years of solitude, is not refreshed by talk, however trivial, that recalls to him the gay time of the world he remembered in his young day, —and recalls it to him on the lips of a friend in youth! But Darrell said nothing; only he settled himself in his chair with a more cheerful ease, and inclined his relaxing brows with a nod of encouragement or assent.

Colonel Morley continued. "But when did you arrive? whence? How long do you stay here? What are your plans? "

DARRELL. —"Caesar could not be more laconic. When arrived? this evening. Whence? Ouzelford. How long do I stay? uncertain. What are my plans? let us discuss them. "

COLONEL MORLEY. —"With all my heart. You have plans, then? —a good sign. Animals in hibernation form none. "

DARRELL (putting aside the lights on the table, so as to leave, his face in shade, and looking towards the floor as he speaks). —"For the last five years I have struggled hard to renew interest in mankind, reconnect myself with common life and its healthful objects. Between Fawley and London I desired to form a magnetic medium. I took rather a vast one, —nearly all the rest of the known world. I have visited both Americas, either end. All Asia have I ransacked, and pierced as far into Africa as traveller ever went in search of Timbuctoo. But I have sojourned also, at long intervals, at least they seemed long to me, —in the gay capitals of Europe (Paris excepted); mixed, too, with the gayest; hired palaces, filled them with guests; feasted and heard music. 'Guy Darrell, ' said I, 'shake off the rust of years: thou hadst no youth while young, —be young now. A holiday may restore thee to wholesome work, as a holiday restores the wearied school-boy. '"

COLONEL MORLEY. —"I comprehend; the experiment succeeded?"

DARRELL. —"I don't know: not yet; but it may. I am here, and I intend to stay. I would not go to a hotel for a single day, lest my resolution should fail me. I have thrown myself into this castle of care without even a garrison. I hope to hold it. Help me to man it. In a word, and without metaphor, I am here with the design of re-entering London life. "

COLONEL MORLEY. —"I am so glad. Hearty congratulations! How rejoiced all the Viponts will be! Another 'CRISIS' is at hand. You have seen the newspapers regularly, of course: the state of the country interests you. You say that you come from Ouzelford, the town you once represented. I guess you will re-enter Parliament; you have but to say the word. "

DARRELL. —"Parliament! No. I received, while abroad, so earnest a request from my old constituents to lay the foundation-stone of a new Town-Hall, in which they are much interested; and my obligations to them have been so great that I could not refuse. I wrote to fix the day as soon as I had resolved to return to England, making a condition that I should be spared the infliction of a public dinner, and landed just in time to keep my appointment; reached Ouzelford early this morning, went through the ceremony, made a short speech, came on at once to London, not venturing to diverge to Fawley (which is not very far from Ouzelford), lest, once there again, I should not have strength to leave it; and here I am. " Darrell paused, then repeated, in brisk emphatic tone, "Parliament? No. Labour? No. Fellow-man, I am about to confess to you: I would snatch back some days of youth, —a wintry likeness of youth, better than none. Old friend, let us amuse ourselves! When I was working hard, hard, hard! it was you who would say: 'Come forth, be amused, '—you! happy butterfly that you were! Now, I say to you, 'Show me this flaunting town that you know so well; initiate me into the joys of polite pleasures, social commune,

"'Dulce mihi furere est amico. "

You have amusements, —let me share them. '"

"Faith, " quoth the Colonel, crossing his legs, "you come late in the day! Amusements cease to amuse at last. I have tried all, and begin to be tired. I have had my holiday, exhausted its sports; and you, coming from books and desk fresh into the playground, say, 'Football and leapfrog. ' Alas! my poor friend, why did not you come sooner? "

DARRELL. —"One word, one question. You have made EASE a philosophy and a system; no man ever did so with more felicitous grace: nor, in following pleasure, have you parted company with conscience and shame. A fine gentleman ever, in honour as in elegance. Well, are you satisfied with your choice of life? Are you happy? "

"Happy! who is? Satisfied, perhaps. "

"Is there any one you envy, —whose choice, other than your own, you would prefer? "

"Certainly. "

"Who? "

"You. "

"I! " said Darrell, opening his eyes with unaffected amaze. "I! envy me! prefer my choice! "

COLONEL MORLEY (peevishly). —"Without doubt. You have had gratified ambition, a great career. Envy you! who would not? Your own objects in life fulfilled: you coveted distinction, —you won it; fortune, —your wealth is immense; the restoration of your name and lineage from obscurity and humiliation, —are not name and lineage again written in the *Libro d'oro*? What king would not hail you as his counsellor? What senate not open its ranks to admit you as a chief? What house, though the haughtiest in the land, would not accept your alliance? And withal, you stand before me stalwart and unbowed, young blood still in your veins. Ungrateful man, who would not change lots with Guy Darrell? Fame, fortune, health, and, not to flatter you, a form and presence that would be remarked, though you stood in that black frock by the side of a monarch in his coronation robes. "

DARRELL. —"You have turned my question against myself with a kindliness of intention that makes me forgive your belief in my vanity. Pass on, —or rather pass back; you say you have tried all in life that distracts or sweetens. Not so, lone bachelor; you have not tried wedlock. Has not that been your mistake? "

COLONEL MORLEY. —"Answer for yourself. You have tried it. " The words were scarce out of his mouth ere he repented the retort; for Darrell started as if stung to the quick; and his brow, before serene, his lip, before playful, grew, the one darkly troubled, the other tightly compressed. "Pardon me, " faltered out the friend.

DARRELL. —"Oh, yes! I brought it on myself. What stuff we have been talking! Tell me the news, not political, any other. But first, your report of young Haughton. Cordial thanks for all your kindness to him. You write me word that he is much improved, —most likeable; you add, that at Paris he became the rage, that in London you are sure he will be extremely popular. Be it so, if for his own sake. Are you quite sure that it is not for the expectations which I come here to disperse? "

COLONEL MORLEY. —"Much for himself, I am certain; a little, perhaps, because—whatever he thinks, and I say to the contrary—people seeing no other heir to your property—"

"I understand, " interrupted Darrell, quickly. "But he does not nurse those expectations? he will not be disappointed? "

COLONEL MORLEY. —"Verily I believe that, apart from his love for you and a delicacy of sentiment that would recoil from planting hopes of wealth in the graves of benefactors, Lionel Haughton would prefer carving his own fortunes to all the ingots hewed out of California by another's hand and bequeathed by another's will. "

DARRELL. —"I am heartily glad to hear and to trust you. "

COLONEL MORLEY. —"I gather from what you say that you are here with the intention to—to—"

"Marry again, " said Darrell, firmly. "Right. I am. "

"I always felt sure you would marry again. Is the lady here too? "

"What lady? "

"The lady you have chosen. "

"Tush! I have chosen none. I come here to choose; and in this I ask advice from your experience. I would marry again! I! at my age! Ridiculous! But so it is. You know all the mothers and marriageable daughters that London—*arida nutrix*—rears for nuptial altars: where, amongst them, shall I, Guy Darrell, the man whom you think so enviable, find the safe helpmate, whose love he may reward with munificent jointure, to whose child he may bequeath the name that has now no successor, and the wealth he has no heart to spend? "

Colonel Morley—who, as we know, is by habit a matchmaker, and likes the vocation—assumes a placid but cogitative mien, rubs his brow gently, and says in his softest, best-bred accents, "You would not marry a mere girl? some one of suitable age. I know several most superior young women on the other side of thirty, Wilhelmina Prymme, for instance, or Janet—"

DARRELL. —"Old maids. No! decidedly no! "

COLONEL MORLEY (suspiciously). —"But you would not risk the peace of your old age with a girl of eighteen, or else I do know a very accomplished, well-brought-up girl; just eighteen, who—"

DARRELL. —"Re-enter life by the side of Eighteen! am I a madman?"

COLONEL MORLEY. —"Neither old maids nor young maids; the choice becomes narrowed. You would prefer a widow. Ha! I have thought of one; a prize, indeed, could you but win her, the widow of—"

DARRELL. —"Ephesus! —Bah! suggest no widow to me. A widow, with her affections buried in the grave! "

MORLEY. —"Not necessarily. And in this case—"

DARRELL (interrupting, and with warmth). —"In every case I tell you: no widow shall doff her weeds for me. Did she love the first man? Fickle is the woman who can love twice. Did she not love him? Why did she marry him? Perhaps she sold herself to a rent-roll? Shall she sell herself again to me for a jointure? Heaven forbid! Talk not of widows. No dainty so flavourless as a heart warmed up again."

COLONEL MORLEY. —"Neither maids, be they old or young, nor widows. Possibly you want an angel. London is not the place for angels. "

DARRELL. —"I grant that the choice seems involved in perplexity. How can it be otherwise if one's self is perplexed? And yet, Alban, I am serious; and I do not presume to be so exacting as my words have implied. I ask not fortune, nor rank beyond gentle blood, nor youth nor beauty nor accomplishments nor fashion, but I do ask one thing, and one thing only. "

COLONEL MORLEY. —"What is that? you have left nothing worth the having to ask for. "

DARRELL. —"Nothing! I have left all! I ask some one whom I can love; love better than all the world, —not the *mariage de convenance*, not the *mariage de raison*, but the *mariage d'amour*. All other marriage, with vows of love so solemn, with intimacy of commune so close, — all other marriage, in my eyes, is an acted falsehood, a varnished sin. Ah, if I had thought so always! But away regret and repentance! The future alone is now before me! Alban Morley! I would sign away all I have in the world (save the old house at Fawley), ay, and after signing, cut off to boot this right hand, could I but once fall in love; love, and be loved again, as any two of Heaven's simplest human creatures may love each other while life is fresh! Strange! strange! look out into the world; mark the man of our years who shall be most courted, most adulated, or admired. Give him all the attributes of power, wealth, royalty, genius, fame. See all the younger generation bow before him with hope or awe: his word can make their fortune; at his smile a reputation dawns. Well; now let that man say to the young, 'Room amongst yourselves: all that wins me this homage I would lay at the feet of Beauty. I enter the lists of love, ' and straightway his power vanishes, the poorest booby of twenty-four can jostle him aside; before, the object of reverence, he is now the butt of ridicule. The instant he asks right to win the heart of a woman, a boy whom in all else he could rule as a lackey cries, 'Off, Graybeard, that realm at least is mine! '"

COLONEL MORLEY. —"This were but eloquent extravagance, even if your beard were gray. Men older than you, and with half your pretensions, even of outward form, have carried away hearts from boys like Adonis. Only choose well: that's the difficulty; if it was not difficult, who would be a bachelor? "

DARRELL. —"Guide my choice. Pilot me to the haven. "

COLONEL MORLEY. —"Accepted! But you must remount a suitable establishment; reopen your way to the great world, and penetrate those sacred recesses where awaiting spinsters weave the fatal web. Leave all to me. Let Mills (I see you have him still) call on me to-morrow about your menage. You will give dinners, of course?"

DARRELL. —"Oh, of course; must I dine at them myself? "

Morley laughed softly, and took up his hat.

"So soon! " cried Darrell. "If I fatigue you already, what chance shall I have with new friends? "

"So soon! it is past eleven. And it is you who must be fatigued. "

"No such good luck; were I fatigued, I might hope to sleep. I will walk back with you. Leave me not alone in this room, —alone in the jaws of a fish; swallowed up by a creature whose blood is cold. "

"You have something still to say to me, " said Alban, when they were in the open air: "I detect it in your manner; what is it? "

"I know not. But you have told me no news; these streets are grown strange to me. Who live now in yonder houses? once the dwellers were my friends. "

"In that house, —oh, new people! I forget their names, —but rich; in a year or two, with luck, they may be exclusives, and forget my name. In the other house, Carr Vipont still. "

"Vipont; those dear Viponts! what of them all? Crawl they, sting they, bask they in the sun, or are they in anxious process of a change of skin? "

"Hush! my dear friend: no satire on your own connections; nothing so injudicious. I am a Vipont, too, and all for the family maxim, 'Vipont with Vipont, and come what may! '"

"I stand rebuked. But I am no Vipont. I married, it is true, into their house, and they married, ages ago, into mine; but no drop in the blood of time-servers flows through the veins of the last childless Darrell. Pardon. I allow the merit of the Vipont race; no family more excites my respectful interest. What of their births, deaths, and marriages? "

COLONEL MORLEY. —"As to the births, Carr has just welcomed the birth of a grandson; the first-born of his eldest son (who married last year a daughter of the Duke of Halifax), —a promising young man, a Lord in the Admiralty. Carr has a second son in the Hussars; has just purchased his step: the other boys are still at school. He has three daughters too, fine girls, admirably brought up; indeed, now I think of it, the eldest, Honoria, might suit you, highly accomplished; well read; interests herself in politics; a great admirer of intellect; of a very serious turn of mind too. "

DARRELL. —"A female politician with a serious turn of mind, —a farthing rushlight in a London fog! Hasten on to subjects less gloomy. Whose funeral achievement is that yonder? "

COLONEL MORLEY. —"The late Lord Niton's, father to Lady Montfort. "

DARRELL. —"Lady Montfort! Her father was a Lyndsay, and died before the Flood. A deluge, at least, has gone over me and my world since I looked on the face of his widow. "

COLONEL MORLEY. —"I speak of the present Lord Montfort's wife, —the Earl's. You of the poor Marquess's, the last Marquess; the marquisate is extinct. Surely, whatever your wanderings, you must have heard of the death of the last Marquess of Montfort? "

"Yes, I heard of that, " answered Darrell, in a somewhat husky and muttered voice. "So he is dead, the young man! What killed him? "

COLONEL MORLEY. —"A violent attack of croup, —quite sudden. He was staying at Carr's at the time. I suspect that Carr made him talk! a thing he was not accustomed to do. Deranged his system altogether. But don't let us revive painful subjects. "

DARRELL. —"Was she with him at the time? "

COLONEL MORLEY. —"Lady Montfort? No; they were very seldom together. "

DARRELL. —"She is not married again yet? "

COLONEL MORLEY. —"No, but still young and so beautiful she will have many offers. I know those who are waiting to propose. Montfort has been only dead eighteen months; died just before young Carr's marriage. His widow lives, in complete seclusion, at her jointure-house near Twickenham. She has only seen even me once since her loss. "

DARRELL. —"When was that? "

MORLEY. —"About six or seven months ago; she asked after you with much interest. "

DARRELL. —"After me! "

COLONEL MORLEY. —"To be sure. Don't I remember how constantly she and her mother were at your house? Is it strange that she should ask after you? You ought to know her better, —the most affectionate, grateful character. "

DARRELL. —"I dare say. But at the time you refer to, I was too occupied to acquire much accurate knowledge of a young lady's character. I should have known her mother's character better, yet I mistook even that. "

COLONEL MORLEY. —"Mrs. Lyndsay's character you might well mistake, —charming but artificial: Lady Montfort is natural. Indeed, if you had not that illiberal prejudice against widows, she was the very person I was about to suggest to you. "

DARRELL. —"A fashionable beauty! and young enough to be my daughter. Such is human friendship! So the marquisate is extinct, and Sir James Vipont, whom I remember in the House of Commons—respectable man, great authority on cattle, timid, and always saying, 'Did you read that article in to-day's paper? '—has the estates and the earldom? "

COLONEL MORLEY. —"Yes. There was some fear of a disputed succession, but Sir James made his claim very clear. Between you and me, the change has been a serious affliction to the Viponts. The late lord was not wise, but on state occasions he looked his part, — *tres grand seigneur*, —and Carr managed the family influence with admirable tact. The present lord has the habits of a yeoman; his wife shares his tastes. He has taken the management not only of the property, but of its influence, out of Carr's hands, and will make a sad mess of it, for he is an impracticable, obsolete politician. He will never keep the family together, impossible, a sad thing. I remember how our last muster, five years ago next Christmas, struck terror into Lord's Cabinet; the mere report of it in the newspapers set all people talking and thinking. The result was that, two weeks after, proper overtures were made to Carr: he consented to assist the ministers; and the country was saved! Now, thanks to this stupid new earl, in eighteen months we have lost ground which it took at least a century and a half to gain. Our votes are divided; our influence frittered away; Montfort House is shut up; and Carr, grown quite thin, says that in the coming 'CRISIS' a Cabinet will not only be formed, but will also last—last time enough for irreparable mischief—without a single Vipont in office. "

Thus Colonel Morley continued in mournful strain, Darrell silent by his side, till the Colonel reached his own door. There, while applying his latch-key to the lock, Alban's mind returned from the perils that threatened the House of Vipont and the Star of Brunswick to the petty claims of private friendship. But even these last were now blended with those grander interests, due care for which every true patriot of the House of Vipont imbibed with his mother's milk.

"Your appearance in town, my dear Darrell, is most opportune. It will be an object with the whole family to make the most of you at this coming 'CRISIS; ' I say coming, for I believe it must come. Your name is still freshly remembered; your position greater for having been out of all the scrapes of the party the last sixteen or seventeen years: your house should be the nucleus of new combinations. Don't forget to send Mills to me; I will engage your chef and your house-steward to-morrow. I know just the men to suit you. Your intention to marry too, just at this moment, is most seasonable; it will increase the family interest. I may give out that you intend to marry? "

"Oh, certainly cry it at Charing Cross. "

"A club-room will do as well. I beg ten thousand pardons; but people will talk about money whenever they talk about marriage. I should not like to exaggerate your fortune: I know it must be very large, and all at your own disposal, eh? "

"Every shilling. "

"You must have saved a great deal since you retired into private life?"

"Take that for granted. Dick Fairthorn receives my rents, and looks to my various investments; and I accept him as an indisputable authority when I say that, what with the rental of lands I purchased in my poor boy's lifetime and the interest on my much more lucrative moneyed capital, you may safely whisper to all ladies likely to feel interest in that diffusion of knowledge, 'Thirty-five thousand a year, and an old fool. '"

"I certainly shall not say an old fool, for I am the same age as yourself; and if I had thirty-five thousand pounds a year, I would marry too. "

"You would! Old fool! " said Darrell, turning away.

CHAPTER IV.

Revealing glimpses of Guy Darrell's past in his envied prime. Dig but deep enough, and under all earth runs water, under all life runs grief.

Alone in the streets, the vivacity which had characterized Darrell's countenance as well as his words, while with his old school friend, changed as suddenly and as completely into pensive abstracted gloom as if he had been acting a part, and with the exit the acting ceased. Disinclined to return yet to the solitude of his home, he walked on at first mechanically, in the restless desire of movement, he cared not whither. But as, thus chance-led, he found himself in the centre of that long straight thoroughfare which connects what once were the separate villages of Tyburn and Holborn, something in the desultory links of revery suggested an object to his devious feet. He had but to follow that street to his right hand, to gain in a quarter of an hour a sight of the humble dwelling-house in which he had first settled down, after his early marriage, to the arid labours of the bar. He would go, now that, wealthy and renowned, he was revisiting the long-deserted focus of English energies, and contemplate the obscure abode in which his powers had been first concentrated on the pursuit of renown and wealth. Who among my readers that may have risen on the glittering steep ("Ah, who can tell how hard it is to climb! "*) has not been similarly attracted towards the roof at the craggy foot of the ascent, under which golden dreams refreshed his straining sinews?

*['Ah, who can tell how hard it is to climb The steep where Fame's proud temple shines afar? BEATTIE.]

Somewhat quickening his steps, now that a bourne was assigned to them, the man growing old in years, but, unhappily for himself, too tenacious of youth in its grand discontent and keen susceptibilities to pain, strode noiselessly on, under the gaslights, under the stars; gaslights primly marshalled at equidistance; stars that seem to the naked eye dotted over space without symmetry or method: man's order, near and finite, is so distinct; the Maker's order remote, infinite, is so beyond man's comprehension even of what is order!

Darrell paused hesitating. He had now gained a spot in which improvement had altered the landmarks. The superb broad thoroughfare continued where once it had vanished abrupt in a labyrinth of courts and alleys. But the way was not hard to find. He turned a little towards the left, recognizing, with admiring interest, in the gay, white, would-be Grecian edifice, with its French grille, bronzed, gilded, the transformed Museum, in the still libraries of which he had sometimes snatched a brief and ghostly respite from books of law. Onwards yet through lifeless Bloomsbury, not so far towards the last bounds of Atlas as the desolation of Podden Place, but the solitude deepening as he passed. There it is, a quiet street indeed! not a soul on its gloomy pavements, not even a policeman's soul. Nought stirring save a stealthy, profligate, good-for-nothing cat, flitting fine through yon area bars. Down that street had he come, I trove, with a livelier, quicker step the day when, by the strange good-luck which had uniformly attended his worldly career of honours, he had been suddenly called upon to supply the place of an absent senior, and in almost his earliest brief the Courts of Westminster had recognized a master, come, I trove, with a livelier step, knocked at that very door whereat he is halting now; entered the room where the young wife sat, and at sight of her querulous peevish face, and at sound of her unsympathizing languid voice, fled into his cupboard-like back parlour, and muttered "Courage! Courage! " to endure the home he had entered longing for a voice which should invite and respond to a cry of joy.

How closed up, dumb, and blind looked the small mean house, with its small mean door, its small mean rayless windows! Yet a FAME had been born there! Who are the residents now? Buried in slumber, have they any "golden dreams"? Works therein any struggling brain, to which the prosperous man might whisper "Courage! " or beats, there, any troubled heart to which faithful woman should murmur "Joy"? Who knows? London is a wondrous poem, but each page of it is written in a different language, —no lexicon yet composed for any.

Back through the street, under the gaslights, under the stars, went Guy Darrell, more slow and more thoughtful. Did the comparison between what he had been, what he was, the mean home just revisited, the stately home to which he would return, suggest thoughts of natural pride? It would not seem so; no pride in those close-shut lips, in that melancholy stoop.

He came into a quiet square, —still Bloomsbury, —and right before him was a large respectable mansion, almost as large as that one in courtlier quarters to which he loiteringly delayed the lone return.

There, too, had been for a time the dwelling which was called his home; there, when gold was rolling in like a tide, distinction won, position assured; there, not yet in Parliament, but foremost at the bar, —already pressed by constituencies, already wooed by ministers; there, still young—O luckiest of lawyers! —there had he moved his household gods. Fit residence for a Prince of the Gown! Is it when living there that you would envy the prosperous man? Yes, the moment his step quits that door; but envy him when he enters its threshold? —nay, envy rather that roofless Savoyard who has crept under yonder portico, asleep with his ragged arm round the cage of his stupid dormice! There, in that great barren drawing-room, sits a

"Pale and elegant Aspasia. "

Well, but the wife's face is not querulous now. Look again, — anxious, fearful, secret, sly. Oh! that fine lady, a Vipont Crooke, is not contented to be wife to the wealthy, great Mr. Darrell. What wants she? that he should be spouse to the fashionable fine Mrs. Darrell? Pride in him! not a jot of it; such pride were unchristian. Were he proud of her, as a Christian husband ought to be of so elegant a wife, would he still be in Bloomsbury? Envy him! the high gentleman, so true to his blood, all galled and blistered by the moral vulgarities of a tuft-hunting, toad-eating mimic of the Lady Selinas. Envy him! Well, why not? All women have their foibles. Wise husbands must bear and forbear. Is that all? wherefore, then, is her aspect so furtive, wherefore on his a wild, vigilant sternness? Tut, what so brings into coveted fashion a fair lady exiled to Bloomsbury as the marked adoration of a lord, not her own, who gives law to St. James's! Untempted by passion, cold as ice to affection; if thawed to the gush of a sentiment secretly preferring the husband she chose, wooed, and won to idlers less gifted even in outward attractions, — all this, yet seeking, coquetting for, the eclat of dishonour! To elope? Oh, no, too wary for that, but to be gazed at and talked of as the fair Mrs. Darrell, to whom the Lovelace of London was so fondly devoted. Walk in, haughty son of the Dare-all. Darest thou ask who has just left thy house? Darest thou ask what and whence is the note that sly hand has secreted? Darest thou? —perhaps yes: what then? canst thou lock up thy wife? canst thou poniard the Lovelace? Lock up the air! poniard all whose light word in St. James's can bring into fashion the matron of Bloomsbury! Go, lawyer, go, study briefs, and be parchment.

Agonies, agonies, shot again through Guy Darrell's breast as he looked on that large, most respectable house, and remembered his hourly campaign against disgrace! He has triumphed. Death fights for him: on the very brink of the last scandal, a cold, caught at some Vipont's ball, became fever; and so from that door the Black Horses bore away the Bloomsbury Dame, ere she was yet—the fashion! Happy in grief the widower who may, with confiding hand, ransack the lost wife's harmless desk, sure that no thought concealed from him in life will rise accusing from the treasured papers. But that pale proud mourner, hurrying the eye over sweet-scented billets; compelled, in very justice to the dead, to convince himself that the mother of his children was corrupt only at heart, —that the Black Horses had come to the door in time, —and, wretchedly consoled by that niggardly conviction, flinging into the flames the last flimsy tatters on which his honour (rock-like in his own keeping) had been fluttering to and fro in the charge of a vain treacherous fool, —envy you that mourner? No! not even in his release. Memory is not nailed down in the velvet coffin; and to great loyal natures less bitter is the memory of the lost when hallowed by tender sadness than when coupled with scorn and shame.

The wife is dead. Dead, too, long years ago, the Lothario! The world has forgotten them; they fade out of this very record when ye turn the page; no influence, no bearing have they on such future events as may mark what yet rests of life to Guy Darrell. But as he there stands and gazes into space, the two forms are before his eye as distinct as if living still. Slowly, slowly he gazes them down: the false smiles flicker away from their feeble lineaments; woe and terror on their aspects, —they sink, they shrivel, they dissolve!

CHAPTER V.

The wreck cast back from Charybdis.

Souviens-toi de to Gabrielle.

Guy Darrell turned hurriedly from the large house in the great square, and, more and more absorbed in revery, he wandered out of his direct way homeward, clear and broad though it was, and did not rouse himself till he felt, as it were, that the air had grown darker; and looking vaguely round, he saw that he had strayed into a dim maze of lanes and passages. He paused under one of the rare lamp-posts, gathering up his recollections of the London he had so long quitted, and doubtful for a moment or two which turn to take. Just then, up from an alley fronting him at right angles, came suddenly, warily, a tall, sinewy, ill-boding tatterdemalion figure, and, seeing Darrell's face under the lamp, halted abrupt at the mouth of the narrow passage from which it had emerged, —a dark form filling up the dark aperture. Does that ragged wayfarer recognize a foe by the imperfect ray of the lamplight? or is he a mere vulgar footpad, who is doubting whether he should spring upon a prey? Hostile his look, his gestures, the sudden cowering down of the strong frame as if for a bound; but still he is irresolute. What awes him? What awes the tiger, who would obey his blood-instinct without fear, in his rush on the Negro, the Hindoo; but who halts and hesitates at the sight of the white man, the lordly son of Europe? Darrell's eye was turned towards the dark passage, towards the dark figure, —carelessly, neither recognizing nor fearing nor defying, — carelessly, as at any harmless object in crowded streets and at broad day. But while that eye was on him, the tatterdemalion halted; and indeed, whatever his hostility, or whatever his daring, the sight of Darrell took him by so sudden a surprise that he could not at once re-collect his thoughts, and determine how to approach the quiet unconscious man, who, in reach of his spring, fronted his overwhelming physical strength with the habitual air of dignified command. His first impulse was that of violence; his second impulse curbed the first. But Darrell now turns quickly, and walks straight on; the figure quits the mouth of the passage, and follows with a long and noiseless stride. It has nearly gained Darrell. With what intent? A fierce one, perhaps, —for the man's face is sinister, and his state evidently desperate, —when there emerges unexpectedly from an ugly looking court or cul-de-sac, just between Darrell and his pursuer, a slim, long-backed, buttoned-up, weazel-faced policeman. The policeman eyes the tatterdemalion instinctively, then turns his glance towards the solitary defenceless gentleman in advance, and walks on, keeping himself between the two. The tatterdemalion stifles an impatient curse. Be his purpose force, be it only supplication, be it colloquy of any kind, impossible to fulfil it while that policeman is there. True that in his powerful hands he could have clutched that slim, long-backed officer, and broken him in two as a willow-wand. But that officer is the Personation of Law, and can stalk through a legion of tatterdemalions as a ferret may glide through a barn full of rats. The prowler feels he is suspected. Unknown as yet to the London police, he has no desire to invite their scrutiny. He crosses the way; he falls back; he follows from afar. The policeman may yet turn away before the safer streets of the metropolis be gained. No; the cursed Incarnation of Law, with eyes in its slim back, continues its slow strides at the heels of the unsuspicious Darrell. The more solitary defiles are already passed, —now that dim lane, with its dead wall on one side. By the dead wall skulks the prowler; on the other side still walks the Law. Now— alas for the prowler! —shine out the throughfares, no longer dim nor deserted, —Leicester Square, the Haymarket, Pall Mall, Carlton Gardens; Darrell is at his door. The policeman turns sharply round. There, at the corner near the learned Club-house, halts the tatterdemalion. Towards the tatterdemalion the policeman now advances quickly. The tatterdemalion is quicker still; fled like a guilty thought.

Back, back, back into that maze of passages and courts, back to the mouth of that black alley. There he halts again. Look at him. He has arrived in London but that very night, after an absence of more than four years. He has arrived from the sea-side on foot; see, his shoes are worn into holes. He has not yet found a shelter for the night. He has been directed towards that quarter, thronged with adventurers, native and foreign, for a shelter, safe, if squalid. It is somewhere near that court at the mouth of which he stands. He looks round: the policeman is baffled; the coast clear. He steals forth, and pauses under the same gaslight as that under which Guy Darrell had paused before, —under the same gaslight, under the same stars. From some recess in his rags he draws forth a large, distained, distended pocket-book, —last relic of sprucer days, —leather of dainty morocco, once elaborately tooled, patent springs, fairy lock, fit receptacle for bank-notes, *billets-doux*, memoranda of debts of honour, or pleasurable engagements. Now how worn, tarnished, greasy, rascallion-like, the costly bauble! Filled with what motley, unlovable contents: stale pawn-tickets of foreign *monts de piete*, pledges never henceforth to be redeemed; scrawls by villanous hands in thievish hierolgyphics; ugly implements replacing the malachite penknife, the golden toothpick, the jewelled pencil-case, once so neatly set within their satin lappets. Ugly implements, indeed, —a file, a gimlet, loaded dice. Pell-mell, with such more hideous and recent contents, dishonoured evidences of gaudier summer life, —locks of ladies' hair, love-notes treasured mechanically, not from amorous sentiment, but perhaps from some vague idea that they might be of use if those who gave the locks or wrote the notes should be raised in fortune, and could buy back the memorials of shame. Diving amidst these miscellaneous documents and treasures, the prowler's hand rested on some old letters, in clerk-like fair calligraphy, tied round with a dirty string, and on them, in another and fresher writing, a scrap that contained an address, — "Samuel Adolphus Poole, Esq., Alhambra Villa, Regent's Park. " "To-morrow, Nix my Dolly; to-morrow, " muttered the tatterdemalion; "but to-night, —plague on it, where is the other blackguard's direction? Ah, here! " And he extracted from the thievish scrawls a peculiarly thievish-looking hieroglyph. Now, as he lifts it up to read by the gaslight, survey him well. Do you not know him? Is it possible? What! the brilliant sharper! The ruffian exquisite! Jasper Losely! Can it be? Once before, in the fields of Fawley, we beheld him out at elbows, seedy, shabby, ragged. But then it was the decay of a foppish spendthrift, —clothes distained, ill-assorted, yet, still of fine cloth; shoes in holes, yet still pearl-coloured brodequins. But now it is the decay of no foppish spendthrift: the rags are not of fine cloth; the tattered shoes are not the brodequins. The man has fallen far below the politer grades of knavery, in which the sharper affects the beau. And the countenance, as we last saw it, if it had lost much of its earlier beauty, was still incontestably handsome. What with vigour and health and animal spirits, then on the aspect still lingered light; now from corruption the light itself was gone. In that herculean constitution excess of all kinds had at length forced its ravage, and the ravage was visible in the ruined face. The once sparkling eye was dull and bloodshot. The colours of the cheek, once clear and vivid, to which fiery drink had only sent the blood in a warmer glow, were now of a leaden dulness, relieved but by broken streaks of angry red, like gleams of flame struggling through gathered smoke. The profile, once sharp and delicate like Apollo's, was now confused in its swollen outline; a few years more, and it would be gross as that of Silenus, —the nostrils, distended with incipient carbuncles, which betray the gnawing fang that alcohol fastens into the liver. Evil passions had destroyed the outlines of the once beautiful lips, arched as a Cupid's bow. The sidelong, lowering, villanous expression which had formerly been but occasional was now habitual and heightened. It was the look of the bison before it gores. It is true, however, that even yet on the countenance there lingered the trace of that lavish favour bestowed on it by nature. An artist would still have said, "How handsome that ragamuffin must have been! " And true is it, also, that there was yet that about the bearing of the man which contrasted his squalor, and seemed to say that he had not been born to wear rags and loiter at midnight amongst the haunts of thieves. Nay, I am not sure that you would have been as incredulous now, if told that the wild outlaw before you had some claim by birth or by nurture to the rank of gentleman, as you would had you seen the gay spendthrift in his gaudy day. For then he seemed below, and now he seemed above, the grade in which he took place. And all this made his aspect yet more sinister, and the impression that he was dangerous yet more profound. Muscular strength often remains to a powerful frame long after the constitution is undermined, and Jasper Losely's frame was still that of a formidable athlete; nay, its strength was yet more apparent now that the shoulders and limbs had increased in bulk than when it was half-disguised in the lissome symmetry of exquisite proportion, — less active, less supple, less capable of endurance, but with more crushing weight in its rush or its blow. It was the figure in which brute force seems so to predominate that in a savage state it would have worn a crown, —the figure which secures command and authority in all societies where force alone gives the law. Thus, under the gaslight and under the stars, stood the terrible animal, —a strong man imbruted; "SOUVIENS-TOI DE TA GABRIELLE. " There, still uneffaced, though the gold threads are all tarnished and ragged, are the ominous words on the silk of the she-devil's love-token! But Jasper has now inspected the direction on the paper he held to the lamp-light, and, satisfying himself that he was in the right quarter, restored the paper to the bulky distended pocket-book and walked sullenly on towards the court from which had emerged the policeman who had crossed his prowling chase.

"It is the most infernal shame, " said Losely between his grinded teeth, "that I should be driven to these wretched dens for a lodging, while that man, who ought to feel bound to maintain me, should be rolling in wealth, and cottoned up in a palace. But he shall fork out. Sophy must be hunted up. I will clothe her in rags like these. She shall sit at his street-door. I will shame the miserly hunks. But how track the girl? Have I no other hold over him? Can I send Dolly Poole to him? How addled my brains are! —want of food, want of sleep. Is this the place? Peuh! —"

Thus murmuring, he now reached the arch of the court, and was swallowed up in its gloom. A few strides and he came into a square open space only lighted by the skies. A house, larger than the rest, which were of the meanest order, stood somewhat back, occupying nearly one side of the quadrangle, —old, dingy, dilapidated. At the door of this house stood another man, applying his latch-key to the lock. As Losely approached, the man turned quickly, half in fear, half in menace, —a small, very thin, impish-looking man, with peculiarly restless features that seemed trying to run away from his face. Thin as he was, he looked all skin and no bones, a goblin of a man whom it would not astonish you to hear could creep through a keyhole, seeming still more shadowy and impalpable by his slight, thin, sable dress, not of cloth, but a sort of stuff like alpaca. Nor was that dress ragged, nor, as seen but in starlight, did it look worn or shabby; still you had but to glance at the creature to feel that it was a child in the same Family of Night as the ragged felon that towered by its side. The two outlaws stared at each other. "Cutts! " said Losely, in the old rollicking voice, but in a hoarser, rougher key, "Cutts, my boy, here I am; welcome me!

"What? General Jas.! " returned Cutts, in a tone which was not without a certain respectful awe, and then proceeded to pour out a series of questions in a mysterious language, which may be thus translated and abridged: "How long have you been in England? How has it fared with you? You seem very badly off; coming here to hide? Nothing very bad, I hope? What is it? "

Jasper answered in the same language, though with less practised mastery of it, and with that constitutional levity which, whatever the time or circumstances, occasionally gave a strange sort of wit, or queer, uncanny, devil-me-care vein of drollery, to his modes of expression.

"Three months of the worst luck man ever had; a row with the gens-d'armes, —long story: three of our pals seized; affair of the galleys for them, I suspect (French frogs can't seize me!); fricasseed one or two of them; broke away, crossed the country, reached the coast; found an honest smuggler; landed off Sussex with a few other kegs of brandy; remembered you, preserved the address you gave me, and condescend to this rat-hole for a night or so. Let me in; knock up somebody, break open the larder. I want to eat, I am famished; I should have eaten you by this time, only there's nothing on your bones. "

The little man opened the door, —a passage black as Erebus. "Give me your hand, General. " Jasper was led through the pitchy gloom for a few yards; then the guide found a gas-cock, and the place broke suddenly into light: a dirty narrow staircase on one side; facing it a sort of lobby, in which an open door showed a long sanded parlour, like that in public houses; several tables, benches, the walls whitewashed, but adorned with sundry ingenious designs made by charcoal or the smoked ends of clay-pipes; a strong smell of stale tobacco and of gin and rum. Another gaslight, swinging from the centre of the ceiling, sprang into light as Cutts touched the tap-cock.

"Wait here, " said the guide. "I will go and get you some supper. "

"And some brandy, " said Jasper.

"Of course. "

The bravo threw himself at length on one of the tables, and, closing his eyes, moaned. His vast strength had become acquainted with physical pain. In its stout knots and fibres, aches and sharp twinges, the dragon-teeth of which had been sown years ago in revels or brawls, which then seemed to bring but innocuous joy and easy triumph, now began to gnaw and grind. But when Cutts reappeared with coarse viands and the brandy bottle, Jasper shook off the sense of pain, as does a wounded wild beast that can still devour; and after regaling fast and ravenously, he emptied half the bottle at a draught, and felt himself restored and fresh.

"Shall you fling yourself amongst the swell fellows who hold their club here, General? " asked Cutts; "'tis a bad trade; every year it gets worse. Or have you not some higher game in your eye? "

"I have higher game in my eye. One bird I marked down this very night. But that may be slow work, and uncertain. I have in this pocket-book a bank to draw upon meanwhile. "

"How? forged French *billets de banque*? dangerous. "

"Pooh! better than that, —letters which prove theft against a respectable rich man. "

"Ah, you expect hush-money? "

"Exactly so. I have good friends in London. "

"Among them, I suppose, that affectionate 'adopted mother, ' who would have kept you in such order. "

"Thousand thunders! I hope not. I am not a superstitious man, but I fear that woman as if she were a witch, and I believe she is one. You remember black Jean, whom we call Sansculotte. He would have filled a churchyard with his own brats for a five-franc piece; but he would not have crossed a churchyard alone at night for a thousand naps. Well, that woman to me is what a churchyard was to black Jean. No: if she is in London, I have but to go to her house and say, 'Food, shelter, money; ' and I would rather ask Jack Ketch for a rope."

"How do you account for it, General? She does not beat you; she is not your wife. I have seen many a stout fellow, who would stand fire without blinking, show the white feather at a scold's tongue. But then he must be spliced to her—"

"Cutts, that Griffin does not scold: she preaches. She wants to make me spoony, Cutts: she talks of my young days, Cutts; she wants to blight me into what she calls an honest man, Cutts, —the virtuous dodge! She snubs and cows me, and frightens me out of my wits, Cutts; for I do believe that the witch is determined to have me, body and soul, and to marry me some day in spite of myself, Cutts; and if ever you see me about to be clutched in those horrible paws, poison me with ratsbane, or knock me on the head, Cutts. "

The little man laughed a little laugh, sharp and eldrich, at the strange cowardice of the stalwart dare-devil. But Jasper did not echo the laugh.

"Hush! " he said timidly, "and let me have a bed, if you can; I have not slept in one for a week, and my nerves are shaky. "

The imp lighted a candle-end at the gas-lamp, and conducted Losely up the stairs to his own sleeping-room, which was less comfortless than might be supposed. He resigned his bed to the wanderer, who flung himself on it, rags and all. But sleep was no more at his command than it is at a king's.

"Why the —— did you talk of that witch? " he cried peevishly to Cutts, who was composing himself to rest on the floor. "I swear I fancy I feel her sitting on my chest like a nightmare. "

He turned with a vehemence which shook the walls, and wrapped the coverlet round him, plunging his head into its folds. Strange though it seem to the novice in human nature, to Jasper Losely the woman who had so long lived but for one object—namely, to save him from the gibbet—was as his evil genius, his haunting fiend. He had conceived a profound terror of her from the moment he perceived that she was resolutely bent upon making him honest. He had broken from her years ago, fled, resumed his evil courses, hid himself from her, —in vain. Wherever he went, there went she. He might baffle the police, not her. Hunger had often forced him to accept her aid. As soon as he received it, he hid from her again, burying himself deeper and deeper in the mud, like a persecuted tench. He associated her idea with all the ill-luck that had befallen him. Several times some villanous scheme on which he had counted to make his fortune had been baffled in the most mysterious way; and just when baffled, and there seemed no choice but to cut his own throat or some one else's, up turned grim Arabella Crane, in the iron-gray gown, and with the iron-gray ringlets, —hatefully, awfully beneficent, —offering food, shelter, gold, —and some demoniacal, honourable work. Often had he been in imminent peril from watchful law or treacherous accomplice. She had warned and saved him, as she had saved him from the fell Gabrielle Desmarets, who, unable to bear the sentence of penal servitude, after a long process, defended with astonishing skill and enlisting the romantic sympathies of young France, had contrived to escape into another world by means of a subtle poison concealed about her *distinguee* person, and which she had prepared years ago with her own bloodless hands, and no doubt scientifically tested its effects on others. The cobra di capella is gone at last! "*Souviens-toi de ta Gabrielle*, " O Jasper Losely! But why Arabella Crane should thus continue to watch over him whom she no longer professed to love, how she should thus have acquired the gift of ubiquity and the power to save him, Jasper Losely could not conjecture. The whole thing seemed to him weird and supernatural. Most truly did he say that she had cowed him. He had often longed to strangle her; when absent from her, had often resolved upon that act of gratitude. The moment he came in sight of her stern, haggard face, her piercing lurid eyes; the moment he heard her slow, dry voice in some such sentences as these: "Again you come to me in your trouble, and ever shall. Am I not still as your mother, but with a wife's fidelity, till death us do part? There's the portrait of what you were: look at it, Jasper. Now turn to the glass: see what you are. Think of the fate of Gabrielle Desmarets! But for me, what, long since, had been your own? But I will save you: I have sworn it. You shall be wax in these hands at last, " —the moment that voice thus claimed and insisted on redeeming him, the ruffian felt a cold shudder, his courage oozed, he could no more have nerved his arm against her than a Thug would have lifted his against the dire goddess of his murderous superstition. Jasper could not resist a belief that the life of this dreadful protectress was, somehow or other, made essential to his; that, were she to die, he should perish in some ghastly and preternatural expiation. But for the last few months he had, at length, escaped from her; diving so low, so deep into the mud, that even her net could not mesh him. Hence, perhaps, the imminence of the perils from which he had so narrowly escaped, hence the utterness of his present destitution. But man, however vile, whatever his peril, whatever his destitution, was born free, and loves liberty. Liberty to go to Satan in his own way was to Jasper Losely a supreme blessing compared to that benignant compassionate espionage, with its relentless eye and restraining hand. Alas and alas! deem not this perversity unnatural in that headstrong self-destroyer! How many are there whom not a grim, hard-featured Arabella Crane, but the long-suffering, divine, omniscient, gentle Providence itself, seeks to warn, to aid, to save; and is shunned, and loathed, and fled from, as if it were an evil genius! How many are there who fear nothing so much as the being made good in spite of themselves? —how many? who can count them?

CHAPTER VI.

The public man needs but one patron; namely, THE LUCKY MOMENT.

"At his house in Carlton Gardens, Guy Darrell, Esq., for the season. "

Simple insertion in the pompous list of Fashionable Arrivals! the name of a plain commoner embedded in the amber which glitters with so many coronets and stars! Yet such is England, with all its veneration for titles, that the eyes of the public passed indifferently over the rest of that chronicle of illustrious "whereabouts, " to rest with interest, curiosity, speculation, on the unemblazoned name which but a day before had seemed slipped out of date, —obsolete as that of an actor who figures no more in play-bills. Unquestionably the sensation excited was due, in much, to the "ambiguous voices" which Colonel Morley had disseminated throughout the genial atmosphere of club-rooms. "Arrived in London for the season! " — he, the orator, once so famous, long so forgotten, who had been out of the London world for the space of more than half a generation. "Why now? why for the season? " Quoth the Colonel, "He is still in the prime of life as a public man, and—a CRISIS is at hand! "

But that which gave weight and significance to Alban Morley's hints was the report in the newspapers of Guy Darrell's visit to his old constituents, and of the short speech he had addressed to them, to which he had so slightly referred in his conversation with Alban. True, the speech was short: true, it touched but little on passing topics of political interest; rather alluding, with modesty and terseness, to the contests and victories of a former day. But still, in the few words there was the swell of the old clarion, the wind of the Paladin's horn which woke Fontarabian echoes.

It is astonishing how capricious, how sudden, are the changes in value of a public man. All depends upon whether the public want, or believe they want, the man; and that is a question upon which the public do not know their own minds a week before; nor do they always keep in the same mind, when made up, for a week together. If they do not want a man; if he do not hit the taste, nor respond to the exigency of the time, —whatever his eloquence, his abilities, his virtues, they push him aside or cry him down. Is he wanted? does the mirror of the moment reflect his image? —that mirror is an intense magnifier—his proportions swell; they become gigantic. At that moment the public wanted some man; and the instant the hint was given, "Why not Guy Darrell? " Guy Darrell was seized upon as the man wanted. It was one of those times in our Parliamentary history when the public are out of temper with all parties; when recognized leaders have contrived to damage themselves; when a Cabinet is shaking, and the public neither care to destroy nor to keep it, —a time too, when the country seemed in some danger, and when, mere men of business held unequal to the emergency, whatever name suggested associations of vigour, eloquence, genius rose to a premium above its market price in times of tranquillity and tape. Without effort of his own, by the mere force of the undercurrent, Guy Darrell was thrown up from oblivion into note. He could not form a Cabinet, certainly not; but he might help to bring a Cabinet together, reconcile jarring elements, adjust disputed questions, take in such government some high place, influence its councils, and delight a public weary of the oratory of the day with the eloquence of a former race. For the public is ever a *laudator temporis acti*, and whatever the authors or the orators immediately before it, were those authors and orators Homers and Ciceros, would still shake a disparaging head, and talk of these degenerate days as Homer himself talked ages before Leonidas stood in the pass of Thermopylae, or Miltiades routed Asian armaments at Marathon. Guy Darrell belonged to a former race. The fathers of those young members rising now into fame had quoted to their sons his pithy sentences, his vivid images; and added, as Fox added when quoting Burke, "But you should have heard and seen the man! "

Heard and seen the man! But there he was again! come up as from a grave, —come up to the public just when such a man was wanted. Wanted how? wanted where? Oh, somehow and somewhere! There he is! make the most of him. The house in Carlton Gardens is prepared, the establishment mounted. Thither flock all the Viponts, nor they alone; all the chiefs of all parties, nor they alone; all the notabilities of our grand metropolis. Guy Darrell might be startled at his own position; but he comprehended its nature, and it did not discompose his nerves. He knew public life well enough to be aware how much the popular favour is the creature of an accident. By chance he had nicked the time; had he thus come to town the season before, he might have continued obscure, a man like Guy Darrell not being wanted then. Whether with or without design, his bearing confirmed and extended the effect produced by his reappearance. Gracious, but modestly reserved, he spoke little, listened beautifully.

Many of the questions which agitated all around him had grown up into importance since his day of action; nor in his retirement had he traced their progressive development, with their changeful effects upon men and parties. But a man who has once gone deeply into practical politics might sleep in the Cave of Trophonius for twenty years, and find, on waking, very little to learn. Darrell regained the level of the day, and seized upon all the strong points on which men were divided, with the rapidity of a prompt and comprehensive intellect, his judgment perhaps the clearer from the freshness of long repose and the composure of dispassionate survey. When partisans wrangled as to what should have been done, Darrell was silent; when they asked what should be done, out came one of his terse sentences, and a knot was cut. Meanwhile it is true this man, round whom expectations grouped and rumour buzzed, was in neither House of Parliament; but that was rather a delay to his energies than a detriment to his consequence.

Important constituencies, anticipating a vacancy, were already on the look-out for him; a smaller constituency, in the interim, Carr Vipont undertook to procure him any day. There was always a Vipont ready to accept something, even the Chiltern Hundreds. But Darrell, not without reason, demurred at re-entering the House of Commons after an absence of seventeen years. He had left it with one of those rare reputations which no wise man likes rashly to imperil. The Viponts sighed. He would certainly be more useful in the Commons than the Lords, but still in the Lords he would be of great use. They would want a debating lord, perhaps a lord acquainted with law in the coming CRISIS, —if he preferred the peerage? Darrell demurred still. The man's modesty was insufferable; his style of speaking might not suit that august assembly: and as to law, he could never now be a law lord; he should be but a ci-devant advocate, affecting the part of a judicial amateur.

In short, without declining to re-enter public life, seeming, on the contrary, to resume all his interest in it, Darrell contrived with admirable dexterity to elude for the present all overtures pressed upon him, and even to convince his admirers, not only of his wisdom, but of his patriotism in that reticence. For certainly he thus managed to exercise a very considerable influence: his advice was more sought, his suggestions more heeded, and his power in reconciling certain rival jealousies was perhaps greater than would have been the case if he had actually entered either House of Parliament, and thrown himself exclusively into the ranks, not only of one party, but of one section of a party. Nevertheless, such suspense could not last very long; he must decide at all events before the next session. Once he was seen in the arena of his old triumphs, on the benches devoted to strangers distinguished by the Speaker's order. There, recognized by the older members, eagerly gazed at by the younger, Guy Darrell listened calmly, throughout a long field-night, to voices that must have roused from forgotten graves kindling and glorious memories; voices of those veterans now—by whose side he had once struggled for some cause which he had then, in the necessary exaggeration of all honest enthusiasm, identified with a nation's life-blood. Voices, too of the old antagonists over whose routed arguments he had marched triumphant amidst applauses that the next day rang again through England from side to side. Hark! the very man with whom, in the old battle-days, he had been the most habitually pitted, is speaking now! His tones are embarrassed, his argument confused. Does he know who listens yonder? Old members think so, —smile; whisper each other, and glance significantly where Darrell sits.

Sits, as became him, tranquil, respectful, intent, seemingly, perhaps really, unconscious of the sensation he excites. What an eye for an orator! how like the eye in a portrait; it seems to fix on each other eye that seeks it, —steady, fascinating. Yon distant members, behind the Speaker's chair, at the far distance, feel the light of that eye travel towards them. How lofty and massive, among all those rows of human heads, seems that forehead, bending slightly down, with the dark strong line of the weighty eyebrow! But what is passing within that secret mind? Is there mournfulness in the retrospect? Is there eagerness to renew the strife? Is that interest in the hour's debate feigned or real? Impossible for him who gazed upon that face to say. And that eye would have seemed to the gazer to read himself through and through to the heart's core, long ere the gazer could hazard a single guess as to the thoughts beneath that marble forehead, —as to the emotions within the heart over which, in old senatorial fashion, the arms were folded with so conventional an ease.

CHAPTER VII.

Darrell and Lionel.

Darrell had received Lionel with some evident embarrassment, which soon yielded to affectionate warmth. He took to the young man whose fortunes he had so improved; he felt that with the improved fortunes the young man's whole being was improved: assured position, early commune with the best social circles, in which the equality of fashion smooths away all disparities in rank, had softened in Lionel much of the wayward and morbid irritability of his boyish pride; but the high spirit, the generous love of independence, the scorn of mercenary calculation, were strong as ever; these were in the grain of his nature. In common with all who in youth aspire to be one day noted from the "undistinguishable many, " Lionel had formed to himself a certain ideal standard, above the ordinary level of what the world is contented to call honest, or esteem clever. He admitted into his estimate of life the heroic element, not undesirable even in the most practical point of view, for the world is so in the habit of decrying; of disbelieving in high motives and pure emotions; of daguerreotyping itself with all its ugliest wrinkles, stripped of the true bloom that brightens, of the true expression that redeems, those defects which it invites the sun to limn, that we shall never judge human nature aright, if we do not set out in life with our gaze on its fairest beauties, and our belief in its latent good. In a word we should begin with the Heroic, if we would learn the Human. But though to himself Lionel thus secretly prescribed a certain superiority of type, to be sedulously aimed at, even if never actually attained, he was wholly without pedantry and arrogance towards his own contemporaries. From this he was saved not only by good-nature, animal spirits, frank hardihood, but by the very affluence of ideas which animated his tongue, coloured his language, and whether to young or old, wise or dull, made his conversation racy and original. He was a delightful companion; and if he had taken much instruction from those older and wiser than himself, he so bathed that instruction in the fresh fountain of his own lively intelligence, so warmed it at his own beating impulsive heart, that he could make an old man's gleanings from experience seem a young man's guesses into truth. Faults he had, of course, —chiefly the faults common at his age; amongst them, perhaps, the most dangerous were, —firstly, carelessness in money matters; secondly, a distaste for advice in which prudence was visibly predominant. His tastes were not in reality extravagant: but money slipped through his hands, leaving little to show for it; and when his quarterly allowance became due, ample though it was, —too ample, perhaps, —debts wholly forgotten started up to seize hold of it. And debts as yet being manageable were not regarded with sufficient horror. Paid or put aside, as the case might be, they were merely looked upon as bores. Youth is in danger till it learn to look upon them as furies. For advice, he took it with pleasure, when clothed with elegance and art, when it addressed ambition, when it exalted the loftier virtues. But advice, practical and prosy, went in at one ear and out at the other. In fact, with many talents, he had yet no adequate ballast of common-sense; and if ever he get enough to steady his bark through life's trying voyage, the necessity of so much dull weight must be forcibly stricken home less to his reason than his imagination or his heart. But if, somehow or other, he get it not, I will not insure his vessel.

I know not if Lionel Haughton had genius; he never assumed that he had: but he had something more like genius than that prototype, RESOLVE, of which he boasted to the artist. He had YOUTH, —real youth, —youth of mind, youth of heart, youth of soul. Lithe and supple as he moved before you, with the eye to which light or dew sprang at once from a nature vibrating to every lofty, every tender thought, he seemed more than young, —the incarnation of youth.

Darrell took to him at once. Amidst all the engagements crowded on the important man, he contrived to see Lionel daily. And what may seem strange, Guy Darrell felt more at home with Lionel Haughton than with any of his own contemporaries, —than even with Alban Morley. To the last, indeed, he opened speech with less reserve of certain portions of the past, or of certain projects in the future. But still, even there, he adopted a tone of half-playful, half-mournful satire, which might be in itself disguise. Alban Morley, with all his good qualities, was a man of the world; as a man of the world, Guy Darrell talked to him. But it was only a very small part of Guy Darrell the Man, of which the world could say "mine. "

To Lionel he let out, as if involuntarily, the more amiable, tender, poetic attributes of his varying, complex, uncomprehended character; not professedly confiding, but not taking pains to conceal. Hearing what worldlings would call "Sentiment" in Lionel, he seemed to glide softly down to Lionel's own years and talk "sentiment" in return. After all, this skilled lawyer, this noted politician, had a great dash of the boy still in him. Reader, did you ever meet a really clever man who had not?

CHAPTER VIII.

Saith a very homely proverb (pardon its vulgarity), "You cannot make a silk purse out of a sow's ear. " But a sow's ear is a much finer work of art than a silk purse; and grand, indeed, the mechanician who could make a sow's ear out of a silk purse, or conjure into creatures of flesh and blood the sarcenet and *tulle* of a London drawing-room.

"Mamma, " asked Honoria Carr Vipont, "what sort of a person was Mrs. Darrell? "

"She was not in our set, my dear, " answered Lady Selina. "The Vipont Crookes are just one of those connections with which, though of course one is civil to all connections, one is more or less intimate according as they take after the Viponts or after the Crookes. Poor woman! she died just before Mr. Darrell entered Parliament and appeared in society. But I should say she was not an agreeable person. Not nice, " added Lady Selina, after a pause, and conveying a world of meaning in that conventional monosyllable.

"I suppose she was very accomplished, very clever? "

"Quite the reverse, my dear. Mr. Darrell was exceedingly young when he married, scarcely of age. She was not the sort of woman to suit him. "

"But at least she must have been very much attached to him, very proud of him? "

Lady Selina glanced aside from her work, and observed her daughter's face, which evinced an animation not usual to a young lady of a breeding so lofty, and a mind so well disciplined.

"I don't think, " said Lady Selina, "that she was proud of him. She would have been proud of his station, or rather of that to which his fame and fortune would have raised her, had she lived to enjoy it. But for a few years after her marriage they were very poor; and though his rise at the bar was sudden and brilliant, he was long wholly absorbed in his profession, and lived in Bloomsbury. Mrs. Darrell was not proud of that. The Crookes are generally fine, give themselves airs, marry into great houses if they can: but we can't

462

naturalize them; they always remain Crookes, —useful connections, very! Carr says we have not a more useful, —but third-rate, my dear. All the Crookes are bad wives, because they are never satisfied with their own homes, but are always trying to get into great people's homes. Not very long before she died, Mrs. Darrell took her friend and relation, Mrs. Lyndsay, to live with her. I suspect it was not from affection, or any great consideration for Mrs. Lyndsay's circumstances (which were indeed those of actual destitution, till— thanks to Mr. Darrell—she won her lawsuit), but simply because she looked to Mrs. Lyndsay to get her into our set. Mrs. Lyndsay was a great favourite with all of us, charming manners, —perfectly correct, too, —thorough Vipont, thorough gentlewoman, but artful! Oh, so artful! She humoured poor Mrs. Darrell's absurd vanity; but she took care not to injure herself. Of course, Darrell's wife, and a Vipont— though only a Vipont Crooke—had free passport into the outskirts of good society, the great parties, and so forth. But there it stopped; even I should have been compromised if I had admitted into our set a woman who was bent on compromising herself. Handsome, in a bad style, not the Vipont *tournure*; and not only silly and flirting, but (we are alone, keep the secret) decidedly vulgar, my dear. "

"You amaze me! How such a man—" Honoria stopped, colouring up to the temples.

"Clever men, " said Lady Selina, "as a general rule, do choose the oddest wives! The cleverer a man is, the more easily, I do believe, a woman can take him in. However, to do Mr. Darrell justice, he has been taken in only once. After Mrs. Darrell's death, Mrs. Lyndsay, I suspect, tried her chance, but failed. Of course, she would not actually stay in the same house with a widower who was then young, and who had only to get rid of a wife to whom one was forced to be shy in order to be received into our set with open arms, and, in short, to be of the very best monde. Mr. Darrell came into Parliament immensely rich (a legacy from an old East Indian, besides his own professional savings); took the house he has now, close by us. Mrs. Lyndsay was obliged to retire to a cottage at Fulham. But as she professed to be a second mother to poor Matilda Darrell, she contrived to be very much at Carlton Gardens; her daughter Caroline was nearly always there, profiting by Matilda's masters; and I did think that Mrs. Lyndsay would have caught Darrell, but your papa said 'No, ' and he was right, as he always is. Nevertheless, Mrs. Lyndsay would have been an excellent wife to a public man: so popular; knew the world so well; never made enemies till she made an enemy of poor dear Montfort, but that was natural. By the by, I must write to Caroline. Sweet creature! but how absurd, shutting herself up as if she were fretting for Montfort! That's so like her mother, —heartless, but full of propriety. "

Here Carr Vipont and Colonel Morley entered the room. "We have just left Darrell, " said Carr; "he will dine here to-day, to meet our cousin Alban. I have asked his cousin, young Haughton, and—and, your cousins, Selina (a small party of cousins); so lucky to find Darrell disengaged. "

"I ventured to promise, " said the Colonel, addressing Honoria in an under voice, "that Darrell should hear you play Beethoven. "

HONORIA. —"Is Mr. Darrell so fond of music, then? "

COLONEL MORLEY. —"One would not have thought it. He keeps a secretary at Fawley who plays the flute. There's something very interesting about Darrell. I wish you could hear his ideas on marriage and domestic life: more freshness of heart than in the young men one meets nowadays. It may be prejudice; but it seems to me that the young fellows of the present race, if more sober and staid than we were, are sadly wanting in character and spirit, —no warm blood in their veins. But I should not talk thus to a demoiselle who has all those young fellows at her feet. "

"Oh, " said Lady Selina, overhearing, and with a half laugh, "Honoria thinks much as you do: she finds the young men so insipid; all like one another, —the same set phrases. "

"The same stereotyped ideas, " added Honoria, moving away with a gesture of calm disdain.

"A very superior mind hers, " whispered the Colonel to Carr Vipont. "She'll never marry a fool. "

Guy Darrell was very pleasant at "the small family dinnerparty. " Carr was always popular in his manners; the true old House of Commons manner, which was very like that of a gentleman-like public school. Lady Selina, as has been said before, in her own family circle was natural and genial. Young Carr, there, without his wife, more pretentious than his father, —being a Lord of the Admiralty, — felt a certain awe of Darrell, and spoke little, which was much to his own credit and to the general conviviality. The other members of the symposium, besides Lady Selina, Honoria, and a younger sister, were but Darrell, Lionel, and Lady Selina's two cousins; elderly peers, —one with the garter, the other in the Cabinet, —jovial men who had been wild fellows once in the same mess-room, and still joked at each other whenever they met as they met now. Lionel, who remembered Vance's description of Lady Selina, and who had since heard her spoken of in society as a female despot who carried to perfection the arts by which despots flourish, with majesty to impose, and caresses to deceive—an Aurungzebe in petticoats—was sadly at a loss to reconcile such portraiture with the good-humoured, motherly woman who talked to him of her home, her husband, her children, with open fondness and becoming pride, and who, far from being so formidably clever as the world cruelly gave out, seemed to Lionel rather below par in her understanding; strike from her talk its kindliness, and the residue was very like twaddle. After dinner, various members of the Vipont family dropped in, —asked impromptu by Carr or by Lady Selina, in hasty three-cornered notes, to take that occasion of renewing their acquaintance with their distinguished connection. By some accident, amongst those invited there were but few young single ladies; and, by some other accident, those few were all plain. Honoria Vipont was unequivocally the belle of the room. It could not but be observed that Darrell seemed struck with her, —talked with her more than with any other lady; and when she went to the piano, and played that great air of Beethoven's, in which music seems to have got into a knot that only fingers the most artful can unravel, Darrell remained in his seat aloof and alone, listening no doubt with ravished attention. But just as the air ended, and Honoria turned round to look for him, he was gone.

Lionel did not linger long after him. The gay young man went thence to one of those vast crowds which seemed convened for a practical parody of Mr. Bentham's famous proposition, —contriving the smallest happiness for the greatest number.

It was a very good house, belonging to a very great person. Colonel Morley had procured an invitation for Lionel, and said, "Go; you should be seen there. " Colonel Morley had passed the age of growing into society: no such cares for the morrow could add a cubit to his conventional stature. One amongst a group of other young men by the doorway, Lionel beheld Darrell, who had arrived before him, listening to a very handsome young lady, with an attention quite as earnest as that which had gratified the superior mind of the well-educated Honoria, —a very handsome young lady certainly, but not with a superior mind, nor supposed hitherto to have found young gentlemen "insipid. " Doubtless she would henceforth do so. A few minutes after Darrell was listening again; this time to another young lady, generally called "fast. " If his attentions to her were not marked, hers to him were. She rattled on to him volubly, laughed, pretty hoyden, at her own sallies, and seemed at last so to fascinate him by her gay spirits that he sat down by her side; and the playful smile on his lips—lips that had learned to be so gravely firm— showed that he could enter still into the mirth of childhood; for surely to the time-worn man the fast young lady must have seemed but a giddy child. Lionel was amused. Could this be the austere recluse whom he had left in the shades of Fawley? Guy Darrell, at his years, with his dignified repute, the object of so many nods, and becks, and wreathed smiles, —could he descend to be that most frivolous of characters, a male coquet? Was he in earnest? Was his vanity duped? Looking again, Lionel saw in his kinsman's face a sudden return of the sad despondent expression which had moved his own young pity in the solitudes of Fawley. But in a moment the man roused himself: the sad expression was gone. Had the girl's merry laugh again chased it away? But Lionel's attention was now drawn from Darrell himself to the observations murmured round him, of which Darrell was the theme.

"Yes, he is bent on marrying again! I have it from Alban Morley: immense fortune; and so young-looking, any girl might fall in love with such eyes and forehead; besides, what a jointure he could settle! . .. Do look at that girl, Flora Vyvyan, trying to make a fool of him. She can't appreciate that kind of man, and she would not be caught by his money; does not want it.   I wonder she is not afraid of him. He is certainly quizzing her. . ... The men think her pretty; I don't. . .. They say he is to return to Parliament, and have a place in the Cabinet. . .. No! he has no children living: very natural he should marry again. . .. A nephew! —you are quite mistaken. Young Haughton is no nephew: a very distant connection; could not expect to be the heir   It was given out, though, at Paris. The Duchess thought so, and so did Lady Jane. They'll not be so civil to young Haughton now. Hush—"

Lionel, wishing to hear no more, glided by, and penetrated farther into the throng. And then, as he proceeded, with those last words on his ear, the consciousness came upon him that his position had undergone a change. Difficult to define it; to an ordinary bystander people would have seemed to welcome him cordially as ever. The gradations of respect in polite society are so exquisitely delicate, that it seems only by a sort of magnetism that one knows from day to day whether one has risen or declined. A man has lost high office, patronage, power, never perhaps to regain them. People don't turn their backs on him; their smiles are as gracious, their hands as flatteringly extended. But that man would be dull as a rhinoceros if he did not feel—as every one who accosts him feels—that he has descended in the ladder. So with all else. Lose even your fortune, it is not the next day in a London drawing-room that your friends look as if you were going to ask them for five pounds. Wait a year or so for that. But if they have just heard you are ruined, you will feel that they have heard it, let them bow ever so courteously, smile ever so kindly. Lionel at Paris, in the last year or so, had been more than fashionable: he had been the fashion, —courted, run after, petted, quoted, imitated. That evening he felt as an author may feel who has been the rage, and without fault of his own is so no more. The rays that had gilded him had gone back to the orb that lent. And they who were most genial still to Lionel Haughton were those who still most respected thirty-five thousand pounds a year—in Guy Darrell!

Lionel was angry with himself that he felt galled. But in his wounded pride there was no mercenary regret, —only that sort of sickness which comes to youth when the hollowness of worldly life is first made clear to it. From the faces round him there fell that glamour by which the *amour propre* is held captive in large assemblies, where the *amour propre* is flattered. "Magnificent, intelligent audience, " thinks the applauded actor. "Delightful party, " murmurs the worshipped beauty. Glamour! glamour! Let the audience yawn while the actor mouths; let the party neglect the beauty to adore another, and straightway the "magnificent audience" is an "ignorant public, " and the "delightful party" a "heartless world. "

CHAPTER IX.

Escaped from a London drawing-room, flesh once more tingles and blood flows. —Guy Darrell explains to Lionel Haughton why he holds it a duty to be an old fool.

Lionel Haughton glided through the disenchanted rooms, and breathed a long breath of relief when he found himself in the friendless streets.

As he walked slow and thoughtful on, he suddenly felt a hand upon his shoulder, turned, and saw Darrell.

"Give me your arm, my dear Lionel; I am tired out. What a lovely night! What sweet scorn in the eyes of those stars that we have neglected for yon flaring lights. "

LIONEL. —"Is it scorn? is it pity? is it but serene indifference? "

DARRELL. —"As we ourselves interpret: if scorn be present in our own hearts, it will be seen in the disc of Jupiter. Man, egotist though he be, exacts sympathy from all the universe. Joyous, he says to the sun, 'Life-giver, rejoice with me. ' Grieving, he says to the moon, 'Pensive one, thou sharest my sorrow. ' Hope for fame; a star is its promise!

"Mourn for the dead; a star is the land of reunion! Say to earth, 'I have done with thee; ' to Time, 'Thou hast nought to bestow; ' and all space cries aloud, 'The earth is a speck, thine inheritance infinity. Time melts while thou sighest. The discontent of a mortal is the instinct that proves thee immortal. ' Thus construing Nature, Nature is our companion, our consoler. Benign as the playmate, she lends herself to our shifting humours. Serious as the teacher, she responds to the steadier inquiries of reason. Mystic and hallowed as the priestess, she keeps alive by dim oracles that spiritual yearning within us, in which, from savage to sage, —through all dreams, through all creeds, —thrills the sense of a link with Divinity. Never, therefore, while conferring with Nature, is Man wholly alone, nor is she a single companion with uniform shape. Ever new, ever various, she can pass from gay to severe, from fancy to science, —quick as thought passes from the dance of a leaf, from the tint of a rainbow, to the theory of motion, the problem of light. But lose Nature, forget or dismiss her, make companions, by hundreds, of men who ignore her, and I will not say with the poet, 'This is solitude. ' But in the commune, what stale monotony, what weary sameness! "

Thus Darrell continued to weave together sentence with sentence, the intermediate connection of meaning often so subtle that when put down on paper it requires effort to discern it. But it was his peculiar gift to make clear when spoken what in writing would seem obscure. Look, manner, each delicate accent in a voice wonderfully distinct in its unrivalled melody, all so aided the sense of mere words that it is scarcely extravagant to say he might have talked an unknown language, and a listener would have understood. But, understood or not, those sweet intonations it was such delight to hear that any one with nerves alive to music would have murmured, "Talk on forever. " And in this gift lay one main secret of the man's strange influence over all who came familiarly into his intercourse; so that if Darrell had ever bestowed confidential intimacy on any one not by some antagonistic idiosyncrasy steeled against its charm, and that intimacy had been withdrawn, a void never to be refilled must have been left in the life thus robbed.

Stopping at his door, as Lionel, rapt by the music, had forgotten the pain of the revery so bewitchingly broken, Darrell detained the hand held out to him, and said, "No, not yet; I have something to say to you: come in; let me say it now. "

Lionel bowed his head, and in surprised conjecture followed his kinsman up the lofty stairs into the same comfortless stately room that has been already described. When the servant closed the door, Darrell sank into a chair. Fixing his eye upon Lionel with almost parental kindness, and motioning his young cousin to sit by his side, close, he thus began,

"Lionel, before I was your age I was married; I was a father. I am lonely and childless now. My life has been moulded by a solemn obligation which so few could comprehend that I scarce know a man living beside yourself to whom I would frankly confide it. Pride of family is a common infirmity, —often petulant with the poor, often insolent with the rich; but rarely, perhaps, out of that pride do men construct a positive binding duty, which at all self-sacrifice should influence the practical choice of life. As a child, before my judgment could discern how much of vain superstition may lurk in our reverence for the dead, my whole heart was engaged in a passionate dream, which my waking existence became vowed to realize. My father! —my lip quivers, my eyes moisten as I recall him, even now, —my father! —I loved him so intensely! —the love of childhood, how fearfully strong it is! All in him was so gentle, yet so sensitive, —chivalry without its armour. I was his constant companion: he spoke to me unreservedly, as a poet to his muse. I wept at his sorrows; I chafed at his humiliations. He talked of ancestors as he thought of them; to him they were beings like the old Lares, —not dead in graves, but images ever present on household hearths. Doubtless he exaggerated their worth, as their old importance. Obscure, indeed, in the annals of empire, their deeds and their power, their decline and fall. Not so thought he; they were to his eyes the moon-track in the ocean of history, —light on the waves over which they had gleamed, —all the ocean elsewhere dark! With him thought I; as my father spoke, his child believed. But what to the eyes of the world was this inheritor of a vaunted name? —a threadbare, slighted, rustic pedant; no station in the very province in which mouldered away the last lowly dwelling-place of his line, — by lineage high above most nobles, in position below most yeomen. He had learning; he had genius: but the studies to which they were devoted only served yet more to impoverish his scanty means, and led rather to ridicule than to honour. Not a day but what I saw on his soft features the smart of a fresh sting, the gnawing of a new care. Thus, as a boy, feeling in myself a strength inspired by affection, I came to him one day as he sat grieving, and kneeling to him, said, 'Father, courage yet a little while; I shall soon be a man, and I swear to devote myself as man to revive the old fading race so prized by you; to rebuild the House that, by you so loved, is loftier in my eyes than all the heraldry of kings. ' And my father's face brightened, and his voice blessed me; and I rose up—ambitious! " Darrell paused, heaved a short, quick sigh, and then rapidly continued,

"I was fortunate at the University. That was a day when chiefs of party looked for recruits amongst young men who had given the proofs and won the first-fruits of emulation and assiduity; for statesmanship then was deemed an art which, like that of war, needs early discipline. I had scarcely left college when I was offered a seat in Parliament by the head of the Viponts, an old Lord Montfort. I was dazzled but for one moment; I declined the next. The fallen House of Darrell needed wealth; and Parliamentary success, in its higher honours, often requires wealth, —never gives it. It chanced that I had a college acquaintance with a young man named Vipont Crooke. His grandfather, one of the numberless Viponts, had been compelled to add the name of Crooke to his own, on succeeding to the property of some rich uncle, who was one of the numberless Crookes. I went with this college acquaintance to visit the old Lord Montfort, at his villa near London, and thence to the country-house of the Vipont Crookes. I stayed at the last two or three weeks. While there, I received a letter from the elder Fairthorn, my father's bailiff, entreating me to come immediately to Fawley, hinting at some great calamity. On taking leave of my friend and his family, something in the manner of his sister startled and pained me, —an evident confusion, a burst of tears, —I know not what. I had never sought to win her affections. I had an ideal of the woman I could love, —it did not resemble her. On reaching Fawley, conceive the shock that awaited me. My father was like one heart-stricken. The principal mortgagee was about to foreclose, —Fawley about to pass forever from the race of the Darrells. I saw that the day my father was driven from the old house would be his last on earth. What means to save him? —how raise the pitiful sum—but a few thousands—by which to release from the spoiler's gripe those barren acres which all the lands of the Seymour or the Gower could never replace in my poor father's eyes? My sole income was a college fellowship, adequate to all my wants, but useless for sale or loan. I spent the night in vain consultation with Fairthorn. There seemed not a hope. Next morning came a letter from young Vipont Crooke. It was manly and frank, though somewhat coarse. With the consent of his parents he offered me his sister's hand, and a dowry of L10,000. He hinted, in excuse for his bluntness, that, perhaps from motives of delicacy, if I felt a preference for his sister, I might not deem myself rich enough to propose, and—but it matters not what else he said. You foresee the rest. My father's life could be saved from despair; his beloved home be his shelter to the last. That dowry would more than cover the paltry debt upon the lands. I gave myself not an hour to pause. I hastened back to the house to which fate had led me. But, " said Darrell, proudly, "do not think I was base enough, even with such excuses, to deceive the young lady. I told her what was true; that I could not profess to her the love painted by romance-writers and poets; but that I loved no other, and that if she deigned to accept my hand, I should studiously consult her happiness and gratefully confide to her my own. "

"I said also, what was true, that if she married me, ours must be for some years a life of privation and struggle; that even the interest of her fortune must be devoted to my father while he lived, though every shilling of its capital would be settled on herself and her children. How I blessed her when she accepted me, despite my candour! —how earnestly I prayed that I might love and cherish and requite her! " Darrell paused, in evident suffering. "And, thank Heaven! I have nothing on that score wherewith to reproach myself; and the strength of that memory enabled me to bear and forbear more than otherwise would have been possible to my quick spirit and my man's heart. My dear father! his death was happy: his home was saved; he never knew at what sacrifice to his son! He was gladdened by the first honours my youth achieved. He was resigned to my choice of a profession, which, though contrary to his antique prejudices, that allowed to the representative of the Darrells no profession but the sword, still promised the wealth which would secure his name from perishing. He was credulous of my future, as if I had uttered not a vow, but a prediction. He had blessed my union, without foreseeing its sorrows. He had embraced my first-born, — true, it was a girl, but it was one link onward from ancestors to posterity. And almost his last words were these: 'You will restore the race; you will revive the name! and my son's children will visit the antiquary's grave, and learn gratitude to him for all that his idle lessons taught to your healthier vigour. ' And I answered, 'Father, your line shall not perish from the land; and when I am rich and great, and lordships spread far round the lowly hall that your life ennobled, I will say to your grandchildren, 'Honour ye and your son's sons, while a Darrell yet treads the earth, honour him to whom I owe every thought which nerved me to toil for what you who come after me may enjoy. '

"And so the old man, whose life had been so smileless, died smiling."

By this time Lionel had stolen Darrell's hand into his own—his heart swelling with childlike tenderness, and the tears rolling down his cheeks.

Darrell gently kissed his young kinsman's forehead, and, extricating himself from Lionel's clasp, paced the room, and spoke on while pacing it.

"I made, then, a promise; it is not kept. No child of mine survives to be taught reverence to my father's grave. My wedded life was not happy: its record needs no words. Of two children born to me, both are gone. My son went first. I had thrown my life's life into him, —a boy of energy, of noble promise. 'T was for him I began to build that baffled fabric, 'Sepulchri immemor. ' For him I bought, acre on acre, all the land within reach of Fawley, -lands twelve miles distant. I had meant to fill up the intervening space, to buy out a mushroom earl whose woods and cornfields lie between. I was scheming the purchase, scrawling on the county map, when they brought the news that the boy I had just taken back to school was dead, —drowned bathing on a calm summer eve. No, Lionel. I must go on. That grief I have wrestled with, —conquered. I was widowed then. A daughter still left, —the first-born, whom my father had blest on his death-bed. I transferred all my love, all my hopes, to her. I had no vain preference for male heirs. Is a race less pure that runs on through the female line? Well, my son's death was merciful compared to—" Again Darrell stopped, again hurried on. "Enough! all is forgiven in the grave! I was then still in the noon of man's life, free to form new ties. Another grief that I cannot tell you; it is not all conquered yet. And by that grief the last verdure of existence was so blighted that— that—in short, I had no heart for nuptial altars, for the social world. Years went by. Each year I said, 'Next year the wound will be healed; I have time yet. ' Now age is near, the grave not far; now, if ever, I must fulfil the promise that cheered my father's death-bed. Nor does that duty comprise all my motives. If I would regain healthful thought, manly action, for my remaining years, I must feel that one haunting memory is exorcised and forever laid at rest. It can be so only, —whatever my risk of new cares, whatever the folly of the hazard at my age, —be so only by—by—" Once more Darrell paused, fixed his eyes steadily on Lionel, and, opening his arms, cried out, "Forgive me, my noble Lionel, that I am not contented with an heir like you; and do not you mock at the old man who dreams that woman may love him yet, and that his own children may inherit his father's home. "

Lionel sprang to the breast that opened to him; and if Darrell had planned how best to remove from the young man's mind forever the possibility of one selfish pang, no craft could have attained his object like that touching confidence before which the disparities between youth and age literally vanished. And, both made equal, both elevated alike, verily I know not which at the moment felt the elder or the younger! Two noble hearts, intermingled in one emotion, are set free from all time save the present: par each with each, they meet as brothers twin-born.

CPSIA information can be obtained
at www.ICGtesting.com
Printed in the USA
BVHW080905151121
621685BV00004B/55